Outing the
Mermaid

Also by Ann Medlock:

Arias, Riffs & Whispers:
Words Written for Voices

Outing the Mermaid

by Ann Medlock

Published by Blooming Twig Books
New York / Tulsa
2017

"I seem stark mute but inwardly do prate.
I am and am not, I freeze and yet am burned, Since
from myself another self I turned."

—Elizabeth I

"The prince asked her who she was, and where she
came from, and she looked at him mildly and sorrow-
fully with her deep blue eyes; but she could not speak."

—from "The Little Mermaid"
by Hans Christian Andersen

"Eppur si muove"—And still it moves.

—Galileo

Table of Contents

Rowing in Eden

In the late-arriving darkness of the long solstice day, in the old house filled with sleeping-child silence, Lee flipped the wall switch that turned on the reading lamps, pulled the drop cloths off the floor and the slant-top desk, and turned the radio up just far enough to fill this one small room with the "Ride of the Valkyries," thundering southward from WQXR.

She smiled encouragement—ride, sisters, ride. She knew she had to hurry too, must get on with it. Go, no go—sign, don't sign. Tonight. The papers in the morning mail. Or not. *Eppur si muove*—the earth still moved. Seasons began and ended, doors opened and closed, whether she went through them or not.

Crescents of dark earth tipped each paint-speckled finger as she spread the pages out to be read one last time. In this day's early hours, before the sun had moved above the trees and driven her indoors, she'd planted a dozen flats of impatiens, making edges of salmon and coral giggles along the curving brick walk to the front door.

Looking from the sidewalk to the door of 99 Underwood Road, she'd decided to plant the salmon blooms on the left of the walk, the coral on the right. The salmon would line a mellow brick road for strangers to follow to the door of a house for sale. Just another real estate deal, one small ratcheting up the Gross National Product for 1977. The coral curve was, instead, her declaration of permanent ownership. This way to my house. Mine. She turned up another spade of earth. Her earth.

That afternoon, with lunch finished, Gabe down for a nap and Tobias practicing guitar chords, two fans had blown droning kisses at her damp skin while she painted this long-locked room just off the foyer, making it her color. Watching the room change beneath her brush from a sky blue to a sea green, she realized that any lingering fingerprints made by the room's previous occupant were being coated over. Exorcism could take many forms.

If she didn't sign the papers and the check, she would keep making this room, this house, truly her own. She would move her files down here from the upstairs bedroom she had long used as her office, take her Selectric off the door she had used for a desktop and put it here, on a typing cart, next to the Dickensian mahogany desk. She would open the cartons she and Toby had hauled down the stairs, cartons full of treasured books. She would make shelf space for them and for the incoming manuscripts she would have to take in from her Princeton neighbors, writers and professors, each one awaiting her editorial eye for logic and sequence, for clarity, for ways to keep a reader turning pages.

This evening she had moved the household accounts here, and paid all the bills. In years to come, she could work here, in her office, in her house, tinkering with other people's ideas and words, helping Gabe with homework when he got old enough to have some, making calls to Toby in the apartment he'd be sharing with fellow students at Hunter College, checking in with Rory to see when she and her sculptor husband would be coming down again.

She would see to it that there would always be a grad student in the attic studio to help with chores, and the guest bedroom and den to rent for extra cash. She'd make sure there would always be tomatoes and string beans from the garden, fresh or put up for the winter, the jars in bright rows on the pantry shelves.

It was damned good duty—unearned, but she was here, a guest in Eden, done with the compass, done with the chart. Lee and her sons. Home. Home free. *Olly olly oxen free* rang in her head, quickly overridden by *Hojotoho* as the Valkyries' voices filled the small room. She tested a newly painted shelf; her finger came away green. It might take days for paint to dry in this weather.

"Home," in her childhood, had looked to her like the big old houses on shady streets in the coastal towns near the Navy bases where her family lived—in tiny Navy quarters. She'd told her father she loved being a nomad, always moving on. She did not tell him that she wished she were one of the people who lived happily ever after in houses that looked like good old 99.

Now, she had been one of the old-house people for seven years, the time it took to renew every cell in a body, making her a different being than the one who had moved into the then derelict house on Underwood Road.

Now, she could hold this ground for her sons, Tobias about to start college, Gabriel approaching kindergarten. She and the house would be the still point around which their lives danced, bringing their children here for Easter egg hunts and Christmas feasts. Gabe would grow up and she would grow old in this gracious old house, sustained by thick plaster walls and quartered-oak floors, living to the soundtrack of the mourning doves, unseen, who filled the trees surrounding this place.

Nothing untoward would happen here, nothing frightening. Not now. Not ever again. She would not need to be a Valkyrie, armor on, spear in hand, shrieking at the world.

If she signed the papers arrayed across the leather desktop, if she wrote the check, it would be another story. A future cast off from this perfect mooring would be—what? There were no sea charts to show possible bearings, ultimate landfalls, to tell her where the shoals were and the hidden riptides, to mark the places where there be monsters.

"Do *what?* Leave *Princeton* to live in the *city* with your *kids?*" That wasn't the way the tide flowed. People upgraded to Princeton, after proving themselves in New York. For Lee, that was the rub. She'd landed on Park Place, as baggage, a camp follower. Year after year, the wonderfully honest property tax bill from the state of New Jersey had arrived addressed to "Joseph V.H. Montagna, *et ux.*" Lee Palmer Montagna had been in this house as her husband's anonymous property, *et uxorem.*

If she signed the lease, she'd need a grubstake. Starting over anywhere took some cash; in New York it would take suitcases full. And she could only get that much money by selling Home. House hunters would come down the walk, taking in the handsomely restored place, solid, simple, but winking its chocolate shingles at them, flapping its peach shutters. They would be new department heads at the University or New York Achievers ready for the great move to this ubersuburb, taking their rightful places among the winners. They would stand in the two-story front hall, absorbing a 1911 solidity they would never find in new, thin-walled construction.

Lee could see them outside the door of this room she was shaping to her needs—or preparing for theirs. Step this way if you will. This was, for the first half of the century, the office of the town's most beloved family physician. Perfect for any at-home work you might want to do, or for seeing clients, patients. And let me show you the kitchen, completely renovated, so charming, perfect for the serious cook.

How Norman Rockwell, they would think it all, not seeing scenes played on this set that were instead pure Edvard Munch, the text not *Saturday Evening Post* but *Journal of Abnormal Psychiatry*.

She breathed deeply into a small movement of air that reached her through the window screen, bearing the scent of watered topsoil from out there in the heavy dark. The newly grounded plants must be settling in along the walk, sending small white feelers out to hit not the walls of nursery flats but open soil, inviting, yielding, limitless.

There would be no more digging and planting if she signed the lease. They didn't let you do that in Central Park.

She wiped her damp hands on the seat of her cutoff jeans, careful not to smudge the papers as she read, yet again, the ponderous terms and conditions, and the changes and deletions she'd made in them. She had ferreted out every problem, she was fairly sure, though she'd left in the attorneys' grammar errors, not wanting to seem a smartass. Now it was time to sign, or lose to another apartment-hunter. When—if—the building's owners countersigned despite her changes, she would put her copy on file so they'd never get away with telling her she'd agreed to something she hadn't.

She smoothed creases out of the tea towel that kept her from sticking to the wooden chair she'd carried in from the kitchen, and cursed the New Jersey summer for invading her beautiful town, weighting and boiling the air as if this were Saigon or Leopoldville. It was past midnight and she was still sweating, still fighting to get some oxygen from the wet stuff that enveloped her. The air couldn't hold much more heat and water, would have to burst soon into rain. There were Wagnerian rumblings to the north and flashes of blue light, the Jersey night harmonizing with the sounds of Bayreuth. She aimed her pen at the window. Cue the lights! Her other hand rose palm up. Bring up the thunder! The night obliged, with flashes and with rumbles that drowned out the radio. Sing louder, sisters!

Laughing, she moved the pen to the signature page of the almost-memorized document. "No one reads that stuff," the agent had said. "It's meaningless. Just boilerplate." But Lee was not willing to be sliced and fried by New York; she had taken the lease away unsigned and parsed it word-for-word, pen in hand, making notes. Reviewing her edits, she felt solid, a responsible head-of-household, shaping the two-year life of this contract. Only two years. She thought it was likely to take four. She'd need four years to see if she could play jacks with the big kids, on her own. Four years and she could be a woman with an established career and one remaining nestling.

Or. Or she would be a woman who had taken her shot and failed, one who had confirmed her place way back in the queue, a woman no longer filled with foolish longings, but resolved, accepting, resigned. She might be able to get back into this fine town, as a renter—of a tract house. Or of rooms in this neighborhood of solid old houses.

The checkbook was in the top right drawer, along with the financial records she'd learned to keep. She'd have to send a check for the first and last months' rent and a security deposit. It was more than it should be, but everything was. She tore out a check and put it next to the nine-by-twelve envelope that would carry the document to the city via certified mail, return receipt requested. If she actually did this.

The city glowed nor'-nor'-east, unseen, invisible but insistent, a huge centripetal force field, though she was alone in feeling it. Toby had already committed to Hunter College, quite rationally; no magic, magnetic pull had been needed. He'd been asking her if she'd made up her mind yet. There were major consequences for him either way, and he had to know soon. Gabe understood only that something big was up, something maybe not good. Lee's mother, on the line from South Carolina, was filled with the economic and safety reasons to stay put, mystified as always by her peculiar daughter, sure she could not affect this wayward offspring's decision, finally saying only, "But sugah, you'd be so lonely."

The fears assumed by neighbors and family did not include the one that most frightened Lee, the fear of being proven, finally and irrevocably, second-rate.

If she signed the papers and sent them northward, into the force field, these pages splayed out in front of her would put her, in a matter of weeks, at windows that looked out not on this silent, sycamore-lined street but on the roaring heart of Manhattan. A person looking out from those high windows would not be able to hide. A person seeing the sun hit those glittering towers every morning would know she was "on." Exposure. She would be exposed, the city looking back at her, daring her to try her hand. The city waited now, indifferent, there where the thunder rumbled and the blue light flashed.

She found herself talking to the radio again. "*Hojotoho* yourself." A warrior woman she was not.

She put the pen down and stared out at the lamplit, blossom-lined walkway, the walk that led to home, and away from it.

Knight's Gambit

Lee put the box of LBJ portraits down and stared into Jack Kennedy's steady, unwounded gaze, looking back at her from the wall above her desk. "I wanted to work for you, damn it." She took the official Presidential engraving down, hung a photograph of Lyndon Johnson in its place, picked up her carton of photos and moved out into the hall.

She had dreamed high—unreasonably high, she knew—when she sent her resumés to dozens of agencies and offices in Washington, expecting a response from some grim, obscure bureaucrat deep in Commerce or Interior, but dreaming of a call from the Kennedy White House for a spot, however small, in the realm of those who would come to be known as the best and the brightest.

She knew the dream was just that; this was a town full of women with real experience in government and degrees from good colleges, younger women who did not have small kids, expecting, needing their attention. The dream, however, was irresistible.

No White House call had come, but she interviewed at the Democratic National Committee in early November for a press assistant's slot. The job's occupant was leaving in a month to get married and stay home, as nice girls did when they earned the much-sought honorific, "Mrs." The job's salary was pitiful and the duties trivial, but that was going to be true of any job that opened to Lee, and this one was at the Committee, a place that was first cousin to Kennedy's White House.

In January of a new and solemn year, Washington was no longer Camelot but just a government town again, with one new role—capital of the world's mourning. Lee hooked the wire behind Lyndon Johnson's jowly face onto a nail from which Jack Kennedy had looked over the Committee's conference room for a little more than a thousand days. She tugged at the wood frame until it hung straight, then moved on with her box of faces.

Looking repeatedly into JFK's engraved eyes pulled Lee's thoughts to Arlington, to the gravesite, where Toby had held this same image in one small hand, a bouquet in the other. Mother and son had watched the honor guards from all the armed services as they took wreaths and baskets of flowers from people at the picket fence that surrounded the muddy site. The young warriors carried each offering in slow, straight lines and perfect square corners, and laid them on and around the grave.

When Lee and Toby had come to the gate in the fence, her son handed his five daisies and three yellow roses to a Marine in full dress blues and a closed, determined face that came undone when he reached down to the child. Tears inching down his cheeks, the Marine had given Toby's flowers the full military drill, placing them at the top of the grave right, Lee realized, at John Kennedy's head. Not the fine head that was filling the carton at her feet, but one that was obscenely shattered.

Seven frames to go.

On most days of this terrible winter, Lee had been at her desk in the press officer's anteroom, answering phones and catching typos as the cast changes were completed. Incoming Texans tried to be tactful as the Yankees gradually found other places for their wounded souls. The Boston reporter she was supposed to assist in getting out releases to the press and stock speeches to party candidates had been replaced by the owner of some Texas newspapers, a man who had never written anything himself. He had need of her English-major skills.

Southwest twangs were replacing New England honks, boots replacing Hush Puppies, but deep into gray January, one highly visible thing had not changed: Jack Kennedy's portrait still looked out from every wall, and Lee's sense of the rightness of things couldn't be silenced.

"C.T.? Have you got a minute?" Lee handed her boss his coffee and waited as he reached for the mug and kept on reading the *Washington Post*.

"Hunh? Oh. Well. Sure. What's on your mind, precious?"

> *Well, first thing on my mind is I wish to hell you'd stop the*
> *precious and the darlin' and all the talking to me like I'm*
> *some kind of pet.*

"What's on my mind is all these portraits of Kennedy. They may be sending the wrong message, you know? It's as if the Committee isn't really behind the President and here he is running against Goldwater, with people so upset about the assassination and wishing Kennedy were alive to run again. Shouldn't the pictures be changed? So we look like Johnson's team?"

"Well, sure we should, darlin'. We got the danged photos of Lyndon, but there's no Texan gonna take that on. These Yankees already think we don't have any class or 'sensitivity.'" He made the word sound as if it came with a cup of *ma hwang* tea and a watercress sandwich.

"You're not from Texas." He squinted up at her. "You do it."

She had a full carton of Jacks under her desk and a pocket stuffed with damp tissues as she went back to answering the phone, typing up memos from C.T.'s hand-scrawled notes, fixing his grammar mistakes. It had not been a good morning, beginning with Toby's insistence that he didn't want to get on the school bus to his kindergarten, then her old car taking forever to start, almost making her late, and now this mournful task. She wondered if she could find the vanished Yankees and give them the engravings. She pulled out her notes on the day's tasks, the appointments C.T. wanted her to set up for him and those to cancel, the filing that needed to be done of his correspondence....

"Hey, Mizzz Pitt!"

Lee looked up, putting a silent finger at the place she had reached in her list. Joe Montagna was leaning, backwards, into the office door, off center, his lower body ready to rush on. His position was gravity-defying, his words mystifying.

"Pick you up at two on Saturday—that's tomorrow. You got that?" She laughed uneasily. "You're assuming you and I have plans."

"*I* do. Now *you* do. So yeah, *we* do."

She wondered what he was doing here, so far from the Department of Labor. And if there shouldn't be a question somewhere in what he was saying.

He grinned a white slash in his dark Italian face, his unlikely pale blue eyes narrowing to pleased crescents of sky before his solid, sport-coated body hurtled out of the doorway.

"Hey! Uh—wait?" She thought she might not have spoken loudly enough, but he was back, grinning, arms folded nonchalantly as he leaned against the doorframe.

"Yeeess?"

"You don't understand. I am one of those working single mothers people talk about—we have to find sitters before we can go out the door and that involves considerable advance notice."

"I know about the kid. Boy, right? Five years old?" He reached into his jacket pocket and fanned out three tickets. "He's going to love this. So you'll cancel anything else you thought you were doing."

Lee looked down, shaking her head in disbelief, looking back up with a string of questions for Montagna. The doorway was empty.

She stared at the vacated space, amazed by this odd man's enormous confidence. What did she know about him? A college classmate had introduced them at a cocktail party just the evening before. Being well married herself and appalled by Lee's divorce, Louise had made it her cause to get Lee safely back into the marriage fold, recruiting Harlan, her own kind husband, to help scout for likely candidates, all of whom Lee had found most *un*likely, as were the men she had met at work.

There was the pudgy freshman Congressman with the non-stop monologue on the magnificence of his legislative ideas, the intense wire service reporter who assumed she would find stories at the Committee and leak them to him, the statistics professor from American U who smelled of onions and thought the analysis of data made for fascinating conversation.

It had been almost two years since Timothy Pitt had left Washington for another tour at the Saigon embassy and Lee had stayed behind, filing for divorce, asking for personal support only until she could find a job. The job had happened sooner than she had feared, but it was taking longer to factor men back into her life. She had been on half a dozen once-only dates in recent months, choosing to read her way through many a long, quiet evening rather than repeat the experiences.

It wasn't just that she hadn't found the men attractive. She sensed in each of them a disturbingly familiar attitude that one woman was as good as any other as long as she was pretty and willing to offer assistance. Lee was willing to be a backup player, trained for the position by her upbringing and the times, but she wanted to do the part as Lee, as her particular self. To Tim Pitt, struggling Foreign Service staffer, she had been My Wife and The Mother of My Son. Lee was sure anyone could have filled the part as written, as long as that someone was willing to constantly shore up a man who was daunted by the world.

There had been so many moments when the next move was clear—to her, but not to Tim—so many times when she had whisper-coached him, only to realize that she could not do that at every necessary juncture. Her husband, Toby's father, the man they counted on, had no idea how to be their protector, the role that was assigned to men, husbands, fathers.

She had married him because he was handsome, as husbands were supposed to be, because he was sweet, because at 21 all her friends were married, because she couldn't imagine he would not be up to the role.

In their early years, it was acceptable to Lee to be a template bride, young helpmeet, then a new mom, the one with a handsome husband who had an exotic job. They looked wonderful together in photographs, riding in a carriage during a layover in Rome, attending a reception in Leopold-ville, climbing a stupa on vacation in Bangkok, backpacking Toby through the hills around Dalat. But she became more and more discomforted by the Tim behind the appearance—that picture was not wonderful. Behind the image was a man who was constantly at a loss, a sweet-natured, passive man who was content with his lot, whatever it was, and with his pretty, helpful wife, whoever she was.

It was better, she told herself, to be clearly alone than to seem to have a husband when she actually had two dependents. A dependent child was welcome, deserving, adorable; a dependent husband was not acceptable in the world as she knew it.

She could not save this drowning man, but she had a chance to save her son from being confused and overwhelmed by the world, as his father was.

She had a chance, a slim one, to save their lives, hers and Toby's, and she had taken it, becoming Lee Palmer Pitt, working single mom in Washington DC, rather than Mrs. Timothy Pitt, My Wife and The Mother of My Son, in Saigon.

It was a temporary holding action. She knew she was not equipped to provide for Toby longterm, to be both mother and father to him, but she could, she hoped, hold things together until she found the right husband, the right model of a man's life for her son. She was of her time, programmed for assisting, for backing up the right man despite a recurring, nagging thought that there might be something off-kilter about all this. But clearly, from all the evidence around her, it was she who was askew. The way things were was natural, inevitable, right.

Through these post-Tim, pre-Someone days, she walked a narrow line between hope and fear, with never enough money or time, with her confidence waxing and waning. From the other side of the world, Tim sent a monthly child support check that didn't cover their son's clothes and food. Her own salary had to cover more than it possibly could. She became a consummate penny-pincher, avoiding all unnecessary expenditures, doing her own house repairs, changing the oil and anti-freeze in her old Volkswagen, making and mending clothing.

She fretted about unforeseen calamities that might shoot the wings off the fragile two-seater plane she was learning to pilot, some calamity that would plunge her and her son into the abyss of poverty. Her days were rounded by nightmares of being homeless, her trusting son in rags, looking up at her with uncomprehending eyes, nightmares that she ran from, waking herself to walk the dark house until it might be safe to return to sleep.

On better nights there was a dream she had never understood, the one in which her lifelong fear of water disappeared and she was under the sea, confident, happy, moving freely, and singing in a voice that seemed not hers. The joy and freedom of the dream made Lee reluctant for the night to end and the day's fears and restrictions to return.

But the days did come and she faced them, repetitious days filled with her son, her menial job, a few friends, household chores, and the occasional once-only dinner or drinks with another man who would prove to be a poor substitute for an evening with an Austin or Didion book and Hovhaness on the stereo.

Harlan had described his new find, this Joe Montagna, with something approaching awe. The guy, Harlan explained, was an ace negotiator who had been brought into Labor to settle a dock strike, but only after he'd negotiated a deal for himself that was so exceptional, it took a special act of Congress to set it up. This cocky man, this blue-eyed Italian, came to town and within weeks settled a dock strike that had tied the whole country in knots for close to a year. And, in Harlan's admiring words, "He didn't even break a sweat."

He was a bit much in the bravado department, but good-looking, funny, clearly competent, and he'd included Toby in his cheeky plan, whatever it was—he seemed eminently worth checking out. The tickets in his pocket had to be for something more interesting than the Saturday she was thinking of, making macaroni and cheese for Toby and a kindergarten buddy.

Her hands burrowed under layers of paper and found the phone. "Louise, that guy Montagna, at your party after work yesterday? He works with Harlan at Labor, right?"

"He runs the whole section, Lee. Hold on. Is this an actual expression of interest? Well, well. Charming, handsome, smart, polite—could it be this one's actually got your attention?"

"I do thank you both yet again for your tireless efforts at fixing up the picky divorcée. You are saints of patience. Now I just need this one's extension at the Department so I can give him my address, and I don't have a Labor directory here."

Her friend laughed. "He got your address from me last night, after grilling me about you for twenty minutes. And how come you don't have every number in Washington there? The DNC is supposed to know all see all in this town."

"It well may. But I'm a peon here, remember? I don't know anything." What she did know was that Joe Montagna had shifted the day 180 degrees. She checked "Change POTUS pictures" off her list and added, "Tell Toby we have a date."

Joe Montagna was grinning at her over her son's head as they sat in the stands at the Armory. "I told you he'd love it."

Toby's huge green eyes were fixed raptly on the antics of the Harlem Globetrotters, when they weren't taking curious looks at this new and strange person who had come to his house in a much nicer car than his mother's rusty Beetle and had let him hold his own ticket all the way to their box seats.

Their date was wearing a sweater the same light blue as his eyes, and black slacks. Lee was annoyed with herself for noticing that both had the sheen of synthetics. Taste in clothes had to be secondary to his startling presence; even sitting still, there was a bright urgency about him, a sense that he was being charged by an invisible power source that could at any moment illuminate him and everything around him.

One of the Globetrotters hid the ball under his shirt and strolled with extravagant nonchalance toward the basket.

"Excuse me, sir, but is he allowed to do that?"

"Good question, Tobe. In a real game, you're right, the players can't fool around like that, but this is only for fun so it's OK."

"I wonder why anyone agrees to play them." Lee smiled at her son. "The other team looks so foolish."

"It's OK, Mom. It's just for fun." Toby turned to Montagna. "Right, sir?"

"It's fine with me if you call me Joe. That is, if your mom says that's alright." Montagna and Toby both looked to Lee for her approval. She smiled assent and Montagna extended a hand to the boy. "Me Joe. You Tobe. Deal?" Toby's small hand disappeared into Montagna's broad grip.

"It's a deal, sir." He looked puzzled when the two adults burst into laughter, then he joined in, realizing the joke.

At the end of an early dinner at Sholl's downtown cafeteria, Lee watched Toby go into the dessert line with a dollar from their date.

"A silly ballgame, a point-to-your-own-dinner restaurant—you're pretty good at knowing what kids like. How many do you have?"

There were three, living in Atlanta with their mother.

"Rory, she's 13. Maddy's 11 and Van, my boy, he's Tobe's age."

"Miss them?"

"Sure. Especially Van. He's...." He looked away, and found his voice. "He's not strong like your Tobe."

He frowned and seemed to welcome the interruption when Toby arrived with a slice of chocolate cake and two quarters in change that he clinked into a stack next to Montagna's coffee cup.

"Good choice there, guy. Lee, may I get you a slice? Another cup of coffee?"

"How about I make a pot, at our house?"

Their empty cups sat on the coffee table in front of the sofa where Toby was gently snoring. Lee was curled in a club chair at one end of the table; Montagna stretched almost prone in the matching chair opposite her, his hands clasped behind his head, framing lobeless ears, small, with black curls around them. *Treasure Island* lay open face down on the floor beside him where he'd put it when he saw that Toby had fallen asleep. He had read the boy almost a full chapter, after a talk about basketball strategies and the promise of a lesson.

"I'm sorry Toby was so demanding. You may not even like reading out loud and if you don't really want to teach him to play basketball, I can make some excuse...."

"No, no. That was one of my favorite books and I'm actually a hell of a basketball player. *And* he's a great kid. I'd enjoy showing him how we did it on the Lower East Side."

Lee wasn't surprised that he was a New Yorker. And a poor boy, on the rise. Who else had his kind of nerve? Rough edges and all, he'd gotten far, fast. The attitude was traceable, but not the voice. She wondered what had happened to his accent. She could hear her father saying, "Of course I don't still sound like South Carolina. People think you're stupid if you talk like that." Her father had moved up and out of his cotton-mill world. And this man-on-the-move who was making himself so at home in her living room wasn't going to let anyone dismiss him as some dumb New York slum kid.

"This is nice, you know?" He was staring up at the ceiling. "Just being here. Quiet." He pulled himself up in the chair and faced her, his forearms on his widespread knees, his broad fingers interlaced.

"OK, what do I know about you? Lee Pitt 101. Let's see. You grew up on Navy bases and you went to seventeen schools, so you know how to handle yourself in new situations. You worked your way through U Maryland because it's cheap and your old man wouldn't put up any money to educate a girl. Lots of hours on lots of part time jobs and you made honors anyway. So you're smart as hell. The books here... you realize they're everywhere? The shelves are full, there's a stack by your chair—and those piles on the stairsteps. So I think you know a lot. About a lot of things. You did some acting and modeling, so you know how to walk and talk. Your dad was a Commander but he came up through the ranks so you're not a snob, but you've got that officer thing down. And the diplomat stuff too."

Lee told herself to have a word with Louise about her responses to the curious questions of strangers. "I'm sorry but, 'officer thing'? 'Diplomat stuff?'"

"You've got class, lady. Look at this place. Look at you."

Lee considered the modest old house she rented, far into the Maryland hinterlands, its backyard conjoining quiet woods where there was a fine little creek and a child could safely play. There was some decent art on the walls, modern prints and a couple of nice block prints from Saigon. Simple furnishings, but comfortable. Nothing expensive, but nothing ugly. Her clothes were, she thought, unremarkable: gabardine slacks, a white cashmere turtleneck, a silk scarf, your basic Audrey Hepburn-on-the-weekend, all bought at good sales.

"I'm not sure what you mean, *sir*, but thanks."

The Navy had indeed affected her, the constant moving from base to base, learning to adjust quickly, to say what needed to be said, do what needed to be done, in each new place. Again and again, she had been taken to yet another new school and left there to find her way, carrying with her a parental expectation of perfection—perfect appearance, perfect grades and perfect conduct. Each time, she had moved into her observer position, surveying the lay of the land, learning all she could, always knowing she would be moving on soon, to the gift of another beginning.

The settings varied, some delighting, some repelling, but her family was constant. Wherever they hung their curtains and pictures, wherever they found the nearest church and school, there was always the little brother who must be taken care of and protected, his future planned and saved for; the mother pointing out her daughter's every shortcoming, determined to stop any move the girl might be making toward being "just too full of yourself." And there was the father appearing from time to time, frowning, ominously quiet, eternally disappointed in his first-born.

Lee had always found refuge in books. She had absented herself from the world of criticism and frowns, from a marriage that wasn't working, from the loneliness and fears that now beset her. Since her first library card at six, she had read her way through one treasury of books after another.

The evenings she spent reading volumes from the shelves and piles in this quiet house were not evenings lost, though she did worry that there were too many such evenings.

"What else do I know? You've got that independent-woman thing." Montagna held up a hand, as if to stop an expected denial. "But you're not obnoxious about it." He smiled appeasingly. "Resourceful. You've even found something you can do with an English major—that press job at the Committee. You want to mix it up in the world or you'd settle for teaching *Moby Dick* to bored high school kids. And how about brave? Setting out on your own, with a kid, no less. Not scared of anything. How'm I doing so far?"

"Sounds like a combination of Mary McCarthy and Joan of Arc. Good for me."

> *So I look like I know what the hell I'm doing, do I? But*
> *I feel like I'm living the Perils of Pauline and I may not make*
> *it to the last reel. If the car breaks down, if Toby gets sick, if*
> *I lose my job—so many ifs and they all mean Poor. This man*
> *is roaring up from poor, and he's not afraid of falling back in.*
> *He'd never understand obsessing about falling backwards.*

"You're very kind but I'm definitely scared of some things. Like water. I won't go anywhere near water. And New York. I'm definitely scared of your hometown. It's amazing to me that kids grow up there and survive. All that concrete. The traffic. The crowds." She was shaking her head, rejecting it all.

He grinned and picked up the beat of her voice, nodding his head up and down to counter her sideways rejection. "The excitement. The juice. The energy." His face turned serious. "You're right it isn't easy—but it was great. Especially for me. My dad was a union organizer, so he was a really strong guy, surrounded by strong guys. They taught me to be tough, which I had to be, just to get to school and back. Public school all the way through. We never had money for anything else—dad was an *honest* union guy, never on the take. But he made me study and if you do that, New York schools are great, right up through CCNY, which has to be the best college in the world. And free—every bit of it, as long as you kept your grades up, which I did. In psychology. History. Sociology. The only bad thing was writing papers. I was terrible at that.

"Oh, before CCNY I did a stint in the Air Force which was how I got to Georgia, which was how I met Cindy Lou Carpenter. And her father's shotgun. When I started at City I was a dad. Rory. God she was cute. But it meant working nights at a plant in Queens that my old man had organized. And never having enough money and listening to Cindy Lou tell me how much she hated New York every chance she got."

"Hated New York? Maybe she was just scared of it, like I am."

"No way. Why would a person like you be scared of the city? You just haven't given it a chance."

"No way back at you—I've been in and out of New York all my life. Starting when my dad was at the Brooklyn Navy Yard when I was a kid. Lots of trips there since then. And you're right, it's fabulous."

"So what's to be scared of?"

"Well, let's start with the third rail." It was Lee's turn to laugh. "My buddy Izzy in Bay Ridge told me all about getting sliced and fried in the subway. Once my mom got lost in the subway and I was sure she must be in little cooked pieces down there in the dark."

"But she wasn't, right?"

"She made it home. Eventually."

He spread his hands palms up with a "See?" expression.

"Right. That was irrational thinking by a little kid. But I get lost in New York too. It's all so fast and confusing, and it's overwhelming to imagine getting a toehold in a place that big, that intimidating. The music, the art, the theatre, publishers, networks, corporations. It's all so high-powered, you must have to be absolutely perfect or you don't survive."

She was thinking about an enchanting, intimidating week of modeling for a college fashion issue of LIFE magazine, the only time in her life she had felt that her bony body was a plus. The LIFE staffers raved about her auburn hair, the structure of her face, the way the dresses looked on her, even though she was not tall enough to be a professional.

She'd been doing leads in college plays, delighted to discover that she could lose herself completely in being other people. In New York for the modeling job, she was drawn to the theatre district between shoots. She walked the blocks of fabled marquees, wondering how you became one of the people whose names were up there, instead of a ridiculous, gawking onlooker. Taxis rescued her when her wanderings left her on loud corners, completely confused about where she might be, surrounded by intense, purposefully moving swarms of New Yorkers.

Just a year ago she had taken her parents' invitation to let Toby stay with them for a visit and had gone north to see Ariel Pierson, a friend from college theatre days, a friend who tried to convince Lee to move to New York and start her new life there, "in the center ring." Lee was alone in Ariel's third-floor apartment when her friend called from her day job and shouted at Lee to close and lock everything. Two doors away from where Lee was trying to understand her friend's urgency, three young women had been butchered and a blood-drenched man had been seen moving across the roofs. Lee fled, back to her quiet house at the edge of the woods, on a creek in Maryland, where everyone was safe. No, New York was far too dangerous, and too tough an arena for imperfect people.

"What I see, Ms. Pitt, is 'absolutely perfect.'" He was not smiling but looking at her seriously. When she moved a nay-saying hand in front of her face, uncomfortable with his intensity, he reached for Toby's ankle, rubbing it gently, and broke the moment.

"OK. You asked why I'm in DC. Well, I figured I could end the dock strike from here and that's not a bad thing to have on your record. Also wanted to case the place, see who runs what, who's got the keys to the kingdom. But I don't know how long I'll stick around. New York is just better, you know? You should think about going there too."

"Not a chance. I don't want Toby fighting his way to school and back. I don't want us to live in the old tenement I could afford—if I found a job there at all. Not a *chance*."

Montagna seemed undaunted, looking at her with wry certainty. "If you were that easy to scare, you'd be a schoolteacher. And you'd still be married."

She was silent, remembering the confusion she'd caused in her family by wanting to go to college. Girls only went to college so they could be teachers or nurses, otherwise they were just taking time away from the job at hand: finding a husband and starting a family. And walking away from marriage had been even more puzzling to them. It wasn't enough to want a better life for her and Toby; Tim had never hurt them, and that was the only acceptable reason for such a drastic step. She had gone so far as to remind her family that she and Toby had both gotten terribly ill in Saigon, that the war was getting more dangerous by the day, and that staying with Tim meant going back there. But she'd never told them that she left because she refused to accept that at 29 her life was over, and because Toby's life, which had barely begun, must not repeat his father's.

"I think... I think the divorce was about running from what scares me *most*. I was more afraid of joining the living dead than of being out here without a safety net. I stopped *breathing* when I was with Tim. At least I know I'm alive, out here on the tightrope. I felt mean and selfish—I still do—for not staying with him, because Tim is a nice guy, but there *had* to be more than that. I spent those years with him trying to stand shorter than he was—and I just couldn't do it any more. It's not that *I'm* all that great—I am *so* far from perfect—but I'd have to erase myself completely to fit behind him."

> *Oh my God don't cry. And you don't say stuff like that to a*
> *man you don't even know. But would like to know. You're*
> *blowing it. He'll run for his life from a woman that bitchy.*

"I should get Toby up to bed." She brushed away the tears before they could fall and stood, smoothing her slacks.

"Why? He's so peaceful right where he is. Look at that hair. Just like yours. It's called chestnut red, right? Lots of Celtic genes?" Again, Montagna was moving the conversation onto safer ground. She eased back into the chair, no longer curled in it, but perched on the edge, ready to flee if she misspoke again.

"Some people call the color roan, I think the Irish. On the Pitt side, Toby's all Scots and Englishers. The Palmers are completely English, but my mother's half German."

"Not quite as mixed up as my people."

"Yes, I did wonder about a blue-eyed Montagna."

He smiled. "I like the way you say that, the Italian way. Moantanya. We've always said the 'g'—to sound more American, I guess. My dad's first-generation here. His folks came over from Italy. But my mother's Dutch, van Heuvel, old upstate New York family. Farmlands and a graphite mine. You know, for pencils."

"But there was no money for your schooling?"

"Funny you should ask." He grinned wryly, perhaps remembering many a family argument. "My dad wondered about that too. But she got nothing. Punishment for marrying a poor dago."

"And you're the only child of an Italian Catholic father." She eased back into the soft cushions.

"It broke my old man's heart that he didn't have a pack of kids, but there was no way that Presbyterian woman was going to spend her life pregnant. And how did *you* get to be Catholic?"

"Me? I'm not. Well, not now. My mother's Germans were Bavarian Catholics so she raised me in the church, but I bailed years ago." His eyebrows asked for a reason.

"I read a paper on brainwashing and all those Sister Mary Benedicts and Mary Christophers flashed before my eyes with the stuff they'd programmed into my head. Then it was easy to walk away. But what made you think I was Catholic?"

He nodded black curls toward a print of Our Lady of Guadalupe hanging at the bottom of the stairs.

"Oh, her. A confirmation gift. So she's been on the wall since I was 12—if she's on the wall, this must be home. And the picture next to her—the mermaid surrounded by polliwogs? That one too. She goes with me everywhere. It's from my dad's ship, in the Pacific war."

"That's good." He answered her questioning expression. "That you're not Catholic. I'm not either. Anymore. This is good."

This man, Lee realized, was actually listening to her. His focus was intense and complete; there was no one else in his world at this moment but Lee Palmer Pitt—as herself, in the particular, even though she'd revealed things she shouldn't have. He was gentle, quick-witted, he had that electric charge, and he was living up to all that Louise and Harlan had said about him. Joseph Montagna might well be worth more than one Saturday of her time.

In her room, settling into the lemon-scented flannel sheets, hoping Toby would sleep late in the morning, Lee wondered how people got past the fears of sliding back into the lives that lurked behind them. Montagna didn't seem to have the slightest doubt that he could rocket upwards and never fall back onto the Lower East Side. He knew he was making it. He just knew. Sometimes Lee was confident that she could keep her family's upward trajectory on track, but confident or not, it must be done. She must not undo the progress her parents had begun by giving her a life better than their own. She owed Toby no less. She took a deep breath of the sweet sheets, wondering why there were no detergents that smelled of roses.

Her northern grandmother used rosewater in the laundry she took in from wealthy customers. The southern one worked the looms in a cotton mill, where chemicals made the air stink. Both their lives were about outhouses and fried-baloney-in-Wonder-Bread sandwiches and the fumes of kerosene heaters, and about hating the people who might knock loose their shaky grip on the bottom rungs of the ladder. It was eight kids in the two-bedroom row house where her mother grew up, the granddaughter of farmers who had lost their land, the eldest daughter of a floor-finisher who could barely feed his brood. Emily Wellock was assistant to her harried mother until she escaped by marrying, at 16, the handsome sailor she'd met in a night-school accounting class. She had Lee at 18, on a Navy base far from home, as she and her sailor built a new life that would lift them above their harsh beginnings.

Lee twisted in the bed, pressing her pillow into a more comfortable shape, pulling the comforting flannel sheets closer.

Her father's people, the Palmers, had been in the Carolinas since the 1600s, and there were family rumors of great old plantations, but when time came down to the Palmers Lee knew, they were cotton-mill workers, lintheads, the bottom-feeders of the white Southern world. They lived in company houses, got their groceries and dry goods at the company store, and died of company white-lung. Every time Lee had visited the tiny town that circled the massive mill, she'd silently thanked her father for running away to sea, getting himself, and ultimately his children, as far as he could from the great white bales, the reeking dye pots, and the roaring looms. His survival instincts had made it possible for Lee to grow up on the coasts and not drawl. And to take the spoon out of her coffee cup before she drank from it, which none of her grandparents had done.

Now, one of her southern cousins was a Bull-Connor clone, sheriff of a county fighting desegregation, belly hanging over his belt, spoon firmly in his cup, probably wearing a white sheet at night. Lee shuddered at the thought of sliding backwards into her grandparents' world of hopelessness and fear, the world her parents had escaped.

She made herself stop. She was not in a rowhouse, in a slum, or in a mill-town company house, but in the Maryland woods, in a dear old house where her son had a room of his own and a creek to play by. She had a job in an interesting place and the possibility of moving into more responsibilities. She'd just spent a Saturday with a man she had begun to doubt existed, a man who was moving brilliantly in the world, who could see her and hear her and seemed to like everything about her. That had happened once, long before, but she had stopped expecting it could happen again.

This had been one day of surface observations. If this Joe Montagna really knew her, knew everything about Lee Palmer Pitt, would he still think she was a combination of Mary McCarthy and Joan of Arc? Hardly. Lee knew better. Her family knew better. Especially her mother.

Emily Palmer had aligned with all the nuns who imbued Lee with a longing to be holy, doing what God wanted her to do, despite the fact that this would not be easy, given who she was. Mrs. Palmer had made it clear that Lee was too bright for her own good, unacceptably artsy, impractical, unreliable, entirely too drawn to the unconventional. Even Lee's handwriting was too dramatic: not the neat, easy-to-read script it should be. A girl that smart needed to be kept in line so she wouldn't get a swelled head and so she wouldn't have foolish expectations that life would knock out of her, causing her great disappointment and pain.

All that reading and drawing pictures and coming up with outlandish things to do. Like getting the base kids to sign a petition to the commanding officer, asking for a playground. It was embarrassing, and dangerous. Standing out was just inviting trouble. People didn't like girls who stood out. Like the time Lee ran for student body president of her high school in San Diego. Student body presidents were always senior boys, boys who had always lived there, not girls, and not Navy kids who'd been in the school a year. Lee was not only a girl, she was a junior, for heaven's sake. Mrs. Palmer reminded her daughter that the week she'd started tenth grade at this massive school, she'd come home every day weeping, saying she couldn't go to a school that big after the tiny one she'd gone to near their last base, in Maryland. She had to adjust. That's what Navy kids did, just as Navy wives did. The girl should keep her head down and just focus on studying something useful.

But did she listen? She actually said she thought she could do a better job than the other candidates and she went right on, making campaign posters and buttons every night, using her babysitting money to put ads in the school paper. It was ridiculous, but it really didn't matter if she wasted her time on a useless campaign, because her classes were a waste too. Mrs. Palmer didn't expect her daughter to take bookkeeping; she hadn't inherited her mother's ease with numbers, but not a single course in typing or shorthand? Instead of these things she would surely need, the girl was taking Latin and Spanish and every literature course the school had, even all the drawing, painting, "playschool" classes that silly Californians offered their children. Nothing that would help Lee get an office job until she married, and then manage her household properly. Mrs. Palmer warned her, got her father to give her a talking-to, but their daughter went right on being willful and foolish.

It was a constant struggle to keep the girl's feet on the ground, but Mrs. Palmer was up to the job, pointing out her many faults and failures. Like getting so lost in some book that she forgot she was supposed to be helping her little brother, Ernie, with his homework. And not rinsing and stacking the dishes in proper order before she washed them, still in the proper order. The girl wanted to cook and she hadn't even mastered doing the dishes. She wanted to drive but she hadn't read the book her father had given her on the internal combustion engine. Mrs. Palmer didn't know how to drive but they were to entrust the family Oldsmobile to this unreliable girl? It was ridiculous.

On the day of the election at school, Lee had rushed home with her announcement: "I got more votes than all the guys combined—there won't be a run-off!"

Mrs. Palmer had done the right thing. She went right on with her sewing, while giving her daughter a grounding perspective.

"If they knew you as well as we do, they wouldn't have voted for you."

Lee shuddered. If Joe Montagna got to know her that well, he would not come back. Your family *had* to keep you around. Men didn't. Bosses didn't. Lee, if fully known, would spend her life alone. And unemployed. She had learned long ago to mask her fears in bravado, to keep her real thoughts closely guarded. She'd slipped tonight, saying far too much. Montagna said he'd be back. But he wouldn't.

She berated herself for allowing her worst fears to overtake her, spoiling the pleasure she had just experienced. This day wasn't about the past. It wasn't about the future. It was simply a very good day. Right here, right now, she was happy. She stretched, turned on her side, and dropped into sleep smiling.

C.T. was at his desk, not looking up at her, not calling her "precious." "Lee, I'm looking at a speech you did here and this War on Poverty piece...."

All through the spring, Lee had filed, proofread, and answered phones for him, finally asking for and getting some trial writing assignments when the reporters the Committee had brought in as staff writers couldn't keep up with campaign-year demands. Thousands of Democrats all over the country were running for office, and the Committee was providing them with position papers and stock speeches on civil rights, the Great Society, the war. There were model letters to the editor and columns for local papers that were supposedly written by well-known Democrats. When C.T. raged that the ghostwriting wasn't getting done fast enough, Lee had asked for a try at it. She'd worked hard on each piece, hoping they would be her way out of the girl-assistant ghetto, up to the kind of assignments—and salaries— the staff writers were getting.

The day had begun for Lee with the end-of-the-world gloom that always preceded her period, a gloom she never recognized as hormone-induced until the flood began and the world returned to a nonmalevolent neutral, allowing possibilities both fair and foul. Listening to C.T., her mind ruled by premenstrual angst, Lee felt total darkness closing in.

"They aren't very good, Lee. I'm going to have to ask you to move on to some place that would suit you better."

Lee stared at his mouth, opening and closing above his yellow tie and his short-sleeved shirt. He wasn't moving her up. He was firing her.

She nodded and hurried out of his office. At her own desk, she steadied herself with both hands, fighting to stay composed.

"Lee, what's happening? You look sick." Hannah Rivers, the widow of a renowned political columnist, was staring at Lee, her arms full of her reports on the voting records of Republican Representatives and Senators.

"I just got fired." Her voice was barely audible. She nodded toward C.T.'s door. "He said my work was no good."

The older woman's eyes narrowed. "Hold everything." She disappeared into her office across the hall, returning with her coat and bag. "Grab your stuff, dear. We're getting out of here."

Lee was propelled into the Cosmos Club, where Hannah's membership had continued after her famous husband's death. In its handsome old bar, Hannah slid a double martini in front of Lee. "Now you listen to me. That man is a fool and a scoundrel. He had no need to say what he said. I know good copy and those pieces you showed me were good. He just didn't have the guts to tell you the truth."

"The truth?"

"Yes, and it's simple. You're out because you have no patron and somebody who has one wants a job. It's not about your competence. Lee, do you hear me?"

Lee did hear, but she didn't believe.

"Listen to me, Lee. In the years I've been there since my Jerry died, they've tried to dump me five times! But I just call Bobby Kennedy and within the hour I've got my job back, and God knows I need the job. You don't have a Bobby, so some chippy from Texas is going to get your desk. Wait. Did that jerk ever make a pass at you?"

Lee shrugged a Doesn't-matter.

"But there it is, Lee. The jerk wants a harem and you wouldn't play. Now I *know* it's about bringing in a chippy. Or a big contributor's daughter. Maybe she'll be both. I tell you what. You don't even have to go back there. Just tell me what you need from your desk and I'll pack it up for you."

"I need to *work*." Lee took a gulp of the martini. "Toby's outgrowing everything and my car needs new brakes and I don't know what the hell I'm going to do."

She could see no glimmer in the darkness. Just when she had begun to hope she could do real work in the world, she'd been declared mistaken. Proven unworthy. Found out. Her only recourse was to admit defeat and tell Joe Montagna that a half year of dating was enough, that he must marry her immediately, to take care of her and Toby, before she completely messed up her son's life and they would soon be wandering the streets, a bag lady and her starving child.

"Let me make a couple of calls. I've got some ideas." Hannah was patting Lee's hand reassuringly.

In the following days, the flooding brought Lee the light-headedness of a plummeting hematocrit, and a slow mental corking-up to the brightness of a world in which there were, once more, options. It was good to have an ally like Hannah. It was good to have Joe Montagna telling her over lobster *vol au vent* at the Rive Gauche that she was way too smart for that dumb job anyway. It was good to get a call from the White House, where Hannah had managed to get Lee's resumé into a newly created office there.

An Ivy League intellectual had been brought in to create some Kennedy-style class for Lyndon Johnson. The professor would choose composers, writers, playwrights, and painters who would be salted into White House events. He would bring in prestigious speakers and performers. He needed an assistant.

In the suffocating June heat, Lee went through the great iron gates, showing her ID to the guards, watching them find her name on their list of the favored few with business inside.

She was there. Wrong time. Wrong occupant. But it was the White House. The professor noted Lee's experience as a Foreign Service wife/hostess, her knowledge of American literature and music, her carefully thought out appearance. She was startled to see that the professor had copies of the ghost writing she had done at the Committee—Hannah had done more than send Lee's resumé.

" This article you wrote for the Speaker of the House—the cadences, the allusions—you made him sound like Winston Churchill."

" Too literary, you think?"

The professor grinned. "Maybe for those bozos at the Committee, but here, literary is good. Hannah Rivers says you're the perfect companion at an art exhibit—you're savvy and discerning. And you've read every American writer we've got *and* you know David Diamond and Lucas Foss."

"Well, I don't know *them*. Just their works. Serious new music interests me. Especially Samuel Barber. And Alan Hovhaness."

The professor was looking at her with a bemused smile. He leaned forward and said in a conspiratorial whisper that the interview period had not closed, but that he would very much like her to accept the job, if she was interested.

Over dinner at the Old Ebbitt Grill, Joe opined that Lee was the best thing that could ever happen to that Ivy League guy and his chances of doing a good job.

"It's going to happen again, I know it. There's going to be a Buffy or a Mimsy from Smith or Vassar whose daddy gives the Party trainloads of money and she'll have artsy connections out the kazoo and I'll be out again. I don't even have the *clothes* for this job."

Lee's fork moved rice kernels back and forth on her plate.

Joe reached across the table and stopped her hand. "Lee, listen to me. The job's officially in play until next week, right? OK, I can get away for a few days so let's take Tobe to your folks and then head out to Hilton Head to think it all over. What do you say?"

It was a good plan. There would be a sea breeze on the island and she could think all this through. Joe always seemed to have a good plan.

He was the man who called her several times a day, the man who had pulled her away from her eat-at-the-desk home-packed brown-bags to eat real lunches in restaurants with tablecloths. He was the man who had taken her to dinner every Friday evening since they'd met, each time sending over a sitter he had screened and paid. He would arrive equipped with a book the sitter could read to Toby, and he would take Lee to dinners and theatre performances that were way beyond her own budget.

He was the playful, charming, entrancingly physical man who had nailed a hoop over her garage door and spent Saturday afternoons teaching her son to dribble down the driveway, then lifting him high enough to sink the ball. Lee watched her son's emerging skill and his delight at each achievement. And she tried not to stare at the raised veins on Joe's knotted, bare arms as they emerged from a gray T-shirt with the words "CCNY Athletic Department" across his broad chest. She got the joke—there was no athletic department at the brainy City College of New York.

He was the courtly family man who would run a finger along her neck, lightly, slowly, watching the gooseflesh appear, but welcomed Toby if he came into the room, with an open, available smile. "Hey, Tobe. How's the jumpshot coming? You get in any practice time after school?" After their Friday evening dinners, when he and Lee went to his high-rise apartment downtown, there was never a thought of letting the sitter stay the night with Toby. Always, Joe would drive her home and head back to town. "Tell Tobe I'll be over around eleven, OK? He said he wanted to show me a chipmunk nest back by the creek. You think chipmunks really make nests?"

The first time they had gone to his glass-walled apartment, Lee was caught in counter-currents of fear and longing. She had to enfold this electrifying being and if she did, she was sure she would lose him. Everywhere they had gone on their evenings together, she'd seen women follow him with lustful eyes, women who saw what Lee saw, the taut, muscular body that moved with such assurance, the startling contrast of crowblack hair and skyblue eyes in dark skin. The women offered, in return, the lush figures that men clearly preferred to spare specimens such as herself.

Lee knew she was a fraud, a faux woman. She had managed to warn Joe that even the small curves she manifested were a deception, attributable to the padded bras she'd worn since realizing that Mother Nature was never going to come forth with secondary sex characteristics for this one forgotten daughter. In all her years of adulthood, she had been pregnant only once, despite years of unprotected married sex and an affair when she was a student. Lee appeared normal but was sure that she was not.

"Don't worry about it, Leedle. I'm a leg man myself and I'm looking at those beautiful gams of yours. And what about that face? You're gorgeous."

Still, she did not believe him until that first time in his apartment when he had laughed and moved two broad hands under her blouse, under the false front that allowed her to pass as womanly.

"Hmmm. I hear Spencer Tracy saying, 'Not much meat on 'er but what's there is choice.' Let me take this armor off so I can see you. Please?"

Lee nodded a frightened Yes, shivering in the warm apartment as the huge windows filled with the swirling flakes of a rare snowfall. He held each of her nipples between his thumbs and forefingers. "God, Leedle, look at you. Look how responsive you are." He laughed in delight, watching the reaction he was causing.

She thought she would implode if she didn't draw in every part of this beguiling man. She wrapped herself around him on his leather sofa, forgetting snow, forgetting fear, lost to any thoughts at all. He shouted as if he'd been shot, was still a moment and then was saying words to her that she could barely decipher. "Good God. I'm so sorry. But you are... that was... OK, don't come back, stay there, I'll get you down." She wanted his tongue in her mouth but he pulled back to watch her as his hands kept her nipples erect and found their way into her depths. Every muscle in her body tightened and exploded, tightened and exploded, until there was nothing left to give and she was sobbing, returning slowly to an apartment looking out over Washington DC on a late Friday night in February of 1964, holding Joseph van Heuvel Montagna in her arms and legs and heart.

On that night and on all the others that followed, Lee longed to stay with him in the severely modern apartment, to follow their lovemaking with a long night of dreaming on his shoulder, of waking in the night to enfold him again. But she knew that a sitter could not stand in for her in Toby's world, come morning. Good parents didn't do that, no matter how much they might want to dream the night away with their lovers.

She imagined full nights with Joe, with no child needing her to come home. She felt sea breezes and heard the long talks they would have on the beach at Hilton Head—it would be the perfect break from work, from worry, from parenting.

She knew his children now—Rory, Maddy and Van—since the early spring day when he had said out-of-the-blue, "My kids have come up to visit and I'm wondering, could they stay with you and Tobe? Your house is so much bigger than my apartment and it's, you know, homier. The girls can watch Tobe so you won't need a sitter." He was nodding the Yes he wanted from her, and grinning the up-on-the-right-down-on-the-left smile that Lee loved to see.

It was a logical and practical idea, and one of many signs that Joe Montagna was planning ahead, though the word "marriage" had not come up at all in their many long talks. Lee filled that vacuum with assumptions. For the divorced, she had mused, meeting the children might be equivalent to a younger couple's introductions to parents—a sign of seriousness.

It would be a chance for Lee and Toby to get to know these kids Joe must miss terribly. Lee would get the house set up—Van could bunk in Toby's trundle, Rory and Maddy could sleep in the guest room where there were twin beds fitted out in Bamberg-lace-trimmed linens. Lee would have to make a run to the Giant supermarket. And she was short one pillow;

Toby had never had a sleepover guest so there was no pillow for the trundle. She'd probably need more towels as well. There was a linen store not far from the Giant. Then she would pick up a tourist brochure and see what concerts and exhibits might be on that she and Joe could take all four of them to see.

"Of course they can stay at the house."

Joe stopped alongside a line of parked cars in front of his apartment building. "That's great. I'll circle the block while you go up and get them."

"Right now? Wait. Do they know about this? Won't they have to pack up all their stuff? And they haven't met me yet. Won't they be startled that you're moving them to my place? How do I explain this?"

"Donworry aboudit." His grin turned his eyes into little arcs of sky. "Just introduce yourself and tell them I said to hustle because I'm driving around and around down here."

Introduce myself? They don't know about me? Oh my God.
I'm the Unknown Girlfriend. The reason their dad hasn't
come home. This is not good. This is not good at all.

"Wait, Joe, wait. I don't know about this. How about *I* drive around and around and you go up and get them?"

"C'mon, Leedle. They're just kids. Good kids. You can do this. For me."

And so she had. Rising to his requirements, she went to the ninth floor and rang his bell. The door was opened by Rory, his fourteen-year-old, a tiny blonde with a stern expression and an angular body that was clothed in jeans and a tight purple sweater.

The girl responded to Lee's explanation of her mission with a resigned sigh and a directive to equally blonde Maddy and little brother Van to get their stuff together "right now!"

Joe's normally stark apartment was a disaster scene. The steel and leather furnishings that had come with the place were draped with jeans and shirts, skirts and underwear. Damp towels and crumpled snack wrappers lay where they'd been dropped and an open, horizontal Coke bottle had spilled half its contents onto the pale beige carpeting.

Maddy was slowly stuffing clothing into a plastic suitcase. Lee found it hard to believe she was only 12; the girl was already an assemblage of S curves, from her baby-lamb curls to her burgeoning breasts and hips. She moved languorously, reluctantly. And she was wearing makeup, lots of it.

Van came into the living room, flailing at the air with bent arms, creaking and clanking across the room in a metal body brace that encased him from armpits to heels, trying to reach for things on tables but missing them, knocking them over. "Rory, don't forget my radio. I have to have my radio!" He spoke clearly, though with some hesitations between his words.

Lee knew she had to find a way to talk to Toby before she and Joe arrived with what she feared was a trio of Visigoths. She didn't think Toby knew that Joe's boy had cerebral palsy, and she was sure Toby had never encountered a child with an external metal skeleton and uncontrolled head-bobs and arm-waves. Her son would need some preparation for this.

She asked Joe to pull his loaded-to-the-gunnels car into the supermarket parking lot so she could run in for extra groceries, going first to the pay phone just inside the door.

When she and the Montagnas trooped into the house with suitcases and grocery bags, Toby had already gotten the sitter to help him pull out the trundle and make it up; his own pillow was at the head of the bed.

By the morning that Joe drove his children to National for their flight back to Georgia, Lee was deeply grateful that their mother had custody. It had begun when Maddy looked into Lee's kitchen, which was a cornucopia of fresh fruits and bakery breads and jugs of juice and varied cheeses and tins of cashews and almonds, and had moaned loudly, "Theah's nothin ta eat in this house."

Lee found Joe in the dining room, teaching the boys to play Go Fish, and asked him, after smiling nervously at Van, what in the world his children ate.

"Cokes. Chips. Oreos." Seeing Lee's disapproving frown, he'd added with his up-down grin, "Think Southern, Leedle. Dr. Peppers would be good. Guess we can't get Moonpies here, but they like Twinkies." He winked at Van. "Waddya say, guy? Twinkies, right?"

Toby looked expectantly at his mother, sure that this was her cue to explain how damaging processed flour and sugar were to children's health. She said nothing.

Maddy watched soaps and sitcoms that she played so loudly they made conversation impossible in the living room. She used the extra-long cord on the downstairs phone to make calls from the front porch, looking up defensively if anyone came within earshot, which Lee did often on her runs out for more supplies. The phone bill later confirmed Lee's assumption that the girl had been reporting to her mother, in hours-long detail.

Van's radio was an audio counterforce to Maddy's television-watching, the boy blasting country and western songs over the organ music and laugh tracks of "Maddy's programs." He seemed puzzled by Toby's simple board games and found the terrain behind the house too hazardous to join in on sorties into the woods. Van returned always to the pleasure of the twanging voices and strong beats from his radio, beats his head and arms tried ineptly to follow.

Rory, seemingly the only sibling who read, was not interested in any of the books in the house. When she asked Lee where she kept her magazines, Lee told her that the current *Atlantic Monthly* was under the *Washington Post* on the living room coffee table. Frowning, Rory flipped through the pages and tossed it back unread. "I mean *magazines*, like *LOOK* or the *Saturday Evening Post* or *LIFE*." Lee had picked up copies on her way home the next day.

The girl sighed a great deal and issued endless orders to Maddy to do various services for Van. Professing boredom with every outing Lee suggested, Rory at least seemed to like Toby, ruffling his hair and calling him a cute little Yankee. Lee noted with relief that Rory was the responsible one, keeping an eye on what the others did, ordering them to stop anything that might be injurious to them, although property damage didn't seem to be on her list of things to prevent. Lee decided she could deal with the chaos as long as it was temporary and as long as no one was hurt; she would not have to insult Joe by calling in a sitter for the boys.

Toby trailed after both girls, trying with little success to engage them in the games and walks that Van could not do. After days of being substantially ignored, Lee came home from work with an imported recording for Maddy and Rory, and books for Van and Toby.

"We can read yours tonight, if you like, Van. Toby always loves to hear a good story, so what if you read this out loud...."

Van closed stiffly curled fingers around the thin book and creaked away from her. She watched him lurch his way to the kitchen and winced at how difficult every move was for him. If her son had such overwhelming physi cal problems, she doubted that manners would be at the top of her agenda for him.

She put the 45 on the turntable. "This just came in at a record shop near my office. A group in England. I thought you girls might like them."

As "Love Me Do" bounced out of the hi fi, both girls rolled their eyes and announced that they were walking to the community pool for an evening swim and a dinner of hot dogs.

Lee could imagine no reason Cindy Lou Montagna hadn't civilized these two perfectly healthy children. Switching the stereo to WGMS classical, Lee put two of the thick chops she'd brought home into the freezer. Her toe encountered the book she'd just given Van, Tolkien's *The Adventures of Tom Bombadil*. Wiping sticky pink Dr. Pepper from the pages, she noted that she would have to do better at figuring out who these children were and what they might like.

Every time Lee looked a question at Joe, he responded with the grin and the upturned hands that said Kids will be kids. But she was to make changes, nevertheless. At a band concert in Rock Creek Park, their improvised family of six sat behind a well-dressed couple and their daughter, a ten-year-old in a pinafore, her Alice-in-Wonderland hair tied back with a bow. As Joe's kids ignored the program and stared off into space, and Toby studied the horn players and the conductor, the little Alice sat in amazement at all she saw and heard.

Joe leaned close to Lee and whispered, "I want my girls to be like her. You could do it." But these days of observing Aurora Belle and Madelena Lucinda Montagna had convinced Lee that they had an excess of attitude to match the excess of vowels in their names. She would never teach them anything, nor she thought, would anyone else. Smart, suspicious Rory had a self-generated surround of ice separating her from any influences at all, much less those of some woman her father was dating. In Lee's company, the girl said little to nothing, always watching the scene, a chronic frown on her small face. And not-bright Maddy, the budding Wife of Bath—Lee thought she'd have as much luck changing her as holding back a dam that had already cracked. Lee wondered about even getting her to understand the simplest things—Maddy grabbed food from across the table and talked with her mouth full.

Joe beamed at Lee. "They see how you are. You can teach them to be ladies, like you." She'd laughed, thinking he couldn't be serious.

And there was Van. The boy named "of." Lee had looked up *heuvel* and found it meant hill; Joe's Dutch ancestors were "of the hill." And his son was Van Heuvel Montagna, Of-the-Hill Mountain. Names meant something. They not only should sound good, they should have good meanings. Like Tobias Andrew Pitt. Three syllables, two, then one. His given names meaning "Goodness of God" and "Manly." Even Toby's initials pleased her. At least Joe's mother had known to give her son a real first name. Lee hated being so critical of Cindy Lou, a woman she'd never met, but surely it must have been hard for someone as bright as Joe to be married to the woman he described as a dumb-as-a-brick cracker.

Lee wondered what Van's level of comprehension might be, whether he understood anything she or anyone else said to him. There was a look in his eye that conveyed not intelligence so much as cunning, a modus operandi a child so handicapped might develop to survive. Lee saw no way past his limitations and his calculations.

But the three of them had left. Their mother had custody. Georgia was far away. Joe's kids would only come to Washington from time to time. In all the other times, she would have just Joe and Toby and the sweet, strong life they were making together, a life that foretold a happy marriage.

For now, after they took Toby to her parents, it would be, for a little while, just the two of them, Joe and Lee, caring about each other, figuring out how she would make a go of the White House job, planning a future in which she, Lee Palmer Pitt—or Lee Palmer Montagna—would be going through the great iron gates every morning of the week, not a tourist but a staffer, an insider, at the hub of power, even if she were the one insider who was hoping not to be propelled back out the gates, an imposter among the powerful.

Mrs. Palmer, her plain face carefully made up, was dressed in a frilly blouse and bright suit as if she were on her way to St. Mary's for Sunday mass.

"So you're the young man Lee's told us so much about."

For heaven's sake, Mom. I just told you about him day before yesterday. Don't make it sound like I've been gushing, or like you and I chitchat every morning before breakfast. And 'young

man'? What are we here, 17? Still, she's trying. She's being
friendly. Which is more than I can say for Dad.

"Yes he is. Mom, Dad, this is Joe."

Joe reached a hand toward Commander Palmer, who shook it seriously and briskly, just once, as if he were returning a junior officer's salute. He was taller than Joe, and even with his hair white and his skin lined by years, he was still the handsomest man Lee had ever seen. "Welcome to South Carolina, Joseph."

"Thank you. I'm glad to be here. It's a pretty town, from what I saw of it as we drove in."

"Mom, can we put Toby's bag in the back room?"

"Yes, of course. And yours? I made up both the beds in there. You are staying the night aren't you? After the flight and the drive from Augusta? You must be tired. And we have this new sofa bed in the den, Joe. It's really very comfortable." Mrs. Palmer was smiling an entreaty at Joe, trying uneasily to head off any thought that he and Lee might share a room in the tidy little brick house to which the Palmers had retired. Lee was sure there had been a serious conversation earlier that included the shouted words from her father, "I don't care how old she is, in my house there's no shacking up!"

"That's sweet, Mom, but, like I told you on the phone, we're booked on the island starting tonight, so we'd better get going." She knew she couldn't bear further delay in having Joe's arms around her. There was no more comforting thought than imagining her head in the hollow of his shoulder through a night of sea sounds outside their windows. She would absorb his strength, take in his courage, making her strong enough to march right into the White House job and know that she would do it well.

Her mother looked relieved; there would be no confrontation. The Commander eyed Joe warily, making curt responses to this stranger's overtures, which Lee knew were overly casual; Joe was making himself too at ease in a house where he was an unknown quantity and to her father, it seemed, a highly suspect one at that.

Still, Joe was clearly charming her mother, who was going to the kitchen for the coffee she insisted he'd need for the rest of the drive.

How about me? It's OK if I doze off and drive into a tree?
Oh, that's right. Women don't drive if there's a man in the
car.

"Not me, Mom. I had a cup on the plane, so I could drive here." She ordered herself to stop, to not get caught up in the old discordant dance.

Mrs. Palmer handed Joe a mug of the coffee Lee knew was chicory-laced and strong, the way Ernest Palmer liked it. Mrs. Palmer turned away, blocking Lee's view of the tray that Lee had already seen did not hold another mug.

Toby took his grandfather's spotted hand. "Granpa, can we go to the lake? Quick? Before it gets dark?"

The Commander winked at his grandson and beckoned him out the kitchen door and into the garage. They returned quickly, Toby carrying a small fishing rod, his grandfather looking down on him with total delight.

"Mom! Joe! It's just like Granpa's but small so it fits me. And he's got a new boat. So we're going right now."

Lee stopped herself from telling her son to change into old clothes, and watched through the sheer living room curtains as he clambered into his grandfather's red truck.

"Well! That wasn't very polite of my husband. I do apologize, Joe."

"It's fine, Emily. And it's nice that Tobe's so excited to be here."

Lee wondered if her father could have left any faster, though she knew departure was better than the inquiry he might have begun had he stayed. *What are your intentions, Joseph? And your prospects?* It was also just as well that Joe did not have the chance to address her father as "Ernie," which she was afraid he might do.

What were Joe's prospects? Well, he was going to be the Secretary of Labor someday, that's all, and he'd do a fine job of it. Lee knew that such aspirations were not understandable in this household. Here, success was keeping your head down and the mortgage paid, being nice to the neighbors, never missing Sunday services. A Cabinet post, or even a minor job at the White House, was just a way to be conspicuous, to act as if you were better than other people.

A sharp pinch on her arm made Lee pull away from her mother, but Mrs. Palmer stayed close and whispered, "Don't scowl like that. It's not pretty at all. That's probably why you lost your job—no one likes a girl who's always grouchy."

> *Well, I'm not always. Not everywhere. Just here, where every-*
> *thing I do is the wrong thing.*

"Sorry, Mom. Thanks for taking care of Toby. We better get going."

Joe was giving Mrs. Palmer the up-down grin and the skyblue crescents as he pulled himself out of the chair, and she was beaming at him.

"Are you sure you can't stay a little while, when you come back for Toby? Lee never comes home. Ever."

"Mom, I keep telling you, I never lived in this house. Or this town. The house in San Diego was home."

"But *we're* here. And your dad's family is all over this valley. So you should come. Your brother came for Easter. Joe, you'll bring her back to stay a while, won't you?"

Lee smiled to herself at the mention of her little brother. She'd wondered how long it would take her mother to put him forth once more as the exemplar of the good offspring. Her brother, the one whose college education her parents were saving for in the years Lee was working her way through Maryland, the one who dropped out after one disastrous semester, the one who had joined the Army rather than the Navy, but who went to mass every Sunday and came home for Easter. The one who was doing just fine.

Lee would have to call him now. They'd never had much to say to each other, being too far apart in age for conversations beyond "Get out of my room!" and "I'm going to tell Mom you're drinking coffee!"

Now that he was a my-country-right-or-wrong soldier who did not like Lee's opinion of the growing war, they had even less to say to each other, but joking worked. Lee smiled at the thought of calling him to say, "Mom always liked you best," in a Smothers Brothers voice.

Joe laughed on his way to the door. "I'm at her command, Emily. At her command."

As Lee followed him toward their rented Buick, her mother pinched her arm again. "You be nice to him, you hear? That's a very sweet man."

One that I of course don't deserve, being so unsweet myself.

"I'll try not to scare him off, Mom."

She opened the French doors, letting in a rush of sweet night air and the sound of waves, small whispering ones, unlike the massive California breakers she remembered, rushing and retreating, but still the sea, the pulsating sea. The long sheer robe she'd packed billowed with the curtains until Joe came out of the shower and pulled her back into the vast bedroom of the suite he'd booked.

"It's late, it's been a long day, it's time to sleep, Leedle my girl."

The lovely suite, her dear Joe, his solid, warm shoulder, the sounds of the waves, the gentle touch of the soft breeze—it was so perfect she tried to stay awake, taking it all in, breathing quietly, not thinking about the serious matters that they would be wrestling with tomorrow. For now, tonight, there was only the sea, and Joe.

"What is it? Leedle? What's wrong?"

She was sitting up, her breath coming in rapid gasps, her hair damp with perspiration. "They're drowning! I can't reach them!" She shook her head rapidly and stared in horror out the open doors to the moon-glittered water.

"It was a nightmare, just a nightmare. Everything's fine, nobody's drowning."

Burrowing into his warm chest she told him what she had seen, what she saw on so many terrifying nights. She was in dark water, unable to breathe and all around her there were drowning men, spiraling downward, their arms and legs moving with loose, hideous grace. She struggled to reach the surface, to find air to breathe as the men circled all around her, moving inexorably down, pressed by the weight of the water. Their eyes bored into her, demanding to know why she was not lifting them with her, up to the light and the air they needed to live. A voice, a woman's voice, encircled her, but she could not understand what it was saying.

"Don't cry, Leedle. Don't cry. It's not your fault. Shhh. Shhh. Sleep. Everything's fine. I've got you. Nobody's drowning. You're safe. You're safe." He wrapped her in his beautiful, veined arms, gently cradling her into a peaceful sleep, without dreams or nightmares.

Joe was diving into the breakfast that had been laid out on the balcony of their suite, pouring himself coffee, adding more bacon to his plate, not looking at her.

"Do you remember what you told me last night, your nightmare?"

She smiled at him. "Thank you for bringing me out of it. Sometimes it's hard to believe it's not real, hard to get back to sleep. But I slept so well... thank you."

"You were really upset. Hell, you were frantic. I felt terrible for you."

"And you were wonderful. I've had that nightmare since I was a little kid. And you made it go away."

He put down his coffee and leaned on the table, watching her intently. "You can't save those men, Leedle. But you can save me."

"You? And what would *you* need saving from?" She watched a butter pat melt into her warm biscuit and reached for the honey pot.

"From being a lonely old bachelor. In New York."

She looked up, a spoonful of honey poised in mid air.

"I've got a job offer, too. In New York. There's this guy I met and he wants to start a consulting business with me. He's got the capital and I know all the people we need to get government contracts." Joe was talking rapidly, pouring coffee, dispatching his omelet. "We'll be doing Great Society work, important stuff that'll help working people get some breaks. We're calling the company Montagna & Altridge Associates, MAA. Good, isn't it? And there's this apartment, the bottom half of an old brownstone on the West Side. Big. Lots of room for Tobe, and for my kids when they visit. Thick walls so it's quiet. It's even got a garden. You'll love New York, I promise. My divorce will be final in two weeks. Marry me, Leedle."

Lee could not keep up with this deluge of information. Joe was not divorced. He was going to New York. All this time, he had never said he was not divorced but surely he had realized that she assumed.... He'd just said Marry me. He had made all these moves, started a business, found an apartment, all without saying a word to her.

It was a done deal and it was not the dream. The dream was being Lee Montagna, yes, but in Washington, making a go of the White House job, living in the dear old house she had chosen, the one by the creek, with her Joe and her Toby, making the life she had begun complete, perfect. The dream was not upending everything and starting over in OhMyGodNewYork.

A sound that was not quite a voice was reaching to her from the sea. It felt of rage and sorrow, but she couldn't make out the words, nor understand the warning. Joe pulled her up from her chair, wiped the tears from her cheeks and held her. His voice was close, reassuring, drowning out the whispered message from the sea.

For Those in Peril
On the Sea

It was to be a civil ceremony, in the tiny garden of the brownstone. When Joe brought Lee to see the place for the first time, she stepped into the small brick courtyard and was amazed to see that the low-wall beds rimming the space were newly planted with Sterling roses, the lavender ones she had always loved. She thought it might be a sign. A sign that this terrifying move was right, that a man who would do this was worth a few abandoned plans.

"I know they're your favorites, Leedle. I thought you'd know this is your place if they were here waiting for you. And don't worry about keeping them alive. I hired a gardener."

Their apartment was on the bottom two floors of the house, its hundred-year-old carved wood and ornate plasterwork beautifully restored by the gay couple who owned the building and lived across the street, in another brownstone they were restoring. The landscape-designer partner had designed the courtyard; the interior-designer one had done the building restoration, and all of it was beautiful.

Joe had thought of everything: the place was close to a grammar school for Toby, to the 81st Street transverse that Joe took to the MAA office on the East Side, and to the Columbus Avenue shops Lee would need to keep the household running. It struck her that he was making the move a great deal easier than her father had ever done for his constantly transplanted family. As imposed moves went, this one was going exceptionally well.

The Palmers arrived for the wedding and to take Toby home with them during the honeymoon that Joe was keeping super-secret, telling Lee only to pack clothes for warm weather. Her parents were leery of the city, and the Commander remained leery of Joe, causing his wife to make an even greater fuss over her daughter's catch, to make up for her husband's reserve. Emily Palmer may have found it hard to accept a marriage that could not be sanctioned by the Church, but her willful daughter would no longer be alone in the world, and that seemed to trump Church rules.

Standing in the handsome kitchen of the apartment, Mrs. Palmer was effusive. "I don't know about this neighborhood, Lee, but the house, this kitchen, they're just beautiful and I'm so glad you'll have time to enjoy them." She frowned, looking out at the backs of the buildings that surrounded the courtyard. "You'll keep the doors locked, won't you?"

"Time to enjoy them? Because I'll be married? C'mon, Mom. You know I've always had some kind of job. Since I was 13, babysitting. Even in Saigon, I taught English classes and I had that editing job at *Viet Nam Presse*. You *know* I've always earned some money. I'm not suddenly going to plop on my butt now and leave it to Joe to keep everything going. I have to find a job I can do in New York so I'm not a dead weight." Lee immediately regretted her words, disrespectful as they were of her mother's lifetime as a homemaker.

"It's a new time, Mom. Lots of women are going out to jobs even if they've got husbands."

"And I'm not sure that's a good idea. You should take care of Joe and Toby. And their home."

Their home. What am I, a guest? No, of course not. I'm just a servant.

"I will, Mom. I will. Just not every minute, OK?

Lee assumed that for such a small wedding, she would make a light meal herself, but Joe brushed the thought away. "My bride doesn't work at her own wedding. You've seen how many restaurants there are around here. Just pick one and have them come set it all up."

The only relatives he invited were Gert and Big Joe, his parents, whom Lee had met only once, for dinner in Little Italy. Gert, Joe explained, did not take well to guests in their Queens apartment. Lee saw very quickly that the played-out maternal line had surely been recharged with life force when Gertrude Agnes van Heuvel, student nurse, met Joseph Vittorio Montagna, union organizer. Big Joe had been sneaking into factories, pretending to be a worker, while he talked people into signing union cards. Dodging company goons who were out to kill him, Big Joe had kept on handing out cards and hope, until he was founding president of one of the most powerful trade unions in the country. Lee was entranced by her soon-to-be father-in-law, loved the stories he told of organizing and of plotting the labor movement's next actions with Red Mike Quill, Joe Curran, and Harry Bridges, giants of the labor movement. It was a time in modern history that Lee had always found fascinating, and Big Joe was one of its heroes.

And his son was smarter, driving even harder. Nobody knew more about working people, nobody cared more about making sure they got a fair shake. Watching Joe, Toby was seeing how a man functioned in the world, just as Joe had learned from Big Joe Montagna.

Big Joe was as warm and effusive as Gert was chilly and constrained. Anticipating a clan of enthusiastic Montagna cousins and uncles, Lee was startled that none were invited to the wedding.

"You don't understand, Leedle. I've been vetted by the FBI for all the government work I've done. And want to keep doing. And those guys... they're not exactly legit. I have to be able to say I haven't seen them in years, or the company could lose contracts." He grinned at Lee. "Besides, they got no class, y'know? I don't think you'd like them."

Joe's best man had, however, considerable class. Tate Altridge, Joe's new business partner, was scion to a Civil War-era fortune. A skinny, pale man in his thirties, his combination of WASP nonchalance and liberal social conscience had led him to invest some of his trust-fund money into establishing Montagna Altridge & Associates, consultants on labor issues in this new era of the Great Society. MAA already had a staff of seven and Department of Labor contracts to study the status of black entrepreneurs, and of household and dockworkers of all colors. When the staff had finished the research and assessments, Joe would make MAA's recommendations for federal action. Since his writing was ungrammatical, he'd be calling on Lee to edit the final texts. It was important work, much more important, she had reluctantly agreed, than trying to make Johnson's White House look "artsy." She was pleased that Joe trusted her to be part of the MAA team, even in this small, unpaid way. Now she just had to find a day job where there was a payroll.

Lee had expected to ask her college roommate to come down from Vermont to be matron of honor, and to invite some Foreign Service friends as guests, a few Maryland neighbors, and Hannah Rivers, who had been so disappointed when Lee had not taken the White House job, but Joe dismissed them all.

"It's all new, Leedle. A new start. Just get that actress you know. She's right here in New York, right? Or nobody. We only need one witness on the license, you know, and we've got Tate. This is about us. Me, you, and Tobe. We don't need anybody else."

Lee erased her images of surrounding herself with friends and allies; Joe was being romantic and dear, keeping the focus where it belonged, on their new little family and its future.

Still, she was glad the garden was tiny so this handful of people filled the space. Ariel Pierson had responded with some surprise to Lee's invitation to be maid of honor, being just as aware as Lee was that they had never been best friends. She arrived for the ceremony wearing a purple jersey dress that clung unfortunately to the indentations her underclothes made in her large, cushioned body, contrasting absurdly with the best man's Ichabod thinness.

The judge came into the garden wearing his black robe, which Lee had not expected. She wondered if it made him look priestly to her mother, who was already applying a handkerchief to her eyes. Priestly or not, he planted himself resolutely in the center of the little courtyard, lavender roses winging to his sides.

Joe and Lee took their places in front of him, Joe in a navy blazer and white linen slacks Lee had helped him find, Lee in a short dress of pale green chiffon. She reached back to Toby, helping him find his place between Tate and Ariel. The sun had risen over the surrounding roofs and was blazing into the courtyard; Lee could feel her skin growing damp, starting to burn. She wanted no sun, some music, a sense of ceremony, of community and ritual, in a private place, not a courtyard surrounded by strangers' windows. But this was what it was, and it had to be accepted.

Ariel held the bride's bouquet of lavender roses as Lee gave Joe his wide gold ring. When the judge asked Joe to produce Lee's, it came first from Toby's tightly clasped fist, into Tate's palm, and then to Joe, leaving Toby clearly pleased by the achievement of an important task. He was watching Joe intently, a small smile on his face that burst into a grin when the words "man and wife" were said and Joe's left arm encircled Mrs. Joseph Montagna while his right reached down to include Toby. There was applause—coming from all around and above the garden. Delighted faces were looking down from the windows on all sides, laughing, giving them thumbs up, clapping. Lee curtsied in each direction, smiling; Joe grinned and bowed. It seemed there was a community in attendance after all.

Commander Palmer and Big Joe Montagna each opened a champagne bottle and filled Lee's crystal flutes for toasts. Toby held an empty glass up to his grandfather, who winked and poured him an inch of bubbles.

Ignoring the best man's prerogative, the Commander took charge, standing to solemnly offer up, "To the bride and groom. Long life and happiness." Lee thought he could have added a little happiness of his own to the moment, but he was at least being coolly gracious.

Gertrude Montagna, wearing a dark gray dress that hung unevenly on her skeletal frame, exchanged brief words with the Palmers and with Tate, nodded at Lee and Joe, and ignored Toby, not once unknotting her face into an expression of pleasure. Looking uncomfortable in a too-small suit and a too-wide tie, Big Joe engulfed Lee in a bear hug before they sat down to lunch at a table under an awning that extended from the back of the house. Lee eased into the shade gratefully.

Looking around the table at this party of nine—the judge had hurried away, Joe's envelope tucked quickly into his jacket pocket—Lee found herself wishing that Ariel were an ingénue rather than a character actress; the customary wedding party romance was certainly not going to click between the fairly attractive Tate, and Lee's big-jawed, heavy-set classmate. Mrs. Palmer was trying valiantly to engage Gert in conversation, smiling at her, chattering more and more desperately as her new relative replied in monosyllables. Emily looked hopefully around the table for help that she did not get as the men struggled to find some conversational meeting point other than the fine character of Tobias Pitt. Toby, proud of his grownup seersucker suit, was even more pleased to be the object of so many questions and comments by grown men. Gert tugged at Big Joe to leave, though Emily Palmer was still talking to her and Big Joe was engrossed in his food.

"Stop it, woman. Have some of the chicken parmigian and the gnocchi. Really good."

Gert responded with a wrinkled nose as though she smelled something repellant. She condescended to sample the fenuccio and escarole salad and sipped the espresso that followed, ignoring the cannoli.

Lee spoke quietly to Joe as they sat on the low garden wall, her espresso cup held in front of her mouth, the skirt of her dress spilling softly around her and across one of Joe's white-linen legs.

"I think your mother hates me. She obviously did *not* want us to get married." She tried not to stare at the gaunt woman who had barely spoken to her new daughter-in-law.

"Hate you? Not you in particular. She's like this to everybody." Lee drew back her chin and raised her eyebrows.

"As in she's a bitch. Ignore her. This is *our* day, Leedle. And that woman's a black hole. Don't let her drag you in there."

Their day ended in a room on the north side of the Plaza Hotel, the windows filled with the lights rimming the park, lights in the windows of millions of New Yorkers unknown to Lee. She thought they just might allow a place for her here, now that she was consort to a blue-collar prince, on Montagna home turf, New York, New York, the center ring, the place that had lured and repelled her all of her life.

She could see the moon reflected on water down in the park, not open water, not moving, pulsating life-filled water, but flat, still water, water put there for all these New Yorkers to walk past, row on, sit by. There was no mystery in such domesticated water, no voices straining to be heard with messages dire and wise.

When she and Joe returned from whatever warm place they were headed, she would have to buy Toby one of the miniature sailboats she'd seen boys sending across that pond.

Joe's honeymoon surprise was revealed to Lee at a dock in Nassau as they stood before a handsome three-masted sailboat, its hull marked *Second Chance*.

"Is this class or what? It's ours, Leedle! Complete with crew and chef— we don't have to do a thing but eat and sleep and..." he dropped his voice to a whisper, "make love. All the way to Tortuga."

He beamed at her as three crewmen came up from below, their white shorts and green tee shirts coordinated to the boat's paint job. He was wait- ing for her thrilled response, his black eyebrows raised in anticipation. "I thought you'd appreciate the name, you being a word person and this being the second try for both of us." Lee thought his skin had already tanned darker and his eyes had gone an even lighter blue in the time it had taken them to walk the long dock.

> *I'm a redhead. He knows I burn. He knows I'm scared of*
> *water. What the hell is this?*

"It's a beautiful boat, Joe, and it has a perfect name. Thank you."

She knew he deserved her gratitude; this was indeed "classy," and she did appreciate the wit of honeymooning aboard the *Second Chance*. She would beat back her fear, focus on the stunning beauty of the sky and sea, and on the kindness of her Joe. She had packed cool linen slacks and long- sleeved shirts. She would find spots of shade on the deck or stay below until dark, coming up to enjoy the night skies. She would stop herself from thinking of the depth of the waters they would cross, of the unspeakable secrets those depths might hold. She would ask Joe, when it did not seem a criticism, how they could afford such extravagance.

She stepped onto the ramp that rose to the deck of the *Second Chance* and reached out for the extended hand of a crewman.

"Welcome aboard, Mrs. Montagna."

Standing on the foredeck the third night out, she reveled in the force of wind-caught-in-canvas driving the hull through the water. She moved easily with the dips and rises, the heeling and righting—her father had taught her how to deal with a deck's movement.

She had slipped out of the mahogany-walled cabin to listen to the wind, to enjoy the sun's absence. She loved the taut white sails, the boat moving through the dark, covered over and upheld by stars doming above the sails and carpeting the seatop—the top of a solid thing, like a street or a field; there was nothing below this bespangled surface.

There was even, to her wonderment, a benevolence emanating from the night sea, a woman's voice that seemed to welcome her, telling her she had nothing to fear from the water.

Lee imagined that tonight she could walk the moonpath across the solid sea; she did not believe the water's promise that she could move into and through it safely.

In the cabin, her Joe was sleeping in the bright moonlight that had awakened her. It played across the sculptured chest and arms that had escaped the rumpled sheets, reminding her of her favorite Michelangelos, the unfinished male bodies emerging from their white marble blocks in Florence's Academy.

This was the male body that held her life safe now, his skin, smelling of sun and salt, an extension of hers. Joe who had seen Lee Palmer Pitt and chosen her, giving form and validation to her being. If the seatop should open, despite her decree that it be solid, should the boat begin to fall through, her life would matter to him and he would save her, which she would not be able to do herself.

Her father had tried, just once, to teach her to swim, when she was small, when all the other children were learning. Her parents had taken her to a pool in the Brooklyn Navy Yard—it must have been a family day on the base. Ernest Palmer jumped into the water himself, turned and held his arms up to his daughter. She laughed and leaped, and he was not there. Sputtering to the surface, she saw him yards away, his arms still outstretched. "Come on, come on! I'm right here." But "here" was too far away. She thrashed, kicked her feet, swallowed chlorine-flavored water, tried to wipe it from her stinging eyes, and sank.

"Well that's the way *I* learned. My dad threw me in a pond and I got myself the hell out of there."

"Ern, she's just a little girl." Emily Palmer, who was deathly afraid of water herself, was patting a towel around her shivering daughter as she sat coughing and weeping on the cold tile edge of the pool, not wanting to look up at her father. He had expected something of her and she had failed, the first enactment she could remember of a script that would play out a thousand times more: a simple expectation, and her failure to meet it.

Not wanting Toby to inherit her fear, she had taken him to a swimming class when he was a toddler. The instructor at the *Cercle Sportif* in Saigon was known for making his lessons fun for the children; she wanted Toby to think that water was fun. The classes required a parent's presence so she went, assuming her role would be as dry-land encourager, but the young Frenchman beckoned the mothers into the water with their various offspring and, first instruction, told everyone to sit on the bottom of the pool together.

Even now, her lungs full of cool night air, Lee stopped breathing at the memory. Her face could not be in water. Water had to be controlled, tamed, edited—she even washed with a cloth rather than letting quantities of water touch her face. She had gestured urgently to Tim, sunning after doing laps, to take her place, which must be done quickly, before her panic spread to their son. With Toby transferred to his father, Lee walked into the clubhouse with as much dignity as she could assemble, turning to wave and smile at Toby, who proceeded to become a stellar student, loving water just as Lee hoped he would.

Water. It was everywhere around her now, and it was everywhere in her family's life, always in waking sight of the base houses where they had lived, ever filling her nights with dreams of the dying men under the sea. The sea had upheld her father's ship throughout a naval war. She wondered if Ernest Palmer had ever gone to the bow of that ship, and watched the night sea rush by. Had he ever imagined there were soft voices speaking from the waters? Lee heard them now as she stood on a deck, enchanted by the beauty of the night.

In the newspapers, in *LIFE*, in the *Saturday Evening Post*, there were stories and pictures of defeat, of death marches, and of sinking ships.

Her father's ship had burned at Pearl Harbor, one of the great hulls billowing black smoke in all the newsreels as Roosevelt's voice declared war on the Japanese. Chief Warrant Officer Ernest Palmer had been on shore leave when it happened, home with them on Coronado, an island in San Diego Harbor that was half navy base and airfield, half charming civilian town filled with Navy families. But they had not seen him since voices on the radio had ordered all military personnel to report immediately to their ships and bases. Buses moved slowly along San Diego's palm-lined streets, loudspeakers blaring, stopping at corners to pick up every uniformed man in that town filled with uniforms.

Commissioned as a line officer and reassigned to another ship, Ensign Palmer had flown to Pearl, where the ships were burning, where the Japanese might land troops, where Lee knew that Navy friends had been killed in their backyards and in their cars by strafing Zeroes.

San Diego Harbor, normally filled with great warships, had emptied out, the carriers, battleships, cruisers, and destroyers steaming past Point Loma and into the Pacific, leaving the harbor bereft, the city unguarded, vulnerable.

She sat with her mother and her baby brother in their green stucco cottage with the drapes drawn over the closed wooden blinds and a blanket shielding one small lamp. There must be no light to guide enemy pilots to the North Island base, or to this fragment of a family, sitting stunned in the Stateside town nearest to Hawaii.

In the long months after that, Pete, the too-old-to-be-drafted mailman, became the most important human on Coronado Island, a modern Mercury, carrying messages to and from the war. Every day her mother had a letter ready for him to take, a letter that smelled always of the sweet peas she grew, picking each day just one to send into the war. Most days the letters she received were things she shuffled quickly through and dropped unopened on a chair or the kitchen counter. And Lee would find her mother listening to songs on the radio like "I'll Be Seeing You" or "When the Lights Go On Again," as she mended Ernie's clothes or grated American cheese into macaroni, and quietly wept.

Then there would be a day when Pete—Mr. Cameron to Lee—came down the walk beaming, and Mrs. Palmer would run into the house with a stack of tiny V-mails, sorting them out to read in order, one for every day that had passed since the last batch that had come. But the sad songs on the radio still made her cry.

Drawers full of V-mails later, one came that said, "I've decided to shave my mustache next month, maybe before Halloween," and, "Why don't you and the kids go see Liz and Danny Bailey for your birthday?" Since Mrs. Palmer hated mustaches and her husband always grew one at sea and shaved it off before coming home and the Baileys lived in San Francisco and her birthday was in late October—she understood the message. The *Delius* was coming home.

In the next few weeks, Lee worried about her mother's behavior. Posters everywhere warned that a slip of the lip could sink a ship, and there her mother was, not saying anything exactly, but laughing too much and arranging for a friend to weed the victory garden when they would be in San Francisco, buying makeup and perfume that she didn't open, and making a lot of new clothes that she didn't wear. She stood in lines for stockings and had four pairs in packages on her dresser, 54 gauge, 15 denier, but she kept painting on leg makeup. She made an awful suit with big shoulders that she told Lee she would need for going out in San Francisco, which was an elegant city, almost Eastern. Then she made a red silk blouse with no back and a black satin skirt that she didn't sew up one side, and she didn't tell Lee what that was for.

Lee was sure her mother was a security risk. She didn't seem to understand that the *Delius* was a mother ship, a submarine tender, the rallying point for subs that would leave her to move below the surface of the Pacific, on the prowl for enemy battleships and carriers to sink. Sink the *Delius* and you'd cripple the submarine fleet. The enemy must not know that the tender was headed toward San Francisco.

Lee tried to make amends for her mother by doubling her red-wagon rounds of the neighborhood, collecting coffee cans full of used cooking grease, clattering piles of flattened tin cans and stacks of newspapers that left the dresses her mother made for her gray with ink. She pulled all of it dutifully, ritually, to the corner gas station where she placed her offerings on the piles of precious junk that would be scooped up by trucks from the base for conversion into explosives and tank treads.

Saturday mornings she would walk to the shadowy antique store on Orange Avenue and trade *Classic Illustrated* comics with the owner, a fierce, white-haired woman who looked remarkably like the parrot that hung near the stacks of comic books, assailing Lee every week with, "Tell me a story!

Tell me a story!" She would make her trade, an *Arabian Nights* and a *Don Quixote* for a *Les Miserables* and leave, getting quickly away from the Parrot Lady and her demanding bird. The comics were previews for Lee; if she liked the story she would get the real book from the stacks at the Coronado public library.

The next stop was the 9-cent matinee at the Strand, hours of Abbott and Costello, Flash Gordon, and of Humphrey Bogart winning the war on land and sea. Sitting over a lemon phosphate at the drugstore counter after the show, she silently ran and re-ran images of ships with guns erupting fire clouds, ships lowering away lifeboats after being torpedoed, ships slipping under the seatop. She would not play in that sea, would not even walk on the beach, knowing that the water was filled with drowned men who might be her father.

On the days she deemed her war efforts worthy, he would be safe. She knew he was not in danger the week she hauled two threadbare tires to the rubber mountain at the service station, and one week when collections were slow, she carried over her new Magicskin doll, just to be sure. If she got the yellow dye squeezed evenly through the disgusting sack of white margarine, he was safe for at least a morning. When the practice air-raid sirens screamed and she ran home under the fragrant oleanders and eucalyptus trees, it meant that no planes were diving on his ship—she was drawing their fire away from him.

Their own little house was well protected; housing was impossible to find, and families all over Coronado were taking in servicemen's families. Her mother had moved out of the room with the double bed and into Ernie's room, sleeping on a folding cot next to his crib, so the most beautiful couple Lee had ever seen could move into her parents' room—a tall Marine pilot based at North Island, and his small blonde wife.

Mrs. Palmer was terribly upset when the pilot's wife spilled a bottle of ink on her hand-crocheted bedspread, but Lee loved the days when the pilot swooped his F4U down over their tile roof and waggled its wings. If the Japs tried to hit Coronado as they had Pearl Harbor, the little house on C Street would have its own air defense.

When Ernie Junior cried, Mrs. Palmer would check his diaper, change it if necessary, then leave the room she shared with him, making herself a cup of Lipton's or folding laundry in the kitchen until he stopped wailing or the clock moved to his proper bottle time. There were rules that must be obeyed. Children couldn't be allowed to get attention every time they wanted it, or to do things imperfectly and think that was all the world expected of them. They would grow up to be people who thought they could have anything they wanted, be anything they wanted to be, and that was clearly not true. The responsible mother must steel herself and resist the urge to soothe and comfort a fretful baby. Even babies had to learn, Emily Palmer explained, that they could not have food if it was not time for food, or attention just because they wanted it. That wasn't the way life worked, and she was determined to do the right thing, even if it made her cry to do so.

During this super-dangerous time for her father, Lee stopped speaking to the Chinese kids who lived two houses away because they might really be Japanese who could send out Morse code reports on her mother's revealing behavior, the stockpiled stockings, and the industrious sewing of San Francisco clothes. Lee couldn't be too careful.

The best insurance came at Sacred Heart, where Lee never missed a Saturday morning confession. She had sinned exceedingly in thought, word, and deed, through her fault, through her fault, through her most grievous fault, offending God in some way or another every perilous week. Amends had to be made. She used up most of her allowance on candles she lit at the feet of Our Lady of Guadalupe, blessed Mary ever Virgin, before kneeling to pray that the dirty Japs would not harm the valiant officers and men of the USS *Delius*.

Words kept coming into her mind from the song they sang at Navy ceremonies, a song that wasn't Catholic and so could not be sung here at Sacred Heart, but it was beautiful and filled up her heart with just the words she wanted God to hear, even if they were Protestant—"Oh hear us when we cry to thee for those in peril on the sea."

Every couple in those war years must have had censor-beating codes—when the *Delius* made it safely into port, hundreds of wives and children were there, waiting for them. The women and their children had all beaten gas rationing or impossible crowds at train and bus stations to get there; civilians had no priority on travel space, the seats going first to the droves of military travelers.

Emily Palmer had been lucky. Ernie Junior completely charmed a teen-aged sailor from Ohio who was waiting near them in the mob jamming San

Diego's Union Station. The toddler had been wearing the chubby sailor's hat and getting romper fuzz all over his uniform for an hour before the train going north was finally announced, and the sailor plunged into the crowd, carrying Ernie on his shoulders. Lee and Mrs. Palmer had tried to keep up but were held back by the solid press of bodies. Her mother was calling out to the sailor to stop and give her son back, but the sailor was already on the train steps, talking to the conductor and pointing to Lee and Mrs. Palmer. The conductor waved them through the crowd, to coach seats with Ernie and his friend. "I told him he had to let my wife and daughter aboard, too," he said with a pimply grin.

In San Francisco, Ernie and Lee stayed with Liz Bailey and her son Danny, who ignored Lee, as he always had in all the times their families had turned up on the same bases, once even sharing a house in Long Beach when their fathers had both shipped out on the *Mississippi.*

There was nothing to do but read, help Mrs. Bailey in the kitchen, and chase after Ernie so he didn't get into trouble. "T-Bone" Bailey, a mustang officer now like her own father—which meant he used to be a sailor—was somewhere in the Pacific, on a battleship.

Lee wondered then about the names their fathers had been given by their shipmates. How did a person get to be called "T-Bone"? She knew they called her father "Deacon." She supposed her own name would be "Bookworm" and Danny's would have to be "Stuckup."

But she knew he would have been better named "Beloved." Danny the Unattainable, Danny who would one day come to love her at last, but would go away. She had pined for his attention when she was ten and she had dreamt of him through all the years since he had walked away from her for the last time, when she was twenty.

Since then, Lee had been haunted by a life she might be living in an alternative universe, a life in which Danny had not left and she was Lee Bailey. On days when her life as Lee Pitt felt impossible, she would slip into that unseen parallel world, an infidelity without sin.

On lonely nights in Maryland when she had longed for company, she had only to step out of that world and into the other, unlived one. She had no need of an alternative world now. Her Joe was all she needed and he was a few feet away, in a mahogany cabin on a beautiful boat he had given her, his beloved, for these amazing weeks.

There had been even more to fear during the war than Lee had imagined as she had made her collections and lit her candles. Her father didn't talk about it, but she learned from eavesdropping at the officers' club that a kamikaze had hit the bridge, shells fired from a Japanese destroyer had torn open the forward bulkheads, and some of his friends had died. The part of the story that frightened her even more was the long, slow towing of the wounded *Delius* across the Pacific, all those days that her mother had been preparing for the ship's arrival in San Francisco. Lee knew from the matinees how dangerous such a voyage was, and she wondered how the enemy ships and planes had missed this opportunity to take advantage of helpless Yanks.

At a picnic for the crew and their families, her father and the skipper presented her with a bowl of polliwogs they said had gotten shell-shocked aboard the *Delius*. On the bowl there was a decal of the emblem that Disney had drawn for the ship—Dolly Delius, a mermaid ringed by polliwogs. Lee didn't think deadly submarines were darling polliwogs, and a cute little mermaid certainly wasn't dignified enough for the *Delius's* solemn and dangerous role in the war. Saying none of that, she agreed to nurse the tiny creatures through a peaceful recuperation ashore. And deep into her life as an adult, Dolly Delius, the mermaid, still hung on the wall, wherever Lee lived.

Each day in San Francisco her parents became sadder, more distracted, as the ship came closer to leaving dry-dock, all repairs completed by round-the-clock shifts of shipyard workers.

There were pushcarts full of flowers on San Francisco street corners then, carts that perfumed the city air. Lee could see now the gold braid on her father's sleeve as he paid for a gardenia and pinned it to the broad shoulder of her mother's ugly suit. For the rest of Lee's life the scents of sweet peas and of gardenias would tip her instantly into being both the enchanted observer of her parents' love for each other and their excluded, incidental child. She would remember them in that long-ago time, each fateful day quieter, until they were standing beside the re-floated ship and they were saying nothing at all.

Lee had not seen the *Delius* wounded, but now it loomed above them, whole, strong, a gray wall held taut to the pier with massive hawsers, the ship full of noise and movement and power, ready to go once more in harm's way.

Dozens of families stood in its shadow, each one a tight cluster of colors around a single, dark uniform. The adults did not look at the ship and no one stood near the gangplank, where officers and men whose families were not there hurried aboard.

On the other side of the narrow dock, another ship waited, its gangway already pulled in, its decks lined with Marines in full battle dress, silently watching the scene below. No one was there to see them away. They had made their goodbyes in Idaho or Alabama or New Mexico and now stood witnessing the undoing of the *Delius's* ties to home.

No sun from the pale winter sky reached into the shadow between the ships. A wind that seemed to seek out the families and men swept into the harbor from the sea, shivering the air. The *Delius* began making harsh noises; men broke away from embraces and outstretched arms to move up the gangway.

Her father bent down to give her a hug, his shoulder board scratching her cheek. "You be good now, you hear? Take good care of your Mama and Ernie."

He pulled himself away and her mother moved into his side, her lavender dress soft against his uniform. Then he was climbing up to the ship.

Lee couldn't find him among the figures that banded the decks and the bridge, but she could see that her mother's eyes were fixed on a place directly above her on the ship's superstructure. Lee wondered how her mother could know which of those uniforms to wave to. But one of them waved back in the way her father did, so Lee pointed to him and got Ernie to waggle his small arms back.

There were no men on the dock now and many of the women were walking quickly away, leading or carrying their children back through the gates where the Shore Patrol stood watch.

The gangway was drawn aboard, the hawsers with their metal rat-guards thrown down, and the ship was freed. It throbbed slowly away from the dock. Her mother moved with it as it eased along the length of the pier, her eyes holding to the figure on the bridge while she threaded her way through the women and children who remained.

Lee tried to get Ernie to walk behind their mother, but he cried to be carried. The skipper's wife scooped him up and went with them to the dock's end. Mrs. Palmer's arm was still in the air and, farther and farther away in the harbor, the man who waved like her father still moved his hand back and forth slowly over his head.

"Bastards!" said the skipper's wife. Taller than Emily Palmer, her hair rolled in a high pompadour, she was facing the troop ship, where Marines were laughing and shouting, some of them hanging over the rails and waving.

"Don't worry honey, you'll find another one!"

"How about me, cutie? I'd jump ship for you."

"Hey, there's always the 4-Fs—don't cry too long, babe."

The remaining *Delius* women were glaring at them or pretending not to hear or leaving angrily. The skipper's wife handed Ernie to Emily Palmer and hugged her quickly before hurrying away, high heels making small angry hits along the pier. Ernie thought the Marines were funny and gurgled happily at them. Mrs. Palmer still had not turned away from the Delius, though it had moved so far away that Lee thought it looked like one of the models on her father's desk.

"Mama, I can't see him anymore."

She looked at Lee, startled, perhaps, that she was there.

"But he has binoculars, he can see us."

She turned quickly back to the ship, holding it firm with her eyes, with the intensity of her need to stay linked to Ernest Palmer. Unstoppable in its purpose, in the gravity of its mission, the *Delius* bore him away, beyond her reach, beyond her sight.

Lee had thought her mother didn't hear the Marines, then realized that they had gone silent. Their ship had begun to move, easing away from the dock to take its place in the convoy that was moving under the Golden Gate, out of the soft, sheltering arms of the California hills that enclosed the harbor, moving into the Pacific, and the war.

A voice called out, "Goodbye, dear," and another, "Goodbye—take care." Men began calling down from all over the troop ship, and Lee could not understand who they were talking to.

"Don't worry darlin,' I'll be OK."

"Think of me."

"I love you."

"Goodbye."

"Wait for me."

"Goodbye."

The toy *Delius* gone, Emily Palmer smiled, waved, and nodded her head in answer to the Marines.

She stayed there, still waving, until their ship too, disappeared. Then she walked slowly away, with her children, in the gray light that flooded the empty pier.

Lee saw now the sorrow and dread, and also the high drama of love, encircled by danger. Gold braid, gardenias, and a war playing ominously in the background—it had been a perfect potion of bliss and fear, preposterously romantic, unmatchable in ordinary times.

It was sad but understandable that the Palmers who lived now in the little brick house bore so little resemblance to the handsome lieutenant and the girl who wore those gardenias. Her father had been puzzled by the transition from decks to carpets; her mother had been frayed forever by that time of being on her own, a continent away from her own mother and half a world away from her mate, who was under fire and, for all she knew, already dead.

The home-front blackouts and air raid practices had been constant reminders that the war could come to Coronado at any time, could take her children's lives, and her own. There were dangers everywhere—stories of bad men breaking into houses they knew were unprotected by resident males; Mrs. Palmer locked every door and window, checking them again and again. People got polio and went into iron lungs, if they lived. When there was news of an outbreak, Lee was not allowed to go to the Strand for her beloved matinees.

There was never enough money or ration points. Mrs. Palmer made all their clothes, grew vegetables in the victory garden, added more and more bread to the meatloaf, mended every tear, darned every hole in their socks. As Ernie grew, he was constantly breaking things Emily couldn't replace or repair, constantly getting cut or bruised or sick.

Looking now through her mother's eyes, Lee saw a daughter who was not helping with all this, who was impossible to understand, always in the library or off in a dream world, wanting things she couldn't possibly have, things Emily herself had never had, nor ever dreamed of. When they listened to the classical albums her father had left at home, Lee asked for music lessons, sure she could learn to make such beautiful sounds.

"Cello," she said. "I could play the cello." Lee had been full of ideas that were outlandish to Emily, who desperately needed a proper daughter, an assistant to a worried, exhausted mother.

The child saw only a mother who was constantly angry and impossible to please, a father distant and always moving farther away, unreachable. Looking back, Lee could see the intensity of those years for that long-ago Ernest and Emily, resolving that she and Joe would hold onto the depth of what they had now, sailing together across these waters. They would not lose it to the mundane, to never-to-be-settled scores, as the Palmers had. Her father would not in his lifetime be able to pay the debt her mother felt was owed her for all those lonely years; Emily Palmer kept careful, permanent accounts.

Lee knew she was following her man back to his home territory, just as her mother had done, but what she was doing was different, she was sure. New York was not Ernest Palmer's safe, quiet Aiken; Joe Montagna's New York was the ultimate adventure. She would accept the challenge silently, as she was accepting these days in the sun, on the sea, aboard the *Second Chance*.

She took a last look at the all-surrounding stars, heard the sea rushing by, and felt the almost-spoken presence that said, You are welcome here, here in the depths. You need not be afraid. As she stepped onto the ladder that led down to Joe, a wave of chill air swept over her shoulders, from the sea.

Moxie by Proxy

It was a common thing for lost out-of-towners to pick Lee Montagna out of a sidewalk crowd when they wanted to know which way to the Frick, the IND, or Battery Park. And she knew. In four years of studying the city, she had watched, learned, absorbed the lay of the land and the habits of the natives, taken on the look and feel of being a New Yorker. People did get braver, they did step up and over their fears to move on, even if she herself could not have done so without the broad, confident hand of Joe Montagna.

Some evenings when the horns and sirens and voices and neighbors' radios were particularly loud outside the windows, she thought of the quiet house on the creek in Maryland, where the only sounds were of frogs and wind. When she read about an event at Johnson's White House that sounded as if it had been arranged by the professor and whoever had gotten Lee's job, she did not mention it to Joe. It was best not to speak of such things. She must not seem to have regrets nor allow herself to be wistful.

Her mastery of the city's geography had been greatly accelerated by her aversion to the subways; she was always on the surface, walking or busing, taking in everything she saw. Toby thought the subways were exciting and kept asking to ride them. Trying to explain why she stayed above ground, she described the trains as jackals—ugly, clever, malevolent and fast; to ride them you had to make quick moves, thinking faster than the jackal. She did not tell him that without light, signs, and landmarks to go by, you could pull an Emily Palmer, making wrong subterranean choices and ending up God only knew where, possibly never getting back to known realms. She did not relay to him the description her childhood chum Izzy had given her of unfortunates pushed onto the tracks to be bisected by steel wheels and barbecued by the third rail.

Bumble-bee Checker cabs were their bearers when they were with Joe, but quite beyond Lee's means for her journeys around town with her son or for her daily commute to MacGregor's publishing house, the place where she earned the small paychecks that she could add to her small child-support checks and assume she was contributing to the mysterious Montagna household finances. Joe kept the accounts. Lee had learned to walk softly around such questions as, Might they go to a play that had excellent reviews? or Could she buy new table linens for a dinner party?, angling for ways to have Joe make the suggestions himself.

It seemed to be small mistakes in what she said or did that derailed their pleasant life. She would do a seemingly insignificant thing and it would trip-wire Joe into a person she didn't recognize. Like the time she shelled fresh peas imported from some country where it was spring, and served them dotted with butter, edging a platter of roast beef slices she'd bought at Zabar's, the food-lovers' paradise on Broadway. Lee loved the place, looked forward to forays into its smells and sounds and people, forays that left her delighted with the city, her life, the world.

At Zabar's meat counter, on that day that was starting so well, she had drawn 87; the call was 79. When she heard 85, she wriggled through the throng to stand jean knees against the cold glass, looking over the display. The closest butcher lifted his knife over a brisket.

A peremptory "No!" came from 86, a middle-aged woman standing next to Lee. Small, tightly wound, grimly dressed, she was the kind of New York housewife Lee often found elbowing her out of the way at counters and in aisles. They were fierce in pursuit of comestibles, these women, taking enormous satisfaction in their tiny triumphs over any merchant who tried to put inferior fare into the mouths of their husbands and children. Lee called them the Warrior Wives.

"I don't want the end," this one specified emphatically. "Let me see that piece over there."

"Lady, this isn't the end." The butcher didn't look up, didn't reach for that piece over there, didn't pause in his cutting. "We started at the end. This is the beginning."

Perfectly countered, the woman took her white-paper-wrapped chunk of brisket with an, "Oh. Well. All right."

Lee coughed into her hand to mask her laughter. God, she loved this city.

Recounting the incident over lunch, she spread the delight to Joe and Toby. It was a perfect New York story.

Her guys did the tidying up, singing "The Eddystone Light" off key, letting Lee stay at the table and read as they bustled about, laughing. She loved their voices. It was a wonderful Saturday. And then it wasn't.

She went into the kitchen that evening, thinking to make roast beef sandwiches. There was no roast beef put away. Stepping on the pedal that lifted the lid on the garbage pail, she saw pink beef slices dotted with pale green peas.

Joe was at the freezer, taking out a carton of ice cream.

> *Why in the world would he dump all that beautiful food? I*
> *trek out to get the stuff, spend all that money, prepare it beau-*
> *tifully, and he dumps it in the can?*

"Joe? The roast beef? The fresh peas?"

"The leftovers? I don't eat leftovers."

"But I don't serve leftovers. They're ingredients. For new meals. It took twenty minutes to shell those peas. And roast beef costs a fortune, Joe."

"You're not poor, Lee. We're not living on your ridiculous salary, you know. Stop acting like some goddam immigrant!" His voice was low, under the volume that Toby might hear. He grabbed the quart of ice cream and two soup spoons. "We can even eat all this if we want to, and we want to. Me and Tobe." He tried to slam the kitchen door but it was hinged to swing; she stared as it flapped wildly from the force of his anger.

There had been no moment for her to clarify that she loved luxury and also hated waste. When it was about food, luxury was fresh peas as soon as they hit the market. Luxury was gathering in haddock and blow-fish from Citarella's; bok choy, butter lettuce, and gravensteins at Fairway; from Zabar's *pain au chocolat*, a baguette, a bag of freshly ground Jamaica Blue Mountain coffee, and a chunk of stilton. Luxury was the hand-packed

French vanilla ice cream that Joe and Toby were spooning out of the carton as they laughed in the living room, watching "My Favorite Martian."

Waste was buying such fine things and then throwing them away. Waste was an insult to all the ancestors who had struggled to survive, to the people all over the world who still lived in conditions most Americans could not imagine. Lee had been in the tin shacks on the edges of Saigon and in the Cité, the black slum side of Leopoldville. Material things that she was lucky enough to have were to be taken care of and used well.

She had to see to it that all the days were like their best, the ones when Joe was himself and that raging person did not usurp his place. She just had to know what not to do, what not to say. For one thing, she could avoid another "leftover" crisis by doing the after-meal cleaning up herself, preserving precious ingredients in opaque containers that Joe would not open. Next time, the fresh peas would make it into a soup, a delicious one.

There were so many good days. MAA was thriving, federal and state contracts coming in at a steady pace. Toby loved his school and had made friends in the neighborhood. Lee's job at MacGregor's was dull but not unpleasant. She was grateful to be given the chance to learn book editing, even if the books were dreary and minor, even if the other editors at her level were 22 instead of 35. And the city, the city was endlessly enchanting. Especially on Sundays.

At least once a month they had Sunday morning guests—Joe told her he wanted to show off their handsome apartment and his beautiful, accomplished wife. He invited the movers and shakers he came upon in his work, urging Lee to be especially charming to them, and always there was Tate, Joe's MAA partner, laughing, spilling his coffee, talking politics and, after he married, cajoling his reluctant bride into conversations with his fellow activists. Lee invited her friends from MacGregor's, and parents from Toby's school.

The events came to be known as "the Montagnas' Triple-B Brunches"—Lee served biscuits, bialys, and brioches, along with frittatas she made or cheese quiches with *millefeuilles* crusts from a French bakery on the East Side. The breads were accompanied by herbed butters and imported preserves, and she'd recently added chopped liver to the array. Joe beamed proudly when astonished New Yorkers said their own mothers didn't make better. Her secret, she readily revealed, was in adding a generous tot of brandy.

Many of the city's secrets were being opened to Lee by Judith Bridges, a born-and-raised New Yorker who had been coaching Lee since they'd met at a fundraiser for Cesar Chavez. Judith was Lee's briefer on the ins and outs of politics in New York, and invited the Montagnas into rooms where the connections were even more abundant than the food. So far, three major MAA contracts had come directly out of evenings at Judith's vast Fifth Avenue apartment. Most recently she had introduced Lee to a renowned political scientist who seemed interested in Judith's extravagant introduction of Lee as a fine editor of nonfiction books. Lee had hopes.

Judith, tiny, intense, firm on her feet, had an impact on the small stuff too, the little pleasures of New York. She knew what time to arrive on a Saturday morning at which East Side bakery to get heavenly warm jelly doughnuts right from the oven. She knew who was a charlatan and who was a great internist or physical therapist. She knew about the little French bakery that made the *millefeuilles* quiches. She knew where to find well priced, not-quite-antiques, good pieces from the twenties and thirties that Lee felt she could afford.

It didn't make much sense to pay top dollar for new furniture when the old stuff was cheaper, better made, and didn't depreciate. Judith had introduced Lee to Parke Bernet's low-end auction house, PB 84, teaching her what to look for at the pre-sale, how to bid, what mover to call to get the goods to the brownstone unscathed. She took Lee on searches of antique shops in Jersey and Connecticut, Judith leaving her furs on the seat of her limo, telling her driver to wait for them out of the shopkeepers' sight, to keep the asking prices down.

Judith was a good teacher and Lee had a good eye; the Montagnas' brownstone apartment was furnished with chests, chairs, tables, armoires, a sideboard—all solid and mellow, like the paneled rooms themselves. Lee had even become a scout for Judith's own purchases, spotting the picture of an 18th-century Hudson River packet boat that now hung over the main fireplace in Judith's upstate farmhouse, and numerous treasures that sold well in Judith's East Side shop.

For her own home, Lee had made the best coup of all, in one of Judith's don't-tell-anybody places. On a Saturday morning, passing the jammed, dirty shop window on Broadway, Lee noticed in one corner a place setting of her favorite flatware pattern.

"Henry, have you got any more of that thread-and-shell, or is it just the one setting?"

The shop owner held up one stubby, just-a-minute finger, saying nothing, and disappeared into a storeroom. Lee moved meticulously through the dangerously stocked shop, wondering what the annual losses to breakage were. One too-sudden turn, one misplaced foot or elbow, and you could shatter hundreds of years worth of exquisite china, plates stacked in columns, teacups and saucers piled in cardboard boxes, soup plates filed vertically on bowed shelves.

The street display window was walled off from the shop, so the only daylight came from the glass upper half of the front door, abetted weakly by three bare light bulbs hanging from cords above the shop's almost non-existent center aisle. The bulbs were clear glass, the elements visible, emitting what looked like 20 watts apiece; Henry had mole instincts. He seemed content in all this gloom and clutter, never dusting, never propping the door open, always smoking his pipe, always smiling. The smell of Prince Albert was linked in Lee's mind with Limoges and Wedgewood, and with potentially destructive sneezes.

Kleenex at the ready, elbows pressed close to her sides, she inched through the darkness, finding French cobalt and gold dinner plates in a four-foot-high column listing dangerously on top of an old steamer trunk. She was counting the gold rims with one careful fingernail when a thud drew her attention back to the wooden counter. Henry moved his pipe from one side of his mouth to the other, then his chubby hands opened a scarred wooden chest, and turned its glistening contents toward her.

"Twelve complete place settings. Lunch and dinner. Hallmarked English sterling. George Angell. About 1850. Serving spoons, fish forks, demitasse spoons, punch ladle, the works." His happy, bearded face beamed at her above the shining knives belted into the lid of the open chest. "Not bad, huh?"

He gave her a price that sounded like melt-weight, not what beautifully crafted old silver should rightfully cost, not enough to cover the history of the patina on each piece, the scars on the battered chest. Judith had explained that the pros often dealt in weight, not history, but still Lee was puzzled.

"I don't get it. I mean what's the catch?"

This was not playing the game well; she wasn't supposed to show such interest, or such receptivity to an asking price.

"Locked in a warehouse since 1933. An estate fight. It was settled. They sold. I bought. So, Lee. You want it?"

"Do me a favor, Henry. Let me borrow this spoon until four o'clock. I have to do some selling too. And don't show it to anybody else before then, OK?"

"With a soup spoon missing? Who'd want it?" He heaved the chest under the counter as she headed for the door. "Lee?" He held up crossed, pudgy fingers. "Good luck. I hope he says yes."

In the brownstone kitchen, at the deco metal table, after warmed croissants, scrambled eggs, Scottish salmon, Blue Mountain coffee dripped in the Chemex, and buttered babka, Lee handed Joe the English soupspoon.

"You're giving me a spoon?" He bounced it up an down on his palm, registering its weight. "Or maybe it's a trowel."

The Queen Anne plated pieces they had just eaten with felt like paper by comparison. Lee talked about the tradition involved, the hallmark, the extraordinary chance to have such a large and complete set for the price of just the metal.

"You're telling me this is a very classy spoon."

"Knock-em-dead classy, dear heart. As if someone in our family trees had left us something of value."

They had been using the sterling every day since. And the cobalt and gold plates for dinner parties and family holidays. When Joe wrote a check on Henry's counter, he had insisted on buying the plates as well as the flatware; Lee had managed to get him out of the store before the check got any larger.

She was sure that every flavor was enhanced by these forks and spoons, but Joe liked it best when they had guests, especially when she served her cranberry/claret punch at Christmas and he could warn guests it might take both hands to lift the magnificent ladle.

Most Sundays, weather permitting, they spent in the park. She would buy the five-pound *Times* and read the front page while she stood in line at H&H, inhaling the aroma of their freshly made bagels. In the park, she and

Joe always spread a blanket and read the paper while Toby bicycled along the nearby paths, Joe reading the business and political sections while Lee went first to what she called The New York Times Review of Books I Didn't Edit. She brought along a thermos of hot chocolate for Toby, one of *café au lait* for her and Joe, and the bagels, with schmears of chive-laced cream cheese. When Joe tired of reading, he and Toby would set up for batting practice, attracting warm smiles from passersby watching the good dad and the happy son.

Sometimes, taking Toby to the boat pond or having a midnight bowl of onion soup at the Brasserie, or peace-marching with Lowenstein and Abzug, she wanted to break into a dance step. She couldn't stay concerned about Joe's sudden rages, the times when he said things that stung. The rages were, after all, avoidable. She need only control her words and deeds.

It was the larger world that was impossible to control, afire with race riots, search-and-destroy missions, famines, high-jacked planes, the poor marching on Washington, the war that was never going to end, and the deaths, so many deaths. It was almost shameful to be privately happy when the news was so desperately sad. Her illusion that "They" must have things properly in hand disappeared as it became clear that the old were lying to the young about the war, sending them to die, pointlessly. Lee learned, along with a generation, that authority must always be questioned, challenged, never trusted.

As the war escalated, the dissension it caused on the home front even boarded the bus Lee took to work every weekday morning after walking Toby to school. When her timing was right, the ride began with a delighted "Good morning!" from her favorite bus driver, the one who made a lie of every tale of the corrosive nature of New Yorkers. This one was mother hen to his passengers, calling out stops with advisories to be mindful of a break in the sidewalk or to get the umbrella ready, noting approvingly when a regular sported a new coat. Lee had even seen him hold at a stop, directing passengers to wake up a rider who always got off there. Though his natural accent was Bronx, he could do a perfect imitation of Laugh-In's little *Wermacht* soldier with his "Ferrry interefting," and of Ernestine the phone operator, even matching Tomlin's snorting laugh as he entertained his rolling audience.

There was a tiny American flag taped to his fare box, a daily reminder to Lee that good people, like this dear man, like Commander Ernest Palmer and Sergeant Ernest Palmer Jr., thought that troops on the ground had to mean full endorsement of the government that had put them there.

When Lee took Toby to visit her parents, she saw in the airport parking lot a bumper that read, America, Love it or Leave it. Just as she said, "Look, Toby, there's one of those bumper-stickers we heard about," her father walked to the car she was pointing to, unlocked it, and gave his daughter the familiar look that said, It's not worth my time to discuss this with you, but you are deeply and permanently wrong.

She began wearing a pin on her coat as a silent return message to the world. It was the American flag shaped into the body of a dove, her favorite graphic of the times, the one that said, I too am a patriot, this is my flag, as it is yours, and I don't believe in this war. She wore it with the open-to-dialogue face that was part of Foreign Service training. Her bus driver responded with increased geniality. There were both glares from other passengers and thumbs-up smiles, all of it making Lee uncomfortably visible. Continuing to wear the pin was her minuscule act of bravery.

Since she boarded uptown, before the bus filled, the odds were high of getting her preferred seat at the window just behind the rear door. There, she had a view of most of whatever happened on the bus as well as the changes in the city as it lurched from the relative quiet of the upper West Side to the high-boil action of 57th as it crossed town to the East Side.

Given the chaos of mornings at the brownstone, getting Joe and Toby out the door and getting herself into some semblance of professional style, the slow trans-Manhattan ride was restorative. Time to think about reporting her progress to her supervising editor. Time to solve an editing problem that had seemed unsolvable the day before.

After eight hours of note-making and page-turning, she took off the high heels that by day's end felt like instruments of torture, threw them into her shoulder bag, put on flats, and took to the sidewalks, the long hike home being her only exercise as well as a private interval between the demands of the day and those that would fill her evening. This time, this long walk, was all hers, and she treasured it. After picking Toby up at the sitter's, there would be helping him with homework, making dinner, tidying up, and working on MAA reports while Joe read Toby to sleep. But this time, and these blocks, were hers alone.

She varied the combination of cross streets and avenues that could get her back to the brownstone, coming to know every doorway, window, and marquee, every tree struggling to survive in its absurdly small opening to the earth below. She still marveled that there was actual soil beneath all the concrete and macadam, revealed in the tight squares for the trees and in the gigantic ones being dug for new buildings. The sight of actual earth was as startling as the first time she'd glimpsed a woman pushing a large pram out of an apartment house door and was struck by the fact that people actually had tender, fragile babies here and raised them, right in all the concrete, glass, and steel.

Those rigid, hard surfaces seemed even harder and more rigid when Lee's eyes were drawn to the passage of clouds overhead, to wind-fluttered flags and leaves, to birds diving and soaring. Still, it was the man-made things that she found most wondrous. Nowhere else was so much excellence so compactly on view. Galleries, restaurants, stores, museums, libraries, magazines, jewelers, networks, and book publishers were shoulder-to-shoulder or stacked one above another, all of them places the world knew, and all of them right here, in the same few walkable square miles.

And the people. People of every color and country-of-origin, people in rags, people in furs, people speaking unknown languages. In other places, you could read about people decidedly unlike yourself; in New York you walked alongside them, sat next to them at counters and on buses, stood with them in lines at the market and the post office. In New York, the poor, the foreign, the super-rich, the famous, the addicts, were not abstractions or statistics; they were your visible reality, all in motion, all within arm's reach.

There were the junkies and drunks, the lunatics, the beggars. There was Greta Garbo on the elevator at Saks, getting off at Lingerie, everyone pretending not to notice. Mikhail Baryshnikov, chain-smoking at the next table in The Gingerman. The Secretary of Defense browsing at Rizzoli. All of them allowed their privacy by New Yorkers, who had seen it all.

Once, on an escalator down from the fifth floor of Bloomingdale's, Lee realized that the man standing on the step below her was Van Johnson. He was still right there on the third-to-second stretch when, giving up her New York cool, she tapped him on the shoulder.

"I think I should tell you that when I was 12, I was absolutely sure I would marry you when I grew up."

He gave her the slanted-grin-amidst-freckles that had so beguiled her younger self and said in his familiar voice, "Well, it seems that you have, and I'm available. Are you?"

The part of the city she was learning particularly well were the blocks close to MacGregor's revolving glass doors on Third Avenue. The avenue was mutating. The "el" had come down, allowing the sun to touch places it hadn't reached in a hundred years. Trains no longer rumbled and screeched past third-floor windows, filling them day and night with a combat-level din. Buildings that housed laundries, hardware stores, fishmongers, candy stores, secondhand shops, used-book dealers, and three or four floors of low-rent, walk-up apartments, had thrived like mushrooms in that noise and darkness. Now they were being eradicated by the buildings' owners, who saw these small-time businesses and apartment-renters as expendable squatters taking up the spaces where corporations were eager to dig deep for parking garages and fill the air above the buried cars with 80 stories of prime glass-and-steel office space.

MacGregor's Publishing House had nurtured, edited, and published writers since the turn of the century in the same charming old building in Greenwich Village. Now, four venerable publishing houses, MacGregor's among them, had been bought up by a corporation and consolidated in the EPNI International Tower, newly arisen on Third Avenue, which was fast becoming Publishers' Row, corporate-style.

Discomfited by being one of the intruders who were destroying a once-vibrant neighborhood, Lee spent her lunch breaks exploring what was left of it. She would take the silent, high-speed elevator down from her hermetically sealed floor of cubicles, all buzzing with fluorescents and electric typewriters, and within minutes would be rolling a ladder along the top shelves of a dusty used-book store, finding an 1898 set of Jane Austens or an autographed Martha Gellhorn.

In an antiques store full of Depression glass and Fiestaware that reminded her of her mother's kitchen, she bought an old engraving. A very young couple walking together on a tropical beach, the boy sheltering the girl with a large palm leaf, he solicitous, she calm, assured. Back on the twentieth floor, she showed the picture, which seemed to be a bookplate, to Pam Pierpont, the artist who designed most of the books Lee edited.

"I don't know who they're supposed to be, but I love this picture."

"Oh, that's from *Paul et Virginie*, you know, the old French story. By de Saint-Pierre?"

Lee didn't know, but the picture pleased her, and that evening she gave it to Joe. "See, he's shielding her, keeping the sun from burning her." He looked at the picture quickly, laughed and put it on the pile of reports and magazines waiting by his chair to be read. She made a mental note to retrieve it before the pile went into the trash.

Joe Montagna might not respond to old book engravings but Lee knew he was her "Paul," the one whose love arched over her, whose arms held the dangers of the world at bay, the man she said gave her moxie-by-proxy so she could survive living in Oz.

There were constant reminders of the need for a protector. Like the Saturday they relaxed into a wonderful lunch at the Fountain in the park, ordering their favorite pail of shrimp and a bottle of champagne. Walking home, arm in arm, they laughed over the prospect of privacy back at the brownstone; Toby was at a friend's until five. They could always make love in their room—the old walls were wonderfully soundproof—but it would be a special thing to walk around the house without robes, to perhaps make love in the living room.

Without warning Joe's voice changed completely. "Look straight ahead. Stay close and don't stop walking." Lee realized that a pack of tough-looking teens was coming toward them. Joe calmly unbuckled his belt and wrapped it around his right hand, looking straight at the kid in the lead, who was much taller than Joe, and heavier. The boy nodded to the others and they fanned out, moving past Lee and Joe, on the watch for someone who would not prepare for combat when they appeared. Lee had not even seen them coming. She wondered how many beatings Joe had endured before learning to stay that aware and to respond so clearly in the language of the street.

On a crisp autumn Monday, Lee found that more old buildings had been razed on a stretch of Third north of MacGregor's and a wooden wall thrown up around the site. Emphatic steel beams had been bolted across obscenely revealed inner walls, bold strokes of industrial power against the fragile humanity of five levels of flowered and striped wallpapers, pink, yellow, and aqua paint, crazily angled hanging pictures. Domestic remnants of generations of people who had lived their lives out in the ripped-away building were exposed to the elements and to staring eyes on the street. A pattern of stair treads zigzagged up the wall from floor to floor, behind the authoritative beams that kept the adjacent building from sagging into the unexpected void that now loomed beside it.

Lee imagined the missing rooms, the people who had moved in them, argued, studied, made love, cooked dinner, raised kids, read the headlines, painted and papered those walls, hung those pictures. She had been in the ground level space; it had been a favorite used bookstore.

She averted her eyes and opened a ground floor door into the surviving building, coming into a musty, chaotic junk store where she found a box of solid brass, art nouveau door knobs, beautifully cast to read "PS 11." She bought them all, at a dollar a pair, though she owned no doors to put them on.

Someday she and Joe would not be renters, perched to move on. They would have their own place, maybe one of the hundreds of derelict West Side brownstones that were being sold and renovated, like the one in which they were renting. They would fix up one of the derelicts, bringing back the beauty that was behind the cheap partitions and the layers of paint that covered beautiful carved wood and molded plaster. They would sand and stain and paint and hang wallpaper. She would unpack the boxes she hadn't opened since Washington, the ones that held her life before Joe, boxes he kept saying he was going to take out of the storeroom and put out at the curb for the sanitation department to pick up. She would shelve all her books and albums, hang her pictures, have an orange and white cat. And when she opened the doors, feeling these heavy brass ovals in her hand, she would know that she was truly and completely at home in New York.

She carried her clattering bag of doorknobs into a candy store—properly pronounced "cenny stoah"—that hadn't changed in decades. Sidewalk piles of newspapers flanked the entry, racks of magazines lined the walls. There were hollows worn into the wood floor by generations of children coming in for Jujubes, Good and Plenties and Necco Wafers, for jacks and tops and jump ropes; by their parents picking up the daily paper and a pack of Luckies; by intellectuals stopping by to read the literary journals and—if they had a teaching gig or had sold an essay or short story—to even buy them. Lee wondered where the current neighborhood residents would go as the bulldozers moved in, whether they would disappear before or after the candy store itself.

The storekeeper, wearing a 1940s' fedora and a moth-eaten sweater, sat reading *Daedalus* at the cash register. When Lee paid for a *Kenyon Review*, he informed her that "The Fugue of the Fig Tree," published years before in the *Review*, was the best short story "evah." When she said, "By Stanley Sultan. I loved the ending, the sound of the nun's robes swinging, the sound of the fig tree swaying," he looked at her with sudden interest.

"You're on lunch? Sit. Sit. You wanna eat? I'm Mort."

Delighted to oblige, she took one of the six stools at the worn marble counter, taking in the long, two-person-wide store.

There were newspapers in Yiddish, Italian, and Greek, tattered boxes of yo-yos, sticks of chalk, clothes line for jump ropes. It was a time warp into the New York Joe had grown up in. She smiled, remembering his lesson in city-kid language: "Jeat?" "No. Jew?" "No. Squeat."

"OK, Mort, pastrami on rye with Russian and a Dr. Brown's Cel Ray."

He squinted at her through smudged horn-rimmed glasses, one earpiece secured with a paper clip. "Not ham and cheese on white with mayonnaise?"

She laughed, hearing her own accent mimicked perfectly.

Mort had one hand on the counter, one on a hip. "Seriously, wadda you know from Russian and Cel Ray?"

"You'd be surprised what I know. You make egg creams?"

"Izza pope Cadolic?"

Reluctantly leaving the reality of the streets, Lee pushed a shoulder into the revolving door at EPNI, crossed the chill marble lobby, fit herself into a crowded elevator, and shot up to MacGregor's nonfiction division. One desk, two chairs, a couple of coat hooks, and her space was full. Chapters of the manuscript she was working on were laid out on the desk, the ones she'd finished to the left, small blue squares glued to almost every page. The unflagged, unread pile to the right was discouragingly high. The historian who had done the draft didn't understand it was a draft, that he couldn't just write down everything that came into his head and call it a book. She was tagging disconnects, errors of fact, confusing progressions, and murky writing. She'd heard that he was great on his feet, a charming lecturer, but

he needed a ghostwriter, not an editor. And she wasn't so sure of his scholarship; her desk was piled high with reference books on Balkan history that
she was using to cross check the professor's version of the facts.

As she pulled her chair into place, her supervisor leaned in the cubicle
doorway, grinning. "I could hear that sigh clear across the floor."

The bone structure in Ramon Sakamoto's Asian/Mayan face was so
strong Lee found herself sketching him in staff meetings, while musing on
the wondrous results of cross-cultural unions. The photos that filled his office of his Asian/Mayan/English/Scots children were even more beautiful,
living testimonials to the joyful conjoining of the world's disparate peoples.

"Yeah, boss man. It's a bear, this one."

"I know it's a piece of crap but I also know you can fix it. The last one
you did came in dross and left the building gold."

"Thanks. I think. But next time, please, somebody who can actually
write?"

"But then just anybody could handle it. I wouldn't need Lee the Miracle Worker."

*Who is he talking about? Miracle Worker? More like Patient
Drudge.*

"Point taken. A raise then?"

She read a page of the manuscript, looked up a name in one of the fat
volumes, and wrote, "R u sur? Cnflcts w Djilas p. 189." She pulled the next
chapter to the center of the desk and was quickly writing yet another blue
tag. "Antcdnt unclr. Who sez?" She did not write "Who crs?" It was going
to be a long afternoon.

She called Joe and asked him to meet her downstairs at 5:15.

When they walked into the candy store, Mort beamed. "Hi, Lee. Two
seconds and they're ready."

Joe was turning on his stool at the counter, grinning, taking in everything in the place, when Mort put the freshly made chocolate sodas in front
of them. Egg creams with no egg and no cream, the perfect New York-native
drink. Joe closed his eyes as he took a deep pull on the straw.

"I bet they've got spaldeens."

Mort heard that. "Over dere inna cohnah. Last place on Toid where
you can ged dem."

And one of the last places in Manhattan where the berl-em-in-erl, toi-ty-toid-street accent could still be heard.

As he hailed a taxi for the ride home, Joe, red-rubber "spaldeen" ball in hand, beamed at his wife. "That was fun, Leedle."

The city was usually fun, not frightening as she had so long thought—fun. So much so that she was reluctant to leave on summer weekends, though the city was far too hot, and the invitations to the Altridge beach house in South Hampton were not to be refused. Tate's parents had given him the house while they were on a world cruise and the Montagnas seemed to be on Tate's must-invite list, though Lee was sure they were not on Pru's.

The Hampton nights could be magic, but for Lee the days were uneasy at best. There was usually a sea breeze at the old house, and she loved sleeping in that beneficent breath as it moved across the bed, smelling of seaweed and brine. Some nights she would slip out of the house alone, going out to the cooling exhalation of the gentle Atlantic surf. Coated with spray and moonlight, she would sit in the damp sand and listen for the voice. The water seemed to whisper, Listen listen listen.

In the canopied bed, next to Joe, the whisper sometimes lured her into the good sea dream, the one where she was in and of the sea, soaring above and through corals, doing a weightless, spiraling dance with great, graceful rays, with clouds of sequined fish. She moved quickly, long hair streaming, iridescent tail powering her in any direction she chose to go, sometimes riding the surface waves, singing into the night air in a wholehearted voice she did not recognize as her own. It made no sense to Lee. How could being in the sea ever be good, even in dreams? That was where the drowning men spiraled around her, demanding she save them, even if it meant drowning herself. Being in any water at all meant choking, gasping, dying. Nevertheless she found herself, at the closing of days when she had triggered Joe's wrath, hoping the good sea dream was waiting for her in the night.

The South Hampton days were sun-beset, the light glaring off water she knew full well to be dangerous, not the benevolent realm of her dream. She would walk out to the beach with Tate, Pru, Joe, and any other guests the house might include, but she remained resolutely landed and umbrella'd, while they gave themselves over to the sun and the sea.

On a particularly hot August day in this summer of being Hamptons semi-regulars, Lee and Joe went with Tate and Pru to a pool party a few houses down the beach. Lee tucked herself under the jutting pool-house roof, wishing she didn't look like someone of another race, so pale among all these healthily tanned people. She was grateful her auburn-haired son was not there to be burned by the sun, not understanding that he, like his mother and grandmother, was not equipped to deal with it. It was the one plus of having her son spend this summer with his father, home on leave, in Washington.

High brick walls around the compound stopped the breeze and captured all the day's light and heat. After an hour of sitting, watching, and yearning for a cool breeze, Lee sought relief, walking down the broad underwater steps, and into the chest-deep part of the pool. As she turned to walk back, the fast-moving bodies in a raucous water polo game swept her into water that closed over her head. She flailed out for solidity—a bottom to push up from, walls to grab—but nothing met her blind feet and hands. Then she was looking at puddles on tile, as urgent hands pushed rhythmically on her back, forcing out the water she'd taken in.

"She can't swim? Oh dear God. She could have drowned."

"I'm so terribly sorry. We were just fooling around. I thought she was in the game."

"Here, wrap her in these towels. She's quite blue."

Coming out of the pool-house bar, Joe stared at his wife, bedraggled, sputtering, surrounded by her rescuers. He shook his head sharply and went back to the bar.

Lee eased away from the party as soon as she could do so without causing further dismay, and walked down the elm-shaded road to the Altridge house, to the room where her things were. She showered away the chlorine, put on dry clothes and sat in the window seat that looked out on the ocean's rush and retreat, hugging her knees, drying tears on the softly worn denim. She had hated to let Tim, home on leave from Saigon, take Toby for the summer, but it was good that her son had not seen her blue and choking. It was good that she could be alone now, just alone, and quiet.

They broke the journey back to the city, as always, with Tate and Joe doing a round at the Greens, a tiny, near-secret golf course that an earlier Altridge and some peers had built on a chunk of Long Island farmland halfway between their South Hampton spreads and their Manhattan mansions. Lee was sure these gentlemen of the past had never envisioned the tract housing that now surrounded this enclave, necessitating a high barrier of boxwood to screen away the unsightliness. The club itself was delightfully dowdy, totally unlike the pretensions and polish of membership golf clubs, or the frantic public courses like the one where Joe had learned to play. Joe teased Tate mercilessly about this quiet course, a cinch to play compared to blue-collar golf. In young Joe Montagna's world you took the subway to Queens, walked to the course, lined up to rent clubs, lined up to tee off. Joe said you had to watch out for guys who'd steal your balls, and swore there were so many people flailing away that he'd worn his union hard hat while he played. Tate begged him to wear it at the Greens Club; Pru looked stricken until Joe had the grace to lie that he didn't have it anymore.

At the Greens there were no redeeming smells or sounds of the sea, and no wave-propelled winds. The women walked the course while their husbands played, Lee's long-sleeved shirt and linen slacks pasting themselves to her arms and legs, the copper wisps that escaped her straw hat darkening into brown commas glued to her forehead and neck. She wondered how Pru managed to avoid looking similarly soggy and bedraggled. The tan that stretched from the hems of Pru's Bermudas down to her sandaled and pedicured feet was evenly golden, and the ash blonde streaks in her Sassoon blunt cut caught and held the sun. Lee thought there was a curse on Anglo-Saxons, on Altridges and Palmers, dropped into tropic climes after being sent into the world with genes for fog and rain; Tate looked as miserable as Lee felt, while their mates seemed to bloom happily.

Joe was making his putt, calmly, his body charged by invisible wiring, moving with the assurance that so intrigued her. He always looked as if he knew the territory, his presence saying firmly and convincingly, This place and everything here is mine. I will tell you what matters and what does not. Just follow me and perhaps it will all become as clear to you as it is to me. If you're smart enough, lucky enough, to be in my world. And Lee knew that not everyone's luck held.

There was the progression of bosses and co-workers, all behind him as he moved on, moved up, heading to where he belonged. There was Cindy Lou Montagna, whose children had come to New York only once in the years his new family had been there. They had trashed the apartment, hated New York, been rude to Lee and Toby. Lee did not know whose decision it was that they had not returned—Joe's, Cindy Lou's or the children's. It was not something Joe chose to discuss.

The ball took a long fast arc to the hole, rimmed it once and sank. Joe crossed the green with the wired stride of someone with direct access to an energy source that would destroy any lesser being who tried to plug in. White slacks covering his short, powerful legs and a pale blue knit shirt tautly spanning his thick shoulders and chest, he reached down with one tanned, muscled, vein-tracked arm, and pocketed the ball.

Watching him move, Lee could see Jimmy Cagney dancing across the screen as George M. Cohan, defying gravity at every step. Joe was Cagney dipped in butterscotch and wigged in crow's wings, her Yankee Doodle Guinea.

His skin's response to summer was a deep burnishing that enriched his midnight hair and set off the noon eyes and white teeth that were now laughing at Tate Altridge. Joe Montagna, alpha male, owned this game, this Club, this heat and humidity, perhaps the sun itself. Watching him, Lee knew that he definitely owned Lee Montagna.

Despite her delight in watching Joe, she announced that she was bugging out. "I'll be the one on the shady porch with the long, cold drink in her hand."

"We won't be long. Promise." Joe put a damp kiss on her forehead.

Tate brushed damp hair out of his eyes and made an effort to tuck in his shirttail. "Pru, why don't you go on back too?"

Lee dropped into a rocking chair on the broad porch as Pru headed into the ladies' room to check her hair and makeup. Lee reached into the basket of paper and straw fans that were the club's only concession to the temperature, pulling out a paper one with coral flowers that matched her shirt.

She pondered the fact that New York's securely rich did not air condition. They simply abandoned their townhouses and 15-room apartments, heading for country places where the terrain was not made of roasting concrete. There, they fanned, they showered, they swam, and they sat on the porches of dowdy clubhouses, anesthetizing themselves with tall glasses of iced, minted vodka and soda, brought to them by solemn, black-tied butlers.

"Claude, you are a most welcome sight. Mrs. Altridge will, I'm sure, have her usual Southside, and I'd like my cognac and soda."

It had been her drink since she'd told the beached-up Legionnaire who owned her favorite bar in Saigon that she hated the cloying Collinses and Pim's Cups that were dispensed at embassy parties. With a gallant grin he had brought her *"Un Gabon, madame, Couvoisier et de l'eau gaseuse,"* and the dry, brisk combination had become her "usual," always ordered in her own country as a pedestrian "cognac and soda" and a secret delight that it was really a *Gabon,* first savored at a great little dive just off the *rue Catinat.*

"Certainly, madam. And the cheese and crackers?"

Lee frowned. "Velveeta and Ritz, right?"

"I'm afraid so."

She rolled her eyes and detected a suppressed upturn at one end of the major domo's thin mouth.

"Very well, madam. I won't bring them until Mr. Altridge arrives."

That was it. That smile. It was the period that ended the summer sentence. As clear as a school bell. Lee had been trying to make Claude smile since June. Mission accomplished. Next week it would be September and The Season would start for Tate and Pru. They would close the beach house and Pru would haul Tate to charity balls and museum benefits. He would tug back and take her to political meetings and fundraisers, to the Westside for the Montagnas' triple-B brunches. And Joe and Lee would not spend a single moment in the parking lot called the Long Island Expressway.

Pru joined Lee, reperfected even to the liner that set off her dark brown eyes. She settled into a rocker and reached for the wedding and engagement pages of the paper. Lee fanned on, staring over the wooden porch rail at a small gray bird staring back at her.

A crumple of paper and a great sigh brought her focus to Pru, whose face was riven by a frown line that stretched from her widow's peak down to the bridge of her long, regal nose. "I can't believe they did that."

Claude arrived with his napkined silver tray and set their drinks beside them. Lee tried to imagine what breach of form was distressing Pru.

> *Have some of the brides married down? Chosen the wrong designers for their dresses?*

"You don't believe who did what?"

Pru smoothed away non-existent wrinkles in her silk T-shirt until Claude was out of earshot.

"Cartwheels on the putting green." Her voice was hushed with disbelief. Our husbands did cartwheels on the putting green. God knows what they'll do out there without us along."

Lee suppressed a smile.

What a hopeless job you've assigned yourself. Tate's never going to give a rap about being proper. And, my God, there are so many things more worth caring about. Heroes have been shot. Blacks are rioting. Chicago just exploded. The Weathermen are blowing things up all over the place. Soviet tanks are in Prague, and the Goddamned war shows no sign of stopping. I think I'm for cartwheels, whenever and wherever. As a small sign of life. No matter what the world is doing.

"Well. Joe did birdie the hole, Pru."

Pru's eyebrows moved toward the widow's peak and Lee saw that she'd taken the wrong tack.

"OK. Look at it this way then. They're behaving normally for a couple of social retards. Really. I think they'll settle down when they finally get over the shock of being friends."

Pru looked at Lee anxiously, as if Lee had surfaced something that wasn't supposed to be brought up.

"I mean, haven't you noticed how rare that is for men? Joe hasn't had a buddy since PS 22, or whatever number it was."

Pru looked relieved, then considered the idea. "Tate had a friend once, at St. Paul's. He's at Ames and Blaine now. Tate says he's a bore."

Lee had no doubt that Tate was right. The most prestigious white-shoe law firm in New York, strictly investments and corporate, nothing political or controversial. Boring work. Boring people. Were her prejudices showing? Tate was adorable, but his fellow St. Grottlesexers, God, they were boring. Pru was boring too. And puzzling. The options for who one could hang out with in Manhattan were so vast, so wonderful. Lee thought of the benefit that July for the United Farm Workers at a downtown gallery. There was an auction at which Joe bid loudly on a print she'd said she liked, paying far too much for it, though it was for a good cause. There was dancing. And the dancers next to Lee and Joe on the jam-packed floor were Gabe Pressman and Gloria Steinem. Pressman was so enchanted he kept saying to them and to other dancers, "Isn't she lovely?" Which, of course, she certainly was. And what about the McCarthy fundraiser last week at Judith's? Surely Pru should have been amazed by the guests.

Lee had talked with an elderly and renowned sculptor, a militant Puerto Rican priest, a network correspondent just in from Vietnam, three liberal Congressmen, a lead dancer at Alvin Ailey, a biographer who'd won the Pulitzer, the director of a new Broadway play, and the principal of an avant garde school—exciting people, doing fascinating work. Lee didn't care where they'd gone to school or who their ancestors were. It didn't matter if they were bastards abandoned in garbage cans. Actually, that would make them even more admirable. Meritocrats. That was it. She was a snob on behalf of the meritocracy. And she was Joe Montagna's wife, so she had a free pass to move among them.

The only member of the Old Guard she'd met and respected was dear Tate himself, "the Altridge boy who was rather odd." His older brother was properly multiplying his inheritance on Wall Street. The younger was a classic playboy, wastreling around Europe and the Warhol scene, chasing models, being charming, artistic, and decadent. Lee loved Tate's summing up of his kid brother: "He's the only guy I know who could be down-and-out in Paris and end up sleeping on Henry Fonda's sofa."

She hadn't asked why he was down-and-out, assuming he'd been a classic remittance man, until he'd so offended the family that even his stay-far-away allowance had been cut off. The photograph he'd sent his mother of himself slumped in an electric chair, feigning death, might well have been the straw that broke the flow of cash.

But Tate, by his family's lights, was even harder to understand. Tate insisted on being concerned about the lower classes and the general well being of the body politic, rather than keeping to concerns the Altridges found proper to the PLU, People Like Us. He simply refused to do what was expected of him, as evidenced by the apartment he lived in when Joe and Lee first knew him.

It was in one of the graceless, white-brick towers on Second Avenue, a deli and a dry cleaner flanking its entrance, the lobby doormanless and decorated with plastic plants, the elevator automatic and the apartments entered through painted steel doors. Tate's place was filled with a random assortment of furnishings gleaned from family attics, a sofa and easy chairs tattered and soiled, all surfaces littered with files, news clippings, and Chinese takeout cartons. There were cigarette burns on Hepplewhite end tables, and a pile of greasy pizza boxes covered the broken seat of an Adams chair.

Tate didn't seem to notice or care. The apartment was near the offices of Montagna Altridge & Associates and roomy enough for the political meetings that helped make such a mess of the place several times a month. He had no further requirements for his dwelling.

His person matched his surroundings. Torn linings hung from the jackets of his off-the-rack suits, and there were food spots on the lapels and the sleeves, no doubt from his penchant for waving his fork to illustrate his points as he gulped down whatever food he was paying no attention to. He had a habit of stirring everything on his plate into one mound, even at *Pavilion*, which was one thing, and quite another when it was dinner at Lee and Joe's. But when Lee suggested that this particular peccadillo was distressing to the cook, who was in that venue herself, Tate just laughed.

That's what he did most, laugh. When MAA lost the bidding for a huge government contract, Tate and Joe both laughed and cuffed each other around like bear cubs, to Lee's complete mystification. She knew how much they'd wanted the job, a Great Society research project aimed at helping more blacks get into trade unions. But they just laughed, Tate doing his usual nasal honk-plus-inhale snort, and Joe his from-the-chest staccato shout, which always sounded to Lee like a slow-motion machine gun. She was sure Joe was mad as hell and would show it later, but she wondered if Tate ever frowned or shouted or wept.

He probably smiled even when Pru the Bride, who knew that Altridges did not reside on Second Avenue, found them proper digs, a rambling apartment on Park, in the 70s. The damaged antiques were picked up by a restorer before they were allowed to make the journey back to PLU country, and the damaged sofa and club chairs disappeared, complete with the good, serviceable, hideously flowered chintz slipcovers that Tate's mother had commissioned for them, as a wedding gift. The senior Mrs. Altridge seemed to think that since Tate had chosen the wrong girl, that girl would not know how things were to be done. But Pru did have her standards, even if they were distressingly chic to her properly unfashionable mother-in-law.

Pru was shaping Tate up, along with the new apartment. Just as Lee had replaced Joe's polyesters with classic cottons, wools, and linens, Pru had eliminated Tate's frayed shirts and stained suits. Now he was custom-fitted and regularly dry-cleaned. Lee thought these artfully staged reforms might be part of Pru's charm for Tate—she'd thrown herself into having servants do things that did make life rather pleasant, even if he didn't care enough to see to them himself. Clean, paired, folded socks lined up in a drawer. A pot of coffee on a tray, with the heavy cream he liked in a small silver pitcher, appearing in arm's reach just when his eyes were beginning to do a four-o'clock droop over the weekend-reading of a report. Tate had even rediscovered breakfast as a meal that could be eaten sitting in a chair, at a table. A well-run household could give one new reasons to smile.

But when it came to casting the personae of their conjoined lives, Lee thought there just might be some frowns, perhaps even some shouts. Tate's friends and associates were not left behind with his sofa, as Pru may have hoped. Instead, evenings at Tate and Pru's became an oil-and-water mix of his social activists and the people Pru courted, people who had the right breeding and schooling, men with jobs at the right law firms and banks; women who knew the right places to lunch and to shop, all of them with clear skin, shining hair, and good teeth. The Blands, as Lee called them to herself, were seasoned with the occasional Countess introduced by Tate's kid brother, whose anti-PLU rebellion took the form of hanging with Eurotrash and people whose income was not from investments, banking, or the law, but from making films, music, or even, to his mother's horror, clothes. The concept of not socializing with one's dressmaker was disappearing, and the senior Mrs. Altridge was not amused. But Tate was a worse offender, wrong in his choice of work, of associates, of friends, and worst of all, of wife.

At his newly elegant digs, Tate ignored The Blands, the chic, and the predators; Pru didn't talk to the activists; no contingent had anything understandable to say to the others. Tate invariably spent these evenings huddled with his cohorts from the political barricades, especially his MAA partner. In the softly lit room with the elegantly striéd walls, the dhurrie rugs and the batik drapes, Joe Montagna held forth, Pru's worst nightmare, at ease, in charge, the subject of Tate's rapt attention.

Lee saw the two men's unlikely alliance as one of the few bright spots in the waning War on Poverty—two smart, caring, and resourceful guys who were going beyond theories and studies to figure out why blacks had gotten stalled at the bottom rung of the economic ladder, and how the Feds could provide a leg up without breaking any bones or allocating vast amounts of money. These days, the two MAA principals were spending endless hours with black entrepreneurs, asking questions, really listening, figuring out what stood in the way of such hardworking people's success.

They were producing good data and good ideas for action. Lee was putting their findings on paper many an evening, after dinner. She was investing in the family business, making sure nothing read like the report Joe had written years before on a controversy at Cape Canaveral. It opened with the words, "This is a descending opinion."

"Joe, did you mean 'dissenting'?"

"Of course. You know me. Could I do some boring official report without goofing around?"

But she knew it had been a gaffe, not a goof. Joe's degrees from CCNY and the New School had given him his ticket away from the Lower East Side, but not an ease with the King's English. He still said "between you and I" no matter how many times she'd said "between you and me" in his presence. It was the verbal equivalent of the raised pinky that Lee wanted to paste a blue tag on every time he drank from a glass or a cup. At least, she reminded herself, he spoke with his mother's upstate voice, not with his father's dese-dem-and-dose accent, the voice of cab drivers and candy-store owners, not of men who would someday help run the country.

She could not abide the idea of such a good man being disdained for his language and manners. Imagining sneering eyes reading his descending opinion, she had resolved that nothing he wrote now would leave him so vulnerable to ridicule. This was something she could give to him, and her shaping of MAA's reports was the most satisfying work she did, making the manuscripts she edited for MacGregor's seem dreary and irrelevant.

Despite Pru's unconcealed frowns, Lee was sure that Tate and Joe would never break up their duo; they were having too much fun. Like the cartwheels. Like the night in December when Tate burst into the Montagnas' West Side living room trailed by a string quintet. He'd seen the musicians with their instruments leaving a gig in midtown and hired them on the spot to play carols for his buddy Joe. Toby gleefully joined them on his small guitar, and she'd made hot chocolate for everyone while Joe and Tate bellowed Deck the Halls and Away in a Manger.

Lee could imagine Tate losing his smile if Pru ever came right out and said that he shouldn't associate with the likes of Joe Montagna—nor she with Joe's wife. Here on the sweltering Greens Club porch, Lee felt the flash of annoyance that always accompanied that thought. She and Pru were stuck with each other and they could make the best of it fairly easily; Pru really wasn't a bad sort and there were things they could come together around. They'd both been English majors, so there was literature to talk about. There was the shared challenge of being married to men who really were rather strange. But always there was Pru's clear wish to be somewhere else, with someone worth her investment of time.

On rare occasions, when they did get onto books or music or an issue of common interest, the two women actually had some good talks. When Pru worked on a survey for an ad agency study, asking people to name the most important invention of these first 68 years of the century, Lee had immediately said, "The Pill, of course," which, she was surprised to learn, no one else had brought up. She started to withdraw her comment, but thought better of it. It just wouldn't do for the Pill and all it meant to be ignored.

"The cotton gin, the internal combustion engine, rockets, transistors—sure they've caused changes, but not like effective contraception. *That's* ass-over-tea-kettled every culture it's hit. It's personal, it changes the I-thou stuff, and it's mega-societal. Making pregnancy optional changes everything—education, business, marriage, *everything.*"

Pru argued long and well on behalf of the machinery, but began to listen when Lee observed that The Pill meant half the human race could now live completely different lives than any of their foremothers. And that every male around them was as deeply affected. "We've been ruled by our ovaries since Eve. We're the first women *ever* who can have sex and still have lives. Forget transistors, this is big."

Pru was concerned that the agency would write her off as a women's libber, but she agreed that the pill had to be in her report somewhere.

It didn't look like there'd be any substantive exchange between the two of them today. Pru was in snit mode, probably thinking Tate's misbehavior was at Joe's instigation. And Lee was marooned here with her on the clubhouse porch, rather than being in the city with her own preferred company—her chums at MacGregor's, or the amazing Judith, or Celeste Papandreou. Lee smiled to herself, imagining her next phone call to Celeste's Butterfield number, the long relaxed conversation they would have about this day, about their concerns and their work, about the latest puzzlements presented to them by Joe Montagna and Stefan Papandreou. It was good to have a real friend.

She wished boring Pru would go talk to some dowager who might do something for her she valued, like getting Mrs. Tate Grovenor Altridge into the Social Register, but as usual, the place was almost empty. Not a grande dame in sight. The Register. The Blue Book.

What was that Vonnegut word? Granfaloon. The Register is a "proud and meaningless association," a perfect granfaloon. And if Lee were in it, Pru would be so eager to please her. Lee imagined sticking a blue tag on Pru's forehead with the notation: Wrng asmptns.

Lee pictured herself as a proper WASP in a Fair Isle sweater, a gold cir-cle pin, and some Debusschere flats, and shivered. Actually, she qualified for the DAR—the Palmers had come to the Carolinas in the 1600's. But when the Revolution hit in the next century, they were Tories—Lee had seen oaths of allegiance to the crown, signed by three colonial Palmers. Did the Daughters of the American Revolution care which side your colonial ancestors had fought on? Lee was willing to wager that it only mattered that they were Over Here, not Back There, with all the dark-eyed hoi-polloi who showed up later, to work in the homes and factories of those who had come early and prospered.

At least Lee was frank about who she'd sprung from, proud of the par-ents who had moved their little family a few notches up the ladder, proud of Joe's leap up from the lower Eastside, proud to be with him. She wished for Pru that she could be proudly Prudence Kranowski Altridge, grand-daughter of the Poznan Kranowskis, as well as Tate's beloved wife. But Pru was running from Poznan, as her parents had. They'd become the Cranes, secular, prosperous American professionals who had given their only child a Pilgrim name and sent her to the best old schools, swathed in cashmere, coiffed and carved to Christian American perfection.

And now she was an Altridge. She'd come out the door at St. James, expecting a *New York Times* camera to be there, as it had been when Tate's brother married Bobo Corley. There were no cameras. And when the next edition of the Social Register was published, there was no Tate Grovener Altridge. WASP princes did not marry granddaughters of the shtetl with-out some punishment from their own kind. Tate thought being cut was funny, and something of an accomplishment. When his mother made her

I-told-you-so call, she'd made his day. Pru was game, laughing with him at the absurdity of anyone thinking the Register mattered. But it did matter to Pru. She had gotten to what she considered the top of the social heap; Tate wasn't supposed to then be deposed, and she wanted him reinstated.

Lee held her icy glass to her cheek.

"This is my idea of a perfect golf round. Sitting right here on the porch and rocking. The whole time." She held up the back of a pinkened hand and started counting the new freckles on it. "At least twenty. Since Friday. I do not think this is what Hopkins meant when he thanked God for all those speckled things."

"I think we should have stayed out there with them." Pru frowned even more severely, ignoring Lee's literary proffer.

Lee was sure that the Greens Club would survive no matter what Tate and Joe did there, but Pru might not. It must be so painful to look so perfectly North Shore and wish that you really were, to have your nose pressed so hard against the glass. Her cause was both silly and futile; Tate could only be fully back in the fold if Pru were not his wife. Since the well behaved Tate she wanted wouldn't have proposed to her, Pru was caught in her own Catch 22. This Tate she had, this good man, had burst the boundaries of his world to work on things that mattered, to have trust-fundless friends who shared his causes, and to marry a woman from a culture that honored intelligence and social conscience, that understood suffering and prejudice and worked to end them. Lee decided they must have courted like Bernstein's Candide and Cunegonde, Tate singing of one life, Pru of another, each thinking they were describing the same marriage.

She did not envy Pru's determination to be accepted. There was a lot to be said for maintaining one's observer status, well learned from her Navy upbringing. She offered up a silent toast of gratitude to the Chief of Naval Operations and all the ships at sea. And to her father, whose gift to her had been freedom from the strictures of place. Her gift to Toby would be knowing what counted. Her son would teach or paint or compose or be a healer—or all of the above. Even spending this summer with his father wouldn't confuse him. The child had Joe to watch the rest of the year, a veritable template for using smarts and drive to do good things in the world.

"What are you grinning about, Leedle?" Joe squeezed her shoulder as he and Tate headed for empty rockers. They swiveled sideways in unison, scanning the horizon for Claude. Both born under the sign of the crab, Lee thought, moving in tandem, sideways. She tucked the picture away to be relayed to Celeste, whose knowledge of astrology was proving valuable to Lee, helping her understand Joe and where his tripwires were.

Pru's silky straight hair had fallen forward, hiding her face. With both hands, she tucked these concealing curtains behind her ears, an unflattering move followed by raising her chin and narrowing her eyes. She picked up the empty glass from her second Southside and peered at Tate and Joe through it, seeming to study the fuzzy, distorted images she was making of them. "Such good little boys, doing right wherever they go, taking such care of the undeserving poor."

Tate sprang toward the handwritten menu that was thumb-tacked next to the screen door behind them. Pru started sharply, almost dropping the glass.

"Hey, there's fried chicken, corn on the cob, and blueberry pie." He smiled at them all. "Let's go!" The door slapped shut behind him.

Joe reached immediately for Lee's hand and pulled her up out of the rocker saying, "What, no mashed potatoes?"

They were back on the safe, playful ground the two men always walked. Lee smiled up at Joe, grateful he wasn't taking Pru's bait.

"Unthinkable! Oh surely, sir, there will also be mashed potatoes."

"As it is written in the prophecies," he answered, extending a firm hand to the tipsy Pru and escorting both women in to dinner.

"You *know* Marshall Poole?" Pru's fork stopped in its ascent from her mashed potatoes. Lee wasn't sure if Pru was impressed or appalled.

"Well, yes. From college. We were in the theatre department together. Played opposite each other in a Christopher Frye one-act, then in *Caesar and Cleopatra*."

Pru stared at her. "You were an actress?"

"Just in college."

"Don't listen to her." Joe was beaming benevolently. "She had offers for Broadway *and* for the movies. She turned them down."

"Why'd you do that?" Tate asked, gnawing on a chicken leg. "Being a movie star would be a gas."

"Looong story. But basically that life takes stainless steel guts and I don't have them." She salted her corn-on-the-cob. "And Joe's exaggerating, sweet man that he is."

She was sure she wouldn't have held form if she'd been the usual fledgling actress temporarily waiting tables; she'd have become a waitress imagining she was an actress. Even if she'd had the nerve to push through the doors that had cracked open for her, even if she'd succeeded and become known, she'd now be one of the emotional basket cases lost in drugs, sequential polygamy, and the terror of aging. To be known was to be caught in the lights, talked about, criticized, to be known was to be found out, dismissed, even hated.

"What about Poole?" Pru urged, leaning for ward. "What's he like, really?"

> *See? There it is. Let's peel Poole, pry him open, reveal his*
> *secrets, roll around in them, so we can be in the know and*
> *assure ourselves we're superior to Mr. Superstar.*

"Aside from being the world's richest hippie?"

Faux hippie, truth be told. The author, composer, lyricist, director, and star of *Boobs*, the defining theatre work of their era, was solidly Silent Generation, "overage in grade." He was 36 and bald and wearing a long wig so he could masquerade as a credible spokesman for the Love Tribe. But what the hell, their own lot was and continued to be dull, dull, dull. They had virgin wedding nights, thought drugs were medicine, and the guys had gone off to Korea without a peep. For God's sake their songs were It's a Lovely Day Today and If I Knew You Were Comin' I'da Baked a Cake. But these flower children—they were trying everything, doing everything, yelling No! instead of doing what they were told, like Lee's generation did. Like she did. Was still doing.

She and Joe had been in one network's coverage of the great Central Park Be-In. They were the "adult" couple in the Irish sweaters, photographed for humorous contrast as they wandered on a bicycle built-for-two through all the flowers and tie-dyes. Lee had squirmed with embarrassment, wishing they'd stayed in some other part of the park instead of providing a cameraman with the perfect visual of the hopelessly uncool.

But Marshall Poole, he'd joined the cool. Marsh-as-Hippy didn't write Whistle A Happy Tune. He wrote songs like Farewell Capricorn and his words were coming out of every radio in the country. But not *Fellatio*, of course. They only played that one and *Boobs* as instrumentals, but everybody knew the words. *Boobs* was an anthem for the anti-war movement.

> *Ole Poole's made messy mix of political defiance and in-your-*
> *face sexuality and fury and terror about this Goddamn war.*
> *And he's hit a nerve, he has, my buddy Marsh.*

"He's actually a fine classical actor. Gentle, and very sweet. He was in a rep company after college, and did some beautiful Chekhov, O'Neill, Shakespeare. But I think he won't do the big stuff any more. His play and the songs have gotten so big, I'm afraid he won't go for the brass ring now."

He was going to be the next Olivier, but now he could afford every drug in the world and he was using so heavily, he sometimes couldn't recognize old friends, much less focus on his art.

Lee took it hard that he'd stared through her when she called to him in front of Bloomingdale's. Marshall Poole was the cherished compeer who had memorized lines with her, planned cast parties, dreamed about the future. They'd even bought each other beers to cry in when they both fell in love with—and were rejected by—the handsome teaching assistant in their general sciences course. And on a New York sidewalk, Marshall Poole had not known who she was. The Marsh who didn't know her that day was someone new and strange. Another classmate had told her it wasn't personal. "Hell, he lived with me, and he doesn't know me either."

But now he'd answered the break-a-leg message she sent him when the show moved uptown from Off Broadway; she'd just gotten a note back—"Legitimate at last. Please come, dear girl,"—and four tickets to the show. Maybe he'd cleaned up. Maybe they were still buds. Maybe he'd do Hamlet someday.

Her first thought had been to invite Celeste and Stefan Papandreou, or maybe Asa and Pam from work, but getting Joe on board wasn't going to be easy. This was a better plan—if Tate wanted to go, Joe would certainly agree to make an evening of it.

"OK, me hearties, I've got four good seats for the fifth of October. Are we on for it?"

Tate honked his nasal laugh through a mouthful of corn kernels. "Hell yes. That'll be a ball." He brandished his cob for emphasis, prompting the immediate appearance of a solicitous Claude.

Pru glared at Tate. "No, no, Claude, we don't need a thing."

She turned to Lee and raised the ante. "We'd have to beg off an opening that night at the Modern, but... do you think he'd go out with us after the show?"

> *You mean me. Would he really want to see insignificant me.*
> *And if he does, can you be right there so you can tell the Blands*
> *an amusing story about dabbling in the counter culture.*

"We have a conflict too—there's a fundraiser that night for Glenn Clay. But we're hosting one ourselves next month, so we'll skip this one. And yes, I'll ask Marsh to join us afterwards."

"I don't know. Let's think a minute. Do we want to give our time to this?" Joe was studying his plate which, given his usual rapid intake, was empty. Lee took it as a good sign that he was questioning, rather than starting at No.

"I mean they don't even print the name of the show in the paper." Joe was speaking from under a monobrow of concern and disapproval. "It's about people taking all their clothes off and they're dancing down the aisles singing about kinky sex, right?"

Pru frowned at him from the heights of her two Southsides. "Oh I think we can avoid contamination. Come on. It's the hottest ticket in town."

Lee had to admit that what she chose to see as Joe's courtliness sometimes tipped over into just being prissy. He didn't approve of a lot of things. When women swore, wore low-cut blouses, or were reported to be promiscuous, his thick brows would join in one black line of disapproval across eyes that became wintry slits.

> *But this is silly. The show is about so much more than nudity.*
> *It's about being against a war that you're against too. It's*
> *about living with love instead of letting people die of hate and*
> *stupidity. It's not about naked breasts, it's about the truly ob-*
> *scene boobs in Washington, those idiots who keep sending boys*
> *off to die for no damn reason. And maybe it's also about all*
> *the jerks who're obsessed with big breasts. That would be good*
> *too. Blue tag: Wrng asmptns. Rethnk.*

She put her hand on Joe's taut brown arm. "The tickets are a gift, love. If you really hated the show you wouldn't have to stay. Tate and Pru could see me home."

Tate slapped the table with one long thin hand, making the plates and cutlery jump. "Hear, hear, the fifth it is. And where shall we supp with this eminent pornographer?"

Carrying Queens

"Joe, I promised. You wouldn't want me to go back on my word." He looked at her, startled, until understanding broke through to separate the conjoined black eyebrows, widen the slit eyes.

"No. I wouldn't want you to do that." His tease-grin pulled up one corner of his mouth. "But you could say Toby's sick. No? How about your parents have decided to visit?"

"C'mon. I'm not going to lie either, smart guy." She had to cajole him out of this request that she do something he would normally disdain. What did it mean that her straight-laced husband was urging her to lie? He could be serious, or just testing her. They were talking about the fundraiser they were giving for Glenn Clay. Joe had agreed that it was a good idea when she'd suggested it, reminding him that his union contacts and MAA clients could make all the difference for their friend's faltering campaign. Joe himself had made the offer to Clay and accepted a bear hug of thanks from the handsome brown man, who towered over compact Joe, the almost-as-dark demi-Italian.

Now Joe was asking her to get them out of the commitment. It didn't compute.

"It's this Saturday afternoon, Joe, five days from now. The election's coming up fast and I sent the invitations out weeks ago."

"And the union guys haven't answered."

"Maybe they don't RSVP."

"Oh no. They're careful about the manners stuff. I think it's because he's black."

Lee wondered why people were called black who so obviously were not. Brown, tan, beige, honey-gold yes, but she couldn't remember ever seeing a black American. She'd understood that when she'd seen a Nubian street vendor, in the Congo. *That* was black skin, so black it gleamed blue in the sunlight.

Antoine Beauvechain, the manager of the Congolese staff at the consulate in Leopoldville, was the only American-looking "local" she'd known. Beige, sharp-nosed, Beauvechain was the son of a Belgian who had acknowledged him and given him his name, though he hadn't deigned to marry his Congolese mother. Manager Beauvechain was not considered African by the local authorities or by his Congolese cousins, but something apart, privileged, better educated, better paid, entitled to an assumption of superiority. According to the colonial government, he was not a Congolese but an *immatriculée*, subject not to tribal but Belgian law, an "adequately civilized" person, constrained to live in a special part of the city, to marry someone no darker than he, to eat European, dress European, speak Flemish and French, send his children to an *immatriculée* school. In return for disrespecting his Congolese genes, he was accepted as a middleman between the black and the white worlds, an intercessor who would carry out the white world's wishes in this colony. He wore his status proudly, ordering about mere Congolese file clerks, gardeners, and janitors with assurance and detachment.

At the consulate's Fourth of July reception, Lee heard him say that he expected his stint with the Americans to earn him the papers to live in their country.

"Dear God, why would you want to do that?" Lee had asked, flashing on her grandfather in South Carolina, his cane coming down on the shoulder of a man of Beauvechain's hue who had not moved quickly enough into the gutter to let the old man and his granddaughter have the full width of the sidewalk. She saw her history teacher in San Diego, a gentle, beloved man, shouting in fury at a brown football player whose arm was around a blonde cheerleader in the parking lot after a game. She saw all the photographs of burned, hung, shot American "coloreds" who had been deemed overly confident in who they were. Men like Antoine Beauvechain.

The Consul General overheard Lee's question and shot her a warning glare. This was not the proper reaction of a representative of the US government, which she was, according to the State Department, despite her lack of title or salary. She smiled at Beauvechain and quietly, as if she were making cocktail chitchat, warned him that in her country all people of any degree of color were treated exactly the same—badly. Her country was full of people as white as he, and more so, and all of them were "negroes" at best, the lightest afforded no more rights by white society than the darkest. He had not believed her; it was too preposterous.

Now here was Glenn Clay, whom she imagined was as much Scot or Cherokee as African, but in America he was just "black," no longer called "negro" by the socially aware.

Blacks and whites. Lee had seen only one truly white person in her life, a Congolese albino walking eerily through the marketplace in the *cité*, a perfect Bantu in features, but with no pigment at all, not peach like her own skin, like the Belgians'. She wondered if blacks might be called browns someday, as the correct term kept evolving. And if white skin would be renamed peach, pulling the rug out from under some unthinking givens in the language. A matter of brown and peach. The peach man's burden. Peach supremacy. That's peach of you. It would make the absurdity so clear.

"C'mon, Joe. How would they even *know* Glenn's black? It's not like his campaign has gotten a lot of coverage."

"You think there's no coverage because it hasn't been in the Times. Those guys read the *Daily News*."

"And?"

"When a black man runs against an Irishman in Queens, the *Daily News* runs pictures. The boys know he's black."

"And about ten times smarter and better qualified than the Irish twerp."

"You know that and I know that. But the twerp is white."

Lee didn't say that he was actually peach.

Saturday at two, the Montagna's oak-paneled living room was filled with potential contributors for the last push of Clay's campaign. They were mostly casually dressed Manhattanites with the means to write sizeable checks. A few of them could write huge checks, though this had to be a convincing event—wealthy Manhattanites weren't normally concerned with the borough of Queens. They had come because Lee had talked to them about Clay, because they knew it was time for more blacks to take their places in Congress, and because Clay was going to need help to get there. They moved freely between the brownstone's living and dining rooms, talking easily with each other, sampling the finger foods, pouring their own wine. In the archway between the two rooms, a knot formed of carefully groomed men in suits and ties, men who pumped Joe's hand and thanked him for being invited to his home, men who spoke only to each other, and waited to be offered drinks and hors d'ouevres.

Lee and Joe exchanged delighted smiles in the Delft-tiled kitchen.

"They came, Joe. I think they love you a lot."

"Not me. Bobby. I talked to them about Glenn's background, then asked them straight out if they were coming and I get, 'The guy worked for Bobby? That's good enough for us.' Him, they loved."

"But he went after Hoffa. I thought the unions hated him."

"Hoffa was scum. Stealing from the members. They know that. Bobby said stuff about sticking up for the little guy. He sounded like FDR, so he got to them."

He winked at her over a loaded tray of stemware and plates, as he backed through the swinging door, admitting the buzz of conversations and the gentle harmonies of the Modern Jazz Quartet from the stereo.

"You are a good man, Joseph van Heugel Montagna." Lee looked up from pulling bottles of chilled Chablis out of the fridge and spoke to the still moving door. "And I love you."

She had been very sure of that as Bobby Kennedy's funeral train rolled toward Arlington. Joe had taken a service revolver out of his closet, the revolver Lee had not known was there, and had spun the bullets out of it into his palm. Toby had come out of his room, huge green eyes spilling over, his arms holding out the toy revolvers and rifles given to him by friends and relatives. The plastic bazooka was from Tim, a rare and treasured gift from the father who rarely reached out to him, but Toby had sat beside Joe on the kitchen floor, the television screen solemn and heartbreaking across the room, the pile of weapons, real and pretend, before them. Piece by piece they destroyed their armory as they watched the train move across the landscape. Then Joe had held Toby, rocking him back and forth as they both wept.

Lee was filled with hope for this evening and for Glenn Clay. Such an honorable and smart man *should* be elected to office. Being a staffer to a Kennedy couldn't be the pinnacle of his career. Clay needed his own place at the table.

The union reps were not the only new people considering his campaign. Judith Bridges had come, and if she liked what she saw of this candidate, she could be enormously helpful. Dick Johnson was in there, shyly reading a campaign flyer. A newcomer to the city and to its politics, Johnson had been a poor boy in Toledo who made it through a state college on an athletic scholarship, then went into managing food service operations for hospitals and corporations. A rich classmate who knew nothing about food bought the Fryin' Freddy's franchise for New York's outer boroughs and made Johnson a full partner, Johnson's only investment being his knowledge of how to move food. Two years into picking sites, building restaurants, converting storefronts, then hiring and training staff, Dick Johnson had serious union troubles that he brought to MAA. Joe had negotiated good contracts with all the parties, and the franchise had grown into the most prosperous in the entire phenomenally successful world of Fryin' Freddy's, so prosperous that the head office had made Johnson and his partner a buy-back offer they couldn't refuse.

That summer Lee and Joe had joined Johnson at a small celebration in the Plaza's Oak Room. There, Johnson's father, in for the occasion from Ohio, stood up in the staid old room and said loudly, "I would like to wager that my son is carrying more money than any other man in the room." All the dark blue suits and wing-tips turned toward the small gray-haired man with the powder blue jacket and white shoes; several smiled and took out their wallets. "I cleaned up," the elder Johnson reported later. "If somebody said that to you, wouldn't you figure they were holding some very high cards?" Indeed, no other man in the Oak Room could top his son's cashier's check for two point two million dollars, giving the bow-tied Ohioan the last word as he headed home. "I'd say this town's full of suckers."

His son, the most unpretentious person imaginable, had looked puzzled when Joe asked him what he planned to do differently now that he was a rich man. "Well, I could start sending my shirts to a laundry—that'd be a good break for my wife." He thought a bit longer. "And maybe the next time we take the kids to visit my folks, we could fly instead of driving."

Now the newly minted multi-millionaire was here, looking seriously at using some of his unneeded riches to support the Montagnas' friend Glenn Clay.

Stefan Papandreaou had more years of wealth behind him; he was well past commercial laundry service and on to antique rugs and modern paintings. And to buying furs and jewels for his glamorous wife. Lee had to say that he was as tall, blond and handsome as Celeste had described him, and he was clearly proud of Celeste, resplendent in fuchsia satin palazzo pants and a green satin blouse. She joined Lee in the kitchen, putting bottles of Chablis and Burgundy on a tray. "Thank you for inviting us. We never get to go to things like this. Is Mr. Clay going to speak?"

"Sure. After everybody's settled in. You think Stefan might support him?"

Celeste giggled. "I've been working on it. Let's see what happens."

An eager young Clay campaign staffer in a miniskirt took the tray of wine bottles, as a timer went off at the stove. In his cage by the window, Toby's bird, Bilbo, sang back at the timer. Lee took miniature crab cakes and bacon-wrapped water chestnuts out of the oven and arrayed them in spirals on the French cobalt platters.

Celeste held the heavy swinging door open for Lee just as Joe called the assemblage to order. The food would go cold on the dining room table, but it couldn't be helped; all attention had to be on Clay now. Celeste moved to Stefan's side as Joe introduced the candidate, both men standing in front of the marble fireplace that Lee had covered with "Help Clay Carry Queens" posters. From a far corner of the room Lee watched Clay speak, eloquently, about his yearning to help carry on the great work that his murdered boss would be unable to complete. With her full view of the room, Lee saw the new leader of Big Joe's union stare at his shoes and an officer of the ILA wipe his eyes. When Clay finished, Joe asked their guests what they were going to do to help this fine man take a seat in the House.

The first person to respond was Ambrose Green, who seemed to have an egg in his hand. Lee braced, wondering what the unpredictable and often stoned philanthropist might be about to say. Wearing a denim jacket and jeans on his stout frame, he put one sneakered foot on the seat of a folding chair and leaned forward, resting a forearm across his bent thigh. Lee recognized the stance, one she'd decided men took when they were trying to be cool and weren't sure they could pull it off.

"This egg was laid this morning on East 73rd Street." Green held it up, then handed it to the puzzled candidate. "And so was my commitment to your campaign. Good luck, man."

Clay uncurled a piece of paper wrapped around the egg and smiled at the crowd. "It's a check for three hundred dollars." He turned to Green and extended his hand. "Thanks for your support."

Lee was annoyed. This was tip-the-doorman money for Green. And how tone deaf did he have to be to get all cutesy with an egg from the cute chickens he raised on his cute mini-farm around his penthouse? He had a couple of sheep up there too. Lee blue-tagged the egg as Green being too clever by half, and too cheap by several magnitudes.

The state rep for the Longshoremen put his hand up for recognition and, at Joe's nod, spoke, chin out, his voice too loud for the room.

"The ILA is in for three *thousand*. And we'll send you twenty guys to help get out the vote."

That was more like it. The room broke into applause. Class warfare was being waged before their eyes and the blue-collars had just laid down a challenge. All seven unions present chimed in with money and people, the other guests quietly writing checks and putting them in the slotted box Lee had covered with Help Clay Carry Queens bumper stickers. Dick Johnson said nothing, but nodded affirmatively at Joe as he put his folded check into the box. Judith pressed a check into Lee's hand and smiled as she headed for the door, no doubt on her way to another political gathering.

Stefan wrote a check and gave it to his wife to deposit. Lee smiled at the spectacular couple. "See you both at 7."

"At the French place, right?" Papandreou did not look pleased with the idea but Joe had insisted on *Le Palais de Glace* for their first evening out as a foursome.

"The food is really wonderful, I promise." Lee smiled at Stefan reassuringly.

By five the Clays and Tate were the only guests left in the high-ceilinged living room. Lee kicked off her heels and rubbed the balls of her feet; Tate punched Joe on the arm, laughing out loud. "That was *so* cool! Those union guys are the best. No messing around. Money and people. That's what it takes and they know it."

"Ashley, will you do the honors?" Joe offered the moneybox to the candidate's tall, lovely wife, a reincarnation of the stunning Dorothy Dandridge.

"I'm afraid to look. What if all those checks are for five bucks each? We're dead."

"They're not, Ashley, I'm sure they're not." Joe took the lid off the box and put it in her lap, along with a pencil and notepad. "Please, do the tally."

"OK, OK I'm looking." Ashley's long tan fingers reached into the box and gingerly pulled up a check. Her head turned away, she held it at arm's length, then squinted at it with one eye and said, "Oh."

Working quickly, she made her way through the box, writing numbers in a lengthening column as the others nibbled at cold appetizers and finished off the wine. Looking out into the garden, Lee saw Admiral Perry, Toby's huge land turtle, tanking across the rose bed on another of his explorations, all of which led to the garden's brick walls. Toby. She must check his room, see if his coach had brought him back from his softball game in the park, find out how his team had done.

She was grateful to see two campaign aides rounding up plates and glasses and heading for the kitchen. If she was really lucky, they'd load the dishwasher and wipe down the counters, leaving her only to vacuum up the crumbs and ashes the guests had dropped on the floors and rugs.

With the last check tallied, Ashley Clay handed the list to her husband, her eyes filled with tears.

"You're not dead, babe."

The evening had brought in thirty-seven thousand dollars, two of them in Fryin' Freddy profits. Judith's check was for a thousand and she had left a note in the box asking Glenn to call her. The candidate pounded Joe on the back, "You did it, Montagna, you did it!"

Tate and Joe, in unison, raised their glasses.

"Clay's gonna carry Queens!"

"To Congressman Clay!"

Ashley Clay caught Lee's eye and mouthed a silent, "Thank you."

Lee was in high spirits when she and Joe met the Papandreous in front of the restaurant that Lee was sure was far too stuffy, though the food really was superb. It was a place she and Joe had been often with Tate and Pru, and one that Lee realized Joe was using to set up his place in a male pecking order, one-up from Papandreou, a fellow graduate of the city's streets. The ante had been raised she knew, by Stefan's thousand-dollar donation to the campaign. Tonight Celeste's Golden Greek was wearing the kind of gleaming suit and white-on-white shirt that Lee had quietly purged from Joe's wardrobe, and Celeste was, as usual, off key. There was something about her that Lee read as innocence, though she knew it would sound absurd to apply the word tonight.

Lee had long ago read the local cues and taken on the dark, elegant severity that said "Manhattan." Celeste remained a poolside Californian, just in town for the shows, overstated, brightly colored, drawing quick dismissive sneers from the bone-thin, dressed-for-grieving New York women, and insinuating stares from their men.

Because they talked on the phone far more often than they actually saw each other, Lee tended to forget Celeste's appearance, thinking of her mainly as the warm, caring voice who could listen to Lee's concerns about Joe and actually understand them, her comforting refrain always, "I know. I know." She and Lee understood things about each other's lives, about being married to street fighters, about fearing their anger, about wanting to keep life steady and safe.

But Lee had to admit that some of her new friend's choices were puzzling. Like tonight, when Stefan took Celeste's sable to check it and she was revealed to be wearing a gold-sequined gauze jumpsuit, her long dark hair teased into a cloud that didn't quite cover her bare-to-the-waist back. A grand emanation of Tabu surrounded her, overpowering Lee's fragile Madame Rochas like a galleon bearing down on a corsair.

Led by the *maitre d'* and followed by their husbands, Lee and Celeste walked the entire length of the room toward a table in "Siberia." Lee, in a black silk pants suit, walked beside her friend, mortified on Celeste's behalf, talking intently with her, hoping she wouldn't notice the gauntlet of frowning grande dames and leering codgers. Lee was tempted to walk in front of her; Celeste wasn't wearing a bra again. Lee's inner editor wanted to blue-tag the transparent jumpsuit, the perfume, and the enormous breasts that were so bizarre on such a slender woman. Lee thought of taking her friend's arm and steadying her so that the swinging weights didn't tip her over. She wanted to tell the smirking New Yorkers that Celeste was not a call girl, and not someone who would steal the silver. She was just from a sunnier, more colorful place and didn't understand the rules here.

A busboy stepped aside to let them pass. He froze, his lips parted in wonderment. Lee could hear Night Train as the soundtrack for their passage, heavy on the drums and cymbals. Maybe Celeste could do a few bumps and grinds. The *maitre d'* kept leading them farther and farther back in the long room.

Lee had met Celeste half a year earlier, on a dare. A voice had been coming up and over the partitions that separated the tiny warrens at MacGregor's, and what it was saying was distracting, annoying. The new editor, somebody named Asa Chandler, fresh out of Harvard, had been talking astrological garbage on the phone for half an hour. When he stopped, Lee walked to the door of his not-yet cluttered cubicle.

"On behalf of your parents, I believe I should lodge a protest."

"My parents?"

"Your parents. I assume they went to some expense to put you through Harvard and here you are, after all those pricy years, your head full of drivel that I'm sure you didn't learn there."

"Sorry I was talking too loudly." He smiled appeasingly.

What is he, 15? Are those pimples? They're hiring children to
do these jobs. Deluded children.

"You weren't. Eventually you get used to these partial walls and you don't talk about anything you don't want everybody on the floor to know. *That's* not the problem."

His flushed, tapioca face broke into a delighted grin and he tugged his tie loose. "How much do you know about astrology?"

"I've seen all that stuff in magazines. So vague it applies to everybody. Complete nonsense."

"Yes it is and that's not astrology. I love to talk about it—as you've noticed—but I can't discuss it with you at the nonsense level. Would you be willing to find out more?"

"Depends."

"Of course. OK, how's this? I give you the number of the astrologer I was just talking to. You call her, give her your time and place of birth. That's all. After you do a session with her, we talk."

"How much?"

"Twenty-five dollars."

"And you don't set her up? Tell her about me?"

"What do I know about you? Nothing. Except that you're funny and you work down the hall. And, the way you talk, you're probably somebody's mom."

"You're on, boyo."

That had been the start of it. For twenty-five dollars, eight words of information, and three hours of her time, Lee received, to her astonishment, a return of faith.

She hadn't been a believer since reading a Philip Wylie essay on brainwashing. She absorbed the implications of his "De Rebus Incognitus" as she walked through Saigon's streets to her office at *Viet Nam Presse*, growing lighter with each step as she recognized that her training as a Catholic had been classic brainwashing. Everything that she had suspected was nonsense was indeed just that. Identifying the programming freed her to feel no qualms whatsoever despite being hard-wired to feel guilt if she doubted any of the rules, big or small; if she thought the accounting system of indulgences and penances was petty and demented; if she could not disdain other religions and their adherents; if she thought the Credo missed Christ's basic points—the really hard parts like forgiveness and loving others as one-self were not even mentioned in this declaration of Christianity, just the tricks, the bells and whistles he pulled out to get people's attention for the message. She had always returned from any cycles of doubt, just as the programming said she would: "Fallen-away Catholics always come back." But not freed-from-brainwashed-bondage got-away Catholics. The wires were cut and she was floating free, at liberty to question, doubt, reject.

And she rejected the concept of order. Life was chaos and you did the best you could. There was nothing more to say. Until Celeste Papandreou had given her those hours of personal information so detailed they included the fact that in her 27th year, Lee had almost died in a foreign country from an ailment of the gut. Remembering the touch-and-go days in the Saigon hospital as the French doctors used heart-stopping toxins to kill off the amoeba that were rioting in her innards, Lee had her road-to-Damascus revelation: if Papandreou had given her three hours of such detail, knowing only her birth time and place—and she had—there was, after all, an order at work in the universe.

After she cajoled a skeptical Joe into doing a session, he had immediately ordered up charts on his kids and Toby. And Celeste told them how all their offsprings' charts interacted with their own. Toby, Celeste declared, was Joe's "astral son," a term that freed Joe from the guilt of loving the healthy, smart boy in the house when his genetic son was flawed and far away. Celeste had arrayed astral charts on the long dining room table and tried to explain what she saw in them, talking about sextiles and trines and parts of fortune and other purportedly good things, but the important thing was that Maddy, Rory, and Van were not connected to Joe, and Toby was. Lee had been overwhelmed with gratitude toward this flashy non-New Yorker.

The two women slid into the banquette and the men took the facing chairs, at a table next to the kitchen door. Though the male patrons at the good tables might have enjoyed more ogling, the *maitre d'* knew that their wives ruled here. Celeste was a non-PLU sideshow, now discreetly hidden from the other diners' view. Lee understood what was going on. They'd always had fine tables when they'd come here with Tate and Pru. They should have taken the Papandreous to the Copa or the Playboy Club, wherever those places were. This wasn't the Papandreous' kind of place. Or Joe's. Or

Lee's, for that matter. There was a new bistro on the West Side where they made great omelets and a mean cassoulet. That would have made more sense. And probably would have better fit the Montagna family budget, the mysterious document Lee feared did not exist. Joe had the family finances handled and she was not to be concerned. When it suited him, there was always money available, some sort of Papa's Bank Account that could fund any expenditure he chose to make, and was in danger of depletion—by Lee—whenever he decided she had exceeded some unknown benchmark.

When she and Joe had come to this bastion of Old New York money with Tate and Pru, Joe had been edgy, ill at ease. Tonight he'd immediately greeted the *maitre d'* as if he were a lifelong regular, slipping him a bill Lee hoped wasn't a fifty. But she knew that it was.

Fifty dollars would never get this party a good table at *Le Morgue*, which was Lee's silent name for the place. She didn't expect Joe's gauche largesse to buy them good service either—but Celeste was having a definite effect. Their hidden table was besieged by an outpouring of staff solicitude.

Stefan was positively preening as he smiled across the table at his glittering wife, but his smile disappeared when a menu was proffered to her with a flourish and a murmured, "Mademoiselle?"

"Madame," Stefan growled. "Madame!"

Water arrived, ashtrays, *crudités*, bread, wine lists, more water for their still-full glasses, lights for Celeste's tinted-paper cigarettes—each offering borne by a different delighted male.

Lee decided that the staff didn't get many opportunities to enjoy themselves. She imagined the waiters back there behind the kitchen door saying to the cooks and dishwashers, "You gotta see this. Here, borrow my jacket."

Stefan directed Celeste to present her new emerald for admiration, a birthday present that had proudly topped his gift of the sable. Her narrow hand looked burdened by the huge stone rimmed with diamonds. Lee wondered if it had been sold by the pound. Stefan should have bought her a sling to go with it. And a bra. She was sure Joe was appalled by Celeste's revealing getup, but he was showing no signs.

"How about melon for openers, Leedle?"

She frowned at him, surprised by his insensitive jape, but saw none was meant. He was studying the menu intensely, as if he could read French.

Celeste looked at Lee in dismay. "There's no English on this menu. Would you order for me?"

"Well, how hungry are you? There's a rack of lamb. Probably from Australia at this time of year. But it's for two so we could share it. You like lamb?"

Celeste did and she also liked the idea of *gougeres*, the cheese puffs that were Lee's favorite appetizer here, then a lobster bisque, the lamb, a salad and after it all, dessert of poached pears and a *café filtre*.

Stefan put his menu down with evident relief. "All that sounded delicious there, girl. Joe, let's double down on what she said, what do you think?"

"And the wines?" The sommelier was looking dubiously at Joe, who shot his cuffs and looked to Lee, his black brows conjoined. "You might as well keep going, Leedle. Tell the man what we're drinking."

This was not an invitation that should be accepted; Lee turned to the sommelier. "I'm out of my depth choosing wines. Would you suggest a nice dry white, and then a full-bodied red? No dessert wine. We may order cognacs with the coffee."

Joe made certain he was deep in conversation with Papandreou, ignoring Lee as if this ordering business were too trivial to warrant his attention. Lee caught the words "portfolio" and "P and E ratios" which Joe could only be using to impress Stefan—and the sommelier—since the Montagnas had no investments, as far as she knew.

As they walked north on Fifth after dinner, the two men strode forward, looking neither right nor left, while their wives strolled, talking, looking in the windows. When the men reached the first cross street, they stood and waited, staring back at the women, far behind them.

"Lee, maybe we should walk faster." Celeste was not, Lee thought, capable of walking faster and maintaining her balance. She'd had far too much of the nice dry white, the full-bodied red, and the cognac.

"But it's a perfect fall evening, the windows are gorgeous, and we're not *going* anywhere. It can't hurt them to slow down."

Lee was remembering another walk, her introduction to the San Gennaro street festival in Little Italy. Joe had taken her hand at the first lighted arch over the street, told her to hang onto Toby—and her purse—and plunged shoulder-first into the throng. She was drawn rapidly forward by Joe's firm hand, often seeing nothing of him but one backward-bent, blue-sleeved arm emerging from the press of bodies all around them. She caught blurred glimpses of booths and games and people laughing together, eating wonderful smelling foods, but mostly she saw backs and bellies or, looking up, women leaning on pillows, looking down from their windows, and people waving from the seats of a ferris wheel rocking high above the crowd. When they emerged, in no time at all, at the end of the street, Lee was amazed by Joe's look of satisfaction.

"But Joe, we didn't see a thing."

"Mom, please, can we go back and do the rides?"

"And get some of those powdered sugar things. Joe, what were they? They smelled heavenly."

They were zeppole, sweet fried dough balls, warm in a grease-stained bag, one of the desserts they chose after backtracking to buy Toby a meatball hero and themselves icy, freshly opened oysters in chilled, dripping shells, and warm calzones stuffed with fontina and prosciutto. Squeezed happily into one Ferris wheel seat, the three of them rose and fell above the lights and the people, waving royally to the throng below, Lee and her guys, licking paper cups full of fresh blackberry gelato and giggling. With a little editing of Joe's first draft, it had been a wonderful evening, after all.

Now Joe and Stefan proceeded briskly past the wonders of Fifth Avenue, looking neither left nor right as the lollygagging women took in the abundance of the Avenue's shining windows, filled with beautifully presented—and safely unavailable—books, jewelry, and clothes. Celeste, her improbable and tipsy body concealed by her ankle-length sable on this night that did not require furs, was just another pretty, pampered woman, no longer a beacon to men's eyes.

"That was a little scary, back there in the restaurant." Lee was frowning. "But maybe I dodged the bullet. I didn't sound too smart-ass ordering dinner, did I? Joe hates to be embarrassed and I sure don't want him blowing up when we get home."

"As Stefan would say, *Tell* me about it. I have to be so careful not to step on that big Greek ego." Celeste cocked her head to one side and appraised the two men walking so far ahead of them.

"But they are handsome dogs, aren't they? Do you think that's why we put up with them?" She took Lee's arm, a companionable gesture that also helped her walk steadily. "I *know* it's a big part of it for *you*, Miss Venus-Conjunct-Sun. Everything around you has to be beautiful or you'll get sick. Literally."

Lee gave her friend a thumbs-up. "Pow! Another direct hit from the Star Lady. Anything that's ugly, I can always see how it could look with a little work. And I have to make the changes."

"That's about more than pretty. That's your Virgo moon, driving you to tidy things up and make everything the way it should be."

"Oh yeah, that's me, the pain-in-the-ass. The editor. Hey, I edit *rooms*. Every space I've ever moved into, I've changed, fixed, all the way back to making curtains out of crepe paper for the windows of Navy temp housing when I was a kid. I edit *hotel* rooms. I line the furnishings up with the axes of the room, move lamps so people can actually read, move chairs so there's a view, and tables so you can put a book down, or a drink. And there can't be any hazards to navigation. I'm very big on clearing the channels so people can navigate safely."

"You don't straighten the pictures?"

"That, m'dear, goes without saying in the modus operandi of us pains-in-the-ass. It makes me feel a little better that you're saying it's about beauty, not just orderliness. I don't want to act like an accountant. But ugly—you're right. I can't stand ugly. You should have seen the house Toby's dad and I rented in Saigon, full of plastic furniture so hideous I got the landlord to haul it all away. I threw big, pretty pillows around a nice rug while I got some simple rattan chairs and tables made. This stuff eats big chunks of my life. And I'm sure it drives other people crazy."

"I know, I *know* you feel that way, but you're being too hard on yourself. People around you get to live in a more beautiful world where everything works. That's not *bad*, Lee."

They were moving past Bonwit Teller's glowing windows, each one presenting a different stunning ball gown.

"Do you realize there are people who actually buy clothes like that?" Lee shook her head in wonder. "I don't get this charity ball stuff where people spend more on a dress than they donate to the cause. Dumb."

"But look how beautiful they are. I'd love to have that red satin."

"And it would be spectacular with your dark hair. But where would you wear it?"

"Oh, maybe walking the dog, if I had one." Celeste was giggling at the image.

"Feh. Dogs. You like dogs? They shed all over the place, bark, you have to walk them, they shit all over the sidewalk." Lee gave an exaggerated shudder. "People are enough trouble. I don't have room for dogs."

"But they're so *cute*. Poodles, Shih Tzus—they're adorable. And I don't have any kids so I've got lots of room in my life to fill up."

Lee smiled, wishing there were a pet store on Fifth so Celeste could fuss over the doggies in the window. Even without pet stores, it was wonderful walking at night in the heart of the city. The sidewalks were delightfully empty, almost private, unlike the daylight's whitewater rush of people. The sparse population this evening made it easy for Lee to spot Milo Hawkins a full block away, walking toward them with a small, attractive woman.

Hawkins was The Enemy, sent into MacGregor's from some industrial branch of EPNI when the multi-national bought the house, sending in the suits, Hawkins in one of the larger ones. A phalanx of managers filled the 26th and 27th floors of the corporate skyscraper. In the evening, when her department's editors and designers waited for their ride to street level and the elevator doors opened on "them," tweeds, beards, jeans, and miniskirts would take note of navy pinstripes, white shirts, and wingtips, and the hip would smirk at the square.

EPNI's corporate personnel department ran all the divisions' hiring and promotions, giving people tests full of "psychological" questions that evidently worked for corporate hires. Within a few months, the new personnel director for their division said that he'd figured it out: if people gave what seemed to be deliberately provocative answers, they'd probably fit in just fine with all the other "nutcases" at MacGregor's.

As one of the resolutely uncorporate, Lee had told Ramon, her supervising editor, that she would be doing a spurt of 12-hour days so she could get the Balkan book to Production, then take three unpaid weeks to drive across Canada with Joe and their kids. Milo Hawkins was outraged.

"You can't do that. Who the hell do you think you are? You have to *apply* for vacation time. I have to see if it fits my scheduling for the department." Then he came up with, "Where's your loyalty?"

Loyalty, she thought, was an interesting demand for dear old EPN International to make. EPNI would at any moment pink-slip everyone in the building, including Hawkins, if it suited the Business Plan. She'd never understood people who said "we" when they talked about corporations they worked for. But then she didn't understand paid vacations and health insurance either. Another-day-another-dollar was as far as her work/money thinking seemed to go.

Within days, a "verbal directive" went through the entire building: No woman could work more than an 8-hour day or a 40-hour week. It was a law. Consequently, but unsaid, no woman could run a major project at any company owned by EPNI—or fast-time a project. It was just a law. What could they do?

Lee asked Ramon for the memo and the text of the law. He told her there was no paper on the ruling, just a spoken directive moving along the management chain-of-command.

But Lee had a labor expert at home; Joe gave her a photocopy of the only remotely relevant law and she underlined the paragraph that specified the jobs covered; all of them were about women doing manual labor. In the resolutely flat-footed memo she attached, she pointed out that women who worked at desks, design tables, and switchboards were not listed. Resisting the temptation to write "FYI, Sucker" across the top, she put the text of the law and her memo in a circulating inter-office envelope, and wrote Hawkins' name in the next blank slot.

Within an hour, Ramon was in her doorway, looking worried. "What did you send Hawkins? He says you have to be in his office at two sharp."

Hawkins, his back to vast windows that glared into his guests' eyes, had counseled her firmly and benevolently on leaving her personal problems at home, since emotional behavior was inappropriate in the workplace. Thrown off stride by the unexpected and illogical advice, she managed a quiet reply. "Excuse me, but there's nothing emotional happening here. The law does not cover us. It should be a simple thing to rescind the directive based on an actual reading of the law."

He'd ordered her out of his office so loudly that it was quickly all over MacGregor's that he'd exploded. Two days later, he appeared on the floor and bellowed at Ramon, "Tell whatsername she can work as many goddamned hours as she wants!"

The directive ceased to be operative for all women in the building except the cleaning staff. When Lee asked Ramon what the hell was wrong with Hawkins, he'd replied with his own *non sequitur.* "Milo's a very hand-some guy."

"What's that got to do with anything?"

"And there's the problem exactly, Lee."

"You're making no sense."

"The other women here flirt with him. Ella and Joyce are sleeping with him."

"He's married."

"What's that got to do with anything?" Sakamoto spread his hands palms up, an amused look on his quite scrutable face.

She was angry with Hawkins, angry with Ella and Joyce and with every woman whose interpretation of sisterhood did not include hands-off other women's men. A married man was the same as an invisible one. But this dim, chauvinistic—and she had to say *emotional*—married man was working his looks, his position, and women's lack of loyalty to each other, to have a harem.

That very Milo Hawkins was now heading toward her, his moderately handsome head tilted down, talking to the woman on his arm, neither Ella nor Joyce nor poor Mrs. Hawkins, but one more pretty, probably intelligent and maybe even kind woman who was, nevertheless, a betrayer, letting the creep set the rules instead of holding her ground. Lee had time to calculate that Hawkins, this boob among boobs, probably had only a vague memory of the bitch who wouldn't play girl/boy games at work, and Joe and Stefan were blocks away—it was the perfect opportunity for payback, and she knew she'd never forgive herself if she didn't take it.

She said quietly to Celeste, "Stand by. I'll explain later." At the moment that Hawkins and date passed by them, Lee lowered her voice an octave and said slow and loud, "Helllooo, Miiilo" and kept walking, eyes straight ahead. She could hear the woman, behind them, demanding, "Who was *that?*" and Hawkins searching fast for some workable answer. Lee wanted to say, Get him, sister. Get it that he's done this before. And get the hell away from him.

She had blue-tagged Hawkins. It felt marvelous.

Boobs Exposed

Jimmy's was not a normal venue for Tate and Pru, but it was across 49th from the theatre where *Boobs* was running, and it was one of Joe's comfort spots, a classic red-check-tablecloth-and-manicotti New York hangout, with no aspirations to sophistication. The walls were covered with autographed headshots of show folk, but the only stars were in their much younger, pre-stardom forms; this was a place for dance company gypsies and bit players, before they hit it big, if they ever did. The tables were still lit by dripping candles stuck in basketed Chianti bottles, the air perfumed with the welcoming, unapologetic smell of thick tomato sauce laden with garlic and oregano. There was nothing of Bologna or Milan on the menu. Here, the food was what Joe called Napolitan or Sigi, the dishes that thousands of mamas on the Lower East Side had made every day in their tenement kitchens, plus specialties they would have prepared only on the most fortuitous holidays, when the family splurged for a wedding or a christening, or in later years when they had made it to garden apartments in Queens or bungalows in Leonia and could eat like dons every day.

Lee liked best the sauces and pastas that ingenious, loving mamas had made delicious on no money at all. A plate of rigatoni, covered in heavy red sauce and dusted with grated reggiano, was so delicious she was sure the children in those tenements couldn't have known it was not the food of kings. When she told Joe she was sorry that he'd grown up on Gert Montagna's meat loaf, her macaroni and Kraft cheese, and iceberg wedges with bottled orange dressing, instead of this lovely, loving food of his father's country, he had waved her concern away, telling her he'd eaten in friends' kitchens a lot.

Lee appreciated the lack of high expectations engendered by Joe's culinary experiences; with such a mother, and an ex-wife whose skills ran to grits and red-eye gravy, he found everything Lee prepared for him something of a miracle. She wished his pleasure in her handiwork led to his eating slowly, savoring what he was taking in, but he still wolfed down every bite as he might have done in those friends' kitchens, looking desperate and deprived. His intake was so rapid that she wondered if he actually tasted anything at all. Though he was several inches taller than Lee, she towered over him at meals; she sitting at her full height, he hunched over his plate as if arms could not be used to bridge the distance between table and mouth. Every rapid bite was accompanied by a sharp intake of air, which he said was his way of cooling the food, though he did it even when he was eating salad. It somehow went with his habit of sucking on uplifted beer or pop bottles, even though the liquid's arrival in his mouth was inevitable, given the reliability of gravity. Lee blue-tagged herself for the annoyance she felt in observing these trivial things. Surely she should be able to ignore such minutia, remembering how many things about this man pleased her greatly.

The Altridges and the Montagnas were finishing their Camparis when Poole arrived, wearing a crisp white Oxford button-down, pressed khakis, and shined penny loafers, his shoulder-length wig tied back neatly, his manners impeccable. He was so unlike the raucous hippie they'd just seen on stage that Joe refrained from letting Lee's friend know that his show was obscene and disgusting.

Joe had sat in the theatre, arms folded across his chest, frowning through every four-letter word, through the nudity, even the anti-war songs. Tate had whooped and chortled and threatened to send tickets to his mother. Now, over the antipasto, Pru announced to Poole that she was running away from home and joining the cast. He graciously promised to let her know when there was an opening in the company. *Boobs*, he told them, would soon be a Major Motion Picture. Pru did not ask for a role in the movie.

For Lee, the exuberant experience of the show was now topped by hearing news of her friend's family, by the Whatever-happened-to's, by telling him that their classmate Ariel was up for a role in a soap that might finally free her from having a day job—she was managing a restaurant in the Village. Lee annotated the dialogue for the others, until they took up their own conversation, attending to their eggplant parmagiano and their braciole, leaving her and Poole to speak in allusions and half-finished sentences that the two of them understood perfectly.

When the cannolis and Strega arrived, so did the dark-haired actor who played the show's sublimely boobish Army recruiter. He stopped just inside the doorway and nodded shyly at Poole, who flushed and stood to make his goodbyes. As he took her hand, Lee knew that he was happy and that his new life was full, his tribe complete. She would not see him again. His eyes challenged her mischievously as he slipped into remembered lines.

"Goodbye, my memory of earth, my dear, most dear, beyond every expectation."

She stood to embrace him and replied in kind. "It will seem like eternity ground into days and days."

She was startled to hear Joe say to the sitter, "That's six hours, right?" It was one in the morning, the alarm would ring in just six hours, beginning a day when she was scheduled to be drained and exhausted by the onset of the monthly flood, a day when she had to meet with her Balkan historian, who was infuriated by the scope of the rewrite that her questions and edits required.

Joe threw his jacket over a chair. Lee let out a great sigh.

"Oh good. You didn't really like it either." There was relief in his tone, pleasure in his assumption of her agreement.

"No, no. I had a great time, I just, I don't know, I just feel pretty low right now."

Joe looked at her questioningly as he unbuttoned his shirt, not seeing the tiny sauce stains that would probably never come out.

"I dunno, luv, I go to a great show, have a wonderful dinner, see an old friend, and I'm dragging around like somebody died." She kicked off her satin sandals. They were beautiful, she loved them, it was a miracle to have found Fiorentinas that matched her pants, and they hurt as if they had knives in them.

She sat on the edge of the bed and rubbed the foot that hurt the most. "Maybe it's just that I'm a failure. There's Marsh with his hit show and his songs, and other classmates—Nate, he's producing Wake Up USA. Lew Walsh's novel is a best seller. And somebody even told me that a B-minus kind of guy who was in a lot of my history classes is the lead counsel on the Sullivan anti-trust case."

She stepped out of the teal hip huggers, admiring them, pleased that she'd worn something so beautiful, so well made, fitting perfectly from hip to knee then flaring into wildly exaggerated bell bottoms. She clipped them to a pants hanger that she hung on a peg inside her closet door. In the morning light, she'd check to see if she needed to drop them at the dry cleaner's, along with Joe's shirt.

"Oh. And remember last year I introduced you to a guy named Perry O'Connor? Class behind me? He's running for Congress from Baltimore now."

Joe still looked puzzled, his black brows tenting over the skyblue eyes. "Well, yeah, it sounds like a pretty talented bunch."

"Right. And what have *I* done? I push people's words around on pieces of paper. These boring books. Well, and the reports for MAA, but still, they're not *my* ideas, not *my* words."

"You've got Tobe. And there's me." Joe grinned expectantly, hopping as he depantsed one solid, curly-haired leg.

"*They* have families too. Well, not Marsh. But I'm talking about making a contribution. Didn't the nuns tell you it was a sin to not use the gifts God gave you?"

"Mortal or venial? I don't remember."

"Don't tease, Joe, I'm serious."

He called out from the bathroom, a toothbrush in his mouth. "But, Leedle, they're all guys."

It was her turn to not comprehend. She leaned against the bathroom doorjamb, the tile floor cooling her wounded feet. "Why does that matter?"

"Well, I didn't hear you mention even one woman's name. Those people tearing up the road are all guys. So why are you so hard on yourself?"

Why am I? I don't know. Good old mom was happy to manage a household and kids. But she didn't get a degree. She never read de Beauvoir and Friedan. She just wanted to be a bookkeeper. Now I'm a book fixer. This is progress? Now it's new rules. No. New game. You make nice about feminism, my dear husband, but I don't think you have any idea what

it's about. Just as well. If you understood, you wouldn't like it.
Not one bit.

"If you were me, would you be satisfied to be somebody's wife, somebody's mom, somebody's sentence-fixer?"

He straightened up from the sink and looked at her in the mirror, wiping toothpaste foam on a hand towel. "If I had half what you've got, nobody would use me, ever."

"No, I don't imagine they would." She turned back into the bedroom.

"So go out for an audition," he called to her over the running water he was throwing onto his face, and the wall behind him, and the floor. "Do something with your sketches. They're good, aren't they? Write something. Your own stuff. Do it."

She reached under the curved shade of a *chinoiserie* table lamp and switched on a soft pool of warmth, then flipped off the glaring chandelier, erasing the sour light and hard shadows it cast over the room. He kept doing that, turning something beautiful ugly. And he didn't even know he had. Maybe she could get the lamps wired to the wall switch, take the bulbs out of the overhead. Then she wouldn't have to come behind him and fix it, over and over.

The costume design prints that hung around her closet door were all askew at different angles. She gave each a tiny nudge in the right direction and the aspect was grounded, serene again. Some things in the world were fixable, but Lee was running out of mental blue tags for this room, this man, her job, her life. It was all too much and she didn't have enough time to do all of it right, and her strength was ebbing away.

She put the peach silk blouse on a curved-shoulder hanger, hung it on the peg with the pants, took off the padded bra that made the blouse fit and made her look female, tucking it quickly into the cloth bag for hand laundering. Here in her closet, where he could not see her, she welled over with tears. He was right. So right. He couldn't say a line, draw a stick figure, even write a coherent sentence. But he had all the nerve in the world. And that was what counted. If he could do half, no a quarter of what she could do, he'd take those little skills and convince the world he was a Barrymore, a Picasso, a Faulkner. But she knew better. She was right where she should be, doing clean-ups for others, helping people with something to say get their ideas on paper, being a good audience for performers, making a pretty apartment and decent food and knowing she could wear peach shantung and teal satin and look good. It was all perfect and it wasn't enough. It was miles away from enough.

There were women who could stand at the center of things, assuming it was their rightful position. Lee had never forgotten the French Consul's wife in the Congo, newly arrived from Paris, walking into a reception with the absolute expectation that the evening would thenceforward be about her. She shone with her own bright and steady light, not reflecting her man's, who may or may not have been a star—he had made no impression. The mystery lay in the Parisian's not being beautiful; she was in fact what her perceptive language called *jolie laid*, her assurance and her clothes and grooming belying an unlovely face.

Lee had never forgotten the French woman's assurance and had wished ever since that she were such a person herself. But she was a reflector, not a source of light. She was lunar, thieving pale fire from the sun; she was the one who watched, who applauded or corrected or silently considered, never the one who set the direction, created the context, called the shots. Her compass needle wobbled here and there, refusing to give her a course setting. She toddled behind people who knew where they were going.

She couldn't talk about this with Joe. He just gave her solutions that wouldn't work and he never understood why she didn't act on them. She pulled on composure with her pajama top. She would put a lid on it. Until tomorrow. She'd talk with Celeste. If anybody could understand this it would be Celeste, the star maven. Lee realized how insane that would have sounded to her a year ago, when she'd been sure astrology was nonsense.

Tomorrow she and Celeste would talk between the rooms, the Montagna's West Side kitchen; the Papandreous' East Side, antiques-filled study. As two women who were both service brats with pasts in California, both transplants in New York, both married to men who'd climbed out of the city's slums and made something of themselves, Celeste and Lee could talk. The empty sister space in Lee's world had been filled by a caring woman who held a map of how the world worked.

Tomorrow Lee would rouse Toby from the astonishingly deep sleep that made it so hard to wake him. Calling to him didn't do it, nor did the hideously loud alarm clock Joe had bought him. Lee had to bounce on his bed and shake his shoulder. But then he would be washing up, dressing, Joe would be gone, and Lee might have a few minutes to talk to Celeste.

Tomorrow Celeste would listen, and maybe she could see if the order of the universe would have it that Lee would always be behind the scenes, watching, thinking, tinkering with other people's creations until they were perfect. It was, after all, her chosen role, except when it looked like a ridiculous way to use her life. Maybe the nuns were right about this one thing— she might be sinning, probably mortally.

The lamp extinguished, the shutters closed, the room was as dark as the city ever allowed it to be. Lines of pale yellow from the neighbors' security lights laddered across the floor and the bed, holding at bay the full darkness of the moon, the darkness that welcomed her monthly fall from reason. Her feet stabbed at her, her back had begun to ache, her life was a disaster.

"You're crying? You're *crying?*"

She thought he was asleep and that she'd been making no sound.

"What have *you* got to cry about?"

"Nothing. It's nothing."

"You're damn right it's nothing. Lee has it made, doing whatever she wants, any time she wants, am I wrong? Nobody else matters. Just Lee the Good. More like Lee the Bitch."

His voice hissed through the space between their pillows; yellow light lined the side of his face, turning the eye she could see a pale green. His breath smelled of Strega. She rose warily to sit on the edge of the bed and said in a voice that had no timbre, "I don't understand."

"Well maybe I can explain it to you." He hurtled out of the bed, flipped the chandelier on and wrenched open her closet. Lee shielded her eyes as she stared at him.

"You looked really great in these, you know?" He was holding the satin pants. "And you wore them to hang all over that Poole guy. Did you think how I might feel about that? Watching you looking at him, all smiley, talking about old times? Saying stuff I have no idea what you're talking about?"

> *Here it comes. The train wreck. But maybe I can stop it. Maybe if I say the right things, I can pull him out of it.*

"You know he's a homosexual, Joe," she said softly. "He's a *friend*."

"Oh sure. And people at Jimmy's are supposed to know that? Joe Montagna's wife is fawning all over this big star and I'm not supposed to be embarrassed?" He was whispershouting, hurling the words at her. "Well not in this, you won't. Not again." His broad hands tore at the silk pants until they ripped, once, twice, then again and again. He pulled out the peach chiffon blouse. "What did I pay for this? What did it cost me to watch you wear it with Mr. Tallblondandhandsomefaggotdirtymouth?"

There was no way to reason with this Joe; he would not hear her. While he was turned, yanking more things from her closet, she took her pillow and the afghan from the foot of the bed and slipped into the bathroom, locking the door soundlessly behind her. Joe did not like locked doors. She was not supposed to leave, but it was not possible to stay in the same space with this Joe. She must leave without seeming to leave, saying nothing, making no sound as she moved.

She stepped through the chilly puddles he had left on the floor, lined the tub with the afghan, and settled in as best she could, leaning back against her pillow. Toes against the faucets, she listened to Joe's fist hitting the bedroom wall, to plastic hangers breaking under his feet, to his threats to throw the bitch out of his home, and considered the fact that there were any number of people who thought her the most fortunate woman in Christendom. Never had there been a man so enamored of his wife as her husband was of her. Everyone said so.

"Ah, so you're the incomparable Leedle," said the Senator at the campaign dinner.

"Where can I get one like him?" asked the highest-ranking woman in New York banking, after working with Joe on one of MAA's programs for the poor.

The waitress at the Argos coffee shop where they had breakfast most Saturdays patted their hands, brought them extra Mellocreams, and admonished Lee to take good care of him.

"Every woman should be so lucky."

Witnesses to their lives told Lee that everywhere Joe went, he somehow got his adoration of his wife into the conversation. When other men ogled passing women, he smiled tolerantly. He didn't need such foolishness. Just look at his wife. And did they know that she gave great dinner parties? That she had manners and, you know, class? That she was editing really serious books at MacGregor's? That she could have been a movie star?

His favorite audiences were the staffs at Bloomingdale's, Bergdorf's and Saks. He would steer Lee through their fragrant doors on a Saturday afternoon, pulling her away from the sales racks to the floors with "the good stuff." She would remind him that there were bills to be paid at home and he would say they were just looking, just passing the time.

She enjoyed looking. Cashmere, silk, and fine workmanship pleased her enormously, as if their uncomplicated beauty could heal her life. She reached out to the soothing colors and comforting softness, inevitably finding things that would be wonderful to wear. And just as inevitably there was a solicitous saleswoman, often one who knew them. "Let me bring you that in a six."

Joe would insist that Lee show him everything she tried on. Even things she didn't like had to be shown, front, back and sides, to Joe, rendering judgments from a damask chair.

"That looks too big in the shoulders," he would inform the saleswoman. "Call the fitter, please." Or it would be: "She'll take this and that emerald-colored blouse. It made her eyes look sensational."

The sales staff would kvell, and other shoppers would discretely watch the madly-in-love man buy clothes for the little redhead. Stock clerks would search for extra buttons. Buyers would be called on to help choose between the Blass and the de la Renta, before Joe would wink and say, "I think she needs both of them."

The perfect husband in all his munificence. Pleased and frightened and angry, Lee would play the demure, grateful wife, sometimes not well enough to avoid being tut-tutted by a sleek saleswoman for not being overjoyed. "If I had a husband like that...." Lee thought she'd be glad to hand him over when the bill came and he pitched a Lee-the-extravagant-bitch fit.

At least there would be the crispness of silk and the downiness of cashmere, in her hands, real, giving delight—until she once more fell sickeningly through the looking glass and found herself trying to sleep in a bathtub.

She told herself that she could get through this, again, because this was not the real Joe. The vicious Joe who hissed insults, the taut Joe teetering on the edge of mayhem, the raging, furniture-busting Joe whose visitations had to be endured—that wasn't her Joe. Her Joe was kind, funny, and loving. It was just so hard to keep him present.

Nothing was more important than keeping her Joe from switching off, from reacting to her criticisms and her wrong moves, leaving her to deal with this angry, frightening man. Until she perfected her words and deeds, she would sometimes have to survive the consequences, waiting this Joe out, then hiding the evidence so that nothing would remind Good Joe of what she had said or done to send him away. Whatever chaos he created had to be returned to order invisibly, expeditiously, and without comment from Lee.

She had mastered that part of things. Just once she had left a bill on his desk for the repair of cupboard doors he had ripped off the cabinets in the kitchen. He had brought the invoice back to her, his eyes locking on hers as he crumpled it into a ball.

"Do you want me to do it again? Is that what you want?" He put his third after-dinner cognac on the kitchen table next to her and pivoted toward the cupboard, catching himself on the sink as he started to fall. One hand on the top of the repaired door and the other on the bottom, he wrenched it off its hinges again, both door and frame splintering with the crack of gun fire. As he stepped over the wreckage and fell against the counter, Lee instinctively reached out to steady him. He shook her off, without touching her, and lurched into the living room. Sinatra's "Summer Wind" soon roared through the apartment and, Lee suspected, the block, though she told herself that Toby's astonishingly ultra-deep sleep made him the one person the sound would not reach.

In the morning, she had smoothed out the bill, written a check to cover it, and looked in the Yellow Pages for another carpenter, one who would not note having done this job before.

For weeks, they would deal with Toby, enjoy friends and the city, work on MAA projects together, being exactly the happy couple people thought they were. Then she would do or say something that sent Joe veering off, jumping the tracks, scattering all the cars of their life into what seemed to her an unsalvageable heap of twisted steel.

In the world of her people, the Palmers and the Wellocks, such actions would have become part of the permanent record, never to be erased from the equation between those involved. Her people were slow to anger and long on grudges—two of her uncles had not spoken to each other since 1946. Something about a borrowed car. She understood endless WASP winters, the quiet, serious, solidly built—and enduring—ice. But not Joe's squalls: sudden, baseless, violent, and then, gone. In a matter of hours, there would be no emotional tracks, not a trace—for him. And it was up to her to see that she bore none; in this, she inevitably failed.

He would sleep soundly now, in their big comfortable bed, swathed in the soft sheets and the down comforter, while she lay wide-awake on unyielding porcelain. Staring into the dark, she ran a film on the bathroom ceiling of what might be happening in the parallel world, the one in which Lee Bailey was living, happily, somewhere in California. That imaginary Lee had never tried to sleep in a bathtub.

In the morning, Joe would wake early and dress quickly, stepping over, walking away from, perhaps not seeing, what he had done. He would use his travel kit to shave in the guest bathroom downstairs, as if that were the most natural of things to do.

When she was sure he had left their bedroom, she would begin playing out her part, hiding everything torn and broken, finding something un-damaged she could wear to work and covering the circles under her eyes with makeup. Then it was scramble eggs and toast a bialy for Toby and send him off to school with a hug as Joe puttered about, humming. He would read her a *Times* article about the election campaigns or the war, heat the milk for her coffee, suggest plans for the weekend. Perfectly groomed and perfectly pleasant, she would agree that the world was a mess, the coffee was delicious, and that yes, it would be nice to catch a four o'clock showing of *Rosemary's Baby* on Sunday.

She would then will her way through the Balkan meeting and plod through the opening pages of an economist's manuscript on market forc-es in Asia. It would all be punctuated by sprints to the Ladies' to change soaked maxipads and tampons. She would take a cab home, unable to walk the distance or even to endure the long bus ride between one bathroom and the next. At home she would feed Toby, oversee his homework, and have a candlelit dinner for two on the table at seven thirty.

Joe would look at her in the soft, warm light and say, "Why are you so quiet, Leedle?" He would hold her hand, loving concern filling his eyes, extending a virtual palm frond over her to protect her from the elements. "Did someone at work upset you?"

>   *Ah there he is, My knight on a white horse, ready to do battle*
>   *to protect me. Unless I say the wrong thing, do the wrong*

thing. Then Sir Doppleganger will appear and ride right over
me. I must not correct him or contradict him or embarrass
him, ever.

"No, I'm fine, dear. Just a little tired."

He would smile his most understanding smile, the one that did not include white teeth, just a tilted line that meant, Poor dear.

"You're shivering. It's your period, isn't it? I know how that does you in. Come on, let's go to bed early and I'll hold you."

She would fall into sleep, her head in the hollow of his shoulder, the full length of her body warmed and stilled by this radiant Joe, the Joe she loved. What she had seen and heard and felt must join all the other hidden, torn things that could not see the light of day.

She could do this, almost, when she was awake, moving, able to stay present in her busyness. But in sleep, the nightmare would come. The lost one where there was no warmth, no home, no safety, where she and Toby wandered unnamed, unknown, untethered, in the city, no one noticing their plight, no door opening to them.

She would force herself awake and out of its hold, easing out of bed to walk through the rooms of the brownstone, touching the amber velvet sofa, digging her toes into the wooly rugs, looking down into the garden of flowers and shrubs, touching the cartons in the storeroom that held pieces of her life, things she would unpack one day, when there was time, when there was room.

She would watch Toby, sleeping so deeply in his room, warm and safe, would think herself through the day ahead, picturing all the people she would be with, people who knew her, spoke her name, who had been here, in her home. When she had convinced herself that the nightmare was unfounded, she could slip back into bed, next to her protector, and sleep.

Knowing the nightmare would come again, another night and another, Lee volunteered to help make dinner for homeless women at a nearby church.

She would meet people who were living her worst fears, show herself how different they were from her, how impossible it was for her life to become like theirs.

On the appointed Friday Lee walked up to 86th through rain that came at her horizontally on a hard, chilling wind. Her slicker dripping in a corner of the church kitchen, she stirred cheese sauce and tore lettuce beside church members who knew the routine well. The difficult part was joining the guests, who waited at large round tables, talking quietly. Taking an empty seat, Lee felt like an intruder, knowing nothing about the safest shelters for the night or which hotel lobbies would not chase away a person who lingered too long, a person whose shopping bags were not filled with new purchases.

"If anyone's allergic to cheese, I'd be happy to make another dish for you. There are other things in the kitchen."

Lee's inquiring smile produced demurrers all round the table as the guests dug into the baked macaroni, the salad, and hot rolls. She would not be released to hide in the kitchen. She must make conversation, taking care to not be fooled by appearances into saying anything stupid or offensive; most of the women at the table looked like people she would never have assumed were homeless.

Hedda was a pinched matron with pretty white hair, wearing a gray suit and one of those little silk neck scarves that were supposed to make working women look like executives. Lee thought at first that she was a church member come to play hostess and wondered why she was intently grooming her nails with an emery board, ignoring everyone around her. Gwin was young, perhaps still in her teens, lightly alert for any threatening moves in her direction, dressed as Lee was in jeans and a turtleneck. Of all the women in the basement room, only two really looked the part. Jeanne, an inflated cherub with shaved black hair, wore high-topped basketball shoes and layers of torn, dirty sweaters. She tucked her tattered Bloomingdale's bags under her chair and protected them with widespread, layered skirts, wool plaids, flowered cottons, velvets, all of them tattered. The woman on Lee's left, Ella, was also disheveled, her clothes mismatched, her hair disordered by the storm; she was vice-chair of the church's governing committee.

On Lee's other hand sat quiet Nora, tall, emaciated, still in a soaked sheepskin coat and hat, even though the radiators in the church basement were pouring out heat. Over chocolate cake and coffee that she savored with disconcerting slowness, she confided in Lee that she had been an editor at Harcourt before her luck went bad. When Lee talked to her about recent changes in the business, Nora's eyes looked back at her from another country.

The next morning the light was feeble, barely managing to displace the night. Rain and wind still assaulted the windows. Lee pulled the flannel top sheet up around her ears and felt out with cold toes for Joe. He was there and warm and it was Saturday. She found herself falling back to where she and Toby were marooned on a concrete island that separated loud, fast-moving cars, taxis, buses, trucks, all of them moving purposefully, going somewhere important to their occupants. Toby shivered in a torn sweater, looking up at her, questions filling olive green eyes in a dirty face. She let the wind slap wet hair across her cheek as she looked at her son, knowing she had no answers for him. Across the street, under an awning, Nora watched them silently, her sheepskin coat brown from the rain.

Wrenching herself awake, breathless, Lee peered out from under the mounded quilts and saw the chest of drawers she'd painted with stars, her soft blue robe across her reading chair, *Slouching Toward Bethlehem* facedown at the place where Joe had said, "Are you ever coming to bed?" She was home. Not like Nora, Gwin, Hedda and Jeanne. They were waking at shelters and gathering up their things—all their things—to go back into the icy wet wind lashing through the streets of the city. Lee was waking to a day she would treasure for its warmth and safety, a day she hoped would not end in the same damned dream.

At least she understood it. It was the future she and Toby would have if she did not succeed at the task of being Lee Montagna. She understood the drowning men as well. They had to be men who drowned in the war; her father could have been among them if the diligent child she had been did not say enough Acts of Contrition, did not collect enough scrap metal, or so her child-self had feared. But she would never understand the dream that came on the grace-filled nights when she was safe, strong, and singing with a full voice—under the sea. That was beyond understanding. Still the dream came, unbidden but welcomed, again and again.

In her waking hours, she could choose to open the escape hatch into the life she was not living, the life in which she was Lee Bailey, the life her daydreams told her was safe, steady, never in danger.

Imagining herself safe with Danny Bailey was as irrational as dreaming she was happy under the sea. Being the son of her parents' best friends, he had been part of her life since before she could remember. And he had never meant safety for her.

When she was a baby and he a toddler, their fathers shipped out together, their mothers shared a house, and she and Danny a "youth bed." Her family had pictures of the two of them sound asleep in that bed, Danny against the bars at one end, as far from her as he could get. A later picture showed him on his tricycle, with Lee standing on the bar between the back wheels, her small hands on his shoulders. Lee was smiling, her eyes squinting against the sun; Danny was scowling. She could still hear him doing his too-big-to-play-with-you, "Get off get *off!* You're slowing me down!"

There were no snapshots of the day the earthquake shook the plates off the kitchen shelves in the Long Beach bungalow and their mothers pulled a door ajar and pushed them behind it. Under the splitting and breaking noises there was an astonishing, terrifying growl coming up from somewhere deep under the floor. Lee made herself as small as possible and covered her ears; Danny kept looking around the door to see what was happening. When it all stopped and they were helping their mothers clean up the mess, he called her a stupid crybaby.

The two families kept turning up on the same bases and in the same home ports. On one of her family's many visits to Danny's, he had climbed onto the roof and then fallen off, landing on old boards with rusty nails in them, one of which went all the way through his foot. At lunch, after his trip to the emergency room, five-year-old Lee was still shaken, remembering the long nail sticking through the top of his tennis shoe.

"I bet you won't go on the roof anymore."

"Why not, crybaby?" Undeterred by what she saw as a clear punishment from God for breaking the rules, he held up the ketchup bottle proudly.

"I bet I lost this much blood." Lee looked at her hamburger, at the ketchup sliding out of it, and left the table, crying again.

When Danny became an altar boy, he would do the mass for his friends, speeded up, saying the Latin responses so quickly they sounded like double-talk. Lee, an eight-year-old aspirant to sainthood, told him that was sacrilegious and he should never do it again.

"You know your catechism, squirt? Yeah? Well, what are the chief creatures of God?"

"The chief creatures of God are angels and men."

"You got it. Men. That means I can do what I want."

"You're not a man. You're an altar boy. You have to do what you're told. Does your mother know you make fun of mass?"

"Tell her if you want to. She won't care."

He had a point. Mrs. Bailey was ever unconcerned, no matter what Danny did. It was "just a phase."

Lee had watched him grow astonishingly taller and ever more distant, as his features hardened into manhood. All through her high school years, she carried a picture she had taken of him in a leather bomber jacket that said Yukon Rambler over his heart. Dateless through the entire high school experience, she told classmates the hugely impressive Rambler was her faraway boyfriend. But Danny Bailey was anything but hers.

Six-six since he was 14, he'd happily abandoned his childhood the first time a grown woman mistook him for a grown man. By the time he was 16 he was a smilingly precocious and highly experienced man of the world. After he'd seduced two of his teachers, the principal urged his parents to transfer him to a nearby boys' school run by the Jesuits. The Baileys scraped together the tuition money, but Danny was undeterred—there were still women everywhere but school; he simply shifted his attentions to neighboring housewives.

Mrs. Palmer was horrified that her friend's son had been expelled, even without knowing the outrageous reason. Mrs. Bailey had shrugged.

Lee yearned for Mrs. Bailey's view of child-raising to rub off on her parents, just as she yearned to be more than "that kid" to the elusive Danny. He dragged her around dutifully when he was ordered to, but even when his friends began to flirt with her, she remained invisible to the Adored One.

She watched him watch women, beautiful rounded women who would press their forearms against their sides, making that amazing line form between their breasts. Then they would smile at him very slowly, knowing something important and wonderful that he knew too. Lee hated being all bones, hated all the lush, mysterious women who so intrigued him, hated not knowing the secrets they shared, hated being ignored and knew she deserved to be. He loved women, could only see women. Lee was rightly invisible.

Until he was 22. Two days out of Army Officers' Candidate School, he was on the Palmers' doorstep in Norfolk. All pressed and polished, his new second-lieutenant's bars gleaming on his shoulders, he whipped off his dress hat, snapped it under his arm, ran a huge hand through his clipped brown hair and grinned with delight at Lee, staring up at him on the Palmer's porch. He was the most glorious thing she had ever seen. And he was looking at her. Straight at her.

He had dropped out of his senior year at San Francisco State to sign up for Korea. There was a war on, again, and the next Bailey was ready to serve, for the brief time an infantry second lieutenant in combat would survive. But when his class got their assignments, his was not to Korea. He'd been ordered to a training post, right there in Virginia, near the Navy base where Ernest Palmer was stationed. And the Yukon Rambler, the Unattainable One, had come courting. Was Lee dating anybody? Would she come to a dinner dance at his officers' club? Could he come to the house whenever he could get off the base?

At the dinner dance, Lee tried to adjust to having Danny Bailey facing her full-on instead of turned away, Danny smiling at her, listening, asking questions, telling her stories. He introduced her to fellow officers proudly, instead of trying to ditch her, as he always had. "They're going totally simian, my girl. I'm the envy of every man in this room."

It was incomprehensible. On the dance floor, unable to see over or around him, Lee had to understand what had changed. "What's happened to you? Why are we here? You've been running away from me all our lives."

He stopped dancing and held both her shoulders in his enormous hands as the other couples circled slowly past them. "When I got these orders, it was the first time since this war started that I'd thought I'd live to be 23. I was ready to go and I knew I'd be a good fighter, while I lasted. Then I'm looking at my orders and I see 'Virginia' not 'Korea' and I start seeing your face. I heard your voice. I remembered how you move and how you smell."

He bent down to Lee, tipped her face up toward his and inhaled. Lee laughed and tried to turn away. He held her in place. "You hear what the band's playing? 'Unforgettable.' That's you, Lee. The girl who was unforgettable. Are you hearing what I'm saying to you? You've always been the girl I'd get to later, when it was time to quit fooling around. You aren't a fool-around-with girl. Then I joined up and you were the never girl, the one I wouldn't live to hold. Now, now I'm going to have a life after all and you have to be in it. Stay with me tonight, stay with me all my life. Have kids with me. I love you, Lee Palmer."

Commander Palmer's initial welcome waned when it became clear that T-Bone Bailey's son was finally moving toward the long-held hope of both the Palmers and the Baileys, that their kids would marry. The large lieutenant was living in a BOQ but was back at their house every hour he wasn't on duty or asleep. "That boy takes up the whole living room. And he eats more than the rest of us put together."

"Now Ern, he doesn't eat here all that often. He takes Lee out for dinner a lot, doesn't he? And he took us all out to that fish place last Friday?"

Mrs. Palmer, no longer the beguiled wife who had waited for her man to come home from the Pacific, had moved into a permanent seesaw game with her husband, a game that often kept them from saying what they were actually thinking. She felt obliged to present the up side whenever her husband raged about the down, or the flaws on the rare occasions when he opined that something was good. The Commander might well be thinking now that he'd always imagined sharing grandchildren with his old shipmate, and Mrs. Palmer was definitely worried about what Lee and Danny were doing besides going out to dinner and the movies. But with the Commander declared wholly against, she had to come out totally for, on principle.

The only time she didn't play the game was when he opined about public affairs. She seemed uninterested, but was actually fact-gathering, silently preparing for Election Day, when she would step into the polling booth and cancel out all the Commander's votes.

Her concerns about Lee and Danny were well founded. Before, during and after the dinners, the walks, seeing *High Noon* and *Roman Holiday* and dancing to "Wish You Were Here" at officers' clubs, there was ever and always Danny's all-out assault on Lee's virginal armor.

Lieutenant Bailey followed her, watched her, smoothed her hair, talked to her. His focus was total, noticing everything, responding to everything. He heard every word she said, saw every move she made, and everything he heard and saw he loved and wanted to have, immediately.

He finished her sentences, laughed at her jokes, and bought her the bracelet she had been silently coveting in a shop window. He handed it to her saying, "When I saw this, I knew you either wanted it or just hadn't seen it yet." It was etched gold, shaped into a small belt that he buckled onto her wrist and then covered with his enormous hand. "Mine. This little arm. This little woman. Don't forget who you belong to, Lee Palmer, soon-to-be Mrs. Daniel Q. Bailey."

He was a magnetic field crackling across the table, sitting beside her, en-veloping her on the dance floor, the substance of him solid, warm, his chest pulsing under his crisp summer uniform, under her delighted hand. Wher-ever he was positioned, every cell in her body turned toward him. Danny Q was finally, alarmingly, hers and she had two years of college to finish, two years before they would marry and make love—in that order. In June, she was speaking of "just" two years. By July those years stretched into the future like decades, and her sense of urgency was coming to match Danny's.

Danny came into the kitchen holding a framed picture that had always hung on a wall in Palmer households, in on-base quarters, in rented apart-ments, and now in this modest house near the destroyer base at Norfolk. The picture was one of the touchstones that meant, We live here now, this is home.

"Who's the Gibson Girl? She looks like you."

The Palmers had gone to a Saturday luncheon on the naval base, leav-ing Lee and Danny to watch Ernie, who at eleven was a serious enough child to be safely left at home on his own. Nevertheless, Lee was charged with keeping him out of trouble and with doing the meticulous clean-up of the house that would meet Mrs. Palmer's exacting standards.

Her forearms wet and foamed with dishwater, Lee smiled, glad that Danny could see her in the picture.

"That Gibson Girl is Morgana Gabrielle Lee, my dad's mom, on the day she became a Palmer. And the guy is, of course, grandpa."

More than once Lee had copied the expression of the grandmother in the photograph Danny was examining, modestly lowering her chin while she looked into a mirror with the same mischievous eyes. All her life, Lee had seen this long-dead girl look back at her, the girl who would step out of the moment caught in the photo, leaving the photographer's shop to begin a life married to "the meanest man in Horse Creek Valley." She would move on to have two daughters and a son, to be swept to her death in the influenza epidemic that followed World War I. But in this picture none of that had happened. She had not suffered her husband's contempt for the world, the fear and pain of poverty, the despair of raising children destined for the mills, the deadly, shaking fever that ended everything before she had seen her first gray hair.

For this agonizingly brief moment, she was a girl, playing the modest, obedient bride to the handsome, arrogant man sitting next to her, his head set at a defiant, upward angle. Her groom, her fate, looked off into the distance away from her, his small mouth petulantly down-curved, his fine nose flared, detecting something distasteful in the air, perhaps the stink of the dyes that poured out of pipes set in the mill's outer walls, spewing into Horse Creek, staining the water the colors of the job in progress. He was a man who had nothing but his defiance, a man who would step out of the photographer's studio, take off this Sunday-best suit, and go back into the dye room in his stained overalls. Seated beside him, the girl in the bouffant hair and the tatting-trimmed white dress looked not into the distance but straight into the camera's eye, setting herself to look for decades out of this frame at generations of Palmers and now at Danny Bailey, who held the girl and her groom in one warm, massive hand.

Lee rinsed a plate and stood it in the drip rack, which was filling in the order her mother had prescribed, glassware first, now the plates. The cups and flatware would follow, then and only then, the cooking gear.

"I've always thought she looks like she's put a firecracker in the photographer's back pocket and is just waiting for it to go off. Those are her watercolors, on the wall in the dining room."

They were confidently done botanicals, a lushly gravid magnolia, a muscularly entwining honeysuckle, an aggressively orange azalea, each signed in a swooping, dramatic hand, "Morgana 1905." They were the work of a fifteen-year-old, painting subjects deemed acceptable for a girl, in an unacceptably sensual manner.

"I bet that hair was auburn—no *roan*—just like yours. And she has those corners on her jaw and the same squared-off chin, exactly like you."

Danny's long forefinger was gently tracing a line along the bottom edge of Morgana Palmer's face. He turned Lee away from the sink and traced the same angled line on her damp face.

"So Lee's a family name. I didn't know that."

Lee drew back from the compelling warmth of that hand. "You just think you know everything about me, but I'm double-named after her. My real first name is Morgana. You didn't know that."

He kissed her wet hand and bowed.

"How do you do, Morgana, Celtic enchantress of the sea. That's a wonderful name, girl. The stuff of legends. It's perfect. I'm going to call you Morgana for the rest of our lives."

He dropped to his knees in front of her, his outstretched arms spanning the tiny kitchen.

"Here I kneel, your cavalier, your abject subject. Milady Morgana, I entreat you, never release me from your spell."

"Get up, fool. You call me that, I won't know who you're talking to. Nobody's ever called me Morgana. Mom says it's melodramatic. And Dad, I don't know. He must have wanted me named for his mother but he's always called me Lee. Which is fine because I'm sure no enchantress of the sea. I'm Lee, she who is scared to death of the sea. Just Lee."

"Not to me. Not to the world that awaits you. Thou art Morgana, goddess of all the waters, and someday I'll convince you of that."

Ernie, his crew-cut spiky and his skin shining from a bath, was standing in the dining-room door frowning at the man who was taking up all the space in the kitchen and saying ridiculous things to his sister.

"Are we still going on a picnic? I thought we were going to the beach for a picnic."

Lee handed tea towels to him and to Danny.

"Get busy, gents, and we'll be out of here in two shakes."

She opened the refrigerator and took out sandwich makings and half a watermelon. Danny cocked an eyebrow down at the boy in the Health Tex striped shirt and neatly pressed khaki pants.

"You ever had a watermelon-spitting fight?"

Lee could see that she would have another mess to clean up before her parents returned to assess her execution of her responsibilities. There would be one eleven-year-old boy coated in pink, sticky watermelon juice, little black seeds, and beach sand.

Marla Shay, Lee's College Park roommate, was just across the Sound at a Civil War Army fort where her father was the new commandant, but she and Lee had not seen each other over the summer. Lee's Danny and Marla's Rand were absorbing all their time. Now an invitation had arrived, to the engagement party of Miss Marla Jane Shay and Lt. Randolph Gavin Fairfield. Marla wasn't waiting to make her life move, wasn't going back to do her junior year; she was dropping out to be a pilot's wife. Lee knew that going to the party would add weight to Danny's case for marrying now, but the event was not to be missed, no matter how much she disapproved of Marla's decision.

Lee thought Mar was the best—witty, world-wise, and smart, though struggling with college course work. Most of her schooling had been by correspondence courses sent to her in Germany, China, France, wherever her father had been stationed. And there had always been a willing lieutenant or captain who knew the subject and wanted to make points with the general's beautiful blonde daughter. Marla had them handle all her high school courses, then her college applications, which all combined successfully to put her into University classrooms, in person, without any eager aides to help her through. She knew no basic sciences or math, hadn't read any of the usual high school literature, and was a stranger to American culture. She spoke rapid German and French, but couldn't spell anything and didn't know any grammar, so she had to take first-year language classes, along with Remedial Everything. Determined to fit in, she struggled to learn what her fellow students already knew, but to Lee it all seemed an absurd comedown—Mar knew things their classmates might never learn, had seen the Yangtze and the Marne, had had an affair with an Austrian Count twice her age. Yet, at campus parties, Mar, a cigarette in one hand and a martini in the other, was always mysteriously kind to the fascinated boys who surrounded her.

She and Lee had bonded from the first laugh as the new roommates each asked, "Where're you from?" and answered, "Dad's Army" "Dad's Navy," that saying it all about where they were "from." When panty raiders hit the dorm, Marla saw the ends of a ladder move into their window and looked down to see two grinning boys heading up the rungs. She waited until they were high enough to provide the right leverage, then gave the top of the ladder a hearty shove just as Lee turned from locking their door against the marauders who had made it into the halls.

"My God, Mar. Did you kill them?"

"They're too dumb to die. And they're not stealing *my* drawers. I bought them in Paris."

Lee and Mar were the best dressed coeds at campus receptions and dances, thanks to a Shay auntie who had married into millions and become addicted to couturier clothes that she seemed to wear only once. Auntie boxes arrived regularly and the two girls would pull from them dresses, suits, and evening gowns from Fath, Dior, and Balenciaga.

"Here, Lee, this suit matches your eyes. Why don't you wear it in that play you're doing?"

"And get grease paint on it? That would be criminal. Look at the way these seams are made. And the cording on the lapels and cuffs. It's a work of art."

"OK, OK so how about these evening dresses? Let's wear 'em to the Sigma Chi ball."

Mar was looking into the floor-length mirror on the back of their door, red-painted fingertips holding the straps of an iridescent yellow gown at her shoulders, the yellow matching the glimmers of light in her pale gold hair.

The dress she had tossed into Lee's lap was brick-red *peau de soie*, stiff and soft at the same time, the most sensuous fabric Lee had ever touched. The entire gown, high-cut top, low back, and voluminous skirt, was lined in a fragile, peach crepe and Lee could find no visible stitching anywhere. It had been assembled by magicians.

"C'mon, Lee, we wear them to the ball. And if anybody steps on them..."

"... we beat them senseless with our tiny beaded handbags."

Mar's studies weren't going well, but her social life was *non pareil*. Every male who saw the curvy little blonde with the knowing eye quickly found out her name and was soon on the phone or at the door, sometimes several of them at once. Mar had a habit of over-booking, then needing to make a quick decision between the diplomat at the front door, the French naval officer waiting outside in the Ferrari, and the boy walking over from his frat house. Lee was in charge of holding the losers at bay while Mar slipped away with the chosen one.

And now Marla had decided on the ultimate chosen one, a nice guy, good-looking, from a good family, a nice guy who had been in a lot of their classes and not much of anywhere else. Lee was sure he was insufficiently sophisticated and had urged Marla to choose someone who was more than nice, but her friend was adamant.

"I like nice. Normal is wonderful, Lee. I want to live like real people. I *do*."

Lee was happy her friend had found what she wanted, but it wasn't going to last. Mar was going to get bored. As Lee was going to be in September, back in College Park with a normal roommate. She would miss Marla Shay.

Less than an hour after Danny and Lee walked into the Shays' quarters, he and General Shay were comrades, the old soldier telling the young one hair-raising war stories. "Old One Horse" promptly told his daughter that she should have chosen a real man like that Bailey instead of her Air Force flyboy, who couldn't get a word out of his future father-in-law.

"Did you see his Jeep?" Danny was chortling as he headed his old Chevy back to Norfolk.

"The one with the bullet holes? Mar drove it to the dorm to unload her stuff."

"He was telling me about driving it through machine gunfire in the CBI when he was with Stilwell. Straight through."

"That would explain the holes. But why didn't he go behind them?"

"Where would the fun be in that? Aww baby, you got the glooms? You missed mass to get over there in time, didn't you? Hey I can fix that. I can put in a word with the BVM and I do remember the whole mass, word for word. You want me to...."

Lee laughed in spite of herself, remembering his altar-boy clowning.

"But you really shouldn't call Mary the BVM, you know. That's over the line."

"Well as long as we're 'over the line,' I gotta tell you your friend Mar is getting a lot of good sex. She looks it. That calm, satisfied style."

"Oh, and does *he* look calm and satisfied?"

"Nah. Guys always look horny, no matter how much they're getting."

Lee resisted the impulse to hit him. It was only partly for his raunchy smugness, his certainty that sex was the answer to everything. It was also because part of her believed he might be right about making love. He'd laughed at her Catholic case for chastity, told her she was long overdue for knowing all that stuff was bourgeois crap designed to control the stupid. He'd brought her a book that excoriated the Church for its war against the sensual, against all the God-given joys of being incarnate, in the flesh, enjoying the beauties and pleasures of this world instead of toeing the icy line that was supposed to earn you the rewards of the next.

She could still hear the catechism recitation—"Why did God make us? God made us to show forth His goodness and to share with us His everlasting happiness in heaven." Not here, not in this vale of tears—in heaven. It was beginning to look like too long a wait.

"Lee, don't you see what evil, lying, manipulative bullshit it all is? Be a good little girl. Don't question anything. We know what's right for you. Actually, it's not bullshit. It's elephant shit. Whale shit. You can't believe it."

But she did. Our Lady of Guadalupe had hung over her bed since her Confirmation—seven years of direct oversight by the Blessed Virgin Mary herself. And since First Communion, Mary's image had hung in silver around Lee's neck. Danny would return to the Church; Lee imagined both their mothers must be saying novenas to be sure he did.

There was her mother and Mother Mary, there was also her father and a lifetime of "No excuse, sir!" There were standards to be upheld, there were good people and bad, good women and tramps, promising children and those who weren't measuring up. If she got straight A's and eagerly helped keep the house in precise order, if she was always combed and shining, constantly willing to look after Ernie, always modest, quiet and self-deprecating, the Commander would approve of her, and tell her so. If.

Somehow she was forever earning frowns and silence instead of promotion to Beloved Daughter. She suspected she would never do well enough, that he would always step back, beyond her reach. But she made the leap, again and again, hoping always that it would be far enough.

In the world outside the Palmer household, she knew she was to be quiet, dutiful, and invisible. She must not lead people to expect more of her than she could deliver. Nevertheless, her surface-self kept corking up into the light. Honor roll, student body president, Girls' State, Most Likely to Succeed, leads in college plays, and now Danny, at long last, Danny. Despite what the world told her about herself, Lee believed instead the people who knew her best, the parents who knew how far short she always fell.

On a July Saturday, she and Danny sat in the Palmers' living room, their backs against opposite arms of the living room sofa, bare feet meeting in the center. He was reading *From Here to Eternity*; she was making notes on a volume of John Keats, for a class she would take in September. Danny put his book down, reached out a long arm and took the Keats. She had not seen him looking so serious since he'd talked about expecting to die in Korea.

"They're wrong about you, you know. Your parents. With all that telling you that you aren't OK."

She looked away quickly.

"Listen to me, Morgana. You are smart, loving, funny, and you deserve all the love in the world, from them, from me, from anyone lucky enough to be around you." His broad smile broke through the seriousness. "And, oh Lord, you are so sexy." He tried to interlace his toes with hers.

Lee took back her Keats and her toes, certain he didn't know her as well as her family did, certain he was just trying yet another way to sway her away from what was right and into bed.

"What do you mean 'sexy'? We've never had sex."

"Damn, girl, sex isn't just sex. It's the way you move, the way your voice purrs up from down in your chest, the way you eat a peach, the way you smile. It's the way you're touching the back of the sofa right now."

She put both hands on her book, tucked her feet under a cushion and fixed her eyes on the page. "That's nonsense."

The next weekend he brought her a paperback novel. "You have to read this. Great story. You'll love it."

Lee thus made the acquaintance of Dominique and Roark, watched them operate by their own *ubermenschen* rules, mating like colossi. *The Fountainhead*, a summer night's walk on an Atlantic beach—and three fingers of scotch—were, at last, Danny's winning tactics. The rules were for other people, stupid people, and nothing had ever felt righter than Danny's hands and mouth, the warm, muscular, enclosing presence of him and that presence moving into her, on a beach in Virginia.

"Now, give me your hand. Feel us? Feel me in you?"

What Lee's hand felt was a veritable tree bridging the fuzz on both their bodies as he lay between her legs. She was astonished that flesh could take such a form. What her body felt was filled to the navel, impaled; she thought there might be internal injuries. When the tree retreated, she was relieved—and disappointed. But he came back and then pulled away again, as if he weren't sure if he wanted to be there or not. Even more surprisingly, her body began to move with his.

"No. Don't follow me. Pull back when I pull back."

But she didn't want to. She wanted to stay tight against his belly, feeling the tree fill every part of her. He laughed and turned to sit on the wooly blanket, rolling her easily up against his chest, keeping the connection.

"I knew it. I knew you'd love it." Sitting there, his hands circling her hips as her legs circled his, she stopped breathing, he had gone so deep.

"Easy, babe, easy."

Still one being, they went back down onto the blanket and he lowered himself over her, her entire body touched by his, her face in his chest. She realized that there was so much blood he was moving easily in and out of her, but why didn't she hurt? Instead, something different was happening as he moved now, each moment of the slow inward journey exquisite, the reaching of full depth breathtaking. He would stop there, throbbing against inner places that had never existed before. She wanted him to stay deep forever, except that his moving out brought again the don't-ever-stop pleasure. She began moving counter to his moves, her body holding tightly as he pulled away, opening to him as he glided back. Unable to keep to his slow pace, she accelerated and began to hear a low, loud sound that seemed to be coming from somewhere under the beach.

He arched down to cover her mouth with his. She pulled his tongue in to fill her mouth and twisted so the tree ranged everywhere inside her. The joining of his tongue and hers, of her moaning roar and his, completed the circuit the tree bridge had opened, bringing her to explosive obliteration.

Her eyes came slowly back to stars and moon, her ears to the breakers. She detected unknown odors that must have something to do with what had just happened, and noted that she had heard no mermaids singing. But she had certainly arrived at a new place, on terra that had been incognita.

He was still and silent. She wondered if he was asleep and spoke quietly to not wake him if he were. "I didn't know about the moving."

"What?"

"I didn't know people moved. I mean, was that all right?"

"No. That was not all right."

She knew it. All those women in his life had known what to do. Now he had proof she was not a woman. He would go back to being run-away Danny. Here she was, no longer a virgin and the man she'd chosen, who had chosen her, would now drop her for someone else, someone authentic, choosing one of the luxuriant, real females she so envied. She would be a spinster school marm. Maybe a nun. If they would take her now.

"Not all right." He laughed quietly and slid his hand between her legs. "That was superb. Here, feel this juicy woman."

"That's not blood?"

"A little maybe, but mostly it's you loving sex." He ran a finger along the wetness, triggering a gasp.

"Good Lord. You don't even know about your clit, do you." Soon she did as he brought her to a second explosion, then put her hand on his resurgent tree and asked, "May I?" She found enough breath to say, "Oh my God yes."

But she still had not said yes to marriage. He didn't believe her, bought her *Brides Magazine*, took her diamond shopping; she wouldn't pick one. Danny was dangerous. How could she ever trust a man who loved women that much, who watched and listened that carefully, understanding every word and feeling? If he was that attentive to her, he would be so to other women, women who deserved such attention.

In their movie-going, she could see that he was riveted by Monroe, charmed by Hepburn. Lee didn't want to be a charming Audrey; she wanted to be a riveting Marilyn, to be certain that she had everything he could possibly want.

She tried on a push-up bra, one with padding in the bottom of the cups, but she didn't even fill the remaining space. She wondered what it would feel like to have weight on her chest, moving gently as she walked. She thought it must be a reminder, at every move, that you were a woman, an incarnation of Eve, carrying with you the power to nurture, knowing things men would never know, while drawing in every Adam's attention. Every time a woman passed them on the beach or danced by them at a club, breasts straining against a bathing suit top or a tight blouse, Lee was sure that she was not a match for Danny.

Despite that certainty, the momentum of expectations and the power of his presence moved her steadily toward becoming Mrs. Bailey. She found herself looking at silver and china patterns, tearing out magazine pictures of wedding dresses, longing for him when he was on the post, cleaving to him when he was with her.

In a careful hand, she wrote out, twice, the words, "They who one another keep alive, ne'er parted be." It was Donne for Dan, she told him. He taped his copy on his shaving mirror at the BOQ; she carried hers folded into one side of a gold locket he had given her. He had put it, open to a photo of them together, in her hand and said, "So you'll remember what's important."

She looked in her palm and saw the laughter, and something else, in their faces, in the locket. Her body remembered, and she flushed.

He had set up his camera on a tripod, aimed at an Adirondack chair under an arbor of honeysuckle, to take their first photo together since they were children.

"OK, I'm putting this on a two-minute timer. Ready, set...."

They raced to the chair and he pulled her onto his lap. Settling in, she tucked the back of her head under his chin, his arms went around her, and the tree hardened against her thigh, threatening to burst through his khakis and her skirt. She slipped her hand past all intervening cloth, found his zipper and took in the tree, in broad daylight, in her parents' garden. His left arm stayed around her, but his right burrowed under all the cotton flowers of her full skirt and found her trigger point. Click.

She unclasped the chain of her Guadalupe medallion and put Our Lady in the sock drawer. As he fastened the chain of the golden locket around her neck, the room filled with the scent of honeysuckle. "Mine. My little neck. My little Morgana."

She expected angry visitations from the personage she now couldn't stop thinking of as the BVM, but there were only her parents' worried frowns, her own relief when her periods came, and Danny's clearly stated hope that a pregnancy would trap her into immediate white lace.

To her great relief, she made it back to College Park in the fall, to the wonders of Advanced Shakespeare, Prange's History of World War II, to Keats and Shelley and, at Danny's request, Home Ec 105, a basic cooking course.

At the first lesson, the instructor told her students to open the storage drawers in their mini kitchens. Then the woman recited from memory the placement of each spatula and beater and knife, from drawer one to drawer five, upper left-hand corner across and down the rows of instruments, never making a mistake in describing what was there. The students would also memorize these positions, as their first assignment. Recognizing yet another accountant in the kitchen, Lee dropped the course immediately, substituting a women's PE class in how to shoot a rifle, taught by a nervous sergeant from the ROTC staff.

Danny stormed at her in Virginia on her Thanksgiving and Christmas breaks; he came to Maryland on weekends and railed still more. The fourth time he turned up in College Park, he was driving a new blue Plymouth he'd bought with his engagement-ring fund.

He was still a magnetic force field, drawing her to him and no, she could not come with him now to a small hotel in Annapolis. It was a Friday morning; she had classes, exciting ones; the Japanese pilot who led the attack on Pearl Harbor was visiting Prange's class, which was bound to be fascinating. An actor from the Folger was doing Hamlet's soliloquies in Zeeveld's advanced Shakespeare class and she was eager to hear his interpretations. In the evening there was a rehearsal she couldn't possibly miss—she had the title role in *Dream Girl*. He could meet her at 10 at the theatre, couldn't he? It would be perfect. She would sign out of the dorm for the weekend, leaving a fake address, and they would have two beautiful days together, after these other things that she simply must do.

She waited at the theatre until midnight, then walked back to her dorm praying he was not injured somewhere, but knowing that he had simply been unwilling to wait a moment longer. He was going to live and he had not expected to; living could not wait. She had not respected his urgency, had not loved him as insistently as he loved her. She would make it up to him. She would not stay for her degree. She would marry him. As soon as classes were over in the spring. She told him in letters that it would be only a few more months. He did not answer.

She knew, through the mothers-link, though she found it hard to imagine, that he married, someone he met in a bar the first week he was home in California, after his discharge. Lee wondered if the woman had said yes immediately, wondered if she had breasts. Danny got a job, selling office equipment, had kids, three daughters.

Lee had never seen him again, except when he haunted her days, pulling her away from present pain into an alternate world, the one in which her younger self had chosen his plans over her own and he had not stepped away, beyond her reach. In that world, she was with the man who had known her longest and best and yet loved her deeply, the man who treasured everything she was or did and would never leave her or hurl threats of exile at her, the man she saw now smiling down at her from the ceiling over a ridiculous bathtub in the middle of this night in the too-real life she was actually living.

Life Lines / Trafalgar to Butterworth

Lee had almost hung up when Celeste finally answered her phone.

"Papandreou residence."

"Celeste, hi."

"Lee. Oh good. I'm glad it's you. I was thinking about you."

"You sound out of breath. You OK?"

"Oh yes. I just ran down the hall so I wouldn't miss the call."

"Don't do that. Just let the service take it next time. You could call me back. Well, maybe not. I've only got until Joe gets home—he said he'd be late but I haven't started dinner. If you don't mind some clanging and banging, we could talk now."

"That's fine. Stefan and I are going out so all I have to do is change clothes before I meet him. I've been in the park, all afternoon. New York is very beautiful today."

"Autumn in New York, girl. The song isn't wrong."

"But even when it's perfect, like today, New York is so serious. In California people would come out to play on a beautiful day like this."

"Can you imagine Stefan walking out of the Exchange and going to the park? He's on the floor all day yelling 'Trade or fade!' and you want him to *play?* He wouldn't know what you're talking about. Joe wouldn't either, of course."

"They *could* relax just a little. Oh but that's a silly idea. They have to keep driving. And I do understand wanting to make money. When I did investments, in L.A., I made *pots* of money and it was wonderful. Now that I'm doing astrology, I just have this short list of retainer clients and maybe six or seven consultations a week. If I ever had to pay the maintenance here on my own, it would eat up everything I have left in my stash. I'd be a bag lady in a matter of *weeks.*"

"If Toby and I had to live on what I make at MacGregor's we might be able to live in some hellhole of a walkup in a war-zone neighborhood. But *you* could make real money. You could write a book."

"Me? Like Jackie Collins? Oh I don't have that ability."

"No no. An astrology book. They're selling really well and you know so much about it."

"What would I say in it? I don't know anything I didn't learn from other astrologers' books. And I'd still have to be able to write, even if I did have something new to say."

"I'd tell you I'll help you, but I have to stop doing that. I think. That's what I wanted to talk to you about. I'm *always* helping other people do things that are important to them and I'm not sure if that's a good thing or if I'm just too afraid to do something on my own."

"You are being too hard on yourself again. We can only do the best we can with what we've been given. Remember I showed you your chart is all weighted to the seventh house? It's so full there's practically nothing in the rest of the houses."

"Partnership. The bloody damned house of partnership."

"You aren't designed to solo, Lee. Which doesn't mean you have to be the *junior* partner, or the invisible one. You can be an equal. But you're always going to want partnership. And you have to find water. You have all that earth, some air, a little fire, but the only planet in water is Neptune and that doesn't mean much. It's just a generational thing. The need for water is basic to all life forms, so you seek it out. And partnership."

"Shit. There's Joe the Crab, with most of his chart in water. And Toby's dad was—is—a Pisces. A crab and a fish, good for me. And Joe works with a crab—Tate's one too."

"My concern about you and water people is that they can mess up your good solid earth because they're influenced by so many things that they're just not predictable."

"Don't tell me that, Celeste. I *need* you to predict, to tell me what to watch out for and when, things to be careful about, like reminding me I can't say or do anything around Joe that means I had a life before I met him."

"I know. I know. It doesn't make one bit of sense. It's the same with Stefan. *They* have ex-wives and ex-girlfriends, but if I say anything that sounds like I ever met a man before him, Stefan just explodes."

"I'm remembering how he looked when his arm got caught in his coat sleeve when we were leaving the restaurant that night. He turned bright red and I thought he was going to tear the coat apart. And that was about nothing. If he's got something he thinks is big to be mad about, like you weren't a virgin at 30, he must be volcanic."

"Yes, a volcano would be the right picture."

"So we keep quiet. We do whatever we can to avoid causing them to blow up. And I'm not doing too well at that."

"I know. I know. Joe blew up again, didn't he."

"You did tell me to be extra careful at dark of the moon, but I would like to file a protest with the universe here. When it's also my *period* I would like some kind of priority status. I mean I've got hormones dropping or skyrocketing or whatever it is that happens, I'm fighting off despair because I think the world is ending, just before I start bleeding so hard I think I won't have anything left, like right now, it's a bloomin' flood. On top of it all, my inner bitch is seeing every fault there is in the world and I know I'm being an absolute pain in the ass, but I still want him to hang in with me, not turn on me. I can't cope with him going crazy along with everything else. He's got to pick other times to turn into Mr. Hyde."

"Mr. Hyde?"

"Dr. Jekyll and Mr. Hyde? The good doctor who kept turning into a monster in the old story?"

"Oh, of course. I saw that movie on TV. Spencer Tracy. He got all hairy and murdered people. Well, I know it doesn't sound fair but Joe does get pulled by the lunar cycle just like you do. His chart is so much water. It's like the moon pulling the tides. He can't help it."

"Not fair. This is not *not* fair. *Women* aren't all on the same cycle—Lord, now there's a thought. We could have a world-wide shutdown, maybe at dark of the moon. Millions of women just say the hell with it and curl up to sleep through it."

"Women who live together do get on the same cycle. I read about a study of women in college dorms, or maybe it was sorority houses. They got synchronized after a few months. You and Joe live together, the moon's getting you both, and you've synchronized. And you have to remember that Joe, Stefan too, these boys learned on the streets to be sharks. They can sense weakness and if they sense weakness they attack."

"Good Lord, that is a truly terrible idea, Celeste. Especially because it sounds right. My God, how do we deal with that? I do try, but sometimes I just don't have the energy. It's just too hard. How do you manage with Stefan?"

"I keep thinking I've figured it out and then there's something new that I haven't thought of and I've set him off again."

"That doesn't sound familiar or anything. This time Joe pulled half the clothes out of my closet and ripped them up. The room looked like a rag bin this morning. And he said things that were so awful, it damned near did me in to hear them."

"What set him off?"

"Besides the moon? And my period?"

"Don't cry, Lee. Don't cry."

"It's just that I'm running out of steam. I've changed pads and Tampax a dozen times already today. I think people need *some* blood to keep moving, and I've still got days of this to go."

"I know. I know. Just talk. Tell me what happened."

"Remember I told you we were meeting Marshall Poole after we saw *Boobs?* It just never occurred to me that Joe could be jealous of a gay guy. But somebody at the restaurant might not know that Marsh isn't into women, see, and they'd think Joe Montagna's wife was flirting with this really good-looking man. Face. I just didn't think about saving face, Joe's damned honor. Like those bozos at Jimmy's Ristorante are so important to him. But get this—he didn't lose it until he grokked that I was really depressed about always being the back-up singer, probably because my period was hours away. *Then* he blew. There I was all tied up in my own stupid concerns and I hadn't apologized to him for embarrassing him in public. I don't deserve the clothes he bought for Mrs. Joseph van Heugel Montagna, so he starts tearing them up and ranting about throwing me out of his home."

"*He* bought? *His* home? But you have a job, you make money."

"You'd think I sat here watching soaps for all my working counts with him. But I'm this partnership kind of gal, right? And one divorce is all I can handle. I *will* make this work. Even if I get down to my last jeans and T shirt. Maybe if I eat this damned steak raw, I'll get some strength back and stop weeping. I'm making a *béarnaise* to go on it. Joe loves that."

"And he really does love you, you know. More, I think, than Stefan loves me. Stefan has this Libra on-the-other-hand thing that keeps him changing his mind about me. Well, about everything actually. This week he was not in love at all. I told him he should delay a business trip, because his transits looked like he'd be confined a long time in a small space, so I thought his plane might be grounded at the airport."

"Why would that make him not love you?"

"He still thinks what I do is nonsense, so he yelled a lot and slammed the door on his way out."

"And? Did he get stuck on the plane?"

"No. The elevator froze on the way down and the emergency alarm didn't work. He was stuck right here in our building for three hours and missed his flight. OK you can laugh, but *he* didn't think it was funny."

"I'm sorry, Celeste. Just consider me punch-drunk for lack of sleep. And hemoglobin. I didn't think anything could make me laugh today, but it *is* a funny image. And perhaps an instructional one? Ah, Grasshopper, what should a wise man learn from such a lesson? To listen respectfully to Honorable Wife Astrologer?"

"Oh, but he'd never. Not Stefan."

"Sometimes I think there's no point in speaking to them at all. Here, I make Wife noises or Mom noises that don't have to be heard. At the office I make Working Woman noises and the only reason most of those guys listen is to tuck an idea away so they can bring it up later as their own. Maybe testosterone is a cause of deafness. It strikes me that I've only known one male who could really hear women. Unless you count gays. *They* can hear you."

"I've always imagined that my dad would have listened, but I was only four when he died, so it's just a dream. My mother said he was sweet. Then she married the sergeant, and he was definitely not a listener."

"Ran the family like a platoon?"

"He was pretty strict. 'R.A. All the Way.'"

"Those career guys. I know about that."

"Oh yes. The sergeant said that civilians were poor excuses for human beings. They all needed some good disciplining. But your father was an officer, wasn't he?"

"Mustang. He was the youngest chief warrant officer in the Navy one day, and the next, he was the oldest ensign. He says it was very embarrassing. He spent the rest of his career dealing with the ring-knockers, the Annapolis guys with their class rings. He only finished eighth grade, but he kept the commission after the war—you got better quarters, and he was a good officer. The men he commanded got it when they saw the only ribbon he wore was the Good Conduct. Officers don't get that one. And his had stars on it, so they knew he'd been in the ranks a long time."

"He sounds like a good man."

"Well, he's smart and he's got this natural grace. He's Central Casting's idea of an officer and a gentleman."

"You inherited the intelligence and the grace. And I think it's wonderful that you got a degree."

"My bargain-basement bachelor's? I went to the cheapest place I could find. Used my savings from old War Bonds and birthday checks and after-school jobs and I stacked books in the university library and did gift wraps in department stores at Christmas. My mom slipped me checks to help pay room and board. It was practically free and it was not a great education, but I did get my ticket punched. So I don't have to work in a restaurant or a department store now."

"I went to Katie Gibbs."

"The gloves, the hats, the steno pads? Good Lord. You never told me that."

"Their ads were very attractive. If you learned to type and take short-hand you could meet powerful men."

"And take down every word they said. Now *there's* an offer. Some guardian angel must have whispered to me to stay away from typewriters. I mean I use one every day but I'm really bad at it. If anybody asked me on job interviews about my typing speed, I could honestly say about 20 words a minute and then a lot of erasing. If you said 65, you were doomed to the keyboard."

"Or you got in the door, and you could keep your eyes open for a *good* job."

"Did that work for you? I thought I'd become the Indispensable Miss Palmer, Queen of the Steno Pool. But you got a real job?"

"I did, but not by typing. Don't be shocked now—it was pillow talk."

"You didn't."

"I did. I was working for an investment banker and there he was in my bed, talking to himself really, about deals he was working on and I'd just talk to him about it all, telling him what I thought. Then at work, he was doing things I'd said."

"You were such a sharp business thinker that he promoted you to a real job."

"Oh no. He never even thanked me. Well, not for the business ideas. But he had a client who really liked me. I went out with the client and got the conversation around to some transactions I thought would work for him. They made him a lot of money and he helped me get an entry slot as an analyst at another house."

"What about credentials? I thought those guys all had MBAs."

"Most of them, yes. And there were no women handling accounts. But my new friend and client said he'd bring his account over if they hired me to handle it. They thought he was just humoring the girlfriend, but it was a good account so they did it. They expected me to fail, of course."

"And you didn't."

"Not at investments."

"At?"

"At everything else. I didn't hide my cards. I wasn't suspicious. I really thought they liked me and would help me get going. They were nice, flirting and being charming, but they were thieves. They all stole ideas, and worked them as their own. They'd do a successful deal and wouldn't remember that I'd figured it out, not them. But, still, they were so nice to me."

"Lady, you are too kind."

"But they didn't have any reason to hurt me. I just wanted to make some money. And I was figuring out new ways to do that, so I wasn't taking anything out of their pockets. I didn't think they'd try to crush me."

"Most of the boys I've worked with would. Have. Like that creep Hawkins, the one we passed that night on Fifth? Uppity women, the ones who aren't around just to serve them, must be crushed. But you survived."

"Not really. They couldn't sabotage *all* my deals, so I took my pot of money and I just left. I wanted to figure out why this happened to me. There was something about me and men that wasn't working. I still haven't figured that out, but at least I have Stefan now."

"Stefan the trader. One of your investment clients."

"Oh no. Stefan doesn't need any advice on investments. I was on a date at a Dodgers game in L.A. and he had the seat on the other side of me, this gorgeous blond guy in a beautiful silk sport coat, big wide shoulders, and a Rolex watch. He looked at me, sort of surprised. Then he lit up with that wonderful smile and said, 'This makes up for the Bums leaving Brooklyn.'"

"Now that's romantic. Good for him. See? They can be so adorable, so worth it. Oh damn, the clock. Mine's going to be here any minute now and you have to dress to meet Stefan."

"Yes, it's late. I'll see you soon, and you can call me *anytime*. Lee? Lee, listen to me. I know you're down and you're scared. I know. But you are a strong and good person and you can get through this. Do you hear me?"

The Viennese Hour

Lee squirmed in the pew, hating her panty hose and thick bra. New York's weather gods had sent in a week of belated heat, as if to say that the summer of '69 had not been long enough, awful enough, so they were taking back their Indian-gift of a crisp, chilled half-October.

Fans as tall as men stood on each side of the sanctuary, moving their humming faces slowly from side to side of the gathering congregation, the intermittent roiling of the still air a welcome but all too brief blessing.

Joe looked at her, his wide forehead shining, and patted her hand consolingly.

"I'm sure the reception will be air conditioned," he whispered.

It better be. I don't know how many hours of this I can take.
But damned if you're going to catch me complaining. Not
about your first contact in years with your clan.

She smiled an It-doesn't-matter and kept his damp hand in hers. She would not fail him today, whatever it took. They'd been in their seats since ten minutes before this five-o'clock wedding was to begin, half an hour of struggling for breath and hoping she wasn't pooling perspiration onto the pew.

But the bridal party was late and so, it seemed, were most of the guests, many of them lingering outside the open doors, talking and smoking.

Lee studied the brightly painted stations of the cross, so unlike the mellow carved wood of the stations in Coronado, the ones that had gelled in her ten-year-old mind as the way the story of the crucifixion was told. Here, everything reminded Lee not of any church she knew, but of Hong Kong's gaudy Tiger Balm Gardens. A statue of the Virgin, face garishly made up, looked down on a tilted raft of tiny flames in familiar red glass votive cups. Lee thought of the soft folds in the white marble of the *Pieta* in the Vatican and caught herself up. She mustn't hand out blue-tags here—it was hardly fair to hold a parish church in Queens to the standards of St. Peter's, and even in St. Peter's there were things that fell somewhat short of Michelangelo. Lee shuddered, remembering the enormous mosaic of Roman soldiers winding a live saint's intestines onto a winch. At least there were no guts on these walls. It was all really quite festive, with people gradually filling the pews who were as Technicolored as the saints around them. Lee, in brown silk, and her mother-in-law, in gray rayon, were conspicuously drab.

She was surprised to find herself feeling comfortable that Rory—serious, quiet Rory Montagna—was at home with Toby, not some hired stranger, a small plus to having two of Joe's kids in residence.

Rory and Van had come in June for a visit with their father, who wrestled their enormous bags into the living room, shouting to Lee before she could ask about Maddy, "Kid's been missing a month and nobody tells me!"

Lee looked at the raised chords in his neck and scanned her mind rapidly for any way this might be construed as her doing. She found none and returned her attention to the conversation.

"I didn't mean to spring it on you, Dad." Rory was calm and even-toned. "I thought Mom must have told you. Sorry."

Lee was fairly sure the girl wasn't sorry at all, that she instead felt that all the adults in her world were so absurd they deserved whatever aggravations befell them.

When Toby eased into the living room with a cautious smile, Joe immediately handed him a bag. "Here, Tobe. Help your brother get set up in your room. Lee, you've got those keys for Rory?"

The keys. They would give Rory, for a whole month of the kids' summer vacation, the studio Lee had just rented on the brownstone's third floor, the quiet space she told Joe would help her concentrate on MAA work at night. She had improvised a desk from file cabinets and a door, and the previous tenant had left behind an almost-new sofa bed. Lee had quietly bought a folding cot for Toby and stored it in the back of the studio's closet.

It was perfect: Lee's quiet work space in Joe's mind; a "safe house" in Lee's, the place she and Toby could retreat to if doors started splintering at home. Knowing there was someplace to go—not a bathtub or an imagined sidewalk—had eased Lee's nights; she and Toby no longer walked rain-lashed streets in her nightmares.

This change was to be for only a month, a month in which Lee would have to be doubly careful not to misstep. It was such a small thing to ask. And it had turned into forever.

In their own room, out of their children's hearing, Joe had relayed the news Rory revealed on the way in from the airport.

Maddy had gotten mixed up with a bad crowd, fought with her mother, refused to listen to anyone, stopped helping Van, sometimes didn't come home at night. And then didn't come home at all. The police had been notified but there had been no trace of Maddy and there were no leads. Rory had left her classes at Georgia State; her mother could not manage Van without help. And Van had not been to physical therapy in months. "Bitch! I send her all that child support, for three kids. I send her money for therapists, and she doesn't take him?" Joe rammed a shoulder into the wall. "He's not going back!"

When he'd made his announcement at dinner, Rory put her fork down and gave him a level stare. "Then I'm not either." It was not that she insisted on sticking with her needy brother; it was that Cindy Lou, the girl claimed, had been attacking her—with punches and kicks and the yanking of hair.

It was settled. Van and Rory were now New Yorkers, resident members of the once-manageable Montagna household. Lee no longer had keys to the studio.

Rory declared herself uninterested in college classes; she would attend art school as soon as Lee could find someone to take the girl's place as Van's attendant. Lee scheduled an appointment for her steel-girded stepson at the Rusk Institute, and registered him for fall semester at Toby's school, which happened to have a full therapy program for disabled kids bussed in from all the boroughs, and it was just two blocks from the brownstone. It was all simply what had to be done.

Cindy Lou Montagna, named by Joe The Wicked Witch of the South, was now a woman with no children in her life. Lee Montagna, a woman who suddenly had too many, a woman who needed a break from the tension and chaos of her home, was pleased this hot Saturday to be far from children, at a celebration in a borough as strange to her as another country.

She leaned closer to Joe in his aisle seat, positioning herself to see the ceremony despite the gleaming edifice of lacquered blonde hair in front of her. She wiped her forehead dry and fought off heat-induced torpor.

Sitting behind a blonde. Lee had been sitting behind blonde Rory on their first family night out in New York. Unlike the stiff structure she examined now, her stepdaughter's hair had been perfectly cut and styled, thanks to Lee's hairdresser at Bendel's.

It was the week of the moon landing and they were at a Carnegie Hall concert and light show. Lee's teeth clenched remembering the insanely expensive tickets Joe had insisted on buying for two ten-year-old boys who would probably be bored, and for Rory and a date, some boy she had met in an art supply store.

Sitting behind them in a box high in the elegant hall, Lee was overcome with a fury that distracted her from the music, the light show, the voice of Neil Armstrong, the thrill of the giant step for mankind. She could say nothing to Joe that disparaged his children or limited their actions. She had maintained silence, until she could tell Celeste.

"She puts a hand up to smooth her hair and she's wearing my gold bracelet—that one with the buckle? I've had it forever. Then I'm thinking the scarf *he's* wearing looks *very* familiar. It's not bad enough *Rory* wears my things, now she's dressing her dates in my stuff? I seriously considered reaching over and wringing his neck with it."

Lee was startled that Celeste responded with giggles.

"I'm sorry to laugh, but you are *such* a Taurus. It is not good to invade bull people's space, and it's definitely not good to take things that are theirs. I'm surprised you didn't strangle both of them."

That urge was strong when Rory brought home an enormous wooden easel and moved it into the studio, the space where Joe's bright, talented daughter would now create works that would amaze the world and bring honor to his name. He and Rory had replaced Lee's improvised furnishings on a shopping trip to W & J Sloane, whose elegant truck had delivered a new sofa bed, an easy chair, a small dining set, and various chests, lamps and rugs. The bill was going to be enormous. And the space that had been Lee's, simple, comfortable and handsome, was now carpeted with clothes and food wrappers and magazines left there by a young woman who had no idea she had pushed Lee back into the fear of homelessness. It was not to be borne; it had to be borne.

Lee would not, however, bear the enslavement of her son. She couldn't say that to Joe; he saw a natural alliance between their sons that was somehow an equal one; "the boys" were just fine. It was only in talking to Celeste that Lee could voice what she saw happening.

"I swear, Celeste, Van's out to make a personal servant out of Toby. You know, 'Oooh it's so hard for me, Tobe. Fetch this, carry that.' Toby could end up hating his guts. And Van can do more than he pretends he can. He's used to total service, but he'll have to take care of himself *someday* and if everybody treats him like he's an invalid, how will he ever learn to cope?"

Actually, Lee sometimes could see the whole crutches thing was funny. They'd been in a long line to see *Yellow Submarine* and she'd whispered to Van, "C'mon, Van, look miserable, will you?" An usher quickly waved them right in. And Van got the giggles. People were too solemn around him. Lee thought she could do him some good, if he'd just lay off Toby.

"Did I tell you what he did last week? No, you and Stefan were away. Well, I'm in the conference room with a new writer and I get an urgent call to the phone. There's a crisis at home. Just what every working mother wants to hear. And it's Van. I'm scared to death. Is he hurt? Is Toby OK? Is something on fire? None of the above. I have been summoned by His

Lordship Van Montagna to order my son to make a snack for him. That's the crisis. I tell Van that the two of them have to work it out and he's never to scare me like that again."

"It sounds like that was not the end of it."

"Right. Not ten minutes later, I'm called out of the meeting again."

"He called *again?*"

"Oh no, this time it's Joe. And he's yelling so loud I have to hold the phone away from my head. Van has just pulled *him* out of a meeting—in *Chicago*—and of course that's really important, not like my dumb little meeting and it's all because I can't control my son. Joe is telling me Toby's *supposed* to wait on Van. That's his job. But it's not. Van's perfectly capable of getting his own snacks—I put all the things he likes down where he can reach them. Toby told Van he's not a slave and he's right. And Joe is shouting that I'm to go home and take care of all this immediately. I just sat there and bawled. I mean, I hate this little blue-eyed person on crutches. I hate Tiny Tim. That's just awful."

"Wait. Wait! As Stefan would say, 'What's not to hate? The kid's a snake.' And I'm afraid that would be right. Van is definitely not Tiny Tim. He's a powerful and very negative force. People may like the picture of the little blond boy on crutches, but when they know Van, they have to see he's not sweet at all. What did you do?"

"I went home. I was too upset to work and it's a good thing I got back here. Toby was threatening to run away from home if Van didn't get off his case. I made Van his goddam snack and took Toby in our room and just held him and told him he was OK. But I'm going to have to hire someone to be here after school every day. These kids are old enough to just let themselves in and do their homework, but it's not going to work without a referee."

"OK. Here's what we'll do. My housekeeper has a nineteen-year-old daughter who's very capable. Her name is Luisa and she's got five younger brothers and sisters. She's been in charge of them since she was 12 so I think she can handle *anything*. I'll give you her number. This problem is now solved."

"But your housekeeper needs her."

"The next daughter down is ready to take over at home, and the family needs the money. It's all right, Lee. You don't want to quit your job and be Van's servant, do you?"

"Dear God no. That would be living hell."

"Be careful, my friend. Van is watching all the time. He wants to get rid of you and Toby. Be very, very careful."

"But I'm helping him get what he wants. He's escaped from Atlanta, which he says he doesn't like. He's with his dad. He's getting first-rate schooling and living in New York, which he says he loves. And he loves his doctor. It's just so lucky he's here. The operation he needs is this guy's specialty. If Van didn't have the surgery before puberty, he'd be in a wheelchair the rest of his life, but he's here and he's going to be better, maybe not even in braces. He's got to be happy about that."

"But he thinks he'd have all that and more if you and Toby were gone."

"But he wouldn't. Joe would send him back to Atlanta in a minute if Toby and I weren't here."

"I know, I know, but believe me, Van doesn't see it that way. He sees a perfect life here with just his dad and Rory, and he'll create one crisis after another to make you look bad. That child is the schemer to end all schemers."

Lee was duly on the watch for Van's schemes, but was thinking better of Rory. The girl was *really* getting New York—she had looked sensational when she'd walked out of the brownstone that morning in Lee's black silk shirt, heading out to engage The City. She wasn't like Maddy, wherever she was. Maddy wouldn't have the energy to live in New York.

"That time Maddy was here I kept saying, 'Hey there's a great show at the Modern, or there's a free concert in the Park,' and Maddy would barely move. She'd just say something enthusiastic like, 'Ah've already seen all thet trayash.'"

"That sounded just like her." Celeste giggled. "How'd you do that?"

"Just my southern genes coming out my mouth. And I don't even like drawls. Thank goodness she's the only one who picked it up. Van and Rory don't do it. But Maddy, the drawling one, you never saw anybody less interested in being alive.

"It's not only her nature, her chart shows high susceptibilty to drugs until she's 29, and drugs can only make it worse."

"Rory's sure that's what's going on. But Joe won't hear of it. 'No kid of mine....' All that pride gets in his way of seeing what's right in front of him."

An elbow-jab from Gert Montagna brought Lee back into the sweltering church pew. The older woman nodded and rolled her eyes skyward. Lee turned in the nod's direction to see dyed black hair, a withered face, and bony limbs emerging from a cloud of pink ostrich feathers as a wedding guest teetered down the aisle in the gait of the extremely high-heeled, wisps of pink floating behind her in the fans' currents.

Most of the men were wearing glistening silk suits and white-on-white shirts. The ushers were each in a different pastel suit with darker shades of shirt ruffles down their chests and over their hands. The one in aqua and teal seated a stocky woman coated in magenta sequins, whipped a comb out of his pants pocket, and reset his Elvis pompadour as he hurried back to the church door.

Lee decided to imagine the assembly as they would look if their forbears had not left Calabria, Naples, and Sicily. The Technicolor scene went to black and white. Pink ostrich and magenta sequins became long, black, shapeless dresses, the spike heels were laced flats you could work in, the beehive was replaced by a black kerchief low on the forehead and tied under the chin. The men wore peaked caps, collarless shirts, baggy black suits. Hands were calloused, not manicured. Faces were lined and browned by the sun and without makeup. No one was blonde.

The organist began the wedding march at last, and eight girls in Acrilan organza sauntered past, then Cousin Eileen Montagna, a tiny teen with pale brown hair, smiled her way down the aisle on Uncle Tony's arm. Tony, young enough to be Joe's brother, cased the crowd as he walked, nodding and waving. When his scan reached Joe, he stopped walking and pulled his nephew out of the pew. The bride stood alone in the aisle, an outraged look on her tiny face as her father lifted Joe off his feet in a bear hug.

"Joey, Joey you came to my party. Waddya think of my baby, eh? Ain't she sumthin?"

A high-pitched voice hissed, "Daaaady!" And Tony headed back to the job at hand, still talking to Joe. "You comin to the reception or what?"

"Yeah sure, Tony. We'll be there."

Tony grinned at his brother, Big Joe, said a wary Hi to Gert, looked at Lee, and gave Joe a way-to-go hand waggle, fingers down. "Catch you later, kid."

Lee had known this wedding would be different when the invitation arrived. It was lavender, with raised Gothic lettering in purple. Miss Eileen Louise Montagna and Mr. Edward Fabio Iannelli—St. Charles Borromeo, Rockville Centre, Long Island—Reception immediately following at Grametti's South Shore Dining Rooms.

"We're going? You're accepting an invitation from your family?"

"I think it's time. I mean, with Nixon in the White House what difference can it make? MAA hasn't had a federal contract since that bastard put the brakes on all the poverty work. All the work is with unions and local governments now—they don't give a damn if I have a national security clearance or not. And Tony's a hell of a guy. I'd really like to see him."

Lee was astonished. "This is the uncle who runs all the gambling in area code 516, right?"

Joe whirled on her, poking an imaginary gun in her ribs.

"Listen Ms. Wisemouth, if you wanna stay healthy you'll remember—Tony Montagna owns gas stations. He's a legitimate businessman, got it? Never mind that he's got an awful lot of cash lying around and there are bodyguards outside his bungalow in Baldwin. So he gives waitresses hundred-dollar tips, what's it to ya? You don't unnusteyen free ennerproise? You lookin' for trouble!"

"No sir, I get the pitcher. Yes sir, give me your aunt's number and I'll find out what patterns cousin Eileen Louise has picked. But why isn't her name Teresa or Carmela?"

"Tony married the Irish girl down the block. And what are you talking 'patterns'?"

"You know. Dessert plates. Wine goblets. Pickle forks."

Joe was patient with her, explaining that there would be no registering at Tiffany's and Bloomingdale's for this bride. The only appropriate gift was money.

"We just write a check?"

"No. Money, honey. A wad of it. Just let me handle it."

The ceremony was over in minutes. As the bridal party hurried out, Tony pumped the priest's hand and put a roll of bills in it.

"Guaranteed those were not ones," Joe whispered.

Lee hoped the priest would use the cash to buy air conditioning.

The back of the church was still full of men who hadn't bothered to sit down. There were two no one talked to, two blue-eyed men in Sears Roebuck suits standing just outside the doors, solemnly scanning faces as the guests filed out. Lee realized with a start that they must be FBI. It seemed absurd to be in a crowd being surveilled for mobsters, at a wedding where the funny little father of the bride had left his daughter in the aisle to bear-hug his nephew. Maybe the FBI was part of the comedy. Maybe they had Dick Tracy watches.

At Grametti's South Shore Dining Rooms the volume rose rapidly and the embracing accelerated as bars in each corner of the huge room put forth vast numbers of drinks to the crowd, which had tripled in size. Big Joe Montagna was repeatedly hugged by men who wriggled through the press of bodies to reach him.

"They owe him," Joe explained. "He always had jobs for these guys, like when they were on parole."

Joe introduced his freckled wife to aunts and cousins, to boyhood buddies and to coworkers from his CCNY days, the guys who had covered for him on the night shift while he read textbooks in the latrine.

The women spoke stiffly to her and moved away; the men punched Joe, winked at him, and gave him high signs. "That's our Joey."

"Jeez Joey. An office on Park Avenue and an Inglesi wife. You're too much."

"*Marone*, where you been hiding her? And what's she see in a dumb *paisan* like you?"

"This is Joey, from the neighborhood. He's a big shot. Legit."

There seemed to be no undertone of disapproval for his long absence. They understood, Joe told her. FBI agents had questioned him about his relatives and his boyhood friends when he was up for the job at the Cape, and again before he got the job in DC, the one he'd had when Lee met him.

Inspired by the crowd, a glass of Frascati, and her delight that Joe had taken the job in Washington so they could meet, Lee took his hand and leaned into his side.

"This is fascinating. I wish we'd done this years ago."

He squeezed her hand and grinned. "I'm not so sure we should be here *now*."

Gert appeared with two buffet plates she had filled from a towering ziggurat in the center of the room.

"That thing over there with the waterfalls and the torches? Well, it's got Chinese, Mexican, Polish, you name it. The stuff in the waterfall is champagne but it's so sweet you could die. Here, Joey, Lee, eat. You want some Chivas, Joey?"

"No, Mom, thanks. I've got this Heineken." It was, Lee noted, still in the bottle rather than a glass, which meant Joe was pulling hard on it as he drank. But that peculiar habit didn't seem to matter on the South Shore of Long Island. She made herself stop the mental blue-tagging, overwhelmed by the numbers of them she would need to cover this odd gathering.

Big Joe glared at his wife's back as she burrowed through the crowd and anger rumbled up in his deep voice. "I swear I'm gonna leave that woman. Someday I'm gonna do it."

Lee offered him her plate. "Pop, this must be for you. I couldn't possibly eat all this."

"No no, that's all right. I'll just work on this bourbon. Tony bought Wild Turkey."

The room was filled to bursting, Lee's feet were beginning to throb and Big Joe had sagged into a chair, but there was no sign of the bridal party.

"Joe, your dad looks so tired. If they don't come soon maybe we should ease out."

"He isn't tired. This is hard for him. He doesn't have a pot and his baby brother is throwing this blowout. Pop was the only clean union boss on the planet and he's old and broke and here's the proof that crime does pay. He's not tired."

Big Joe was the real thing, a true believer. He had believed in Labor, had helped the trade unions rocket from persecuted to powerful, bringing in the forty-hour work week, the minimum wage, workmen's comp, paid vacations, medical insurance. It had been noble work. And it had turned to dust before his eyes, in one lifetime. The mills and plants and ships fled organized territory, taking their jobs with them. Other union leaders stole from their memberships, took bribes from management, bought four-hundred-dollar suits, and moved to Boca. Lee wished time had slowed, stretching the glory days through Big Joe's lifetime, waiting a decent interval to turn so sour.

She looked at the big, sad man rolling his glass slowly in his hands and saw him instead the way she would always remember him, leaning into the television screen in the brownstone's den as the evening news reported a threatened wildcat strike of the city's bridge and tunnel workers.

"Yes!" he urged the set. "Go out! Shut it all down."

"Joe, for God's sake think of the mess." Gert was not, had never been, a friend of the working class. "We wouldn't be able to move for the traffic jams. And the stores would be empty."

Big Joe had turned his back on his wife and explained to Lee, "They're getting a raw deal, those guys. And they're invisible. They need to show what they can do. Just shut the damn city down. And all the other unions need to back them up so *nothin* moves. So people *see* who makes this damn city run. A general strike. Just once in my life, let me see a general strike."

Lee had silently joined his prayer, thinking his years of devotion had earned him at least a one-day show of real and righteous force by Labor. But there was no general strike; not even the bridge and tunnel workers had gone out. Lee wondered if their grievances had been resolved or their leaders paid off.

A loudspeaker announcement cut through the din of voices. "The Montagna-Ianelli party will now move into the Orchid dining room. Montagna-Ianelli to the Orchid."

The walls on one side of the room began to roll away, revealing what appeared to be an enormous night club. Round, purple-skirted tables stood on tiers ringing a dance floor, and a 20-piece band was playing "Sunny." The bridal party was seated at a long table on the top tier, Tony standing in front of them, waving people into the room.

"My God," Gert groaned.

Lee was confused. "Joe, this wasn't it? All that food. Everybody's already smashed. What's going on?"

Joe took in the panorama with a grin.

"What's going on is Tony's laid out dinner for a few hundred of his best pals. There will probably be monster shrimp cocktails, filet mignon, and every other goddam thing he can do to knock em dead." He leaned closer to Lee and whispered, "Welcome to Our Thing."

Cosa nostra, of course. This was the New York mafia, assembled and celebrating. She was seeing things WASPs could only read about in books—unless they had married into *La Famiglia*.

With the half dozen jumbo prawns in shaved ice, an MC had announced, in earnest imitation of Bert Parks, the first dance. As the bride and her father danced to "Daddy's Little Girl," Tony's several hundred best friends cheered and clapped. The exhaustingly enthusiastic MC cajoled various Montagnas and Ianellis to join them on the floor, introducing each of them and cueing fanfares from the band.

Lee leaned closer to Joe. "Could he be a little more obnoxious? Who is that? And why is he acting like he's such a big deal?"

"You don't recognize him? He has some game show. Calls himself Jay Fieldson, but he's Johnny Figlio, from Mulberry Street. The Boys have an interest in him."

Oh yes. Very big deal. If I ever break my leg and am laid up helpless, I'll be sure to catch his show.

"Do you know what your new in-law does for a living?"

"Knocks up nice Irish-Italian girls. What else, I don't know."

Big Joe leaned across the table. "The kid flunked out of Saint Augie's, which is very hard to do. Tony gave him a gas station so he can support his new family."

"Well, there's a dowry for you," Gert cut in. "He'll be home every night smelling like gasoline, with black grease under his fingernails. Lovely."

"It's honorable work, woman." Big Joe was shaking his head disconsolately. "Every man has to have work. So he can take care of his responsibilities."

The glare of Gert's pale blue eyes carried the full weight of the decades she had spent watching her honorable husband fail to meet what she considered his responsibilities. Lee wondered why Gert had hitched her wagon to Big Joe expecting anything but the life she got. How had they ever gotten together, the little Yankee nurse and the burly union organizer? How had they stayed together despite Gert's contempt for his world, despite never having any money, despite having only one child while Big Joe's brothers and sisters produced the huge broods that now filled tables here? Big Joe was sure his wife was sitting on a hidden remnant of her family's land-hold-

ings upstate, foregoing the comforts it would buy them, just as she had
withheld from him the sons and daughters he wanted around him now, to
be the wealth he had created in his life.

Lee was glad the stream of well-wishers had not ended. Maybe her father-in-law could see the love he had earned in the fact that a chair pulled
up beside him was constantly occupied, one smiling man after another
sitting own, talking to Big Joe Montagna with shining eyes.

Lee tried to remember Gert ever saying a kind word, about anything.
The woman seemed quite capable of holding onto valuable acreage or a
secret stash of blue-chip stocks while she blamed Big Joe for the miserable apartments they'd shared with cockroaches and rats, for the cheap,
unhealthy food she cooked, perhaps even for their having only one child.
Yes, Lee could definitely imagine her mother-in-law questioning Big Joe's
virility while she secretly used a diaphragm or even aborted the children she
did not want to have.

She wondered how her Joe had survived growing up in Gert's angry
hands, how Big Joe had stayed with her for decades. Lee knew she could
handle only a few hours at a time with her highly toxic mother-in-law.

The MC announced a special surprise direct from Vegas as the O'Ban-
nion Sisters swung onto the bandstand singing what he described as their
latest gold record. They waved to Tony as they took their bows, then shifted
quickly into *Al di La*, for some reason singing not to Tony or to the bride
and groom, but to a tall, white-haired man in a gray silk suit and very dark
glasses. Lee had not seen him at the wedding or at the earlier part of the
reception.

"Joe, who is that?"

"Don't ask."

She had never seen Joe look so uneasy.

The serenade completed, the MC granted permission for general dancing. Joe held Lee close and maneuvered her through the crush that had
filled the floor for "It Had To Be You."

"Don't weddings make you feel all soggy?" She kissed him on the nose.

"Even weddings on Longgisland? You're OK with this?"

"Hey, it's another country. And you know how I love to travel."

He laughed and swung her out in a turn. She felt the impact of another
body on her back; Joe's arms flew up stiffly on each side of her.

"Hold it Frankie. It's OK."

Lee turned to see a heavy, enraged face, bright red and bulging over a too-tight collar, watched the slitted eyes widen in delight.

"Joey izzatchew?"

"Yeah Frankie yeah, it's me. How ya doin?" Joe quickly danced her away.

"What was that about?"

"Frankie Arrabbiato. From the neighborhood. Frankie doesn't like anybody to touch him."

"Oh?"

"Frankie hurts people. Professionally."

Safely back at their table, Joe touched her hand and pointed his chin toward the bridal table. "Here it goes." A queue of men was moving along the edge of the dance floor, to the bridal dais. Each one went up the steps and stuffed an envelope into a white satin pouch that matched the bride's gown, its ribbon ties looped around her wrist. A kiss on the cheek for her, a handshake for the groom, a few words and a bear hug for Tony, who was standing behind the bride's chair.

Joe took a place in the quickly moving line. Gert moved into his seat.

"Disgusting isn't it? Stuffing a bag with money."

"But it's practical. I mean they can buy some furniture instead of starting out with a lot of blenders and dessert plates."

"Furniture? They can buy a condo and a trip around the world. And a Ferrari."

"Oh. Of course. They're getting a *lot* of money." Lee looked around the room. "I don't think I've ever seen so many diamonds in one place."

"Hot," Gert growled. Lee fanned herself in agreement.

"Not the room. The diamonds. They don't buy jewelry in stores. You see that man talking to Joey? That's Dominic, another brother. We don't see him much because he's in jail most of the time. The first time for deserting from the Army. In World War *Two*." The former Gertrude Agnes van Heugel was in high WASP dudgeon. "These people don't pay their way."

Lee guiltily left Gert to focus her rage on Big Joe and her filet mignon, escaping to the dance floor with the new president of Big Joe's union. The band was playing "Night and Day," loudly, as he shouted to Lee. "So little lady, what do you think?"

"About?"

"About Italian weddings. About New York. The whole *megillah.*"

"Overwhelmed, Myron, overwhelmed. Do you know all these people?"

"Most of them. The Boys. They're OK. They don't hurt nobody, you know? They're not into drugs, dangerous stuff. Just gambling. Harmless."

Lee wondered what these harmless men would do to a losing gambler who didn't pay them.

The music shifted suddenly to a tarantella. Lee turned back toward the table, but Myron caught her hand and tugged.

"If a nice Jewish boy can learn this, so can you."

At the edge of the floor he demonstrated the steps, giving her almost no time to get the moves down before he danced her into the thick of the action. An intricate exchange of partners began and Myron handed her off to a short round man who wheeled her away, smiling up at her gleefully. Then it was Frankie, who simply lifted her off the floor so she no longer had to think of the steps. The music was too loud for talking, for which she was grateful since the only thing she could think to say to him was that he was crushing her ribs.

His beaming face suddenly went serious and Lee followed his line of sight. The tall, white haired man in the gray silk suit was standing perfectly still, looking at Frankie, who put Lee's hand carefully into the older man's and backed away, looking at the floor.

The bandleader saw the exchange and stopped the tarantella in mid bar. He called out a shift in plans and the music became "Moonlight Serenade." He looked to the floor with a beseeching smile.

The silver head ignored him, bowed slightly to Lee and began to move her smoothly across the floor, his step light, his lead sure. There was no longer a din and no one to bump into. The dancers who had not gone to their tables rocked gently in place half-watching the expertise of this grave man, dancing with the pale, skinny redhead in a boring dress who had married Joey Montagna.

Lee concentrated on the steps, not wanting to spoil the silent man's confident execution of this dance from his youth. But she soon found there was no need for concern. She was as light and sure as he, gliding, turning, holding for a moment, then slipping back into the pattern, carried by the music and her partner's firm lead. She began to smile at the simple pleasure of it.

The song ended and there was cautious applause as the man put Lee's hand on his arm and escorted her to her table. Joe rose as they approached.

"Thank you, my dear, that was delightful." The man turned to Joe and said quietly, "Joseph, you are a lucky man." He nodded solemnly to Big Joe and left.

Lee was about to tell Joe she'd felt like Rita Hayworth in a 1940s' movie, but she was silenced by the black bar above his narrowed eyes.

"Pop really does look exhausted now. I think we better get out of here."

"My God, Joe. It's one in the morning and the bride and groom haven't left yet. What'll we do?"

"Leave." Joe pushed his chair back. "Mom? Pop? Let's go."

Joe and Lee made their way to Tony. "Pop's usually asleep by 9:30 these days, Tony. I gotta get him home."

"I unnesten. You take cayuh yer old man." He waved a good night across the room to his oldest brother. "But it's too bad, y know? You're gonna miss the Viennese owah."

A sleepy parking valet pulled Big Joe's old Chevy into the buzzing fluorescent light under Gianetti's canopy.

"I'll drive, Pop." Joe opened the back door for his parents. Gert settled in next to the open door. "I can't believe the bride and groom haven't left. Did they expect us to wait all night? What is wrong with these people?" She ignored her husband as he stooped to enter the car.

Both Joes walked to the other side of the car, ignoring Gert's incivility. Big Joe dropped with a great sigh into the cluttered seat beside her.

Joe closed the dented door behind his father, and kicked the nearest tire. "I am a goddamned fool."

Looking at him over the roof of the car, Lee couldn't imagine what he was talking about. "What's wrong?"

"This ugly heap of Pop's. I should've rented him a limo. Like those other bozos. Jesus. Tony even pulled in the Don. We shouldn't have come. I will never mess with these people again."

After parking the Chevy and seeing the elder Montagnas to their apartment, Lee and Joe made their way back to Manhattan in a rattletrap Yellow Cab, Lee dozing in and out of a dream filled with whirling, hoop-skirted waltzers. She would like to have seen the Viennese Hour.

Montagnas,
Coming and Going

Lee was pillowed contentedly in bed, reading, QXR surrounding her with Casal's caress of a Bach sarabande, when the phone intruded shrilly, startling her off the page and out of the reverie. It was almost midnight, and it was Saturday. Toby and Van were safe in their room; it couldn't be a report about them from school or from an emergency room. Joe was working in the living room. Rory had stopped in to say good night to the boys on her way upstairs to her studio. All present and accounted for. She didn't need to pick it up. The service could get it, or Joe. She could keep reading, listening to the music, swathed in flannel and down. On the fifth ring, she picked it up.

"I have a collect call from Maddy Montagna. Will you accept the charges?"

The connection had the hollow sound that meant Joe was on the living room extension. Lee heard him say a terse, "Yes."

The operator went off line to patch the call through and Lee started to put the phone down, but Joe hissed, "Take care of it, whatever it is," and clicked off. His missing daughter was making contact, but whatever problem was now coming at them would be Lee's to deal with.

> *A massive blue tag on that, Montagna. This is your kid, remember?*

She switched off the radio.

"Where are you, Maddy?"

"Texas. Ah'm in Texas."

> *Oh god that cracker accent. Don't let it get you. Just focus on translating. This is important.*

Maddy's voice was even less lively than her norm, as if her battery were too low to spark. Lee assumed the girl was stoned.

"Where in Texas?"

"Eyul Paso."

That made sense. Border town. Easy access to cheap drugs. Opportunities to buy and deal.

"Ah gotta git outta here, Leedle. Tell Dayud ah need to come home. When'll he be bayuck?"

> *Home. Where is that? With the Wicked Witch of the South? With your stepmother in boring New York?*

"Get yourself to the airport. I'll have a ticket waiting at Tri-Air."

"Cain't do that."

"OK, I'll wire you money."

"That's not the problem. There are these paypul lookin' fuh me."

Maddy's listless voice was fading to nothing, as if she were forgetting to speak into the phone.

"Maddy? Maddy, talk to me. Who's looking for you and why?"

"Some paypul ah was crashing with. They think ah stole their stereo, n some othuh crap."

> *Some other crap most certainly, like maybe the inventory of their small-business enterprise. You took their cash and their stash, and probably hocked their stereo, as well. Smart. Very smart.*

"OK. OK, they're looking for you. And they're mad. They have guns?"

"Yayuh."

Lee could hear passing truck engines.

"Maddy, pay attention. Are you in a safe place?"

"Ah dunno. Issa phone bewth."

"Maddy, open the door right now. Open it all the way so the light goes off."

"Then how will ah see the phone?"

"You don't need to see the phone. There's a bright light shining on you. Open the door!"

"Oh yayah. Okay."

The sounds of large engines, bearing down and dopplering away, got louder.

"Now look around you and tell me what you see."

Maddy gave a meandering description of an intersection of highways, a bar, semis passing and, Lee was relieved to hear, a motel. Lee got her to read the highway numbers and the name of the motel.

"OK Maddy, I've got all that. Now you're going to hang up, and go to the motel. I'll get the number, guarantee your room, and call you there. Stay in your room. Do not go *anywhere*."

"But ah'm hungry. Ah'll git somethin' t eat. In the bar."

Lee could picture a low-riding, underlit convertible. From its furry seats, four Tejano braves looked in all directions as they cruised El Paso's streets and bars, looking for the gringa bitch.

"Forget it. You can eat on the plane. Do not leave the room. I'll call you there with further instructions."

"Yayus, double-oh-seven."

> *Bad sign. Smart-alec kid's going to get herself dead. But not*
> *tonight.*

"Maddy, hang up now. I've got to call the motel. You walk over there, as soon as you hang up. No! Wait for the green light, then cross over."

Lee put on a robe, then got El Paso Information and read them the motel name.

"Is Maddy Montagna there?"

"*Si, Senora*, the girl is here." There was an audible leer in the words. Lee wondered what Maddy was wearing and how stoned she looked. Still, it was good news that she'd made it through the semis. Lee gave the clerk her MasterCard number, hoping she wasn't plugging it directly into Crime Central USA.

"Please give her a room with a strong lock that works, OK? If some people come looking for her, you must tell them you haven't seen her. Please? If there is any problem, you call me collect, OK?"

"What kinda trouble you talking about, lady? I don't need the cops here."

"It'll be fine, don't worry. She'll be out of there very soon."

Lee got a call through to a Tri-Air 24-hour number, paid for a ticket, and explained her need for further assistance—or at least as much as she dared to say without triggering a police intervention.

"I do understand ma'am, but I'd have to connect you with our El Paso office about this and the office is closed."

Lee managed to convince the woman that the matter was urgent enough to track down the airline's El Paso manager, who responded to Lee's requests with Oh dears, Oh mys, and Oh boys.

"Ma'am, I will personally drive to the Starbright Motel, which is a truly terrible place, get your Maddy, and escort her myself onto the next plane to LaGuardia. She'll be on Flight 971, landing at 8:10 tomorrow morning."

When Lee thanked the manager for going beyond the call of duty, he sighed. "Mrs. Montagna, this is the third time this month that I have put a runaway on a plane home. I have two kids, 11 and 9. And I know how I'd feel if it was one of them. Which it may be some day, the way things are going in this world."

Lee collapsed back onto the pillows, vowing to fly Tri-Air forever.

Joe insisted on sparing Lee a cab ride in morning rush hour to meet Tri-Air 971. He generously took on the task himself, would welcome Maddy to safety, and of course absorb any gratitude she might feel. And could Lee make sure Rory had made room for Maddy in the studio upstairs by the time they got back? It was so hard to sleep on planes, his daughter would no doubt be tired. And probably hungry. Could Lee leave one of her omelets and some of that good bread in the oven as well?

Everything was ready. Van would go into surgery in the morning, then into weeks of intensive physical therapy in the hospital, and months of at-home recovery and catch-up school work. The World-Renowned Surgeon was optimistic that Joe's boy would not live his life in a wheelchair, which was deemed inevitable without the needed operation.

Lee imagined Van no longer lurching about in the external steel skeleton that he sometimes made into a wearable chair by locking the hip and knee hinges. It was unnerving to find him sitting in mid-air, listening, watching, behind doors, or behind her chair.

An altered future hovered in the shimmering heat of the road ahead, a future in which Van would no longer receive Tiny-Tim indulgences from a pitying world. His teachers had found him to be unable to read at all, unable to do the simplest arithmetic, but even that seemed improvable to Lee. She bought a set of colored rods that a post-operation tutor might use for explaining math concepts to him, and a whole set of Ball-Stick-Bird readers that she knew worked wonders with kids who were finding it hard to decipher written language.

New York abounded in doctors and therapists who could fix his body, and tutors who could help him learn, but was there anyone who could change who he was? Lee feared that Van, even on the honor roll and doing wheelies on a bike, would still be a snake.

She was having trouble getting Joe to talk about the realities that were looming just weeks away. Van would be coming home—to a hospital bed. There wasn't room for another baseball card in the room he shared with Toby. Maybe Joe was planning to set him up in the living room. He couldn't be thinking of moving him upstairs with Maddy and Rory, who were already battling over the territory. Lee's worst fear was that he could be planning to give Toby's room entirely to Van and exile Toby to the sofa. And she'd heard no plans for hiring a nurse. Or a tutor. Luisa, the mother's helper both boys were now in love with, was great with them, but she was neither nurse nor tutor, and worked only in the afternoons, sometimes staying late if Lee and Joe were going out. Lee was at MacGregor's all day, Maddy was wherever Maddy went. Rory was in art classes. Competent people had to be found to tend this child, and Joe kept changing the subject.

Van had been gleefully wired for days, grinning almost constantly, rubbing his dry-straw hair, elbow akimbo, a gesture that always meant he was greatly pleased. He made jokes with Toby and was polite to Lee, even when his father wasn't present.

Now school was out and the eve of the operation was at hand. She'd brought home Van's favorite take-outs from shops on her route home, and set the table for a festive family dinner. As she warmed the dishes, Toby fed Bilbo, the small white bird he'd named after Lee read *The Hobbit* to him; now her son had been reading the book to Van in their room, where it would not be seen that one ten-year-old was reading to another. Van spoke authoritatively about the story and the characters, letting slip no hint of how he had come to know them. Lee wondered if he had ever thanked Toby for taking him on these nightly journeys to Middle Earth.

"What's all this?" Joe frowned at the cobalt plates and heavy silver, the bouquet of lavender roses she'd just picked in their tiny garden, this season's first blooms of the Sterling bushes he'd planted to make her feel welcome in New York.

"It's for Van. We're having those barbecued ribs he likes so much. And the mashed potatoes with the little lumps."

"Well, you can take his place away."

"Oh no. He's too upset to eat?"

"He's having dinner with his mother."

Lee stared at Joe. "She's in New York?"

"Yeah. The Wicked Witch of the South loves her little boy and she wants to be here for his operation. What could I say? 'No, bitch, stay in Georgia'?"

Lee couldn't imagine what she would say to this strange woman who beat Rory, wouldn't take Van to therapy, who drove Maddy to drugs. But she wouldn't have to.

"The bitch isn't coming in here. This is my home."

Van clanked and creaked his way across the living room in his best shirt and pants.

Joe reached out to him. "There's my man. Here, let me fix that collar, sport."

"Is it time yet?" Van's right forearm flailed from the elbow, as if he were fanning away flies.

It was good that he was so excited; the boy loved his mom. Lee could hear Mort of the candy store saying, "So what could be bad aboud *dat?*"

The front door buzzed loudly and Van plunged to the floor, his crutches clattering to the parquet before the terrible metallic impact of his rigid body. An end table toppled with him, a lamp shattering, books tumbling over him.

Head back, eyes white, arms riveted to the floor, Van was having a *gran mal* seizure, nothing like the brief mental absences Lee had wondered about. Joe had never said the boy was epileptic; Lee knew only from films that this was what she was seeing.

Joe was on his knees, the debris shoved aside, taking care of his son with practiced moves. This child's parents knew the drill. Lee ran to the apartment door and asked the Wicked Witch of the South to come quickly.

To Lee's amazement, Van was on his way back within minutes. He was sitting up, on the floor, his mother and father bookended at his sides. Joe held him upright while Cindy Lou wiped his damp face with tissues she pulled from the pockets of a bright pink pantsuit.

"Hayay, li'l feller." She tucked a thin band of dry-straw hair behind her ear and smiled at her youngest child, her gums wide above small teeth.

Lee stood across the room, her arms around a trembling Toby.

"Mom, what happened? What's wrong with Van?"

She stroked his shoulder and spoke softly. "He's OK, see, he's coming out of it and he's OK."

Cindy Lou Montagna looked only at her son, taking Joe's moves for givens as, together, they got Van to his feet and moved him to the sofa.

She was small and alarmingly thin, with the gaunt wiriness of a mill worker, her face just pale skin over skull, her hands bird claws. The suit, her purse and shoes, all looked new and stiffly synthetic. Lee could see her tiny-boned hand moving hangers at Penney's, looking for something wonderful she could wear in fancy-pants New York City, while she helped her boy get well. Lee ordered herself to stop being such a bitch. She was about to ask Cindy Lou if she'd like to sleep on the sofa so she could be near Van, when she realized that she and Joe were helping their son into his sport coat. He wasn't going to bed, he was going out to dinner with his mom, his parents icily formal to each other as they readied him to leave.

At dinner, Maddy sulked, Lee passed the serving dishes, Joe pretended everything was normal, Toby looked from one of them to another. "Is he going to be all right?"

"Tomorrow or tonight?" Maddy sucked barbecue sauce off a bone, her face grease-stained, her voice edgy with challenge. She had refused to come downstairs when her mother asked Joe to call her. Rory had deliberately planned an evening out, knowing her mother was coming to the house.

"He's fine. He's fine now. Those attacks pass really quickly and he's just fine. And he'll be fine at the hospital." Joe was hunched over his plate, glaring at Maddy then ignoring her.

"Lee, let's go see *Easy Rider* next week. Tate says it's good."

"How would we do that? We're going to be doing visiting hours after work every day, and on the weekends, and when he comes home...."

Joe cut her off before she could ask again what was to happen when Van came home. "I think we better plant some more flowers. The shrubs look good but there aren't enough flowers out there." Through the salad and the ice-cream-topped brownies, he gestured at the glass doors into the garden, telling Lee what blooming things he wanted her to find and plant. After dinner, he settled into a living room chair to wait up for Van, a pile of papers from MAA at his side.

Lee woke the next morning to find him sitting on the edge of their bed. He looked like he'd had no sleep, which she could understand, given the tension of the hours ahead, and the fact that his hated ex had actually breached the walls of his domain. But he also was exhaling brandy, which was not understandable. She asked if he wanted her to go with them to the hospital.

"No. That won't be necessary."

"I don't mind, really. Even if I have to deal with his mom, it's OK."

"You just don't get it do you. You never do."

He hurled himself out of the room and down the stairs. She heard the garden door shoved open and looked down to see him pulling out the precious Sterling roses, the boxwood, every plant and flower in the tiny, walled space. This was inexplicable but it was late and would have to be deciphered at another time. Grabbing her robe, she hurried down the hall to wake the boys. She had to get one off to school, the other to a hospital.

Van wasn't there. Lee stared at his untouched bed, her hands on the side rail of the top bunk where Toby snored quietly. There would be no surgery, therapy, tutoring—no new life for Joe's son. He had chosen his mother, Atlanta, and life in a wheelchair. She was stunned. And she began to breathe again.

Ob La Di Ob La Da

"In three words I can sum up everything I've learned about life. It goes on." —Frost
"Lala how the life it goes on." —Lennon & McCartney

The two men stood shoulder to shoulder, both average in height but one massive, his born-large body pushing a belly-presence into the world; the other compact, extending himself out from his muscled frame not with flesh but with a broadcast of command.

"Do you believe this? Look at those kids."

"On Avenue A they'd be dog meat."

"Tell me about it."

Both leaned against an ancient maple on Judith Bridge's Duchess County farm, its abundant, broad leaves roused from summer's torpid green into triumphant scarlet. Watching them, Lee thought Len Levine seemed to draw from the trunk the strength he needed to stand there; Joe Montagna might have been sending force up the trunk into the branches, driving their leaves to burst into flame and fall to the ground.

This morning the assembled guests had witnessed the bar mitzvah of Judith Bridge's son Michael, a milestone they were now celebrating. With the stunningly good taste that made her antiques business such a success, Judith had set up the perfect all-American picnic for her perfectly mannered boy-who-was-now-a-man.

He looked distinctly boyish at this moment, swinging at a softball pitch and missing, his cherubic face flushed and happy, thick brown curls springing his Yankees cap up from his head, ensuring that it would fall off regularly. Lee thought he needed the bobby pins that had held his yarmulke on at the services, but she couldn't remember ever seeing a baseball cap held on that way.

He had much to be happy about, this springy-haired boy-man, surrounded by well-wishers who were the liberal Establishment of the city, high office-holders, renowned lawyers, party officials, journalists, behind-the-scenes power brokers, ranking professors, all of them aware that the bar mitzvah boy-man was the descendant on his mother's side of three generations of political king-makers, and on his estranged father's of a fortune earned from having sold at least one ready-to-wear suit to 11 per cent of all living US males. Michael Bridge had a future, and his mother had much to say about the prospects of anyone who hoped to hold power in New York.

Today, the agenda was private, a time-out from the reasons they were usually summoned by Judith—to plan, to lobby, to mourn. Today it was spouses, political or not, kids, hot dogs, corn-on-the-cob, hamburgers, homemade apple pies, baseball, and sack races on fields surrounding the

18th-century farmhouse Judith had bought and perfectly restored. But the murmuring undercurrent was still quietly political.

Joe took a long pull on his Heineken, his other hand a fist hooked by a thumb into a belt loop on the front of his jeans. Harried by a late-season fly, Len rubbed a huge hirsute arm up his gravity-weighted face, over his naked skull and down to the brown fuzz that hung over his size-18 collar and onto his sloping shoulders.

The hair seemed an unfortunate nod to the times, to hipness—dumpy Len's way of "feelin' groovy." In other aspects, he was clearly a member of the clan Lee thought of as the Shtetl Cousins: the early-balding, fleshy, dark-eyed men who were drawn completely in curving lines. Lee was sure they were all related, back in Eastern Europe, and the family resemblance was holding strong through distant lands and generations.

When they were in shape, the Cousins were attractive to Lee, which she knew was presumptuous of her. She didn't have the nerve to take on a culture that deep and complex. Men, all men, were dauntingly foreign, perhaps impossible to understand. Adding differences of culture made the challenge look overwhelming to the former Lee Palmer, who wondered if she would ever really understand Joe Montagna. He was from a family that struggled with money, as hers had, both of them had been raised Catholic, half his genes were as northern Europe as hers, but he was also Italian, and above all, male. He was, therefore, ever and always, mystifying, a being who could both gift her with her favorite roses and rip them all out of the ground, who could buy her beautiful clothes and shred them, who could both love and revile her, doing all of it for his own unfathomable reasons.

She was silently in awe of the many peach-and-brown couples who moved about the city, and still impressed by the courage of the Vietnamese women she had taught in Saigon, women who had married American men and were going to the other side of the world to live with them, in American houses in Toledo and Birmingham and Montpelier, and raise beautiful Eurasian or Afroasian children. Lee had been charged with teaching the women about life in their new country, about how Americans lived, ate, dressed. But she doubted there was any way to make the mysteries between the cultures dissipate into comfortable understanding, and the gulf between women and men was not even to be assailed.

Living now in a city of Jews, Lee could only admire the Shtetl Cousins, whose sensuality made them almost as attractive as another, smaller Jewish gene pool in America—the Desert Hawks, straight-line, sharply angular men with jutting cheek bones and knife-edged noses, men whose lineage was surely from warriors, not lovers.

Len didn't have a healthy Cousins' physical appeal. He was almost as unattractive as the slug-pale Woody Allen Lee kept seeing shambling along city sidewalks, a mess of long, transparent, orange frizz floating around his head above his surplus-clothed little body.

How did women take in such men? Did all the intelligent and beautiful women who'd lived with Allen find his talent blinding? Was Len's Rachel turned on by his good heart? Len Levine was a true mensch, dedicating his law practice to civil rights cases and to conscientious objectors, defending the innocent, doing constant pro bono work for good causes. Leonard the Lion, champion of the wrongly accused, protector of mothers' sons from an unjust war, a good man. And an ugly one. Maybe he was so good a lover that his protruding belly and dreadful hair didn't matter to Rachel.

Lee tried to imagine opening herself to a man that unattractive, wrapping herself around him. Her guts lurched in revulsion. Not even the most talented of lovers, enduring, responsive, tree-equipped, could get past the halt that could be called by her eyes.

Sitting on the vibrant red carpet that circled the maple, she needed an immediate antidotal image and conjured up Joe in their honeymoon bunk, partially emerged from the drapery of the white sheet. Dots of moonlight gleamed in the crow-black curls that defined his forehead and shaped themselves around his flat, lobeless ears. His eyes pulsed and flickered under his lids as he dreamed, his full lips slightly parted. It would be a wonderful face to paint—strong bones, clean angles, like a carved bust in a gallery of Roman Caesars. She felt the brush work she would use for that mouth, the small square-edge for the pointed upper lip, dipped in a blend of alizarin crimson and yellow ochre, a deep, wide sweep with a rounded sable for the lower. She imagined tracing careful fingertips along the veins that mapped his beautiful arms until he turned, silently, to enfold her in his dream.

"Sheesh! Double error. The Mets they're not."

His voice pleased her too, a light clear baritone that seemed to begin down in his lungs and heart.

"I dunno, Joe, I dunno what the world's coming to." Len's voice was too thin for his mass, and started somewhere in the back of his nose. A voice for hectoring opposing attorneys, not for evoking female goose-bumps.

Even being facetious, they were giving the kids' fumbling too much attention. As if it ranked up there in importance with the Mobe, with the trial in Chicago, with the grim joke of dumping Johnson and getting Nixon. As if it ranked near the saving gleams of grace they were sometimes afforded—men walking on the moon, the pleasure of a new Bergman film or Nabokov novel, the excitement of a woman taking charge as premier of Israel—and of women being part of the bar mitzvah they had just witnessed. Lee wondered if women, even nuns, would ever appear on a Catholic altar.

This trivial matter of sports got none of her attention, neither as participant or spectator, unless her Toby was playing. Then she would watch delightedly, as she was doing now. Pru played tennis twice a week at a club and rode Central Park's trails regularly; it was the thing to do. It had never occurred to Lee to pick up a racket or get on a horse. Other people did such things, not her people, not Palmers. Palmers did not play instruments or travel for fun instead of to visit relatives or move household. Palmers did not expect to excell, to be in any spotlights, at the helm of—anything. Palmers were the quiet, get-by people, heads down, doing the no-frills minimums. Lee was sure her father had never gone to a ball game in his life, not when there were books to read, records to play, something in the house to repair. The Commander had certainly never played a sport. Or danced. But she understood that other people had been brought up to consider these normal activities.

Now here were Joe and Len focusing on the kids as if they were indeed the Mets, the Yankees, or the ever-mourned Dodgers. She was puzzled by the emotional involvement so many men had with sports, particularly with "their" teams. Professional players were hired gladiators, brought in from anywhere to play for the clubs with the most money and the cleverest management, yet some men's pride of place, even their personal self-worth, seemed hostage to the gladiators' performances.

When the Mets had won the series, just days before, Joe—and it seemed every man in the entire city—every one of them was ecstatic. Anything was possible. On losing days, for *any* New York team, Lee had learned not to bring up important matters. And not to reason with Joe that the loss had nothing to do with New York or with him personally; it wasn't as if the players were born-and-bred New Yorkers, proud products of the city's neighborhoods and schools. That logic was met with his observation that she just didn't understand. Which she readily admitted was true.

She wondered if Len's Rachel was concerned about her man's growing girth, if she was steering him toward salads and broiled fish. He looked like a prime candidate for an out-of-the-blue heart attack, which would be a terrible loss, another Good Guy dying young. There had been far too much of that going on.

Eternally skinny Tate Altridge was sprawled on a Navajo blanket in the sun, his empty plate beside him, a smudge of mustard on his chin. His closed eyes and the steady rise and fall of his shirt front suggested that he was not listening to Pru, as she talked to him from a wrought iron lawn chair at the edge of the blanket. Other guests milled and lolled, on this perfect, nippy, blue October Sunday, on a farm so far from and so unlike their normal world that they were released, somewhat unsteadily, from their usual speed and intensity, let loose to move slowly, to talk quietly, to hum along to "Back in the USSR," to fall asleep in the sun, to half watch children playing softball ineptly.

Wild pitches passed over prepubescent batters' heads, fly balls descended unheeded by chatting teen-aged fielders, producing concern in no one but Len Levine and Joe Montagna, who were steadfastly maintaining their Manhattan intensity, with nothing better to apply it to.

Speakers in the trees were playing the *White Album* and Lee was listening intermittently but respectfully. Despite her first failure, with "Love Me Do," she'd bought all the Beatles' early albums for Rory and Maddy, thinking them fit only for kids. Then came "Eleanor Rigby," and these were no longer silly Brits trying to imitate Black rhythm and blues. Suddenly an intelligence was showing. Not on the level of Brubeck, Kenton, or the MJQ, but intelligence. Now their music was worth the attention of both the young guests here and their parents.

At Lee's urging, Judith had invited the Clays to come today, even though Glenn Clay had run in the borough of Queens, which barely counted, and had put no dent in the old machine's ability to hold a Congressional seat. Glenn and Ashley, Lee had assured Judith, were strong on the Big Issues and needed to stay on the radar screen as they looked for another opportunity to serve. They were especially valuable, Lee thought, because their style and humor also made them good company, a relief from the many peace-and-justice workers who were so unrelentingly dour. Lee smiled, thinking of the Clays' Forest Hills house, the first floor and the broad staircase to the second entirely carpeted in purple, huge paintings of Mack trucks hanging on the walls because Ashley considered them icons of American culture. And the campaign's Help Clay Carry Queens shopping bags still made Lee laugh.

Glenn carried over a chair and set it down next to Lee; Ashley sank into it gratefully. Talking over Tate's inert body, Pru asked, "Who's your OB?"

Judith overheard Ashley's answer and paused in her movement from tables to blankets to trees, seeing to her guests. "Oh, dear, you're not using Burnside, that old charlatan!" She spoke as a woman who was accustomed to being heard and heeded for her knowledge, as well as seen and admired for her beauty. She had changed from the silk suit she had worn at the synagogue, now wearing jeans that looked custom made, a pink crepe shirt, and a soft rose jacket. Her perfectly cut black hair backgrounded her antique ruby earrings like a jeweler's silk. It was a pleasure to have a friend whose every move was so well done. Lee never had a moment's temptation to edit Judith Bridge.

"I don't care about his reputation, I could tell you stories.... Get away from him. Best obstetrician in the city is Sam Steinmetz. You remember that now. He'll take good good care of you. You call him right away and tell him I sent you."

Startled but pleased, Ashley laughed and assured Judith that she would consider the switch.

Lee picked up a huge five-pointed leaf and studied its veins. She ran a hand over the grass it had rested on. This elegant green sod rolled endlessly under all the farm's massive trees, right up to their trunks, completely unnatural and utterly beautiful. These were not like the Park's tough, razory blades, bred to stand up to hordes of humans; these were thin, pliant threads that soothed the palm, too tender to survive the pressure of her own thin butt and the heels of her loafers. But some skilled healer/gardener would no doubt be tidying up leaves and revivifying any flattened patches tomorrow—Judith's land was far better maintained than Central Park. She knew how to take care of things. And of people.

Lee had been sure Judith would love Ashley, and take an interest in her husband's career, as she had in Joe's. Maybe Ashley could come along the next time she and Judith went to an auction. And there was no doubt Ashley would switch obstetricians—Glenn's career was important to her, as was the health of her baby; if Steinmetz was the best OB, Ash would want him.

Lee knew that Pru was also seeing "that old charlatan," but Pru would not be calling Steinmetz. Burnside was an Eastside obstetrician with a Blue Book clientele that made the possibilities of his waiting room far too compelling for Pru to abandon. He was the right doctor delivering the right babies at the right hospital. Pru had her priorities.

"Your Tobe's doing pretty well out there, Joe. Good catch on that grounder and a strong throw to first." Len gave Joe's forearm a punch. "You been coaching him?"

"Hey, what are dads for? We practice in the park most weekends. And speaking of good, your Rebecca can *run*. Leedle, you see her beat Michael to second and put him out? Where'd she learn that, Dad?" Joe's white teeth flashed against his fading tan, his eyes laughing slivers of this day's fine sky.

"She's learning to hurdle now. Kid's going to be a track-and-field wonder."

Now there was a good feminist dad, urging his girl into athletics. Lee was sure he wouldn't stiff her on college either. He'd stake her to Swarthmore or Reed. Some place really good. Bright, strong, talented Rebecca who would be a bright, strong, talented woman like her mother. Lee wondered if Rachel had taught him to be like this or had he figured it out himself? Either way, he wouldn't be pushing Rebecca to marry some junior associate at his firm. Raising girls by the new rules. Rules. They didn't matter with Joe's girls. New or old. Lee wasn't doing a good job, either way. Rory seemed impermeable to anything coming from Lee, though intense about her art-school classes; she just might find her way to being a curator or an agent. But Maddy still had the manners of a truck driver and was still without any interests at all.

Lee tried to imagine the bounteous Maddy taking up track and field, running and jumping along with young Rebecca Levine, Rebecca all muscle and bone, Maddy an assortment of orbs—boobs and hips and thighs and buttocks—lifted on the upswings of the pole vault, the long jump, the airborne step of a run, plunging down on impact, bouncing.

"Look at that will you? They've got a real bat and ball and they can't hit for shit."

"We did better with a broomstick and a lousy spaldeen."

"Watch it, gentlemen." Lee brandished her fork like a Mother Superior's ruler. "That's my beloved son out there." She smiled and rerouted the tines into a slice of warm apple pie that had just been brought round by Judith's houseboy. She closed her eyes and disappeared into the perfect blend of crunchy crust, soft, sweet-sour apples, and breathy cinnamon.

"And one of them is my Becca, which makes me realize I have not taught her enough about this game. What do you say, Montagna, should we give them a lesson in how it's done?" Len put on his sunglasses resolutely, and hitched up his sagging chinos with his forearms.

Joe put his beer down, spit on his palms, and rubbed them together. "Make way for the masters!"

They trotted onto the field and each volunteered to captain a side.

"Oh, we didn't have sides." Toby looked part pleased and part embarrassed. "We were just messing around."

"Well, that's part of the problem," Lee heard Joe answer. "You'll play a lot better if you've got something to lose and somebody to beat."

He leaned down and whispered in Toby's ear, no doubt reminding him of earlier pointers. Joe and Len divided the children, Len choosing Toby and Michael for his team, Joe taking Len's Rebecca and half of the tallest boys. They split up siblings and evenly distributed the unathletic. Fairness personified.

The children took their newly assigned positions, looking apprehensive as the two men gave them demonstrations of batting stance and pitching form. Joe made amazingly fast underhanded vertical circles with his arm that turned into fast balls aimed at Len. On the third pitch, Len put all his adult weight into a rapid horizontal arcing of the bat, hitting the ball low and fast into an apple orchard, the source of the superb pie filling that was dissolving behind Lee's smile.

The bar mitzvah boy-man shouted, "It's a home run!"

Ever logical, Toby asked, "How can it be a homer when there's no fence?" But, fence or no, the ball was out of play. Len's team applauded as he sauntered, skipped, and walked backward around the bases, his arms upraised in triumph, while most of Joe's team scoured the orchard for the ball.

"No, no! Go back to your positions!" Joe shooed his players out of the trees.

Rebecca ran jubilantly back to the field holding the ball in the air, to find her father reclining Buddha-style on his side across home plate, one arm supporting his head, as he looked up at Joe. "Your turn, Montagna. Bet you can't hit the side of that barn."

"I can, Levine, if I pretend it's the warehouse down the block."

All the sass-and-swagger of the streets was upon them, as if they were still the Italian kid and the Jewish kid, probably calling each other dago and kike, vying for the upper hand.

Joe went to home plate, Len to the mound. Len's arm made a blurred circle and the ball shot toward Joe. Joe swung and the ball soared high, then arced down to the barn roof, thumping onto it and bouncing down the far side. Len's team disappeared behind the dark red barn. Joe's cheered him to first to second to third as his machine-gun laugh marked his progress around the bases. An assortment of handsome chickens fluttered away from each end of the barn, escaping the marauding children. Running through the cackling hens, a red-haired boy threw the ball toward Len at home plate. Joe slid in, taut arms reaching out to grab the bag as five boys and a small blonde girl jumped on his back. Lee couldn't see if any of them had the ball, but Len stood over the pile, shouting, "Yer out!"

"Am not! Waddya blind? I was safe by a mile."

Pru turned away from the dozing Tate to say quietly to Ashley, "Not exactly the playing fields of Eton." Ashley looked anxiously at Lee who pretended she had not heard, while thinking, Eton shmeaton. Len and Joe were the best, New Yorkers to the bone, street-bred and proud of it.

Lee studied the needlepoint she had brought along. She was copying an art deco pattern she had taken from a Pushpin Studio graphic. There would be exactly 40 squares in it, and she planned to have it finished and made into a cushion for Joe's favorite chair, by his 40th birthday. It was an arduous process, one that she fitted into the evenings she wasn't working on MAA reports, when she sat with Joe as he watched television. She found it impossible to sit as he did, doing nothing, absorbed in a program. The unpainted canvas filled the emptiness for her. She counted the pattern on the white threads, six navy across, four up, shade the corner with gold, yellow, and cream. When she missed the count by even one, the areas that followed went askew and had to be ripped out. But gradually the handsome design was spreading wider and wider across the white canvas, absorbing her attention through sports events and movies full of gunshots and explosions. Joe often talked to her about something they had supposedly seen, and wondered why she seemed not to recall it.

"Why didn't Maddy and Rory come? Are they OK? I mean, you know...."

That is so like you, Pru, bringing up bad stuff to spoil a good time. Where are Maddy and Rory? Out. Somewhere. Not spoiling this lovely day with Joe and Toby. Celeste says it's a fine time on the personal front, no matter how bad the world is. Something about Jupiter, or maybe it's Venus. Toby's got Luisa's undivided and devoted attention after school. Joe hasn't exploded in ages. I'm almost done with the MAA study on the future of trade unions. And the office, that's fine too. The book on the Balkans is selling on campuses and everybody knows the author can't write, so the word is that I did it, I made the book work. If Judith's star poli-sci guy goes with MacGregor, and asks for me, like he said he would, I'll finally work on a book lots of people might read. Yes, things are good. And what I don't know about Joe's girls—or about Van—let's just keep it that way.

"Teenagers. You know how they are. They're not going to be seen dead with boring people like me and their father."

The softball teams agreed that the score was 1-1, and that they'd change sides every time a run was scored. Toby was next up and Lee held her breath, hoping that he'd do well, for his pride, for Joe's. But when the boy swung hard at a pitch, the bat split along a deep crack Joe's hit over the barn had made in the grain. The bat splintered, leaving a shard in Toby's grip.

With the tiniest smirk of satisfaction, Joe called for throwing/catching practice. The teams lined up and Len and Joe hunched down behind them, guiding arms and eyes, giving praise for good moves and counsel for failed ones. Toby sent a fine overhand straight to Becca, the girl snagged it easily, and the two disheveled fathers gave each other hearty thumbs up.

Lee wondered if somewhere behind Joe's proud grin he was thinking that his blood-son, his Van, would never do this. Perhaps no more than she was thinking that Timothy Pitt had not called or written Toby for almost a year.

That night, Lee and Toby sat on his bed, reading alternating paragraphs of *The Lord of the Rings*, until he interrupted the story with a hand on her arm.

"Do you think Michael liked his present?"

Toby had picked out a gray, grapefruit-sized geode, split and mounted as bookends, the cut surfaces polished, the secret, glittering purple interior revealed.

"Absolutely. That was a good choice. I bet he'll still have those bookends when he's an old man."

"I wonder if they were really a million years old, like the rock guy said."

"At least. And who else gave Michael a million-year-old present?"

"I should start studying now. He says it took him two years to get ready."

"For?"

"The bar mitzvah."

"Oh honey, that's only for Jewish boys."

"Yes, I know."

"But you're not Jewish."

He looked at her, puzzled, and then considered this news. "I'm not Jewish." Then he brightened. "But Joe is, so I can be too."

Lee realized that she had never talked to him about religions, somehow thinking he should know all she knew, by osmosis. That would be logical, and fair. He should have it all, everything she had seen and heard. And he should be able to do everything she could do, because he was hers, had come out of her body and still felt like part of her, because he mirrored back to her the same skin, the same hair, nose, fingers.

Of course he should know what she knew. Just as she should know what was in every book she bought. It was only reasonable that the act of acquiring a book should give you the information in it. Why did you have to invest time, when you'd already handed over the money? There were piles of books awaiting that investment of time, lurking behind all the ones that already had bookmarks in them or were turned face down on the lamp tables and chair arms where she had left them, with favorite lines lightly underlined. Someday she would even read past the first five pages of *Finnegan's Wake*.

It hadn't occurred to her that she had to tell Toby about family names, the histories they stood for, the places and religions. He didn't know about confession and Our Lady of Guadalupe, and the near occasions of mortal or venial sin, because she'd never told him. He knew nothing about the theatre, the war in the Pacific, Vespas on the *rue Catinat*, frangipanis in Africa, or mill towns in Carolina. He didn't know about parents who made sure you knew you weren't good enough or about dreams of singing under the sea, and nightmares of wandering in icy, angry streets. This being who was part of her did not know these things she knew.

"No, honey. Joe was raised Catholic. So was I."

They would have to have some long talks. Maybe she would take him to mass, and to some other churches, and to a synagogue, so they could sort all this out.

Before he dropped off to sleep, he asked if Van might come back, his voice a wary mixture of apprehension for himself and concern for Van.

"No, I don't think his mom will let him come again. He'll stay in Atlanta now."

She bent down to kiss his warm forehead. He smelled of the baby shampoo he still used, so his eyes wouldn't sting.

"But he'll be OK down there?"

"Maybe. Sort of. I mean, he's got what he chose—he's with his mom. But he's also got serious trouble with his health. And he's chosen that too."

She touched his silky, freckled cheek. "Sometimes we make choices that aren't the best thing for us and then we're stuck with what happens."

Toby twisted his face up to hers. "You said 'we.' But you don't do that."

"Sure. I always make the right choices. Having you was a really good one."

On days like this one she could talk herself into believing she had also chosen the right life, making no forays into the world she would have lived as Lee Bailey.

Joe shouted over his shoulder, "Call 911!"

"Not Dr. Sondheim?"

"No! 911!"

He was shoving Maddy toward the bathroom. She was ashen, all the natural high color gone from her round cheeks and full mouth, her legs buckling. This time the girl could have done something to herself that was unfixable.

Lee tried to remember what had been in their now-empty medicine chest. She got a sudden picture of the full bottle of codeine that had been in the top left-hand corner for months, since Joe's dental surgery, since he'd refused to dull his pain, choosing instead a deep frown and a foul mood. A full bottle. Were there ten? Fifteen? How strong were they? And the sleeping pills Lee had bought when her mother came last summer and hadn't been able to ignore the late-night sounds of neighbors' radios, of cars clanking over the loose manhole cover in front of the brownstone, of assorted shouts and sirens, and the light that seeped into the windows around the edges of closed shutters and drapes. That bottle could have been half full. Everything was gone, even the aspirin and the Midol. Then there was whatever Maddy may have stashed upstairs, in the studio. The possibilities were immense.

The second time she dialed, Lee finally got a ring, but no one was picking up.

*Come on, damn you. This is supposed to be an emergency
number.*

"Ah yes! We need an ambulance. No. A suicide attempt. She took pills. I think a lot of them." She gave the address and hurried to the bathroom. Joe was holding Maddy's head over the toilet.

"You've got to get it out, Maddy." Joe's voice was coldly insistent.

"Ah cayun't."

"Stick your fingers down your throat."

"No."

"I read something. About drinking detergent...." Lee tried to remember the instructions as she hurried to the kitchen. She fumbled under the sink for the Joy, squirted some into a glass of hot water, then dumped in Coleman's dry mustard and a palmful of salt. Bilbo fluttered in his cage, seemingly aware of the distress in his domain.

"Here, quick. Try this." Maddy was slumped on the floor just outside the bathroom door, her chin on her chest. She sniffed at the concoction Lee was holding up to her pale mouth.

"Jesus, Leedle, ah cayunt drink that. Yew tryin t'kill me?"

The girl pushed the glass away, the slimy mess spilling across the carpet. Joe tried to lift her rubbery body to its feet, but it kept sliding back to the floor.

"Damn it Maddy. You cannot do this. You're not some shit-for-brains hippie—you've got my blood in your veins! I will not allow this."

"Maddy, you've got to throw up. If you don't that stuff could kill you." Lee ran to the insistent doorbell, calling back to the unhearing girl, "And you can't go to sleep. Let your dad help you up!"

She opened the door to the foyer and a hit of January cold. Two uniformed policemen turned quickly from the line of door buzzers and looked at her. The middle-aged white one stomped his feet and blew on his ungloved hands. There was supposed to be more snow tonight. The shorter, younger one, a black man, looked at Lee intently.

"Mrs. Montagna? You called 911?"

"Yes. In here."

"What's her name?" The younger man seemed fully concerned; his partner going through the motions, ones he'd made a thousand times before. Lee thought he looked bored. Paddy Bored and his new partner, Leroy Sincere. She wondered what their patrol-car conversations were like.

The men knelt, one on each side of Maddy, their damp raincoats gleaming, dark blue forms bracketing another Montagna child down for the count.

"Maddy, what did you take?" Officer Sincere asked. "Come on now, we've got to know."

Maddy opened one eye, tried to focus on the black-eye-browed, pink face of the older officer, and managed a glare. "Fuck off, piyug."

Lee suppressed a powerful urge to burst out laughing.

Paddy Bored stood up. "Kids." He took a note pad out of his back pocket and scribbled something, perhaps "Subject hates cops."

"Is an ambulance coming?"

"Yes, ma'am. But we usually beat them to the scene."

On the floor, struggling to get snow boots onto Maddy's limp feet, Lee looked up at the officers. "But why do you come?"

"Suicide is against the law, ma'am." Officer Sincere said tautly, as if he were recalling lessons from his Police Academy classes. "We have to answer all suicide calls."

Lee was startled. If Maddy lived, she'd be arrested? Her mind raced to what the girl might have had in her own pill collection. Acid, speed? Maybe those sunshine tabs laced with strychnine, the new thing in the Park. Oh God, why was Toby standing here watching all of this? But where else could he be? Maybe it was OK. Maybe he'd remember and be too repulsed to mess with drugs himself. There was certainly nothing appealing about what he was seeing.

An ambulance siren screamed into their street, subsiding in front of the brownstone. A red glare beat rhythmically through the bay window, turning them all into intermittent demons as the policemen took Maddy by the arms and moved her out of the house, walking her across the stoop and down the steps, her coat flapping, one boot falling off. When her knees gave way, they joined arms over and under her body and kept her moving, face down.

"Where are you taking the bitch?"

Paddy Bored didn't answer Joe. Leroy Sincere looked at the father of the subject disapprovingly. "Roosevelt, sir. Your daughter will be at Roosevelt. We'll meet you there."

White-clad arms reached out of the ambulance and lifted Maddy in as the officers pushed. The policemen slammed the heavy doors behind her and went to their double-parked patrol car, Paddy getting in after Leroy had started the engine. They pulled out behind the shrieking ambulance, both vehicles hurling gray slush up the sides of the parked cars.

Joe motioned away the faces in lighted windows up and down the block, shouting "Show's over, folks. Nothing to see."

Lee knew this was a nightmare for him—uniforms at his door for anyone to see, coming into his home, hauling away his child. She stood at the curb shivering, as Joe went up the brownstone steps, his sheepskin slippers soaked black from the dirty snow. Maddy was dying. Lee had not figured out how to keep her alive, or even how to know where she spent her days. With all her lazy sass and bass-ackwards motion, Maddy was dying.

And Toby was in the apartment alone. Lee raced back inside and dialed the studio upstairs. Had Rory looked out the window, seen her sister being removed by The Authorities? Had she even noticed her roommate was missing? One arm around Toby, Lee waited five rings before Rory picked up.

"Yes?" That clear, strong voice, from the chest like her father's, and like his, unaccented. It was part of seeming totally unrelated to her drawling, nasal sister; lean, purposeful Aurora; abundant, lost Madalena.

"Rory I need you to come down right away. We've got to go to the hospital because Maddy's really sick and Luisa's already gone for the day so Toby's here alone."

"Well, you can just send him up here. We'll play Scrabble." No questions about her sister, no alarm.

Lee locked the apartment door and watched Toby move slowly up the stairs.

"She OD'd didn't she."

"Yeah, honey. She OD'd."

> *Damn Joe for having these kids, kicking holes in our life. Now this whole ugly world I don't want Toby to even know about. Well, he isn't going to see the emergency room at Roosevelt. Drunks and loonies and gut-shot gang members, everything they've scraped up off the streets, and Maddy right in the thick of it.*

"You stick with Rory now. I'll be back as soon as I can."

"I'll be OK, Mom." The enormous olive-green eyes were close to overflowing. "Just make sure Maddy's all right. Please."

They sat on a worn wooden bench in a pale green, echoing hallway, next to a huge radiator that hissed and belched out a skin-searing heat. Long lines of fluorescents sizzled overhead. Joe leaned forward tensely, his elbows on his knees, his fingers tightly interwoven, staring at the floor. A gurney careened by, a thick male arm hanging down from it, trailing blood and coming within inches of hitting Joe.

An orderly shouted, "Lookout! Cominthrough!" after the gurney had passed. On the bench facing them, a woman so covered in dirt that Lee could not tell her age or color, was unraveling her knitted hat and eating the yarn. Someone had vomited in this hallway very recently and the stooped janitor waving a filthy string mop across the floor seemed to have done a very poor job of dealing with it. A child was screaming from behind one of the curtains. "*Lastima, mamacita,* make him stop! *Lastima!*"

"My God," Joe muttered. "My God."

> *So what did you expect from calling 911? A private sitting room at Doctors' Hospital? If I'd called Sondheim, we'd at least be at Lenox Hill, with our own doctor. Is this supposed to impress Maddy? Scare her out of doing it again? She's not seeing any of this. Won't remember a thing—if she lives. Except the cops. The night Daddy called the cops on me. And isn't this just a grand evening for us all.*

She passed a comforting hand along Joe's arm, saying nothing. This was the second time she'd waited outside a closed medical door for Maddy to emerge, but Joe had been left out of the first experience. It had been Lee's little Christmas present from Maddy, who had come to her, warily, testing the waters.

"Lee, yew cayunt tell mah dad, OK? Ah mean it's impohtant and yew have to help me, but he'd kiyull me so...."

"Maddy, what is it?"

She was pregnant, she didn't want to be, and she wanted to know what she was supposed to do. Lee blessed the times—there was the clinic in Greenwich Village now, legal, staffed with a real MD and RNs. No grapevine leads to backrooms, no need to risk arrest—and Maddy's life. Lee called for the appointment after making sure Maddy wasn't thinking adoption, or motherhood.

"Heyull no. Get all huge en then spend all mah time with a pukey baby?"

They'd gone downtown by taxi, and come home the same way, a few hours later. Lee had waited in the clean, homey outer room, trying to work on a manuscript, but repeatedly pondering the ease with which other people seemed to be getting pregnant.

An amazing number of women in her world were bursting forth in full womanly bloom. Pru. Ashley. Three editors in her department at MacGregor's. Dozens she saw in the building and on her walks home. The woman who lived on the top floor of the brownstone. And Maddy. For a few minutes longer. There were real women everywhere.

It had taken years of marriage to Tim to produce Toby. She'd never imagined having only one child, but Joe wanted no more offspring, so it was not to be considered. Lee, the woman with no breasts, didn't even need to take the Pill to comply with his wishes. As a pseudo woman she seemed to be somewhat immune to pregnancy.

"You want to come in now, Mom?" The gentle gray-haired nurse who had welcomed them to the clinic was standing in the now open door to the surgery.

"She's a little dopey from the anesthetic, but she's just fine." The nurse patted Lee's shoulder reassuringly as she looked with concern at the groggy girl.

"Maddy? Maddy, dear." The nurse shook Maddy's T-shirted shoulder. "Time to go home now."

Maddy opened blank eyes. The nurse looked into them and said, "Maddy? Maddy, you're not pregnant anymore. And you're just fine. Do you understand?"

The blank eyes closed and tears poured from them, wetting the blonde curls and the white pillow. Lights blinked in a small courtyard just outside the window. Christmas lights. Celebrating a birth.

Lee sat with Maddy on a big soft sofa, her arms around the girl until the sobbing stopped.

"Ah'm really OK? Re-ully?"

"Really. And we can go home anytime you're ready."

"And yew aren't gonna teyull Dad?"

"Scout's honor."

So there would be no talking about Maddy's near brush with motherhood. And Lee sensed no memory of it in Maddy. No sadness for the loss, no caution learned, and no affection for the stepmother who had once more pulled her out of a crisis. It became something that had not happened. But now Maddy drugging herself out of reality had happened. Being in this hellhole was happening—and this time Maddy was playing out her drama in Joe's full view.

Paddy Bored came out of the treatment room, shaking his head, his jacket unbuttoned in the stagnant heat.

"She's somethin else, your daughter."

The man's attitude was getting to Lee, she wanted to talk to Officer Sincere, not this uncaring SOB; her voice took on an edge. "What is happening please?"

"Oh, they say she'll make it. She took enough stuff to kill three grown men but they managed to pump her stomach—once they strapped her down. Quite a mouth she's got on her. And she's got a good left."

Joe said nothing until the officer went back into Maddy's "room."

"This does it. We've got to get out of the goddammed city."

"The city?"

But the city's not the problem. Maddy could do this anywhere. The city's good. The mayor calls me Leedle. I'm getting a window office at work. Jimmy Breslin told me a joke last week. Toby's got the best teacher he's ever had and Luisa is the love of his life. We've got season tickets for Paul Taylor.

"Don't look at me like that. Like you don't know what I'm talking about. She's buying drugs in the Park. And you don't care Toby almost got mugged right in front of our own stoop?"

"When? Did they hurt him?"

Joe had her attention. She'd left the Congo so her son could be born in safety; she'd endured dysentery for two years in Vietnam, but when Toby got it she'd booked the two of them home, staying with her parents until Tim's tour was up. She'd left Tim when she realized Toby needed a better model of manhood. Now Toby had been threatened. She would have to leave New York. And she couldn't leave New York.

"We're paying a fortune to live in a combat zone, Lee. In that cramped little half of a row house. We can spread out in the country. The kids can have their own bathrooms."

In the Roosevelt ER, an armpit of her beautiful New York, Lee's shining time went dark. It was over. Joe was adamant and Toby was in danger. She knew she must not cry.

She smiled at him. "Just so it's not New Jersey."

Maybe the Sound side of the Merritt Parkway. Or a year-round house in Sag Harbor. That place we visited there, when Ramon rented it for the summer—nice town. Lots of artists. But the commute....

"I know you don't want to be a Jersey housewife, Leedle. It's not the Bendel's thing to do."

The man had unerring aim at partial truths; enough wrong to be infuriating, enough right to silence her. The tiny ultra-chic store was indeed her favorite, but she was too cautious to buy anything but small gifts there. Still, she was going to miss checking out their windows on her walk home. Was there any other store cool enough to have mannequins with nipples?

She turned her thoughts toward all that would have to be done to make the move. Checking out good school zones in three states. Finding a house. Asking Luisa to come along. Begging her. Packing up the brownstone. Admiral Perry and Bilbo were moveable pets—Toby wouldn't be leaving *everything* he loved behind. Lots of people came into the city every day to work. How hard could it be? And those weekday hours, those lunches, would mean she was not really gone, just sleeping somewhere else. She would manage. She would.

At breakfast the next morning, Joe announced to Toby and Rory that Maddy was going to be OK and the family was moving to the country. Toby looked to his mother for confirmation. She put a hot waffle on his plate.

"Joe and I will have to commute, but we'll work it out. I'll get home as fast as I can."

"He'll be fine on his own. Won't you be fine, Tobe? In a nice old house in the country, where nobody wants to hurt you?"

Her son, courtier to the prevailing power, swallowed his concerns and beamed adoring agreement at his hero.

Rory was another matter. Dressed in head-to-toe New York black, she had her own announcement to make.

"I got a job at the arts supply store across the street from the school. If you people leave, I want to keep the studio. Dad, if you just pay the rent upstairs and my tuition, I can earn the rest."

This was Joe's Rory—efficient, cool, presenting a done deal she'd worked out carefully before making her proposal. With pride in the Smart One, the one who had his blood in her veins, Joe signed off on her plan, but posed her a question.

"Now what about your sister? She'll be home this afternoon and we have to have a plan. I say she stays here with you."

Lee tried to silently transmit a Yes response to Rory. She wanted it to be just Joe, Toby, and herself again. If that was the deal, she'd stop crying about leaving New York, stand by her man like a good Navy wife, pack up quietly.

Rory cut into a waffle she'd smothered in syrup. "No way. I can't handle her and she's under age. She's your problem, Dad."

As if Joe would be the one, would do one damn thing that helped. The family had to leave the city because Maddy was getting drugs in the Park but he was trying to dump her here, two blocks from said Park. Great. Just great.

And Rory. Lee had to give the Smart One points for knowing what she wanted and going for it. Art school, an easy job, a complete escape from Cindy Lou's world, and a free studio all to herself, the one that had been Lee's room of her own, in her New York.

Going South

Joe's eyes were fixed on the cars ahead as they left a party in Connecticut hosted by a potential MAA client, making their way down what Toby called the Dewey Threwy, back to the real world, back to New York.

"Joe, are you having any second thoughts about moving?"

"Aw Leedle, what are you talking about now?"

She had to make her question about his needs, his preferences.

"Those people. I can't picture you living with people like that all around you."

"What was wrong with them? They were nice, you know, good neighbors."

Nice. That was it? They were moving to the burbs to live with "nice." Country clubbers. Interchangeable. No one had said a single interesting thing all evening. Grass seed. Recipes. She couldn't believe Joe hadn't been bored.

"And that was Connecticut, Leedle. If you didn't like them it doesn't matter. We'll be living in Jersey."

As if that were better. Jersey. A bad joke. The seat of everything uncool to New Yorkers. The Jersey Turnpike running through industrial hell. The burned-out cities. Newark. Hoboken. And the little suburban towns. Nice lawns and nice cars and nice suits and nice jobs and Lee was sure she would go stark raving mad. She was a New Yorker. She could not be a bridge-and-tunnel commuter. She did not care if Princeton was a pretty town—it was in New Jersey.

She had to remind herself to breathe as she thought about the ramshackle house they had agreed to buy on the Andy Hardy street in serenely dowdy Princeton. She imagined each door on the beautiful, quiet block being opened by the same woman who had been cloned to fill half the party in Connecticut. They were clean, smiling, well mannered. They smelled good, they voted, they paid their bills, and went to church. And there was no juice in them. Lee's life was about standing up to, leaning into, and drawing from, tense, boiling, juicy New York. The sirens at all hours; the disputatious housewives at every counter; the constantly changing street scene; the mix of every color, class, and attitude; the constant sense that something was up, something new, challenging, exciting. Most of all it was the interactions with admirable people, people who inspired her to do more, try harder, people who found Lee useful in their lives.

She didn't want to be in the city from nine to five, to go slack every night and weekend, in distant, calm exile. Imagining such a life, she felt herself disappearing, becoming one of the nice people whose lives were about lawns and casseroles. Moving into 99 Underwood Road would be the end of existence for the person she had become.

Joe might need this, might need to pretend to be a good burgher, to join the respectable, the solid. It was good for business as MAA increasingly moved into working on the problems of counties and small cities. But she didn't need it and she wasn't going. They must stop payment on the check, take back their notice to their New York landlords, register Toby for his old school for the fall, tell Luisa to stop looking for another job—there was still time to save themselves. She would keep walking Toby to school everyday as she'd done for months now, keep having Luisa walk him home. Lee papered all of Underwood Road, all of the not-New-York universe, in blue edit tags of wrongness.

The next afternoon they again headed into the wilds. The agent who had found their house, a well-connected Princeton matron, had wangled them an invitation to a neighborhood party. They were to meet her at 121 Underwood for a little gathering, hosted by some people the agent was sure they would like. Lee had said yes before the party in Connecticut, before it was clear that they must not leave New York, must not proceed to closing on a house in the kingdom of the Blands.

They drove south on the Turnpike, passing identical highway rest stops, each with the same gas station lit as if to attract interstellar visitors, the same orange-roofed Howard Johnson's, spaced apart by miles of the same fuming industrial complexes. Lee tried not to inhale the clearly toxic air and realized that her leg ached from miles of pressing against an imaginary brake pedal. Her whole body yearned for a u-turn as Joe drove straight ahead, ever deeper into this godforsaken territory.

She had spent months of winter weekends searching for Joe's dream house. Her assignment was to find the place from which he would hold forth, J. vH. Montagna, man of accomplishment, *pater familias*, and gracious host to the growing regional clientele seeking his expertise. It had to be large, a place where he could have an office, where they could have house guests and parties, the way Tate and Pru had people out to South Hampton. Meaning, she understood clearly, that the place and the address had to impress. Her guy was making it in the world and he needed the right setting. MAA was growing; Tate had brought in new capital and Joe had brought in union clients, several companies, and now, municipal governments in three states. The Great Society contracts had vanished; just as Dr. King had predicted, the War on Poverty was being abandoned as the nation's treasure poured into Vietnam.

Joe's specifications had not included a price range. When she asked him what they could spend, he had smiled tolerantly, "You just find the right place and I'll find the money."

She'd called any number of real estate agencies within striking distance of the city, but giving them only Joe's requirements and no price ceiling had brought her dozens of pictures of millionaires' estates. She'd rejected those and gone through innumerable multi-bedroomed houses in Ridgefield, Cos Cob, Short Hills, Dobbs Ferry, Glen Cove. On Sunday evenings she would go through her notes and pictures with Joe and he would say no, no, and no again. There was always something wrong with the building, the grounds, or the town. Never a word about the price that was printed on each description.

She'd realized that the only way to get all Joe wanted, at the unspoken price in his mind, was to find a derelict house in a good neighborhood, and to pretend that this was a choice, not a necessity. The Princeton house was in terrible shape, shingles warping, porches listing, wallpaper peeling, the wiring and boiler threatening, the grounds overrun with weeds and what looked like the attempted return of a forest that may have once stood there. But it was big, old, and on a beautiful, quiet street roofed over by massive sycamores, a street between the University's Graduate School and the Institute for Advanced Study. Lee convinced Joe to come with her to see the place, hoping a look up and down the street would impress him and end her long search. The neighbors, the agent had let them know, were former governors, a Secretary of State, a Nobel Laureate.

Joe had made an offer before the woman could finish her pitch. It was shockingly low, so far below the asking price that Lee was embarrassed by Joe's temerity—and amazed by the agent's immediate, "I'm pretty sure that will work."

Joe had realized what Lee had not, that this ruin of a house had been on the market with no offers, sinking further into decay every season. It was dead-in-the-water, ripe for a piratical offer. And despite the house's daunting condition, Lee could see the moves that would make it habitable soon, and eventually, quite handsome.

Now she would be relieved of that huge undertaking. In the last light of the evening, as the car turned off toward the tree-topping University tower that marked the town of Princeton, she knew that they must tell the agent they'd changed their minds.

"You must be the Montagnas. I'm Sam Howe."

The person in the doorway of 121 Underwood was a girl so startling that neither Montagna spoke for a moment. A wide braid of glistening black hair crowned the palest, most finely modeled face, a face in which black lashes, thick and very real, rimmed eyes that matched her royal blue, floor-length, long-sleeved, "at home" gown, a gown cut low to frame a high, creamy décolletage. This was a picture from another world, another time, and it could not be named Sam Howe.

"Ah, you've met my wife. I'm Rolly Howe. Come in, come in." Lee recognized him, despite the fact that he must be using a decades-old photo on the dust jacket of his newest book. Polly, the agent who thought she had finally sold the disaster at 99, had invited them here without mentioning that their host would be Rollins Howe, counselor to Presidents, television pundit, and author of a shelf of political books. Lee hoped Joe realized who he was; he paid little attention to other men's accomplishments.

Polly, her big-boned WASP face beaming, swooped in and led them into a large, candle-lit room. The far wall was lined with French doors through which Lee could see a formal garden where small spotlights lit banks of tulips and calla lilies in the shade, and tiny ground lights marked out a path to a gazebo. The living room was both warm and formal, with several arrangements of soft, oversized chairs and sofas, pools of light from clustered candles, and walls covered in dark red moiré. On every wall, small museum lights illuminated Renaissance paintings—saints and Madonnas and mythical heroes in ornate gold frames looked out over the living people in the room.

It was tempting to just study the amazing pictures, but Polly was introducing them to any number of equally surprising Princetonians, saying only their names and locations as in, "Oh here, Porter and Claudia Quarmyne, they're two blocks down from you." No footnotes, no comments, but Lee knew. Claudia Havstrom Quarmyne, a reporter for *World Watch,* had been one of Lee's heroes since childhood. And Porter Quarmyne had given up a syndicated political column to write novels that became popular movies.

In a dizzying half hour, they were introduced to the former Secretary of State, a Nobel Prize-winning physicist, a magazine publisher, an inventor of the transistor, various recipients of Pulitzers and National Book Awards, an art historian, poets, editors, painters, economists, novelists, two former governors, a revered anthropologist, an Emmy-winning television producer, and the composer of some of the most popular standards ever to come out of Tin Pan Alley. A few of them were the Howes' house guests; most were The Neighbors.

They all seemed to know each other well, moving easily from one grouping of silky chairs to another, engaging in intense conversations, punctuated by bursts of laughter. They were mostly middle-aged or older, except for Sam and one conspicuously dewy blonde who turned out to be her best friend, former boarding-school roommate, and Rollin Howe's daughter. Which answered the How-did-you-meet question in Lee's mind. Howe had, Polly whispered, married an almost-underage beauty—for the fourth time.

"Oh let me introduce you to Sam's mother and grandmother. Lee Montagna. Marina Seton, Phoebe Vandewasser."

"I see you wondering," Marina Seton said, her eyes and voice verging on laughter. "How could Samira have blonde forebears, right? We're Dutch. Sam's father was Syrian."

Lee was delighted with this woman's open, amused face, her directness. "And I suspect she combines the best of both. She looks exactly like you, just in different colors."

"And shorter than we are, like her father, who was not, I must tell you, a handsome man. Still, there she is, so we Dutch will happily accept credit for her."

The smiling Marina was indeed tall, close to six feet, a woman of perhaps forty-five, her long body athletic, her eyes as royal-blue as her daughter's, her face lightly marked with laugh lines from years of finding the world hugely entertaining. She was a photographer, taking a break from her darkroom where she was pulling prints for a show coming up in May, at a New York gallery. She was also the mother of another child, Samira's half-brother, Connor, who was Toby's age and lived with his parents and grandmother in a house Toby would be able to reach without even crossing a street.

Phoebe Vandewasser, abstract impressionist, looked like an even-paler Louise Nevelson, the sharp angles in her face grooved dramatically by sun and smoke, the royal-blue eyes outlined in broad swipes of black kohl. Wisps of white hair escaped from a headwrap of orange and chartreuse silk that made her as tall as her daughter, despite the curve that age had made in her spine. She tipped toward Lee, leaning on a carved ebony cane, and spoke confidentially in a voice darkened by decades of cigarettes and hard liquor.

"I could not imagine why Samira wanted to marry such an elderly man. Too old for *Marina*, much less Sam. But my dear, has he ever held your hand?"

"Well no. I mean we shook hands at the door but...."

"It is the *most* sensual experience. Extraordinary. You feel like you're being fucked. It must be divine to sleep with him. Do you hike? I do and there's a wonderful trail along the canal, over by Griggstown."

Lee could actually see herself in boots and a backpack, if that was what it would take to spend time with Phoebe Vandewasser.

"Connor will be bored out of his gourd when school's out, just when your Toby arrives." Marina's long, multi-ringed fingers picked a card from a tiny silver shoulder bag. "Please. Call the minute you move in."

Lee talked with the former Secretary of State about a book she was editing on the Soviet Union, confirming her suspicion that her author was off-base in his assessment of *detente*. She knew all the words when the song-writer took over the piano and played a few of the classic popular songs that had made him famous. Timidly, she approached Claudia Havstrom, who would never be a Quarmyne to Lee.

"I can't believe you're standing there, that you're a real person, not just a by-line and a photograph.

"Me?" She had a barking laugh that turned heads toward them. "How's this poison ivy for real?" The hand that held her spritzer was covered with angry red patches. "I thought country living was supposed to be safe. This hurts like hell."

Havstrom listened incredulously as Lee talked about articles the older woman had written for *World Watch*, years before.

"You're kidding. You remember that stuff?"

"A woman covering Adlai Stevenson's campaign? Trekking into the Sierra Maestre to interview Che? Getting an exclusive with Lumumba? Oh yes, I remember. All the women I knew were making tuna casseroles. You were my evidence that there might be something creative I could do besides putting crushed potato chips on top instead of bread crumbs."

Havstrom was wearing a cowl-necked black cashmere sweater, silk pala-zzo pants in a loud Mexican pink, and pink high-heeled sandals. There was a red stain on one pants leg that looked like the sauce from the scallops that were being brought around the rooms by a young man in a tux. With her dark blonde hair uncombed and several fingernails broken, Havstrom looked very real indeed. Lee asked what she was working on, and the older woman's eyes instantly filled with tears.

"Nothing. Bloody goddamned nothing. Being Mrs. Quarmyne, whatever the hell that means." She frowned at Lee. "Polly said you're an editor. Are you a good one?"

Lee thought before answering. It wouldn't do to be coy with a pioneer feminist.

"*Damned* good."

"Attagirl." Havstrom studied Lee's face, then spoke slowly. "There's this piece I've been stuck on for months. I *hate* freelancing. At the magazine... there were all those people working. The typewriters all rattling away. I just jumped in and did it too. Now there's no *World Watch.* Nobody working at other desks. Just me in my damned little home 'office' in a corner of the bedroom. And I'm stuck. The piece is just not coming. Maybe you'd look at it? Help me figure out why it's not working?"

It was Lee's turn to tear up. "I would be honored, Ms. Havstrom, *honored.*"

"Claudia, kid. Just Claudia." She shook Lee's hand, quite formally. "I think I'm very glad to meet you."

Lee looked for Joe. Earlier she'd seen him, nodding, speaking seriously to one of the ex-governors, no doubt describing some issue he was working on with Jersey mayors. Now he was standing in the library, feigning interest in Howe's enormous collection of books. Lee took his arm and moved with him toward the buffet as she told him about finding a playmate for Toby, and perhaps a few for herself as well.

The dining room table presented an enormous still life of artfully arranged salads, braised asparagus in a vinaigrette, roasted red potatoes, tiny lamb chops, pea pods, and the baby string beans and carrots the French call "firsts." A perfect spring meal, the platters and bowls surrounded by bouquets of pink and orange tulips. As Joe filled his plate with chops, ignoring the vegetables, Former Governor One called to him.

"Montagna. Come sit with us out here." He beckoned Joe toward the open doors to the garden. On the terrace, Former Governor Two sat on a canopied bench, his plate on his knees. Lee winked at Joe. "Way to go, guy. I'll see you later."

Plate in hand, she began studying the paintings on the dining room walls as she dipped the tiny firsts into creamy aoli. Her eyes and mouth filled with beauty as she took in the pungent garlic and sweet vegetables and the brilliant colors of a small triptych. The white-haired art historian joined her and said quietly, "That disappeared from a side altar of a small church in Tuscany when Mark Clark's troops went through."

Lee whispered in mock horror, "Are you saying, sir, that our host is a thief?"

"Nothing so direct, I should think. A picture disappears for years, resurfaces at a respectable dealer's, provenance clouded. Ah well. Isn't it lovely?"

It was. Especially the center panel, the Madonna in deep blue velvet and a crown of dark braids—the living lady of the house had been painted hundreds of years before she was born.

"He may or may not be a thief, Professor, but he certainly is a romantic."

With night falling and guests beginning to check the time, the physicist's wife, a grandly overweight and definitely soused dowager in lime chiffon, cognac snifter in plump hand, began proclaiming in a loud, shrill voice that sailed high over the low register of the general conversation, "People, good people, I must tell you that I hate Samira Howe. Loathe the child. Don't you know every man here is wishing he could dump the old dame and get himself such a wife?"

There was much looking about to see where their hostess might be, and relief that she was out of the room, though Lee doubted that the belligerent voice would have desisted had Samira been standing in full view and earshot.

"Well, it's true, isn't it?" the dowager persisted. "Not a line or scar or stretch mark on her and not a criticizing thought in her gorgeous head. She is every old goat's wet dream."

Her sternly dignified husband took one large lime arm and steered her firmly toward the door.

"It is very late, Phyllis, and the old goats of the world must hurry home to bed, perchance to dream."

They made a beautiful exit, stage left to stage right at a forced-march clip, and Lee was tempted to applaud, as if it were the deftly directed curtain for a comedy's first act.

In the car, heading back up the stench alley of the turnpike toward the lights of Manhattan, Lee regaled Joe with reports of her evening; he offered none of his own. She wondered if he had failed to charm the governors, who might be useful allies for MAA.

"So, Leedle. You liked those people."

"Liked them? Oh yes. They were outrageous."

> Outrageous as in great. They were interesting and involved and smart and funny. There wasn't anyone there whose best foot forward would be borrowing a cup of sugar.

He said nothing.

"Come on, Joe. You didn't like them?"

"It's not that. It's that... did you meet any other Italians there?"

"A short round guy from Modena, he's at the Institute for Advanced Study, doing something I didn't understand."

"I mean Italian like me. American Italian."

Lee thought it best not to mention that there had been no vowel-ending names at all the night before, in Connecticut. She brushed past his question to describe the anti-Sam outburst, which Joe had somehow missed. He didn't laugh.

"Trade my Leedle for that kid? What, are you kidding?"

"I don't think she meant you, the perfect husband. She was talking about normal guys. I mean it's an interesting power balance. The beauteous Samira gets to play with people a husband her own age could only *read* about. No gambling for that girl. She'll never have to wonder if her guy's going to make it. He gets to look at a walking, talking work of art—and soak up all that admiration. The way she looked at him, like he was, I don't know, a god. That has to be an incredible ego boost for a guy who's gray and pot-bellied."

"Maybe. If you like that kind of thing. And if you never need a goose in the right direction. If I didn't have your boot up my butt at least twice a week, there's no telling what I'd be doing. Wearing white socks, picking my nose, using the salad fork for the main course...." He checked to see if she was smiling. "I'm just glad you're happy. About the house. I think it's going to be a good place for us, for the business."

It was going to be all right for Lee and Toby as well. Connor had to be an interesting kid, with Marina Seton for a mother and Phoebe Vandewasser a live-in grandmother. Toby would have at least one friend. Lee imagined walking that canal trail with all of them. And working with Claudia Havstrom—Lee, nobody from nowhere, helping a legend break through her writers' block. Then there was Maddy. There might be no right place for Maddy, though at least the possibilities of being pursued by gun-toting drug dealers might be fewer in Princeton.

A moon waxing toward full rode alongside them, filmed over by the haze that shrouded the eastern part of this accursed state. The moon. Veiled by pollution, but still shining faintly, with a light not its own. Without the sun, the moon would go dark, just as Lee feared she would, without bright light around her. She would not go dark in Princeton. Its people glowed in her mind and made her smile up at this moon she understood so well. She might have nothing to say herself, might generate no light of her own, but she could assist these generators, shine their light back to them, play a useful role in their lives.

She imagined the renovation complete, the old house back in plumb, painted, landscaped—beautiful. She would make it the steadying home base that would keep Joe calm and happy.

Lee thought of all the times she'd gone to school friends' big old houses, solid places with lawns and staircases and dormers and guest rooms, houses their grandparents had owned. The Underwood Road house would be all that. It would just take some time. Their children, grandchildren, great grandchildren, would have Christmases and birthdays and weddings and Easter egg hunts in a house that sat where Washington's troops walked away from the Battle of Trenton, where the sidewalks were sheltered by ancient trees, where kids didn't get mugged for their bikes, where a beloved candy store wouldn't be replaced by a heartless skyscraper. And where the meritocracy had one of its most vibrant outposts.

Smiling, Lee saw herself getting out her PS 11 doorknobs, not for the doors of the city brownstone that she'd dreamed of owning, but to give a touch of the city to an old Princeton house. She'd plant a vegetable garden, unpack her boxes, reclaim all her books, her recordings, her photo albums, and mementos. She would lean out the kitchen Dutch door and watch her garden grow. And she would put a big plastic Virgin Mary, maybe with a fluorescent halo, on the front lawn, inside an upended bathtub, painted a nice fluorescent blue. Another Italian-American family makes it to the suburbs. Lafayette, we are here.

"What's so funny, Leedle?"

The long June day had gotten away from Lee; the dinner she had improvised was far too late. It was already dark. She was sure there were candles somewhere in the moving box marked "kitchen/misc." She dug around the sides, coming up with potholders, a paring knife, kebab skewers and, finally, a boxed pair. One had broken. She snapped off the bottom of the unbroken one, making them a rough match, jammed both into the silver holders in the middle of the card table and lit them. She knew it was absurd, but there had to be some acknowledgement that this was a Sunday evening meal, despite its being not a day of rest but of sweaty labor.

Outside the circle of light, walls of cartons loomed, every box of them waiting to be unpacked, then places found for each thing inside. There was no place to put any of it. Not yet. But it was Midsummer's Eve at the start of a new decade, of a new life, the first night they would actually stay in the house instead of going back to the city. The brownstone apartment was empty; all the things of their lives were here now, and she had two weeks of vacation ahead of her to get the whole mess sorted out.

She moved the oscillating fan from the kitchen to the dining room, sat it on the floor, turned it to Low and plugged it in, hoping the old wall socket was safe. Seeing that Bilbo's cage was now in the fan's path, she moved it to a corner where dust couldn't be blown at the cheerfully noisy bird. She wondered how Admiral Perry was doing in his newly expanded territory behind the house.

"Toby, Maddy! Rally in the dining room! Some kind of supper is ready. Toby? Toby, you hear me?"

He appeared in the dining room door, sprinkled with flakes of dry wallpaper paste.

"You got all the wallpaper down in your room?"

"Almost. Connor helped. Can I paint all the walls different colors?"

"The ceiling and the floor too, if you want to. It's all yours."

All his. Even if Van reappeared, there were so many rooms in the old place, Toby wouldn't lose any ground.

"Put the puppy in that pink room upstairs, OK? Give him some news-papers to pee on and crack the window a little so the room isn't so hot for him."

The cool would be relative. All day the heat had turned dust to mud on their sweating skins. The fans she'd bought at the hardware store on Witherspoon got the still air to move, but it remained heavy, damp stuff, pushing back at you when you moved through it, adding heavily to the tasks at hand. A late-afternoon downpour had lightened the air only momentar-ily, until the reemerging sun boiled the puddles into steam, reminding Lee, not happily, of the Congo.

She went to the oven of the gas stove that she suspected had once been a wood-burner, and took out a roast chicken she had picked up on a foray to town, and a noodle casserole. She knew there should be something green, a salad, some string beans, and nine at night was way too late for kids to be eating dinner, but the June light and the enormity of the tasks had kept them working later than she'd realized. Telling herself they'd survive a few less-than-ideal meals, she pictured Joe, crisp and clean, in some restaurant, breathing cool dry air, spinning scenarios to a prospective client over a beau-tifully served three-wine dinner, rounded off with a good, strong espresso.

"Jesus, Leedle. Candles? In this mess?" Maddy was slumped against the doorway, cut-off jeans and T-shirt sleeves fringing her grimy thighs and shoulders. The girl might still have a mouth on her but Lee thanked God that the sounds she emitted were no longer in a languid drawl; she seemed to have remembered that she had spent most of her life in the north.

> *She is such a pretty girl. Look at those big round eyes and those*
> *blonde curls all over her head. She looks like a baby lamb.*
> *Well, not really. Not with those hips and that chest. And the*
> *look in her eye.*

"Sure, candles. The better to go with the fine cuisine. The better not to see the cracked window panes and the peeling paint, so stepmother doesn't burst into tears and high-tail it back to the city."

Not that Maddy would mind if she did. Despite Lee's record as the girl's ally and sometime savior, Maddy seemed to go out of her way to do things that would annoy her stepmother. Lee half expected her to flip the switch for the hideous brass chandelier, just as her father would no doubt do. There were overhead lights in the ceilings of every room in this house, making Lee squint, turning people's faces into sickly masks. Maddy and Toby didn't need the candles, but Lee did. Because the kitchen was being gutted, and the new refrigerator was standing behind them in the dining room. Because workmen had been in, around, and over the house for days, sealing out the water that had stained the ceilings and walls, bringing in the light that had been blocked by untended shrubbery run amok. Men had been booting and banging across the roof, hammering on new shingles; others silently caulking leaks around the doors and windows—silently after Lee had pressed them to turn off the radios that were blasting country and western through the house. Boom boxes, she realized, were not just a scourge of the city's streets and parks; they were everywhere. She was tempted to unpack the stereo and send some Mozart through the rooms, but decided that would be pushing it too far.

The ground floor windows at the front of the house had been entirely blanketed by enormous rhododendron bushes that must have been planted when the house was built in 1911, and not trimmed since. Now they'd been sawn down to waist-high, raw and ugly until they could recover from the shock of losing over half a century's growth. Ivy tentacles had covered many of the other windows, even on the second floor. In the guest room, tiny, determined tendrils had needled into minute cracks, prying open the dead materials of the house. The leafy, living arms reached up the room's plaster walls, even growing into the ceiling fixture and along its wiring, into the attic. Rain had followed into the breaches the ivy had opened. Mother Nature, never off-duty, had been resolutely destroying another creation of humans who had dropped their guard, who weren't vigilantly protecting their handiwork.

Until the new wiring was done, Lee was afraid that plugging in the new appliances would burn the place down. And she mustn't think about the plumbing. Pipes were sticking out of the wall in the kitchen where the old sink had been taken out; she'd been doing dishes kneeling beside a bathtub. The visible parts of the piping were copper; if none of the rest was rusted-out iron they'd be saved from yet another massive, destructive re-do.

She and the kids had taken down drapes that disintegrated in their hands, sending up clouds of choking dust. They were scrubbing painted walls and stripping wallpapered ones, Maddy grousing constantly, disappearing regularly to nap on her new bed, which she hadn't bothered to cover with sheets. Toby took his breaks exploring the neighborhood with Connor, but gradually, the three of them were having an effect on the mess. She looked at the besmudged girl and laughed.

"Maddy, what a face. It really is a good old house, you know. It's going to be OK. Someday."

"There is absolutely nothing to do in this town. It is sooo boring."

There are over 4,000 boys at the end of this street. I'm sure
you'll think of something.

"C'mon Maddy, sure all this work is boring. But this is a college town. That means there are parties and movies and places to hang out because the town is full of students. Give it a chance."

She imagined Maddy would indeed find more than enough to do. Within days she'd find willing bed partners and a local source for whatever drug was now *au courant*. And someday she'd do something that would move her father to notice and to love her, or so Maddy thought.

But he just didn't like bigmouth broads. Maddy wasn't his type and the more she used and dealt and slept around, the more she wouldn't be the darling daughter he wanted. But Rory, Rory was resolutely taking life on, going for the brass ring, in New York. That he liked.

"Come on, Toby! It's getting cold."

He was in the dining room before she said "cold," a delighted smile on his face.

"He loves me, that puppy. He keeps kissing me. Do you think Ivan is an OK name for a Russian dog? They pull sleds, in the snow, in Siberia."

He piled into a card chair and accepted two drumsticks. "What's this?" he asked of the casserole, voice laden with suspicion.

"Seems to be noodles and cheese. It's just not the way I make it. Connor's mom brought it over, so let's give it a chance, OK?"

"Why?" Maddy demanded. "Why did she do that?"

"Because she knows how hard it is to cook at a time like this. And because it's the kind of thing good people do."

"She wants something," Maddy decreed.

Toby asked if his new friend's mother had also brought ice cream.

"No, but I grabbed some Lorna Doones and some strawberries when I went to the store." Toby made an Oh-Mom face.

"The fridge isn't hooked up, Toby."

"Oh. Well, Lorna Doones are OK. But they're better with vanilla soup."

Of course. Toby liked warm ice cream. She could have bought a pint of Haagen Daz for him to dip the cookies in. She and Maddy could have poured it over the strawberries. Here was her son, facing the unknown, a young stranger in a strange land, needing assurances that things were going to be OK. Joe had understood that. And Lee hadn't even thought of vanilla soup.

She had been silently furious when Joe carried a three-month-old Siberian Husky into the chaos of moving men, floating furniture, and mounting boxes.

"He's yours, Tobe. To go with the yard full of grass."

Enraptured, Toby had enfolded the white ball, looking all amazed into its ice-blue, black-ringed eyes. "He has a mask, Joe. It's a Batman dog."

Seeing her son hugging the dog, hugging Joe as she directed the moving men, Lee had asked, "Where's the rest of it?"

"Rest?" Joe winked at Toby and elaborately checked over the puppy, confirming its completeness. "Four legs, one tail, one wet nose. Looks like a whole puppy to me."

Lee stopped a sofa headed into the kitchen. "No no, fellas. The living room's that way. The rest as in water dish, Joe. You know—leash, six-pack of horse meat...."

"Horse meat? My dog won't eat horses."

She was coming off very badly in this. She pet the quivering fluff ball. "OK. Joe can get him a bag of that dry stuff."

"Not me. Gotta go. Big meeting in Montclair."

She'd been right, it was the worst possible timing. But Joe had been righter. She listened to Toby rattling on about his beautiful country dog. It was the perfect gift to celebrate the move, giving Toby some joy to balance the sadness of leaving his New York school and Luisa and his friends. And it was working. Her son was happy. He was going to be OK with this quiet town where kids and their dogs roamed safely, where he could be Andy Hardy.

As Lee bit into a cookie, she was jolted by staccato crashes of wood on the ceiling

"Go see, sweetie. He's knocked over a bunch of stuff up there." Toby called down almost immediately.

"Mom! He's not here!"

An unhousebroken puppy somewhere in all this debris. Just what the day needed. Lee went up the worn wood stairs, calling ahead, "Did you leave the hall door open?"

"No no. It was closed all the way."

She stood in the doorway of the pink-flowered room. Pee-stained newspapers filled the far corner, bed slats that had been propped against the near wall were splayed across the floor. And the window was wide open.

"Uh oh." She went quickly down the stairs and out onto the porch, peering into the night for a fleeing speck of white. He could be blocks away already, propelled by the fright of the crashing slats. She turned to go back in, and caught her breath.

Ivan was hung on one of the cut-back rhododendrons under the kitchen windows, white limbs hanging down, like a baby's Dr. Denton's flung there to dry.

"He's not in the house, Mom. He must be out here."

Lee tried to turn Toby away and push him back inside, but it was too late.

"He's dead! My dog is dead!" He was staring at the dog in the pale light spilling from the windows. "I killed him. I left the window too open. He's a snow dog and I wanted him to be cool."

"No, honey, no. It's not your fault. Nobody could know he'd jump out a win...." Toby began to shriek, his eyes fixed on the rhododendrons. Lee tried to turn his head away but he shouted, "Look look!"

Ivan was moving. His head rotated until the pale blue eyes stared at them.

"Oh my God. Maddy! Maddy come quick!"

Lee hustled the wailing Toby into the entrance hall as Maddy emerged from the dining room.

"Listen to me, Maddy. Look in the phone book and call a vet. Tell him we've got a mortally injured dog and to come quick with a hypo to kill him." Toby wailed louder.

"Toby, listen to me now. There's a stake right through Ivan's body. He's hurt really bad and we don't want him to suffer, right?"

The boy nodded his head and began to moan. "It's my fault. It's all my fault."

"Maddy, make that call. And take care of Toby. I've got to get the dog off that thing."

"But Leedle, I want to see. Are there guts all over the place?"

"Maddy for Christ's sake shut up! Hold Toby and get on the phone. Call the police station too. See if they've got some kind of animal rescue squad. *Now* Maddy. Go!"

Lee stopped a few feet from Ivan. "OK now boy, I'm going to help you, OK? Got to get you out of this fix." When she reached out to lift him up and off the stake, he made an astonishing noise and clamped needle-sharp puppy teeth deep into her wrist. Her mouth went wide in a silent shout—Toby must not hear her screaming. She reached for a loose brick on the ground but couldn't bring herself to hit the dog. Instead she wedged a finger into the hinge of his jaw, pried it open, and pulled her bleeding arm away.

She hurried back into the house, grabbed a dish towel from a carton of linens and an old green blanket that had been wrapped around a glass table for the move.

"Maddy?" she shouted. "Did you get hold of a vet?"

"Yeah yeah. He's coming. And the cops." Lee realized Maddy's calm voice was coming from the porch and so were Toby's sobs. Racing out with the blanket, she found Maddy studying Ivan, ignoring Toby.

"Mom get him off there! Mama please."

"Maddy goddamit get him in the house!"

"But, Leedle, I want to *see*."

Lee put herself in front of Toby and hugged him. "I'm going to wrap him in this blanket and lift him off. He's scared and he hurts, so it's hard to get near him." Toby wrapped his arms around her waist.

"Go with Maddy, Toby."

Maddy was still contemplating the skewered dog. "God, that must hurt like hell."

"In the house, Maddy. Move!" It was important that Toby not see what had to happen now.

As she approached Ivan, the blanket outstretched, a searchlight picked her out of the night.

"Hold on, ma'am! We've got a net."

Three policemen in khaki uniforms took over, deftly, as if they captured crazed, impaled dogs regularly. One slipped a muzzle over Ivan's foaming mouth, the other dropped a net over him before lifting him up and to the ground. A balding man in old clothes and bedroom slippers knelt on the grass next to the net.

"That's Abe Murray, best vet in town." Marina Seton was standing beside Lee. Other neighbors, drawn by the commotion to see if they could help, stood in the yard, talking quietly. "Abe's a good man." Marina put a long arm firmly around Lee's shoulders.

With a sigh of relief, Lee saw the vet slip the deadly shot through the net and into the small fluff ball. He took Ivan's body out of the net and wrapped him in the blanket. He was cradling the puppy like an infant when Lee reached him.

"Thank you for coming. My name's Lee Montagna."

"Abraham Murray."

"We just moved in. Just got the puppy. His name was Ivan. Sorry to meet you this way."

"I know you wanted me to put him down, but I only knocked him out."

"Then he'll die in his sleep?"

The vet shook his head, his eyes filled with tears. "He's a fine young dog, beautiful and strong. He could survive this."

"But that stake went through everything except the skin on his back."

"Please. Let me take him to my clinic. I really think I can save him."

She could still hear Toby's pleas that she help his dog. At least it would be easier on him if Ivan died in this kind man's care, not here, in all this chaos and with Toby's sense of guilt so immediate to him. She looked up at the open window, high over the dreadful stakes, and down to the vet's sad, heavy face. She nodded yes. He gently placed the wooly bundle on the passenger seat of his station wagon and drove away, one protective arm holding Toby's dog from further harm.

Lee thanked Marina and the others for coming, ruefully noting that it was not exactly the housewarming she had imagined.

"It's not an omen," Marina said softly. "This is a good place. You can be happy here."

Porter Quarmyne extended his hand. Lee reached out to shake it and found he had given her a Baggie of grass.

"Figure you could use it. Welcome to Princeton."

Her wrist still wrapped in a towel, she sat on Toby's bed, telling him about sweet, careful Dr. Murray who thought he could save Ivan, telling him things were going to turn out all right no matter what, until the exhausted boy sobbed himself to sleep. She found hydrogen peroxide to pour on her wrist and Band Aids to cover the punctures. Then she went back outside with one of the carpenters' saws.

It was important that Toby not walk out the door in the morning and see the bloody shrubbery. In the thin light from the kitchen windows and the waxing sliver of a moon, she knelt in the muddy earth and sawed the killer rhodie off at the ground.

Joe's Buick pulled into the garage, the thud of the car door triggering a great fatigue in her. Her wrist throbbed, her head ached, and she began to cry. Joe was making his way along the planks they had put down over the mud between the garage and the front porch, his suit jacket over his shoulders.

"Oh God am I glad to see you. Here. I'm over here."

He peered into the dark, stopped, and stared at her. She got up and went to him, dragging the bush, pouring out the story of what had happened, wiping tears on her muddy sleeve. He stood silently on the plank path, his face not responding to what she was saying. Then he charged through the open door of the house, slamming it behind him.

It locked, and Lee wasn't carrying keys. She sat on a tilted, splintery step and collected her thoughts. The rotted board gave way under her. She stood and considered her situation. There had to be a way into the house and there had to be an explanation for Joe's strange reaction. She saw that she'd blown it, tried to think of what she might have done differently. There was no point in thinking she could get Joe to see all this through her eyes. She had to see it through his.

She would figure it out, quietly, without the kids knowing about this new strangeness. She explored the surface of the house, looking for doors ajar or windows she could slide open. The Dutch door to the kitchen pushed open at the top; she reached in and unlocked the lower half.

Joe was in their bedroom, where she had put familiar linens on the bed and turned his side down, to welcome him to this first night on Underwood Road.

"Don't look at me like that. You think I'm going to stay here with a crazywoman? You are a goddamned crazywoman!"

He'd just come from his air-conditioned car, but his shirt was stuck to his arms and shoulders. He yanked his tie away from his collar.

"Tell me what you're talking about, Joe."

"What am I talking about? I come home from a day of beating my brains out. Come *home*. And my *wife* is crawling around on her knees in the mud, in the front yard, the *front yard*, like she's putting on a show for the town, with a saw in her hand and some cockamamie story about cops and vets and dogs jumping out of windows. Do you ask anything about me? If I'm OK? What my day was like? Do you think about anybody but yourself? Crazy bitch."

He charged out into the hall and down the stairs.

"Where you going, Dad?" Maddy was in the foyer, looking frightened.

"Damned if I know." Maddy followed him out the front door. The Buick's engine raced, sputtered, died, started up again. The tires burned rubber in the late-night stillness, and they were gone.

Lee sank into the big bed, but racing thoughts and strange night sounds kept her from sleep. There were no sirens, no horns, no clanking manhole covers, no drunks yelling as they passed by. Instead, she was besieged by assorted droning and clattering insects, a dog barking on some far block, and the mourning birds that she'd heard all through these days, continuing their lament into the night. The country was not a quiet place. She listened until the sunlight came, ending this midsummer night. By the light of day, she knew what her next moves had to be.

Lee and Toby jolted along on the Penn Central, staring through the grubby window at the ghastly "landscape." It was not to be believed. How many times had she said she wouldn't live in the Taj if she had to go through Jersey to get to it? Now she'd be going through it every damn day, commuting to that goddamned mess of a house.

Toby's shoulders were trembling and the new horror of this reached out to her. She took his hand.

"Don't think about it, bubba."

The enormous green eyes spilled over. "I can't stop."

She leaned in front of him, shielding him from other passengers' curiosity.

"I know how new it is and how much it hurts to think about it. I've been making myself think of anything else, but it creeps back to get you, doesn't it." His damp head nodded against her neck. "Try to kick sand over those pictures so you can't see them."

"Do you think the vet can give him something so he doesn't hurt? It must hurt so much."

"Yes, yes of course. You know he's doing that." The sand blew off the image of the small white head swiveling to look at them, ice-blue eyes in a black mask, and she shuddered.

"Pam, bless you. I should be back for him by four."

"Oh, thank *you*. You know how us childless career women are all secretly yearning to be mommies. We'll be fine here."

Pam Pierpont, Lee's favorite illustrator, had left MacGregor to freelance, working out of her loft in Soho. Pencils behind both ears, she smiled at Toby, who didn't smile back. He was taking in the long, echoing loft.

"You live here?"

"Yeah. And work here too. You want to see my drawing stuff?"

"Maybe." He was staring at the long, shining floor that stretched away to frosted, two-story-high windows. "If I take off my shoes, could I slide?"

"If you promise not to break any bones before your mom gets back." Toby dropped to the floor and pulled off his sneakers. At the door, Lee fumbled in her bag for the address of the meeting.

"He really does like to draw. As soon as the novelty of this place wears off, he should settle down with some nice quiet paper. You doing any stuff for kids' magazines, books? He could kibitz. Just don't show him any dog pictures."

"Especially Huskies. I understand. Not to worry. But promise you'll schedule in some time to tell me what the hell's going on with Joe."

"It's not time that's the problem." Lee hugged Pam quickly, awkwardly. "I'm not sure I *know* what's going on. I just know I'll be damned if I'm going to miss that meeting and I couldn't leave Toby in Princeton."

Tate and Joe were already settling into Lawrence Ashburn's office when she arrived. She took the chair next to Tate's while they were placing their coffee orders. Tate smiled hello. As the young secretary reached the door, Lee said to her back, "Black, please. No sugar."

She'd need it. She couldn't afford to be fuzzy-headed now. Joe grinned at the distinguished, lightly graying editor and threw a leg over the arm of his handsomely upholstered chair.

"Why don't we start by explaining who the hell we are and what we're up to?"

"That sounds constructive." Ashburn put the tips of his fingers together and looked over them at Joe.

It was certainly the wrong tone to take with the senior editor of *Our Times*. He wasn't some street kid Joe was playing stickball with. But Ashburn didn't seem put off. Lee wondered if there was some sort of secret handshake that altered the rules of civil interaction.

"All right, Mr. Montagna and Mr. Altridge, just who the hell are you?"

Lee pulled a file out of her briefcase, as Joe proceeded to talk about MAA, using the droll description of the Montagna/Altridge alliance that had gotten them this meeting. Lee had written it, in a query letter she'd drafted for their signatures. Had Joe memorized it? Ashburn would think he was an idiot. The editor had certainly checked the letter to remind himself who he was meeting with at two o'clock.

Ashburn nodded smiling Go-Ons, as Joe talked. Then Tate repeated Lee's rundown of the article they proposed to write, an extract from the book she was ghosting on their black entrepreneurs project. It was an effort to salvage something of their Great Society work, to let the country know that change was possible. Way too quickly for Lee's sense of the necessary timing, Ashburn was saying yes.

"Well, gentlemen, *Our Times* has been looking for a good minority progress piece, and given your credentials, and the quality of the book chapter you sent me, I'd say you have a cover story. How soon can you have the article ready?"

Having no idea, Tate and Joe were silent.

I told them that moving to Princeton would knock my schedule back a month, that I can't get this done until the end of July. Obviously they don't remember and this silence is bad. Like they really are idiots. Uh oh. Joe's opening his mouth. Probably to promise it next Friday.

"In six weeks," Lee said quickly. "You'll have it August first."

Ashburn looked at her for the first time, puzzled. Joe didn't move.

"My name is Lee Palmer, Mr. Ashburn, and I don't follow these fellows to meetings because they're cute—I'm their ghost." She smiled. "I did the chapter you read and I'll be doing the article. Now, I need to know if you want the focus on Jefferson Briggs, as I suggested in the query, or if the piece should take a broader perspective."

Ashburn didn't answer right away, seemingly disoriented by the fact that she was making sounds. Joe examined the end of his necktie. Tate picked lint from his jacket sleeve, smiling. Ashburn watched her mouth, frowning intently, then said to Tate and Joe, "Briggs, yes. The fellow with the lamp factory in Bedford Stuyvesant. Interesting study. Focus on him."

Tate hailed a Checker in front of the Our Times building and held the door open, sweeping them in with a courtly bow. "Madame? Sir?"

Lee climbed into the far seat and looked back to see Joe insisting that Tate precede him. "After you, Alphonse."

Tate dropped into the seat next to her. Joe flipped a jump seat into position and perched on it, facing Tate.

"Tate my man, how do you like that? We're gonna have a cover story in *Our Times* magazine."

Tate was shaking his head in wonder. "You know I got Ds in English? Damn near didn't graduate I had so much trouble writing." He whooped with glee and slapped out a drum roll on his knees. The cab was pulling into traffic. "Hey, where're we going?"

"Oh that," Joe grinned. "We're pointed south. How about Max's for burgers? I'm starved."

Tate nodded a fast yes and Joe shouted "Max's Kansas City!" to the cab-bie. She looked at Joe, beaming at his chosen brother, and quickly looked away. Max's would be good. Only a few minutes from Pam's loft.

Tate didn't seem to realize that Joe would disdain the idea of getting Ds at Yale. Street kids fighting their way through CCNY didn't get Ds in anything. Ever. Without your 3.8 you lost your place. And your chance in life. And Joe wasn't going to lose his. She was sure he'd never told Tate his CCNY bachelor's took him six years of classes by day and a factory night shift, three hours sleep, at the most. He'd never tell Tate anything so per-sonal, or talk to him about how mad he was at Lee for what she'd just done in that meeting. She hoped that Joe at least got it that she was profession-al, Ms. Palmer, not The Little Woman. She wondered if he actually hated Tate, wanted to punch him out for his amusing Ds at Yale. There was no evidence to go on. Instead, there was always this laughing, Tate's inhaled honks, Joe's staccato gunfire.

Now they had a new choo-choo train—they were about to be published writers. If there were room in the cab for cartwheels, they'd be doing them. And if she pointed out that they and their new pal Ashburn had been in-credibly rude, neither of them would know what to say to her. They'd have to pretend she hadn't spoken. For now. If Joe came home, and they were alone, she would get his real reaction, if she could hear it over the sounds of splintering doors and furniture.

Tate was chortling over Joe's description of what Big Joe would do when the magazine came out. "My son The Writer," he'd be saying, giving copies to all the union guys.

Sliding into the booth at Max's, Tate looked over at Joe and said, "You know, you know what I think the article ought to say?" He had become a mischievous child, about to shock the grown-ups. "Heap big liberal do-good-ers work asses off on minority advancement and reach mind-blowing con-clusion." He paused, pushed back the sandy hair that had fallen over his eyes, passed his hand down his face, leaving behind a frown worthy of a grave pronouncement. "The problem, ladies and gentlemen, is that they really are inferior."

Lee reached out a restraining hand, but found herself starting to laugh, dissolving into helpless, exhausted laughter. Richard Nixon was president and nobody cared about black entrepreneurs—white/peach bullshit about black/brown people was absurd—moving to New Jersey was a ghastly joke—the meeting at *Our Times* had been insane—thinking she could handle the article, the book, editing MAA reports, the house, Toby, Maddy, and her job at MacGregor's was lunacy—and the beloved city that had passed by the cab windows was no longer hers. She could not stop laughing.

Joe hooked his thumbs under his lapels and intoned, "Shiftless." Tate solemnly added, "Ne'er do well."

Lee followed, gasping, with, "No account?" and what was left of the Great Society was laid low, years of effort and dedication, giddily flying apart like popcorn hurling itself out of a lidless pot.

They worked it all out, keeping their voices down so no one could hear and perhaps take them seriously. Minority economic development would be achieved by a massive government/corporate program to purchase and distribute thousands of shoeshine kits.

"Entrepreneurial basics, that's what we need to teach 'em," Tate affirmed.

When he left for the men's room, Lee wiped away the slap-happy tears. Tate would be back any minute, and she had to pick Toby up.

"Is Maddy OK?"

Joe responded tonelessly. "She's at her sister's."

"You'll pick her up? Bring her home?"

Joe said nothing.

"We really have to talk about all this, Joe."

He turned his head slowly, looking directly at her for the first time since he had stared at her in front of the house the night before. As she started to say more, the pale eyes fixed on her and narrowed. She shuddered, and stopped. As sky slits locked on her silenced mouth, he took a long pull on his scotch and put the glass down carefully.

"No. We do not. Not here. Not now. Not when we get home. Not ever."

Tate reached into the booth for the check, but Joe slapped an emphatic hand on it.

"Well, my man. Another day—" Joe paused and Tate came in on cue:

"—another stunning victory."

Folie à Trois

The report was due in Bergen County in ten days, but Lee's eyes kept bouncing off the pages of findings; the words were dense and the distractions constant—Toby calling from school to remind her that he had a game at four and she'd promised to come. A heating contractor wanting to know if his bid had been accepted. Ashley Clay thanking Lee for the silver teether she had sent, engraved RMC, for their newborn Robert Martin Clay. Joe wanting to know how the report was coming and if she'd called the dry cleaner about delivering his suits. And Vito Frenare had knocked on the back door twice since eight.

After months of Frenare's slow, careful masonry work around the house, Lee was still disconcerted by the graying immigrant with the face of a Roman senator and the cap-in-hand obsequiousness of a serf. She was sure he was putting her on with all his head-ducking and grinning, imagined his true persona emerging when he walked into his own home, his back straight and his hooded eyes demanding respect and service.

In his first appearance of this chilly day, he had extended in two leathery hands a box of *sfogliatelle* made by his wife, an Italian-American woman who clearly knew how to take care of an Italian man. He asked apologetically if he could put his lunch in the fridge, as if she hadn't said yes dozens of times; an entire shelf was set aside for the brown bags and pop cans the various workmen brought with them every morning.

An hour later, he'd asked her to look at the bricks he'd had delivered, a request for appreciation, she knew; any word about corrections had to come from the master of this house. Fortunately, the bricks were exactly the ones she'd picked out at the brickyard; she smiled and encouraged him to proceed with the pathway he was to make from the kitchen door to the garage.

Now he was at the door again, this time translating for his nephew, Gino, whose English was non-existent and who needed to be paid for sanding and painting the shutters. Lee explained that she was forbidden to hand over Joe's check until young Gino with his sweet, uncomprehending face corrected an error that Joe had seen in his work.

The house's graying, desiccated siding shingles had soaked in a velvety, brown-black oil, the color of bittersweet chocolate. For all the peeling green trim, Lee had chosen paints that picked up tones in the old bricks, a deep terra cotta for the doors, peach for the shutters, and peach lightened almost to white for the window frames. She thought the effect was warm and delicious—Tuscan colors for a Cape Cod-style house. Twice this week, strangers had rung the doorbell and asked where they could get the same paints. She was ready to check off a job well done, except for one shutter on a guest room window, the one Joe might have noticed if it had been painted fuschia.

"That one up there, Gino, see? It's the color of the windows—it's not like the other shutters."

Vito translated. He'd been working on his English since the forties when he'd landed in a New Jersey prisoner-of-war camp that was much visited by the Italian-American families in nearby towns, their daughters bearing home-cooked cannelloni and the possibility of citizenship. No doubt the handsomest man in the camp, Vito had married a girl whose father owned a construction company in Kendall Park. In the decades since, innumerable Frenares had proliferated along Route 27, both by procreation and by immigration. Lee suspected that Vito's village in Puglia was a ghost town, every male blood relative and in-law now working the building trades in the towns between New Brunswick and Trenton, a large percentage of them, she was sure, putting their brown bags in her fridge as the Underwood Road renovation unfolded.

She called Nassau Secretarial, the answering service referred to in this house as Vi the Voice.

"Hey, Vi. I'm crashing on something so don't let any more calls through until maybe 3:30, OK? Unless Joe or the kids need me—you know, the usual drill."

"You got it, Lee. Did I give you the number yesterday for that guy Sacka something who called from the city?"

"Sakamoto. That's my old boss. Yeah, I've got it. Thanks Vi."

Gino's ladder banged against the house. She had to concentrate. What did the stat charts add up to? And these financials? She did some quick calculations on a scratch pad.

Clearly this MAA report, the third she'd done this month, was going to be late. An autumn chill was whispering through the edges of the old window above her desk in the extra bedroom on the back of the house. The heating bills were going to be astronomical when winter started moving through the cracks around all the framed panes in the house. The new storm windows had to arrive before the first heating bill appeared on Joe's desk, because things were going well and she had to keep it that way.

Toby and Connor had worn a groove between the Setons' number 11 and Toby's big, multi-colored room at 99, Ivan the Miracle Dog running between them, restored to Toby by Abe the Vet. Maddy actually had a job, something in a dining hall at the grad school. Rory had come down for a day, bringing along her sculpture teacher, a wiry, dark Croatian whose loft she was now sharing in Soho. Joe and Tate were in high cartwheel form, hiring three new people in their New York office to handle MAA's contracts with local governments and businesses in the tri-state area. Tate ran the office and staff; Joe handled clients' labor relations, spending hours on the phone and days on the road. When he made it home, it was Lee's Good Joe who came through the door, pleased with himself, his family, and with the rapid changes on the exterior and surroundings of the house.

And Lee, Lee was good too, now that Joe had drafted her out of Mac-Gregor's, ending her daily commute. He'd convinced her that the minuscule paychecks she was earning hadn't mattered to the family at all. She needed to focus on helping him and Tate make a go of MAA, where the work was important, unlike what Joe called the "pretentious," unread books she produced at MacGregor's.

She had managed the renovation teams by phone for weeks, trying to picture from her desk in Manhattan what various electricians, plumbers, and landscapers were proposing and doing at 99. There had been many an unpleasant and costly surprise when she made it home and saw what they'd actually done.

It was late July when Joe had talked to her with great concern about how tired she seemed to be from the commute—which was about to get worse—more hours, more pressure. Ramon had offered her another promotion: an office with a window and the work of five editors to supervise. Definitely not a job that could be done in an eight-hour day. She was being promoted into incompetence, moved up and away from her ability to tinker with people's words—there was no way she'd be a competent manager. There would be schedules and budgets to meet, five work-lives to direct, when all she was sure she could manage was her own editing pencil.

If she'd taken it on, the house renovation would have slowed to a halt and Toby would become even more a member of the Seton family than he already was. It just wouldn't work.

Being there for Toby, managing the renovation everyday, doing MAA work there, at home—it was a good plan and good work. Like this study of the labor force in Bergen County. It was important stuff. She frowned as she forced her eyes to look at the single-spaced statistical jargon that MAA staffers had "written." The report was supposed to make the plight of exploited bottom-of-the-ladder workers clear and support County policies that brought more living-wage jobs into the area. But instead of pithy, arresting stories backed up by clear, stunning facts, the pages were ice and mud, dull, impenetrable. She thought that making this mess persuasive to a reader should earn her a medal. Or a fat fee. But this was her contribution to the growth of MAA, to the well being of her family, and to a lot of working people who needed good jobs. There would be no medal, and no fee, though Lee didn't see why a bit of the money flowing into the company couldn't be allotted to her.

MAA's income, like the family's, was Joe's department. He scowled over every bill, telling her she was spending too much, yet money appeared whenever he decided it was necessary, as it had when he had dashed off a check on a personal account for the down payment on 99. Lee had learned to collect at least three bids on each aspect of the renovation, laying them out for him to see and to make the call himself. Invariably, a Frenare, a Bugiardo, or a Incagliarsi got the nod over any non-Italian, even when the Italians' bids were higher and their reputations lower. With them, Joe was a don, not an upstart wop among the WASPs.

Paying all the Vitos and Ginos, the mortgage, tuition for Toby and Rory, child support for Van—everything depended on their continuing to come through for MAA's clients. And this shaping and producing of reports was her part, the least she could do.

She understood, but she missed paychecks, missed working with Pam and Asa and Ramon. She missed the sounds and sights and smells of her walks across the city. She missed her boring writers—she even missed going up against misogynistic corporate managers. Ramon "Sacka-something's" call might be about asking her to come back, or to freelance. She would tell him she was fully booked.

Next up on her to-do list, Lee and Joe had agreed that once the outside of the house was done, she would create a guest room. Joe would invite the Altridges for a weekend; then Lee would ask the Papandreous. Before Christmas. It was autumn. She had to hurry. Eliminate distractions. Keep to the tasks at hand. No more detours like the sheer joy of working that summer with Claudia Havstrom, helping her get on with her stalled article.

"But what's my lede? How do I start this thing off?"

"You said it perfectly, Claudia. Remember? Here, I put it in these notes, it was so good."

They had laughed a lot, talked as they made themselves lunch, adjourned to the Quarmyne's pool where Claudia did laps and Lee sat under a deep awning enjoying the wonder of working with Claudia Havstrom. But now, only MAA mattered.

She rolled a sheet of paper into her typewriter. There wasn't much point in making notes on the report pages; this would have to be a complete doover. She'd call a grocery order to the Food Mart, get something started for dinner before she left for Toby's game.

Maybe, while she organized dinner, she could talk with Celeste.

Lee held an image of a wire connecting her to the lines strung across the countryside, diving under the Hudson, burrowing through subway tunnels to Celeste's phone. Celeste had always helped Lee understand her life; now the phone line back to her felt like Lee's tether to the world she'd lost, the latest one, the New York life she'd come to love, now stored away in the same mental box where she kept a house on a creek in the Maryland woods, and a great job at the White House.

Lee had told Celeste that there had been no more dramas since Ivan went out the window and Joe went out the door, and back in. She took in again and again Celeste's calming, "I know, I know," and her advisories on how the movements of the solar system might impact Lee's world. She could listen to Celeste's assurances that it was good that she'd gotten the kids away from the city, which was far too dangerous.

"Stefan got mugged yesterday."

"Stefan? Mr. Streetsmarts?"

"I'd never say it to him but it was sort of perfect. I was telling him that I've never seen the neighbor that I do errands for sometimes. She has the back apartment on our floor and she's very old. I phone her and ask if I can pick up anything for her when I'm going over to Madison. But I've never seen her. She won't open the door, so I just leave packages for her and ring her bell so she knows they're there. Stefan had a fit. What's she afraid of, it's ridiculous, carrying on and on. I pointed out that he's not a little old lady. He's a big, healthy, confident guy and he can't imagine what it's like to be frightened. He just stormed out, but an hour later the phone rang. He was at the police station looking at mug shots because an addict put a knife against his ribs and took his wallet."

"He's OK?"

"Just angry. He swears he'll have the addict put in jail forever. But it does seem like instant karma, doesn't it?"

"I hope you managed not to laugh."

"Oh, I know better than to do that."

"That's us, the keepers of the peace."

Celeste had echoed Joe in urging Lee to stop commuting, not for MAA's sake but for Lee's. "You've got all those workmen at the house, you're commuting, working full time, taking care of a family and a dog and a bird...."

"But no turtle. Did I tell you we can't find Admiral Perry?" Lee hadn't discussed it with Toby but she was pretty sure that, encountering no garden walls, the Admiral had lit out for the territories.

"Actually, Toby handles Ivan the Resurrected—trained him, feeds him, walks him. He feeds Bilbo too. Even cleans his cage. There's a good dad coming along there. And the kid's in heaven. He's got a best friend right down the block, his dog didn't die, he's in a day school he loves, plays end on the junior varsity, gets to school and back on the new ten-speed Joe bought him. It's all perfect."

"You forgot to mention that he's got a great mom."

"If you say so. But what matters to him is Joe."

"He's been in a very steady time. It looks like it's tied to Joe's ascendant."

"I think everything about Toby is tied to Joe's everything. Ivan follows Toby around, Toby follows Joe. When he's here."

"They have so much to build on. There are trines and sextiles linking all their major planets. But Joe still has some guilt issues about loving him, Lee. He's living with this kind, smart, healthy boy and his own son is so damaged but all he does is send money to him."

"Van had his chance. He could have lived with us. And he could have been repaired."

"I know, I know. Just don't ever forget how heavily Joe carries Van. It can come out in strange ways."

"I'm counting on his sadness or guilt, or whatever it is, losing out to how happy he is with the life we have now. You should have seen his face when Toby asked us if he could change his name to Montagna. Joe was *thrilled*."

"Oh I don't know about changing names, Lee. That can be very complicated and not a good idea at all. You're not going to let him do it, are you?"

"Heavens no. His father's alive and Toby's his only child. There's no way I'd do that to Tim Pitt. But changing your name to fit new circumstances isn't so odd. Women have been doing it forever. You changed to Papandreou. And nobody looking for Morgana Lee Palmer would ever find Leedle Montagna. That Palmer girl is lost and gone forever."

"I never even thought of not changing my name. Children—that seems different. But I can see that Joe would like the idea."

"Are you kidding? It would be a triumph over Toby's dad. And Joe loves a good triumph over another guy, even if he's never met him."

"I'm afraid I will never understand men. Never. Even if I read a million of their charts."

"That makes at least two of us in the pitch dark. I suspect there are more."

When Lee did give Joe the report—in clear, compelling English and ready for printing—he would not thank her, not for work that was late. It wouldn't count that the task was nearly impossible and the deadline had been set without asking her if it made sense. It wouldn't matter that she had been right on time with previous reports and with the *Our Times* article, while directing the massive face lift on Underwood Road.

The chocolate and peach house with its handmade post lights, its planters overflowing with orange and rust mums, its instant green lawn unrolled from the sod farm, now looked as fine as any house on Underwood. No passerby would imagine what ugliness and chaos still prevailed within. The home of Joseph van Heugel Montagna now presented itself properly to the world—if you were just passing by. Someday soon, once Lee had dealt with the still disastrous interior, it would welcome MAA clients to gracious, smoothly run receptions and dinners.

She was getting there; the fireplaces worked and Joe's office, just off the front door, was beautiful, the floor refinished, his grip-and-grin photos of himself with famous people hanging on walls that were now the sky-blue color of his eyes. There was one photo in which an intense LBJ towered over Joe, another of Joe standing beside a smiling John Glenn in Apollo regalia. Around them, he posed with various Senators and Secretaries of this or that part of the President's Cabinet. Lee hung the one she liked best just inside the door, at eye level—Big Joe Montagna standing proudly behind a seated John L. Lewis, who held five-year-old Little Joe on his lap.

She'd used her auction savvy to find a worn rust-and-blue Kerman and an English desk from the early eighteen-hundreds, a desk with a leather-covered tilt top that was perfect for the work Joe did on legal pads with the monogrammed Waterman pen she had given him. Joe did not type. His brown leather swivel chair looked out onto a tiny walled garden accessible only from his office. In one corner of that garden, a stone mermaid now poured water from an amphora into a small pond. Lee had found her in a Trenton junkyard, battered but still beautiful, had hoped Joe would not object to having her in the line of sight from his desk. There was no objection; he seemed not to have noticed the figure was there. In another corner of that small garden, heavy wrought-iron chairs awaited MAA clients who would join him there for weighty discussions come spring, when the rest of the house would be ready.

When he was away, the room was not one that welcomed family members; he kept it locked. When he sat in its center, speaking urgently into the phone, his body tense, the room became the power station from which the force of Joe Montagna was transmitted out into the world. And she had created this setting for her Joe. As soon as the pea-gravel arrived for his garden walk and the banker's lamp for his desk, she would check off another job she could see was well done.

The guest room, as per Joe's priorities, opened for business, and she did it, triumphantly, before Thanksgiving. It was in a small wing of the house, just two rooms, one up, one down, that had probably been added on in the twenties. With Joe's imprimatur to proceed rapidly and "make it good," she'd thrown herself into the task and found herself well pleased as she surveyed the finished space before Tate and Pru, and their Priscilla, were to arrive for the first time.

Like the entire house, it was solid. The floors had revealed themselves as solid cherry, the walls were thick plaster over lathe and four-by-six studs. After she'd pulled down the layers of blistering, peeling wall paper and had the dark woodwork painted white, she picked out a handsome yellow paper with a small pattern of blue and white flowers. The wiry little guy who came to hang the paper had been a joy to watch, cutting, matching, pasting the long sheets he'd cut, a quick and confident master craftsman. She told him how the room had looked, about the leaks and the ivy growing in through the windows and into the light fixture.

"Oh, I'm not surprised. These Princeton people don't care about their homes." He smoothed another panel into position, every leaf and flower aligned seamlessly. "All they're interested in is books and booze."

Given what Lee had been seeing of overflowing bookshelves and well-stocked bars, she suspected he was right.

She had humble blue-and-white-checked gingham made up as lined drapes to border the windows, and hung white sheers over the panes that looked out from under broad eaves onto the new green lawn. She brought in a whimsical *chinoiserie* dresser and double bed she'd found at a garage sale and had painted white, along with an art deco dressing table and mirror. Table lamps of green and white pottery were wired to a wall switch; the overhead wiring and fixture removed. On each side of the now-working fireplace, there were easy chairs with good reading lights. Kindling and splits of dry wood were stacked and ready for burning. Small, grass-green throw rugs awaited bare feet at each side of the bed, which was covered in a blue and white quilt. And in one corner, a white crib with a butterfly mobile awaited Priscilla Altridge.

It was a pleasure to look at. But the sound effects were quite another thing. The mourning doves seemed to never stop their dismal, sad song. Lee joked about firing them and hiring some cheerful songbirds, or getting some nightingale recordings to play outside, so the doves would get the idea. She expected they'd be keeping city guests up all night, yearning for the familiar sounds of garbage trucks and sirens. Lee had yet to sleep through a Princeton night; she hated the doves, all of them sounding like Chekhovian Mashas, in mourning for their lives. It was not a soundtrack for happiness.

On the November weekend when the Altridges became the first weekend guests at 99, Tate appeared with not only his wife and daughter and his usual grin but also with a truck bearing his housewarming gift—the ailanthus he'd raised in a pot on the balcony of his bachelor digs on Second Avenue. Noting that it was a trash tree, the tree that grew in Brooklyn and on every neglected vacant lot in all five boroughs, Pru had banned it from their new apartment; Tate had talked his mother's gardener into keeping it in her Bedford *orangerie,* an urban street-fighter of a tree surrounded by super-groomed French citruses.

"It was a long way from home, but it didn't die, Joe, look at that baby." Tate was grinning at the ten-footer being delivered in the open-bed truck. It took Joe, Tate, and the driver to lift the tree and drag it to the center of the lawn behind the house, the spot where the Montagna's landscape designer had drawn a raised flower garden. Joe brought shovels out of the garage and he and Tate dug an enormous hole in the cold-hardened ground while Lee set up lunch and Toby made monkey faces at tiny Priscilla, in Pru's lap, waving her arms and laughing Toby on.

"Toby, come quick! You'll never believe who turned up." Joe was waving Toby into the yard, a huge grin on his face.

Lee watched from the dining room window as Ivan and Toby arrived at the newly dug hole in tandem. Ivan, now quite a large creature, began pawing at what seemed to be a large muddy rock but was actually Admiral Perry.

"No, Ivan, don't hurt Perry!" Toby tugged on the dog's collar, trying to pull him away from this fascinating object. The great land tortoise knew exactly how to deal with such negative interest and continued to imitate a boulder as Ivan nosed him over twice. Joe got a restraining hold on Ivan as a delighted Toby brought out the garden hose and revealed the long-missing turtle inside the mud coating. Watching them, Lee could not contain her delight. She and Toby would have to look up the life patterns of land turtles and figure out what the Admiral might do next.

"I doubt that this was in your plans for the garden." Pru was standing at another window, patting Priscilla's back and frowning at the two men as they clicked Heineken bottles under the newly planted tree.

"Hmm? Oh, the tree? The best laid plans of wives... but you know, it's kind of perfect. And it's a hell of a fine gift, considering how much Tate loves that thing."

By all the standards of meaning for giver and receiver, it had proved a fine gift indeed. Every evening that he was home, Joe watered the tree himself, dragging a hose out to it, even when it had rained that day. There was no telling when Lee would get Joe's green light to order the landscaping back there, where it couldn't be seen from the street. Drawings of raised flower beds might remain forever drawings, while this gorgeous guttersnipe of a tree hung tough and grew taller in refined Princeton ground.

She slapped the report on the door that she'd used to make a desktop over file cabinets, and went down to the kitchen door.

Vito Frenare stood at the bottom of the three steps he had taken two weeks to build. "*Prego, signora,* look, look. Isn't the path beautiful?"

Frenare had now laid the first yard of the path to the garage—a whole yard in the wrong place and in a pattern that he'd made up instead of the one he'd been given to do.

"Oh yes, it's lovely. But hold it just a minute OK?"

All right all right, I know I'm letting the side down. I should take the time to teach these guys about working for an American woman instead of pretending to be Signora Idiota, but if I go toe-to-toe with them it'll slow things down for years. And what can you expect from first-generation Italians who are so proud that Montagnas have moved into this neighborhood? I have got to get back to the damned report and Vito has got to cut the crap, which he's only going to do if he thinks "Don Montagna" wants him to.

She ruffled through a stack of sketches and notes on her desk and went back down with her drawing of the walkway.

"Look, Vito, this is the picture from Joe, remember? Now we have to do it this way, OK? See how the bricks go together, two this way, two that way? And it's wider, I think. Yes, here. The edges go right to the sides of the beautiful steps you made."

As she spoke, the right opening lines for the report sounded clearly in her head and the rest of it fell into place behind them, the compelling anecdotes, the revealing discussion of data and the call to action were all there, in her mind. She hurried back to the typewriter, suddenly sure that she could get a fine report ready for the printer, in ten days. And the good times would not be disrupted by another of her failures.

She'd cleaned up the shards of the purple cow before Toby joined her in the den, where they were both reading by the fire on a gray winter Saturday. But now she spotted one piece she'd missed, next to a front leg of the big corduroy chair where Toby had settled in with *Dune*.

Lee had found the whimsical porcelain cows in an antique shop in Lawrenceville and brought them to stand on the upright piano just inside the door of this cozy room. They were her wink at being a female Taurus, the bull. Down a twisting staircase from the light, airy guest room, the den was a dark, quiet sanctuary with a low, beamed ceiling, walls of built-in oak bookshelves and furnishings of deep reds, browns and purples, all of it warmed now by fireglow.

Watching Toby concentrating over the book, she hoped that Paul Atreides was in mortal danger on the page so Toby's eyes wouldn't wander to the small purple triangle near his foot. He loved the cows, insisting that they mooed in time with his piano pieces. He'd even made up a tune for the old doggerel, "I never saw a purple cow, I never hope to see one. But I can tell you, anyhow, I'd rather see than be one." She didn't want to lie to him about how one of the cows had been broken.

Joe came to the doorway and stood there, not coming into the room, not seeing Toby tucked into the wingback chair. He was still wearing his black cashmere caftan, the one she had given him, that he wore because it was warm, that she had always loved to see him wear because it fell and moved so caressingly around his stony body, because it matched his blackbird hair and made his pale eyes even more startling.

She didn't want this Joe to be wearing the beautiful garment she so loved to see on *her* Joe. He still had the bottle of Remy Martin in his hand, though Lee suspected it was much lighter than it had been the last time he appeared.

The pale blue eyes looked at her calmly.

"Just in case you didn't get my message the first time...."

He picked up the other china cow, bouncing it in his free hand, then hurled it overhand, full force, at the bricks above the fire, the same spot where he'd thrown its companion. Chips shot back into the small room, one nicking her forehead.

Toby leaped out of the wingback and stood looking at Joe, at the shards, at his mother. "Mom, what's happening?"

Lee had no answer. This was about something she'd done or failed to do but she was not sure what that might be.

She looked toward the door. Joe was not there. Toby brought her a Kleenex.

"That could have gone in your eye, Mom."

"But it didn't. I'm OK."

She saw his bewilderment and knew his world was spinning, the world in which he was safe, loved, and cherished by two good grown-ups. The only Joe Toby knew was a warm and loving man; this Joe was a stranger, and he had just manifested into Toby's perfect world.

Lee reached for him; he pulled away.

"What did you do? Why is he so mad?"

> That isn't fair. But if I tell you that I can't think of anything I did, you'll be dragged through the looking glass and I don't want that for you. I want you back in your wonderland.

"Would you help me pick up the pieces?"

They moved around the room, finding the fragments wherever they'd shot. Toby took the ones he'd collected to the trash basket by the sofa, where he found the debris from the first explosion and looked quickly at the piano.

"He busted *both* of them?"

He was out the French doors and into the icy rain, without a coat, but Connor's house wasn't far, and Toby was running.

Joe's black form filled the doorway once more, arms upraised against the frame, as he surveyed the den.

"Where the hell is Tobe?"

"I'm not certain. But probably at Connor's."

His black brows came together and black lashes hid the sky in his narrowed eyes.

"Not certain. What kind of mother are you? Rotten mother. Rotten wife. Why did he go wherever he went?"

"Maybe he was scared, Joe."

A hint of alarm crossed his face and quickly disappeared.

"Yeah. Scared. His mother's sitting there with blood on her face. What's the *matter* with you?"

He whirled to leave, steadied himself on the doorframe. When she could hear him moving heavily up the stairs, Lee got an umbrella, her coat and Toby's, and headed out to find her son.

Connor's mother, Marina, was one of the people Lee would like to really know in this new place, as soon as there was time. She would take that hike with Marina and her outrageous mother, Phoebe, along the Griggstown canal towpath. She'd learn how Marina got such fabulous effects in the photographs she shot, how she'd happened to marry a Syrian, what it was like to have two kids as far apart in age as Connor and Samira. Someday when there was time, they would be friends. For now, they were Connor's Mother and Toby's Mother, their boys constant companions, classmates at the day school, and the only topic of the two women's conversation.

"Lee, why don't you and Toby stay for dinner? We're having salmon. Mom's in the city for the weekend and Oscar just called that he's working late, so we have plenty."

Lee sensed that Toby hadn't said anything to Connor and his mother, but it couldn't be too difficult to notice that she and Toby were not their usual selves—especially since Toby had arrived at the Setons' coatless and wet.

"Here, you. Looks like you forgot this." Lee handed Toby his winter jacket.

"I did get him to take the soaked sweater off." Toby was wearing an argyle knit of Connor's. "Both you fellas think you're invincible, I know. But it's better not to run around in the rain with no coat." Marina smiled reassuringly at Lee.

It was important to Lee to keep the boys' alliance nice and simple, and to keep the secrets of the Montagna family within the walls of their house. She had to get Toby out of the Setons' before too much was known, before Marina decided Toby's life was not one her Connor should be part of, before this woman she wanted as a friend learned things that could make that impossible.

"May we take a rain check on dinner? We ate early and I promised Toby we'd go to the Garden to see the movie. He must have forgotten. It's *Hello, Dolly*. C'mon Toby, what a face. No really, I saw the play before it had music and it's funny. You'll like it."

"Yeah, Toby. Listen to your mother. Connor's dad and I saw the movie and it was great.

"Mom, can I go with Toby? I hate salmon."

Lee seized on the idea. "Good idea, Connor." Having him with her and Toby would buy Lee some time, time to decide what to say to Toby about this breach in his world. "Marina, what if I get him a hamburger at The Annex? Toby and I can have dessert and the timing will be just right for the first showing."

"C'mon, Mom, say yes. It's winter break. No homework. C'mon."

After the movie and prolonged hot cocoas at PJ's, Lee reluctantly headed back to Underwood Road, dropping Connor off, then parking around the corner from 99. Lights were on all over the house, but she had delayed going home as long as possible; it could be hours before Joe went to sleep. Seeing Maddy's lights blazing, Lee wondered if she was safe, but the girl had a lifetime of dealing with this Joe. In a flash of anger, Lee thought the drunk and the junkie deserved each other's company.

She eased Toby into the house through the back door. It was a short sprint to his room on the ground floor, where they pushed his dresser against the door. He had his own bathroom and there were twin beds—they'd manage. Something hit the floor upstairs and Toby jumped.

With no outsiders listening and no movie to distract him, he got back to what mattered. "Mom, I don't understand...."

She put her forefinger to her lips and whispered, "It's better if he thinks we're still gone. Here, I've got your book in my bag and one for me. We'll just read and be really quiet."

She handed him *Dune*, the place marked where he had left that fantasy world. He took it slowly, his eyes searching her face for answers.

She pulled *Play It As It Lays* out of her shoulder bag and sat at Toby's desk looking at the pages, thinking her life wasn't as strange as those of Didion's people. All through the house doors slammed, heavy things hit floors, metal clattered, water ran, a toilet flushed.

Lee and her son were behind a barricade, waiting for the sounds of violence to stop. It had happened before. In Saigon, surrounded by walls of mattresses, she had held him in her arms, a toddler singing "Boom boom, maman, boom boom," not understanding that the firecracker noises were not from a street festival but an attempted coup. There was a machine-gun emplacement half a block away, firing at the rebels. She had gotten him out of Saigon. She had gotten him out of New York. And still he was not safe.

When the noises stopped and she saw that Toby had fallen asleep, Lee put down her book and stretched out on the other bed. Streisand's voice trumpeted against raining on her parade until it was drowned out by the crash of surf. The scent of the sea filled Lee's lungs and she waded deeper until it was possible to stop walking, stop pushing against the muscular waves. She was soarng, safe, at home.

In the morning, she waited to hear the Buick pull away from the house before they moved the dresser. In the hall just outside his door, Toby found his bicycle, the extravagant ten-speed Joe had bought him, put there now like a hand-delivered message. Spokes had been kicked out, and the wheels were no longer circles.

"Joe wrecked my bike? But why? What did *I* do?"

> *Why? Because you were scared, because you left the ship when you*
> *saw it hit the iceberg, because the world doesn't make any sense.*

"We'll take it to the repair shop and get new wheels. It'll be good as new."

But Toby wouldn't be. Not ever again. He sat at the kitchen table while Lee fixed his Cream of Wheat. When she brought him the brown-sugar-topped bowl, he was sobbing and she sat next to him and wrapped him in her arms, rocking him back and forth, his soft hair against her cheek.

"Honest, in a few days you'll get the bike back and it'll be perfect." He didn't answer. She saw that he was staring into the white bird cage that sat in the bay window of the breakfast nook.

"Mom?" He could say nothing more. The door was open, the cage empty.

"Oh no. It's just a terrible coincidence, Toby. He couldn't have done that. He wouldn't."

But she knew that he had, and that she had to grab Toby and run. Right now. With no stopping to think of where they were going and what they would do. But this was home. This beautiful, serene shell filled with dissonance and fear was home. Their only home. The one she was making with every skill she had. The place where she and Toby were supposed to be. And where they could not be. She could make no sense of this. She needed time, and another place, to find her way through.

"We've never been to the beach, you know, the coast of New Jersey? Let's drive east and see if we find water."

Toby said nothing as Lee rummaged in the hall closet.

"I've got a good map of the state in here somewhere. You can be navigator. And you can play whatever station you want to hear. I promise no classical." She knew it was pointless to try to make him smile, but she wanted the devastation in his face to go away.

She put the map in front of him as she stood beside him, enclosing him with her arms and the map. "Look. Point Pleasant. I say that's where we go."

"It's way too cold for the beach, Mom."

"If you're swimming, yes. But walking a beach in the winter is wonderful. We'll wear warm coats and our slickers over them."

Lee headed her Volvo toward country roads that bore south then eastward, Toby calling the upcoming turns. A pop rock station blasted forth from the car speakers, blessedly making conversation impossible. She didn't have to talk about what had happened or what she was going to do. For now she could concentrate on driving, keeping pace with the rush of cars and trucks on the highways.

But in little more than an hour they were parked, facing the pulsing gray sea through the watery windshield. They would have to talk now. Lee found herself wishing she could make the wipers move at the same tempo as the waves; they were going much too fast, even on the slowest setting.

"It's too early to eat, right? You're not hungry yet?"

He shook his head. "Not for awhile."

"OK there's a hood on your slicker and you've got boots. Let's walk."

The beach was completely empty and almost all the shops along the boardwalk shuttered. Sea and sky and beach were all of the same grayness, making the woman and the boy shine brightly in their glistening yellow coats.

Toby's eyes were down, searching for anything of interest that might have washed onto the sand. His hands filled with shells and sea-worn bits of glass.

Lee tried to find the line between sky and sea but it was as indistinct as the picture of what it was she was supposed to do. She listened for the voice in the water and was sure it was saying Run! as each wave crashed in, Now! as it withdrew.

"Why did he do it, Mom?" Toby threw everything he had collected onto the sand and started kicking each piece as far as he could.

"It." The purple cows. The bicycle. Bilbo. Toby had seen Joe's doppelganger and now she must talk to him about that.

"I've never told you about the times when Joe gets strange because I was always sure I could make everything better, and it would never happen again, so you'd never have to know. And I was sure he wouldn't do anything to make you unhappy."

"But I knew, Mom. He broke *doors*. In New York. I knew *you* didn't do that."

Lee was grateful for the rain so her son would not see the tears that followed his words. She had not protected him from the knowledge that something was terribly wrong. He knew, had known for years. He had simply assumed that she had done things so infuriating that she had caused his hero's explosions. It was true and it was not true and the pain of it was unbearable.

"Yes, he gets terribly angry, but it doesn't have to be something that would make *anybody* mad. It's more like he disappears into his own world where it's all clear to him but not to me. Like you can't see now why he would be so mad at you. It just doesn't make any sense."

They sat on a boardwalk bench, as Lee talked about the way different cultures express anger, about drinking and how it could distort reality and lead to actions that people regretted.

"Can we get him to stop?"

"Not 'we.' Me. I have to figure this out. You're 12 years old and you're not responsible for any of this, the grownups are. You didn't do anything wrong, you got that? You didn't do one damn thing wrong."

On the drive home, Toby turned the dial to WQXR and left it there through almost two hours of Bach cello suites and rain-assaulted roads. Lee kept their speed low, not wanting to aquaplane out of control in the now deep pools of water, as she focused on the surrounding too-fast traffic, and on her options.

She could admit her inability to raise Toby and ask Tim to come for him, to take him to his new post in Karachi.

She and Toby could move into her parents' house in Aiken, and she could find a job there, perhaps as a postal clerk.

She could convince Joe that he was an alcoholic and get him into detox and AA.

She could try to get her old job back in New York, live with Toby in a coldwater flat, fighting rats and cockroaches.

She could invent a reverse Jekyll-Hyde formula that would keep Mr. Hyde from taking Joe over.

She wondered which scenario was the most preposterous. Certainly Karachi was the most painful.

When they arrived back at 99, there was a duplicate of Toby's bicycle just where the damaged one had been. Joe and Bilbo—or his newly-bought twin—were both whistling in the kitchen.

"Ah there you are. I know how much you two like breakfast for dinner, so I thought I'd surprise you."

Lee stared at him. He was asking if they wanted pecans in their pancakes, handing her a cup of hot coffee. He said nothing about the cows, the bike, or the bird. She could see her son's silent confusion, his stifled doubts, his dubious, cautious relief. She could see him beginning to do what she had done again and again, accepting the return of this smiling, beguiling, generous man, setting the boy to wonder if what he'd seen just hours before was real or if he'd imagined it, if he'd had a dreadful nightmare that he could now put behind him.

And she knew that the madness of the secret, dissonant Joe-Lee duet had now become a trio.

Something had to be done. For Toby, she'd left the Congo, left Vietnam, left Tim, left New York. But she could not leave the man who was now bringing her son warmed maple syrup, the man who must realize, this time, what he had done, and was making amends.

She had to find a way to keep this good man present, always. There was no potion, and convincing him to detox and join AA was never going to work. There had to be something else.

"Your turn." Joe smiled and handed her an apple, a pear, and an orange from the basket they had brought, and a new white handkerchief. "It's good," he whispered and beamed at her, squeezing her hand.

She took her offerings into the small room where her initiation as a transcendental meditator would be conducted. Joe was already in the fold, trained to go instantly to his own core radiant being, to hover there outside space and time, and to come back unburdened by stress, by long-harbored fears and causes for anger. Toby would go next, after Lee.

She had found The Answer. Joe would emerge from the light of meditation as only himself, leaving behind the darkness that kept spawning his Mr. Hyde. These followers of the Beatles' guru were lecturing to packed halls at the University, their presentations filled with stats on lowered crime rates, lowered blood pressure, cessation of substance abuse, and higher grade-point averages. All very pragmatic, as though they were not discussing anything in the least spiritual. But the process came out of a religion and a set of beliefs that didn't match those Lee had been taught about the war between darkness and light. She challenged the baby-faced speaker who was describing TM.

"You say that this place in yourself where meditation takes you, that it's a good place, that it's bright and peaceful. What if you got in there and it wasn't? What if it was dark, evil?"

The speaker looked at her kindly. "If you did that, found your center was evil, you'd be the first person in five thousand years. I'd say it's highly unlikely."

So they were here, at the induction ceremony, with their fruits and white cloths, Joe and Lee with checks, Toby with a month's allowance. It had taken some doing, but Toby was game if the Beatles were, and the lecturer's stats had given Joe his own way to say yes.

"My blood pressure's high. So's Dad's. Let's check this out. If it lowers my numbers, I'll get the old man to do it too."

Maddy, well Maddy might get there if somebody told her it was a better hit than her current favorite drug, whatever that might be. But three household members out of four wasn't bad, and Lee was sure that this answer from another culture would mean that she and Toby could live permanently in only one reality. It was worth the world.

Lee handed her offerings to the instructor, a tall, balding man she knew to be a history teacher at the high school. There was a small altar, pictures of the guru and his guru, all surrounded by flowers and new meditators' edible offerings. Her initiator motioned her to his side, then began a long succession of Hindi words until he got to one he repeated, gesturing for her to say it with him. She did, until the sound became internal and she felt some part of herself leaving the room, hovering in a still place where she was simply present, with no analysis or thought, her edges gone, opening her to be seamlessly part of something that was whole and pure and loving.

A sudden percussion in the room brought her hurtling back. A ball. A ball was bouncing against the door. Toby was out there, waiting for her to come out.

No. She had to have this time. Just for the word. Just for herself in this wonderful stillness. She brought the word back to her mind and fell and rose, returning to the good place.

The ball hit the door again and again and she began to sob.

When she emerged, Joe was waiting for her, filled with concern. "What happened? You were in there forever."

"It would have helped if you'd stopped Toby."

"Toby what? I was down the hall talking to these guys about Dad's blood pressure. What'd Tobe do?"

She wondered what it would be like to take a bath without hearing about someone's needs, through the locked door. To read a whole chapter of a book without being asked to solve a problem for a child or a workman or a husband.

But somehow she would get away from all of them. She didn't have to hope for the beautiful sea dream now, she could escape at will. She would get in her car if she had to, and drive somewhere they couldn't find her. And she would think this strange word that would carry her, if only for moments, to "the place where nothing is real, a place you can go where everything flows."

Those Beatles were onto more than music.

In the Land
Of the Silent G

All through the long night across the Atlantic, the passengers' sleep was interrupted by repeated sing-song calls of "Signoreeena," the voices hitting a high note on the "eee." At least a dozen of the seats on the Alitalia flight were occupied by short, black-clad, Italian matrons, all of them requiring pillows, water, extra desserts, blankets, and bits of information.

"Nonna's going home to see her sisters," Joe whispered.

Lee moved her pillow closer to his. "Lots and lots of nonnas. We're surrounded."

"Their sons have made it in America, and they can afford to go home and gloat."

"They've been waiting hand-and-foot on those sons for decades and they're gonna get all that service back, before this plane lands." She put an arm across his chest, glad that he had raised the armrest between them when they reclined their seats. Nothing was going to make this journey an unhappy one, not demanding nonnas, not a long night of trying to sleep in a chair, not the burning in her chest. Lee was determined not to mentally edit a single moment in this time-out from their normal world.

An empty champagne bottle festooned with pink and blue ribbons protruded from the seat pocket in front of Joe. Good old Tate. Lee couldn't imagine how he had managed to have the bottle brought to them as the plane reached altitude over Nantucket. Perhaps the tight security procedures at JFK were just more rules that didn't apply to the Altridges of the world. Tate certainly didn't look like a Cuban highjacker.

Joe, in his delight, had insisted that the stewardess bring glasses for all the passengers in Row 11, exhorting them to toast his wife, the beautiful pregnant wife he was taking to Italy. Lee approved his generosity, glad that it meant there would be only a sip for Joe himself. It was time to believe that Joe really had stopped drinking, that meditation truly had changed him, but Lee was still skittish about alcohol in any form. Even beribboned Dom Perignon.

"Right. Nonna's not going to waste time sleeping. But you have to, Leedle. I want you to sleep."

He smoothed a warm, broad hand along her cheek. Coming to a lock of hair that had fallen there, he moved it back, off her face.

She fitted the bridge of her nose into the curve of his neck. "But have you noticed they never call the stewards?"

"Of course not. Catering to your every whim is women's work."

"Don't you wish." Lee laughed quietly.

It was true that Joe had been the one in attendance for some time now, pampering his adored wife. As a regular meditator and a man who was to be a new father again after thirteen years, Joe was happier than Lee had ever seen him. He seemed to have indeed transcended, rising to be only and always Good Joe, even a Good Joe who thought having another child was a grand and wonderful thing. It would be a girl, Lee's girl, so she would have both a son and a daughter. It was only fair, he told her. And wonderful. There would be a little Leedle.

After months of living with only Good Joe, of being pregnant after years of assuming that as an un-woman she was immune, after months of floating every morning and evening in her mantra-induced calm, Lee knew that she too was happy. She pulled Joe's hand to rest with hers on the small belly she had already made.

"Say good night to Kate. Maybe it'll convince her to settle down."

"Oh. I felt that." Sky eyes crescented at Lee. "Like a butterfly." He mock-frowned at Lee's midsection, the overhead reading light making blue sparkles in his black hair. "Go to sleep, Katiegirl. Your mom needs to rest." He reached up and flipped off the light.

Lee pulled the thin airline blanket around her shoulders and counted benefices. So much good here, with Joe falling happily asleep next to her and Kate somersaulting inside her. They were halfway to Italy, a country she loved, where their name would be the beautiful "Moantanya," not a graceless Montagnuh. Things were even good behind her, back on Underwood Road. Toby and Connor were still inseparable, Ivan the Amazing full grown and their constant companion. Maddy was shaping up. Sort of. She was taking her dining hall job seriously, getting there on time, even working extra hours. A dress code meant she spent most of her waking hours reasonably clad, and the co-workers who had come by the house were fairly normal blue-collar kids, making vigorous fun of the Princeton students they served meal after meal. Maddy had even been seen to smile at Toby, more than once.

The ground floor rooms were nearly finished and the kitchen was done, a huge restaurant stove presiding under a range hood she'd bought with the check from *Our Times*. The nursery was painted a honey yellow, brightly jonquiled curtains caught the incoming sun, a matching quilt covered a single bed next to the white baby basket with its dotted-Swiss canopy, for the nights when their Kate might need a parent close by.

Lee would have all the bedrooms and baths done, maybe by the end of the year, if the money held out, which looked likely. Joe hadn't protested a renovation bill for months, paying them all without comment, even telling her how much he liked the rebuilt kitchen and the way she'd extended the once tiny living room. He had been so even-keeled since becoming a meditator that Celeste was gently campaigning to have Stefan sign on too. Lee wanted her friend's life to be as steady as her own now was.

And there was Dasya. Lee had discovered that most of the huge houses in the neighborhood used their extra bedrooms to house students, in exchange for babysitting and household chores. At Marina's urging, Lee had converted the attic at 99 into a pleasant bed-sitter and bath now occupied by one Dasya Srinigar, an ever-cheerful mathematics student half-a-world away from home. Das was companion to Toby, yard man to Lee, sometime-driver to Joe and—happily—nothing to Maddy. With her years of Southern living, Maddy did not consider the brown young man a possible bedmate and he, resolutely clean and sober, and about twenty pounds short of Maddy's extravagant weight, was suitably terrified of her. Toby liked having a nineteen-year-old big brother, especially one who could help with advanced algebra. It was working out spectacularly well.

Still, Lee had balked at being away for almost an entire month, no matter how much she loved May in Italy. But Marina was adamant that having Toby stay with Connor was a gift, and that she would contact the appropriate number on the itinerary Lee had given her if there were any problems at all, which there wouldn't be, Marina was sure.

All Lee's pending MAA reports were duly edited, printed and delivered to clients; Tate was covering Joe's bases in client-tending. And there was a project of her own, a book she had imagined when her family's experience with meditation began with such astonishingly good fallout. She had proposed a book on new meditators' experiences and there was interest—if the Maharishi, now ensconced near Rome, agreed to cooperate, she would put it together, the first-ever book that would have "by Lee Montagna" on the cover. The plane raced her toward the meeting that would determine the book's fate. It really was all going to work—the book, the trip, the business, the pregnancy, the family, the house. The life.

As thin morning light seeped into the cabin, Lee raised her shade, hoping to see Alps, instead blinking at the bright white tops of mashed-potato clouds. She smelled sausage and gagged. The signoreenas were moving down the aisle with breakfast trays. Joe finished off both their breakfasts, Lee was sipping barely warm tea and eating a cold bun when the captain announced that the baggage handlers at Ciampino had just walked out. The flight crew would do their best to assist in unloading luggage and volunteers would be welcome to join them. Joe laughed out loud.

"Perfect. Welcome to Italy, we're on strike today. *Sciopero*. A fine word I learned at my father's knee."

"And the consequent *chiuso*." Black eyebrows moved toward the bridge of his fine straight nose and Lee quickly added, "Doesn't that mean 'closed'?"

Lee's plans for this month of May included seeming to be as new to Italy as Joe would be. He would be out of his element here, not the cocky New Yorker he'd been among the government types in Washington, not the native son he'd been in New York, nor the somewhat uneasy interloper on Underwood Road. Joe had never left the country before; if he was to enjoy this adventure, Lee knew she would have to share the newness with him. They would be two innocents abroad.

Jet-lagged passengers milled about under the plane's wings and belly as the pilot, co-pilot, and stewards worked the cargo bay, lowering suitcases and boxes into the arms of male passengers. Joe sweated among them, cheerfully playing stevedore as stewardesses helped the chirping nonnas identify trunks and rope-tied cardboard boxes. Lee sat on Joe's bag as the weary travelers gradually dispersed into the terminal, heaving and dragging their belongings with them—the Italian equivalents of Sky Caps had joined the impromptu walkout.

They were the last passengers on the tarmac when Joe told her, "I climbed up there myself, and it's definitely not there."

Lee searched for words she might use to explain to Ashley and Pru that the beautiful maternity clothes she'd borrowed from them were all gone. She tried to get her mind around losing a maternity wardrobe twice in a week, but she couldn't manage it. The first time, it had been her own newly made outfits, a set of pieces she'd sketched and had made by a dressmaker. Three pairs of pants, two skirts, three dresses, two jackets, and a jumper she could wear with her regular shirts, all the new pieces in fabrics and colors that worked together, all beautifully made and all stolen out of Joe's car an hour after he had picked them up.

His solution was an immediate trip to Bonwit's, but after buying the loose jacket and wraparound pants she wore for the flight, Lee had insisted on putting out an SOS. Now Pru's batik dress—ankle-length on Pru, floor-sweeping on Lee—her linen sundress and jacket, Ashley's three-piece silk suit, her knit-front jeans and slacks—every beautiful, borrowed stitch was gone.

Lee and Joe checked into their frescoed and ormuloed hotel and got the concierge's directions to an elegant clothing shop. There Lee found just one garment she thought would work, if only for the weeks they'd be in Italy: an absurdly priced, empire-waisted dress in dark blue jersey with just enough gathers to accommodate a five-month pregnancy. The saleswoman, perfectly fitted into a straight black kidskin skirt and white silk sweater, her nails, coiffure and makeup all camera-ready, informed the flight-bedraggled Lee that she would find no suitable maternity clothes for sale in the city; Roman women had them custom-made.

Before Joe could perform for this formidable new audience, ordering up unneeded, costly things, Lee managed to get him out of the shop and into more mundane surroundings. She needed a toothbrush, underwear, and some washable shirts she could use with the pants suit she was wearing, and might be wearing for most of the weeks ahead. She had basic cosmetics in her handbag, and buying Italian shoes had been on her silent agenda for weeks. The trip would be fine; though apologizing to Pru and Ashley at the end of it would not be. And there was the concern she was brushing away, the one that said there might be a dire message in the rapid disappearance of two entire sets of maternity clothes.

She was their navigator for the city, constantly consulting her Michelin guides, reading out loud from the Green about each point of interest, asking Joe what he wanted to see. He left restaurants to her and she guided them to the ones described in the Red guide as *"tipica romana," "rustica," "trattoria d'habitués,"* or to ones she simply remembered as favorites, but this she never said. Joe's swagger was slipping, trying hard to seem savvy, saying he didn't care about "little details" that could be left to her. In return, she feigned amnesia about this country she'd explored repeatedly. When she wanted to sit in the Piazza Navona and have the perfect chocolate *tartufo,* to sip a Cinzano on the terrace of the Casina Valadier and watch the city turn gold at sundown, to buy her favorite brand of shoes from the small shop in the old wall, to be re-horrified by the picture in St. Peter's of Roman soldiers cranking a live saint's intestines onto a winch—she pretended to have been led to these wonders by the guidebooks.

But neither the books nor her memories had brought them to their luxe hotel. When they'd talked with the travel agent in Princeton, Lee had inquired about *pensiones*. "I understand that they're charming and comfortable. Can you suggest some good ones?"

But Joe had overruled her, to the delight of the agent. "No, no. I'm taking my girl to Italy and it's got to be first-class all the way."

By the third day in Rome she had forgotten her concern about the bills that would be coming in. Whatever it cost, it just might be worth it. She loved the feel of heavy linen sheets, crisply washed and ironed, on the bed every day before her treasured post-prandial nap. Coming in after exploring Caracalla or the Palatine and a long, leisurely lunch, she would adjourn to the shower, where a gleaming, head-to-toe spiral of pipes made movement unnecessary. She considered the possibility that plumbing caused the fall of the Empire. Thousands of Romans in spiral showers had simply refused to come out and take care of business.

She had always been intrigued by small things in foreign places—the doorknobs, the light switches, the phones—all of them strange, reminding her, with everything she touched, that she was not at home. She turned off the strange faucets and left water heaven to pull a huge, heated bath sheet off the strange hot-water-pipe towel rack and drape it around herself, toga style. It was then irresistible to address the steamy, mirrored wall.

"Good Caesar, heed thee now thy concern-ed wife and go not to the Forum today."

"Leedle? Who are you talking to in there? And when are you coming out?"

Wearing one of Joe's T-shirts, she propped herself up on the plump linen-cased pillows, knowing that a horizontal angle would bring the lunch she had so enjoyed burning into her chest and throat.

Joe wasn't interested in siesta breaks, but assured her that he would meditate before plowing into one of the Department of Labor reports he'd brought along to study. She knew he'd be too tired, again, to last through a properly late Roman evening. He settled into the easy chair where she had moved the room's best reading light. It had become Joe's Chair, hers being the one she'd pushed up to the window that looked down on a lovely park and the vivid Roman street scene. She wasn't much interested in reading these days, but she watched people for hours, hoping their lives were working out well.

After brief consideration of the angels on the ceiling and a short encounter with her mantra, she dreamt of wild strawberries and splashing fountains until Joe woke her at five, eager to begin the evening.

"I went for a walk. Everything's *chiuso*. How do they get anything done?"

"Maybe they've already done it. I mean, everything's built, found, sculpted, painted, accomplished. Maybe they just want to enjoy it all. And to snooze in the afternoons."

Joe's tempo meant he was hungry when Romans were not even thinking about dinner. Lee ordered up room-service cheeses and breads in the evening, hoping they would keep him going until 9 when the tavernas and trattorias would begin filling with Romans, enjoying their city.

Dressing on their third morning, Joe shot his cuffs and buttoned his blazer. "Thank you for looking like that."

She'd put on a new yellow shirt and her full-cut jacket, which covered the unusable lower buttons of the shirt. She was clean and rested, her lipstick was on straight, but she wasn't sure what he meant.

"I thought you'd go all to pieces. You know, slop around with stringy hair."

"Because I'm pregnant? Why would I do that?"

To Lee, being pregnant was all the more reason to heed her appearance. For all the relief of living week after week with Good Joe, she knew something else was happening, something that held him distant. And she didn't want to move him any farther away. He was playing *Paul*, holding the virtual palm branch over her, sheltering her from harm, but he was not touching her. He had stopped raging, but he had also stopped wanting her, whether her hair was combed or not.

She accounted it to a knightly nervousness about causing harm, or perhaps some off-putting memories of his first wife pregnant. Still, he was obviously enjoying the 'good-for-you' looks he was getting as waiters and taxi drivers and desk clerks fussed over his pregnant wife. He was a lucky man and a potent one. She was his proof, even if not presently his lover.

She was concerned, but her body was not. It was fully occupied with the gestation job at hand and with the mellow colors and textures of the city, with the sensual pleasures of sheets and showers, crusty breads and pungent sauces and fresh-fruit *gelatis*. And there, with her, was a charming and predictable Joe. Fretting about anything at all seemed ungrateful, and could even be an opening for the wonders to cease.

She pretended to learn the words *"fragolini con panna,"* and for her own pleasure, said them at every opportunity. Beaming waiters couldn't move fast enough to bring the tiny wild strawberries heaped with whipped cream to *la rossa incinta*, the pregnant redhead.

Five days after they'd landed, it was Christmas in May—her suitcase appeared on a luggage rack in their room, with an apology from Alitalia. Somehow the bag had made its way to Tel Aviv. Suddenly she had scarves, jewelry, slippers, nightgowns, and Pru and Ashley's wonderful maternity clothes.

"Well, my beauteous Leedle, we have to celebrate this. Give me that book."

"Oh, are you sure? I mean, I don't mind being the researcher."

"And you've been doing a good job, too good. Let's blow some money, honey."

Reluctantly, Lee handed over the Michelin red guide.

It was only seven o'clock but the decibel level in the many-crossed-forks-&-spoons restaurant was off the chart, the air was solid smoke and the lights were an assault. The captain pulled out a table along a banquette and Lee squeezed in between two strangers as Joe took the chair in the busy aisle. Settling her bag into the inch of space at her side, she realized that she could hear no Italian in the din. German and American voices were all around them. She leaned across the minuscule table.

"What did the guidebook recommend here?"

"I don't remember. I'm going to order the veal."

Pointing to the menu, he asked their waiter to explain *lombartine* and *al cartoccio*. *Vitello* he knew. The man's response was an eye roll. Lee ordered the *abbacchio al forno* and asked that the Valpolicella Joe had ordered be brought before the meal—it might stop him from ordering a pre-dinner Scotch.

She talked about the wild Roman drivers whipping around the traffic circles in their tiny Fiats. "It used to be Vespas—in the movies—now it's all cars. No more pretty girls on the backs of bikes with their skirts blowing up." She noted the Italian peacock culture that put so much money on everyone's backs. She asked if Joe would mind setting out for Fiuggi by nine the next morning, and shared her hope that this trip to the Maharishi's encampment would win his imprimatur for her book.

"Thanks for understanding how important this is to me. With Dasya helping at home and my work leveling off at MAA, I'm actually going to be able to do this. It's wonderful. Really exciting."

Joe fussed that the contractors might not have delivered the enormous attic fan they wanted installed before summer, when Lee would need the cooling air currents it would make in the house. The previous summers in the Jersey heat had been hard enough for her; a pregnant Jersey summer would be far worse. He fretted that Tate would need his help at a meeting Tuesday in DC, that Maddy might be thinking up a new disaster, worried that Toby might be lonely.

"At Connor's house? He *loves* it there. Connor's his best friend ever. And he's got all those art projects with Phoebe. Best of all, Marina lets them stay up till midnight watching television."

"Well, that's not good. He'll get too tired for his morning classes. Maybe we should call." Joe looked around for a phone.

"Come on, luv. She only does it on the weekends. And have you calculated the time in Princeton? We can send him a postcard tomorrow. I've sent cards to him and the girls, to the Setons, Tate and Pru, Celeste and Stefan, the Clays, Judith, Dasya, the MacGregors gang, everybody. We can send Toby a picture of the Coliseum. Tomorrow."

At last the waiter appeared with their wine, uncorked it, dripped a trail of red dots across the sleeve of Joe's camelhair jacket as he poured two glasses without waiting for Joe to taste it, offered no assistance, muttered something, and disappeared. Lee quickly soaked her napkin in her water glass and passed the cloth to Joe as the red stains grew larger.

"What was that he said?"

"It's not important."

"Your face turned red."

"OK, OK. He called me an American ass. In Italian. I wasn't supposed to know what he'd said."

Lee knew that Joe, Mr. Labor, was not going to say anything that would get a working man into hot water, but this was just too much to take silently. She looked around the huge, reverberating restaurant and motioned to the captain.

"Do not send that waiter back to this table. He has ruined my husband's jacket and insulted him."

The captain served their meal himself, beautifully, without further incident. Nor was there further conversation after Joe, his face flushed, hissed, "You just got that guy fired—he's going to lose his *job*."

"Well, if he hates tourists so much, maybe he'll be happier doing something else."

> *Ohdamnohdamn. It doesn't matter if I'm right. If I'm sticking up for my guy. I think I just killed the good times. Me and my big mouth.*

Joe kept his eyes on his food for the rest of the meal. Lee pushed morsels of lamb around her plate, yearning to breathe better air and to move her atrophying legs, yearning to get away from the noise and glare and smoke, and from Joe's hard silence.

When their places were cleared and she reached for her bag, Joe ordered a double cognac and sat his ground, staring past her at the wall as he finished it off, very, very slowly. Not even meditation was strong enough to change Joe. It was over.

She had planned to be up and ready for breakfast by seven thirty, but she saw it was eight when she opened her eyes. The loss of her new certainty that life was safe had kept her conscious until exhaustion took her down into the safety of the seaworld where there were no dangers, where she wanted to stay and not wake up to the day. She sat up in the linen-swathed bed.

Joe was gone. She dressed quickly and headed down to the dining room, hoping he would be there, that he wasn't blowing off the excursion to Fiuggi, that he hadn't gotten on a plane, leaving the bitch who got poor working stiffs fired to fend for her bitch self.

Standing in the ornate lobby, watching her descend in the lace metal cage, Joe made no response to her wave, to her too-bright smile. She knew the drill. Approach with caution, make no reference to recent unpleasant events. Be cheerful. Chipper even. Amusing. This time was not out of joint. And she had been born to set it right.

"My, but you're looking dapper there in your suedeness. Could you be Gianni Agnelli perchance? At least an Orsini."

"We can't go."

"We gotta go, *caro*. I have to be in Fiuggi by noon and we have to allow some time for finding it."

"We are not going anywhere."

Lee saw the strong old house on the street roofed by sycamores, saw Joe holding Kate in the white wicker rocking chair, saw Toby's graduating class partying in the flower-filled garden, saw all the scenes and rituals that were to come, the trimming of Christmas trees and the wedding receptions and the Easter egg hunts, all of it sliding away, never to happen. There was no "we." She would not spend the rest of May as Signora Montagna here. And she wouldn't be Lee Montagna, beloved wife and mater familias in her own country, in her life. She and Toby—and Kate—were on their own.

She took a step back toward the elevator. Joe put his hand on her arm.

"Bastards are telling me the only car they've got is some dinky sports car. You did tell them I wanted a full-size four-door?"

She was too startled to know the answer, then remembered that there was proof, in her shoulder bag, proof that would end this minor matter. Their lives were intact.

"You want to see the confirmation they sent?"

"Yeah give it to me. I'll make the son of a bitch eat it."

In the shade of the hotel's vast porte-cochere, a thin, irritated young Italian tossed a set of car keys into the air impatiently as he leaned against the side of a low, white Maserati.

"That's the car?" The look on the young man's face as he saw Joe answered her question.

"But we didn't pay for anything like that. Just for an ordinary car."

"That's what *he* said. Like I should be pleased."

She nodded at the Maserati's keeper as Joe briefed her on the crisis. It seemed the agency had run short of cars, too many in the repair shop they said. This was a personal car of the agency's owner, commandeered to accommodate Joe this morning when he insisted they find him a goddam car.

Lee pointed out that there was a luggage rack on the back and a space behind the two seats. She was sure she could fit everything in when they began their touring, and for this quick overnight trip, they had only the shoulder bag she was holding, with their toothbrushes and clean underwear. Surely they could manage. But Joe was adamant. He didn't know why the guy was even hanging around. They were going back into the hotel and to hell with Fiuggi.

"Joe, it took me weeks to set up that meeting and that's the most beautiful car I have ever seen so why don't we just try it out...."

She started toward the car, but he reached for her arm again, pulled her close to him and said, *sotto voce,* "I don't think I can drive the friggin thing."

Joe who could do anything. Joe who was always in command. She caught her breath, knowing that pushing him into such an admission might have moved her back onto a precipice.

"Neither can I, luv, but how hard could it be? We can figure it out and it's mostly nice wide highway according to the map. We just have to avoid death getting out of Rome."

She started to laugh and it worked. A gleam appeared in the pale eyes.

"What the hell." He grinned, grabbed her hand and fairly bounded to the car. He took the keys from the Roman in mid-toss. "*Molto grazie,* pal." He stuffed a 10,000 lire note into the startled man's shirt pocket. "Take a cab."

Despite some much too visible lurching, wincingly audible gear-grinding, and one hair-raising experience of entering a street marked *senso unico,* they made it onto the pedal-to-the-metal *autostrada,* to endure much irate honking by the Italians rocketing past them. When they exited onto the first minor road that would lead them to Fiuggi, they pulled off in a village and sat for awhile on a park bench, celebrating their survival, thus far.

"I come from a long line of madmen. That last Ferrari must have been doing over a hundred."

"I think you disappointed him."

"What?"

"You wouldn't play."

"Me?"

"Yeah. You in the hot new Maserati. The guy wanted to race and you're poking along at 70. You're no fun at all."

"That's me. You can take the boy out of his Buick...."

Fiuggi had been taken over by the Maharishi's entourage and hundreds of transcendental meditators. Lee's contact was the press officer of the operation, a young German baron, gracious and eager to introduce her to the spokesman for His Holiness, not so keen on the possibilities of a meeting with the Maharishi himself.

"You will please this afternoon attend *darshan*. After that, we will talk more. Now, you will rest from your journey."

They were assigned a simple room in a private house, all the town's public accommodations having been filled with young Europeans and Americans who spent their time meditating in their rooms, coming out only for meals and for *darshan*, the sessions when the Maharishi sat on a deerskin, surrounded by flowers, answering questions and leading group meditations.

As Lee and Joe were escorted to front row seats by the baron, the Maharishi beamed at Lee, pressed his palms together, and nodded. *"Jai guru dev jai guru dev jai guru dev."*

She returned the little man's gesture and looked her question to the baron, who whispered that he would explain, later.

"Maharishi, you have said that anyone who meditates will become better at what he does. But what if the person is a thief?" Lee turned to see that the Scandinavian-accented question was from a tall blonde in a sari.

The guru seemed pleased, a star batter swinging at a home-run pitch. "To be a better thief is no longer to be a thief." The assemblage laughed quietly.

"Maharishi, there is criticism in the press, especially in this Catholic country, that the west has its own religions, that Eastern religions are not needed here. How do you answer those critics?" The questioner was a teenaged boy who spoke with the hard r's and flat a's of Chicago. "How do *I* answer my *parents?*"

There was louder laughter and what felt like a collective leaning forward. The tiny dark-skinned man in white robes, surrounded by pale Western faces, was silent a moment. He was not, Lee thought, looking for an answer but considering how much to say of what he was thinking.

"Western religions teach, Be good and you will see God." Another silence. "It is very difficult to be good." The listeners murmured their agreement. "Eastern religions show you God." A small smile and a twinkle. "It is then quite difficult to be bad."

Lee took in a gulp of air at the realization that this might be the truest thing she had ever heard. The glowing place of rightness that she entered with her mantra was affecting everything, making it easier to do what was right to do, even when she was frightened. Joe too was seeing God and it had become difficult to be that other Joe. Not impossible, she realized, just difficult. But with more meditation, more time with God, it might become impossible.

After more questions and answers that she missed in her thoughts about the effects of seeing God, the Maharishi led a meditation and then was escorted away. The young German began to talk about arranging a meeting with Jimmy, the Maharishi's Number One. She touched his arm. "That was the deepest I've ever gone in a meditation. Is it him or being with all these people? Or was it what he said—about seeing God?"

"It was perhaps all of those things. Perhaps it was also that he was giving you a special blessing. I have never heard him greet anyone as he greeted you."

"All that jaigurudeving? He could have been greeting a TM baby. This girl started the week after we began meditating." She began to say more about meditating being the key, but seeing Joe's frown she decided not to give the wise little man any credit there.

That evening they joined the guru's inner circle for dinner at Jimmy's villa, a lovely old place with exquisite tile floors and a courtyard filled with flowers tumbling out of pots and boxes. Clearly Jimmy, a balding American in a business suit, was one important fellow in this realm.

The Maharishi, Jimmy reported, would like to talk with her in Boston in July. Would she be available? Everyone seemed to think this was marvelous. But she had already come to Fiuggi. Ah, but Thursday, tomorrow, was a regular day of silence for everyone, and His Holiness had decided to stay in silence himself for the next six weeks.

Joe immediately began to negotiate with Jimmy, asking if a large donation would get the guru to look at Lee's proposal now.

"He doesn't have to look. He says she's the right person to do the book. I'm to give you the addresses and phone numbers of any transcendental meditators you would like to interview and he's recommended several well known people who might be very interesting to readers."

Joe began to say more but Lee thanked Jimmy warmly and tugged Joe toward the buffet.

"I bring you half way around the world and the little creep stiffs us? I don't believe it."

"No no, I've got what I wanted. *Without* talking to him. In Boston, I'll interview him and ask him to write a foreword. It's OK, *really.*" She surveyed the impressive array of vegetarian dishes, spooned pasta in a green sauce onto Joe's plate and her own. "Lovely. It's basil. Mmm and garlic. Smell."

While Joe read through Jimmy's magazines, Lee talked with a rock guitarist from Belfast, a French nuclear physicist, and Bunny, a tiny, white-haired heiress who would be hosting the Maharishi in Boston. Bunny had already decided which of the 14 bedrooms in her house would be Lee's. It was all set.

Lee approached the most exotic person present, a tall, brown woman swathed in bright colors and patterns, from her wrapped head to the belled hems of her silk palazzo pants. She was, Lee discovered, an American dancer named Jamuna, now the Maharishi's driver. Best of all, she had been in a road company of *Boobs* and was delighted to share stories about Marshall Poole as she and Lee ate peanut butter cookies and sipped cardamom tea.

When Lee and Joe began making their good-nights, Bunny and Jamuna stopped them.

"You have a car here?" Jamuna was talking very quietly.

"Yes, of course."

"No one has cars here," Bunny whispered. "Except Maharishi. Are you going back to Rome tomorrow?"

After months in Fiuggi, the women couldn't take another silent Thursday if playing in Rome was a possibility. With the boss going into seclusion and therefore having no need for his driver, they figured they could get away with a quick disappearance. The tiny Maserati, they insisted, was not a problem.

"We're both very skinny." Jamuna pressed her voluminous clothing close to her sides to demonstrate. Bunny, all bones in her trim gabardine pants suit, laughed. "We'll fit quite easily behind the seats."

Joe agreed graciously, pleased, Lee thought, to aid and abet in the breaking of some of the "little creep's" rules. He would have the hotel make up two beds in the sitting room of their suite. No problem. They were his guests.

After breakfast the next morning, the two women wedged themselves behind the Maserati's seats, keeping their heads down until the car was well out of town. Bunny and Jamuna knew a different Rome than Lee's. Joe bowed out, leaving the three females to laugh their way through facials and shampoos at Elizabeth Arden, lunch at the Hassler, a sweep through the city's most elegant shops, and a visit to a gypsy fortune teller Jamuna swore had saved her life.

The dancer showed Lee an oddly marked amulet that the gypsy had given her, pulling it from the array of beads and scarves that swathed her neck above the sweeping, silk body draperies that fluttered around her when she walked.

Her head wrapped in emerald, sapphire, and ruby twists of cloth, her face broad and brown and beautiful, Jamuna was a literal traffic-stopper in Rome. Drivers hung out of car windows, veered toward oncoming trucks— there was much screeching of brakes. Cars waiting at red lights did not move after she floated past them and the light turned green.

On the narrow sidewalk that led to the gypsy's house in Trastevere, the women walked Indian file, Lee bringing up the rear. A chubby bald man stepped into the street to let them pass and stared open-mouthed at Jamuna. As Lee passed him he was murmuring in wonderment, "*Que bella negra!*"

Jamuna reported to the bleached-blonde fortune teller that she'd been wearing the amulet as directed. Was she out of danger? The woman looked into her client's teacup, studying the leaves intently.

"The evil forces have retreated but they are not gone. You will wear the amulet for three more months, but its powers must be restored."

For the payment of a great many lire, she would give Jamuna the needed instructions.

Lee was disappointed that the woman hadn't asked that her palm be crossed with silver. When Jamuna handed over the bills, the gypsy wrote something on a small piece of paper.

"Here, signorina. At midnight at next dark moon, two nursing women must sit close, one looks north, one looks south. They must each put milk in silver cup. You must put amulet into cup and say words on this paper."

Jamuna, as nonchalant as if she'd just been given directions to the super market, pocketed the note and thanked the gypsy graciously.

"Bunny, don't you have something to ask—about that problem you're having on the Cape?" Bunny, in the dark suit and pearls of a proper Back-bay matriarch, shifted uncomfortably on the hard kitchen chair. "Oh my goodness. No, not really."

Jamuna turned to Lee, who shrugged, palms up. The gypsy stood to show them out, then looked intently at Lee.

"Boys. I see three boys, three men."

Back on Via Veneto, Jamuna and Bunny introduced Lee to Café Hag, the first coffee Lee had drunk since learning she was pregnant. "The caffeine makes me too jumpy so it can't be good for the baby and Sanka is disgusting, so I just gave it up." But Café Hag was both decaffeinated and delicious. Lee sipped and puzzled over the gypsy's words. What did three boys and three men mean?

"You better figure it out, girl. That woman knows her business." Jamuna's evidence was that the unseen evil forces had still not shown themselves in her life.

Lee thought that was akin to being grateful elephants hadn't flattened your house in Indianapolis. Joe did not want a boy. He already had a boy. So did Lee. Joe said this had to be a little Leedle, so she would have both a daughter and a son. This baby was a girl and that gypsy was full of crap.

"Lee, promise you won't ever tell Maharishi we went to a fortune teller. He would be just furious." Bunny seemed sincerely concerned. Lee responded, trying to be as serious, that she couldn't imagine the subject ever coming up. Although if Jamuna managed to get two mothers milking at the next dark of the moon, the news just might get to him along the grapevine. Lee had a sudden image of Jamuna driving the holy man along some highway as she hummed "Fellatio." It seemed a long way from *Boobs* to enlightenment.

In the morning, halfway back to Fiuggi, they stopped at an inn to stretch their legs and have a bite to eat at an umbrella'd table on a sunny terrace. Lee moved her chair a few degrees across the flagstones so her legs escaped the umbrella's shadow. As warm weather began each year, inevitably she considered having tanned legs—with enough caution and patience, it might work. But by late June it was always too hot and her willingness to sit was long gone. There had always been too many more interesting things to do. But now. Now it was May in Italy and she was creating when she sat slug-still. She was still productive if her mind went to mush for days on end. This year she could have tanned legs and a baby by fall.

She folded her hands over the fine round pot that was, for a change, not in motion, and listened for a moment to the conversation. Instead she heard a wondrous concert of bird songs, all of them sounding delighted with their little lives. She wanted to record these merry creatures and play the tape for the damned doves at 99 so they'd quit with the endless mourning and live it up a little.

Her eyes settled on the valley below the terrace. Was it the Po? No, that was farther north. But she didn't have to know. She was pregnant. She didn't have to attend to Bunny and Jamuna. She could let Joe handle it all. She would smile and sit. She was pregnant.

He was doing well. Charming the socks off them. Good war stories about labor unions. He was funny and solicitous and warm. The perfect host. He had even become quite the Maserati handler, not fazed by the autostrada maniacs. She smiled, remembering how he'd brought the hot little car to a fast, smooth stop on the inn's gravel driveway. Atsa mah Giusep. It was all a foolproof performance. As usual. No one in Bunny's world had ever socialized with a labor-movement princeling before. Jamuna might know some Actors' Equity reps, but they were hardly blue-collar.

Lee saw the fascination in the women's faces, knew they would go back to their boss with glowing tales of the charming, generous, exciting fellow who had just come into their lives, a Halley's comet of competence and promise.

The innkeeper appeared in a flurry of apologies. They must forgive him. The hour was late. He had not been expecting more guests before dinner. But if they would bear with him, his son would catch some trout in the stream behind the garden and his wife would bring in some tomatoes and radicchio from the garden and he had a nice oil from the grove over there....

Lee took in the fragrance of broiled butter, studied the moist white chunk of trout balanced on her fork tines. There had never been a more perfect fish, and no tomato had ever matched the tomato-ness of these red slices sparkling with golden oil on a bed of purple leaves beside the small, fat trout. The tumbler beside her plate held a pale, fragrant Frascati, light and fresh as a May morning. She wondered if she could be happier. Then the innkeeper said he had *fragolini*, picked this morning, and life was perfect. *Abbondanza.* Her cup was definitely running over.

"Lee, dear, I can't stand it." Lee focused carefully on Bunny's excited little face. "Here I've been frantic with worry about some properties on the Cape. Big tax mess that I can't deal with from over here. And your Joe has it all figured out. He's going to straighten it out in Washington for me."

Jamuna was equally delighted. She actually had a problem with Equity and Joe knew the guy in charge in New York. It was all going to come out fine, thanks to Lee's wonderful Joe.

Lee managed to swallow a mouthful of the chilled wine. Did seeing God cover all this? Joe would actually do all the things he was promising, instead of forgetting about them? That would be truly miraculous. She smiled at them, one and all, silently wishing them well.

Back on their own, Joe and Lee fit their bags into the Maserati and set off for the north, meandering their way to Como to celebrate her birthday in a four-hundred-year-old villa where roses as large as hats were blooming on bushes so old their stems were small tree trunks, where sudden lake breezes were prevented from ruffling the hair of terrace diners by the silent, automatic raising of shimmering glass walls.

Joe bought the *International Herald Tribune* at every opportunity, poring over reports on Vietnam, on Northern Ireland, on Nixon this and Nixon that, and on the aftermath of the killing of Joey Gallo in a New York clamhouse. Lee could not bring herself to read any of it, though she did note a headline that said George Wallace had been shot. The Italian papers and television news were not interested; they were focused on what they saw as a more important story than an assassin's attempt to kill an American segregationist—some crazy person had attacked the *Pietá* with a hammer.

None of it meant as much to Lee as the omnipresence of *fragolini con panna* and of the wildflowers and grasses all along the roadways, small red poppies the brightest among them. In Florence, she found every May wild-flower and grass silk-screened onto a Gucci scarf at a fraction of the cost of Gucci silks in New York, the perfect memento of the trip, to go with the two decals she had found in a petrol station. One was a peace sign with the words, *"Fate l'amore, non la guerra;"* the other a snorting bull saying, *"Oggi mi sento un toro."* Those she would keep, but she was gathering in small presents for friends and for the kids, tucking the packages under the seats of the Maserati. For Joe, she ordered a suede-lined briefcase that would be made and sent before his birthday, a discreet JVHM tooled under the handle. He hadn't much liked the pillow she'd made for his 40th; maybe this gift would be more to his liking. On the *Ponte Vecchio*, she found an oval of pale pink coral set in a ring of gold flowers and leaves. Joe bought it and disappeared it, telling her he would put it on her hand when she was holding Kate.

On their last afternoon in Florence, Lee sought out Galileo's tomb and sat beside it in Santa Croce, reading a pamphlet on this favorite character in history. As she read the familiar account of his abjuration, tears smudged the words. She had never been able to read dispassionately as he swore "that I have always believed, believe now and, with God's help, will in the future believe all that the Holy Catholic and Apostolic Church doth hold, preach and teach." That would have to include not only that the earth was the center of the universe, but also that all other religions were demonic, that God kept accounts of indulgences and penances, that women were temptresses drawing men away from God and must be kept away from all things sacred, and that no one could ever leave the Church.

In Galileo's times they could kill you if you deviated from the Church's views, threatening to take this man's life, as painfully as it is possible to imagine, if he did not submit. They tried to kill his work and his spirit with the humiliation of this abjuration, this promise to not believe or teach what he knew to be true, even making him swear to inform the Inquisition if he found anyone else speaking scientific truths.

Outgunned, frightened, he caved to an overwhelmingly larger force. And lived to work on, in silence, in secret, despite them. Lee fervently hoped it was true that as he walked away from his submission, the old heretic said under his breath, *Eppur si muove.* And still it moves. She cheered now, silently, for the dear, magnificent coward. True remained true, no matter what the bastards made you say, no matter how much firepower they aimed at you. They could shut you up, push you to your knees, but we know what we know, always.

And now the old heretic was entombed grandly inside the Church, brought here a century after his death, his Inquisitors no longer alive to protest. A marble bust depicted him looking sadly skyward, above a carved tribute that included the words *Hic bene quiescat*.

Why didn't she believe that he was resting here in peace? Being displayed in this great church, with all the marble gewgaws, wasn't enough of an apology to produce peace. He should be buried up on a hill outside the city, where he could sit on his tombstone and watch the earth turn around the sun, just as he knew it did.

"Leedle, I found something over there that says he isn't all here."

She looked at Joe, trying to understand what he was saying.

"Part of him is across town in a science museum. Look."

He handed her the little booklet, the pages open at a picture of a glass bell with a gilded form inside. The translation read, "This is the finger with which the illustrious hand covered the heavens and indicated the immense space. It pointed to new stars with the marvelous instrument, made of glass, and revealed them to the senses." And that's not all it did, she wanted to add, as she read that it was the great man's middle finger right hand, now gilded and erect, for all time.

"This is funny? Sheesh, Leedle, you have a really weird sense of humor."

They drove through paintings, the little white car winding through the backgrounds of all the portraits of Renaissance Madonnas and grandees on the museum walls. Lee wondered which of the churches they passed had light patches on their walls that matched the frames at the Howe's house in Princeton.

The poplars, the churches, the soft round hills all sang to her. She loved the crumbling villas, the molds staining the old stucco walls, loved the flowers that burst forth from every balcony and windowsill, loved the multiple times of the place, the lifeforce of all the years and of this moment, all present, all around her, loved that every living face she saw had been sculpted centuries before.

Sitting in a town square on the worn marble steps of a church that had once been a Roman temple, she smoothed a hand across the softly curved stone, imagining the millennia of climbing feet that had shaped it. A small boy eating a gelato sat down at the other end of the step and smiled at her, dark eyes sparkling in the face of a Leonardo *putti*.

In old churches, she sketched the floor mosaics in a notebook, along with drawings of loggia-lined courtyards. With their repeating arches opening onto gardens filled with the scents of flowers and the movements and singing of birds, loggias welcomed and accommodated humans, sheltering them from sun and rain. They were, she realized, the perfect way to be both outside and inside, architecture for the sun-shy.

Everywhere they went, people knew not to pronounce the g in Montagna and the words *Signora Montagna* were as beautiful as they should be, even though the *signora* was feeling the strain of so many long days of one-on-one with the *signore*. He seemed to have forgotten her anti-workingman faux pas with the waiter in Rome and was back to being courtly, making jokes, often even enjoying himself. Still, Lee found herself sleeping more, not wanting to take the chance of saying or doing something that would again break his meditator's calm.

Charging up a hill into a walled town, the Maserati jolted to a halt in the town's gateway, the engine still racing but for some reason causing no forward movement.

"What the hell?" Joe was looking straight ahead, not down at the road where the underside of the car was caught on the sharp crest of the hill. As the car began to seesaw, all four wheels spinning in the air, they were surrounded by a pack of laughing young men in red hats with long pointed bills who simply picked the car up, the open-topped Maserati presenting the astonished Americans face-to-face to their rescuers. As the liberated car skittered away into the city's streets, Lee twisted in the seat to throw kisses and wave wildly at the laughing students.

"Did that really happen? We just got rescued by a bunch of Pinocchios?" Joe maneuvered deftly into a parking space in front of an attractive *ristorante* and slapped the steering wheel. "Damn, I love this country!"

They headed south, toward the parts of Italy Joe claimed had nothing to do with the Montagnas. They'd been northerners, he insisted, though the dark skin, barrel chest, and stocky legs Joe had inherited argued otherwise. How many Italians, Lee wondered, had left Lombardy or Umbria to struggle in turn-of-the-century New York? She hadn't recognized many people on the streets of Bologna, Parma, or Milan, but as they drove south, more and more people began to look familiar, like people who might be seen filling a church for a Long Island wedding.

Sitting in a floating restaurant at the edge of the Bay of Naples, Lee noted that the food was also familiar, the heavy red sauces, the fried cala-mari and the cannoli—it was like eating in Little Italy. Even the voices from a large table at the center of the room could have been heard on Mulberry Street. She listened, then made a slightly elaborate show of not listening.

"What's the matter? Your lunch didn't agree with you?"

"No, not at all. Lovely *stracciatelli*. And the salad had fennel in it—won-derful. But those guys...." She took the dessert menu and began pointing dishes out to Joe, smiling. "Don't look, but there are five Americans in silk suits sitting across the room, behind you, heavy New York accents. Dia-mond pinky rings. The whole bit. They look like your uncles." She turned the menu over. "And they're talking about Lucky Luciano."

Joe leaned back in his chair, seemingly ruminating on his choice. Then he stretched across the table and took Lee's hand. Smiling, whispering, like a man in love.

"Damn. What are they, idiots? They're running off at the mouth in a public place about a meeting they've got with the most notorious criminal in the world."

"Maybe they think nobody here understands English. As soon as I heard his name and Joey Gallo's, I decided I don't speak it myself." The waiter appeared for their dessert orders.

Joe said, *"Zabaglione,"* speaking with the inflections of Italy, not New York, and handed back the menu.

Lee asked only for her usual Cafe Hag, then saw with delight the bowl of beautiful fruit next to the pastries on the waiter's cart.

"Y *una peche, piacere.*"

"*Pronto, signora.*"

It was a good sign—the waiter hadn't said, "Yes, madame." Relieved, Lee was captivated by the peach as she sliced into it, revealing a perfect red pit in a ground of white, red-freckled flesh, and releasing a fragrance that was the bright essence of peach. With the first sweet, smooth bite, she knew she was experiencing peach perfection, a peach for the ages.

She was brought back to the room by the sight of an ancient, bent-in-half nun slowly coming down the gangplank and into the restaurant, a small box in her gnarled hands.

"*Elemonsina, per favore, signori.*"

Perhaps in Italy nuns too old to do the work of their orders were sent out to beg. No one seemed to mind; the waiters nodded to her, the patrons dug into their pockets and purses, dropping coins noisily into the box.

Joe folded some lire notes and laid them on top of the coins. The old nun tilted her head up from its horizontal position over the box and smiled. "*Grazie, signore.*"

A few shuffling steps and she was holding the box toward the five silk suits. Lee didn't pretend not to look as each of them pulled out money rolls the sizes of their fists and began peeling off bills. Bill after bill. Lire. Dollars. Every time the ancient nun said, "*Grazie, signori, molto grazie,*" they grinned and stuffed more bills in the box.

The nun began to cry, and Lee to clap. Joe reached out to stop her, but it spread in an instant across the restaurant. People were applauding, even calling out "*Bravi!*" and the mafiosi were taking little bows that looked almost shy. The one wearing a yellow tie winked at Lee.

Joe joined in the applause, grinning, and leaned close to her. "Think they put in enough to make it to heaven?"

The question took on more import the next morning when Joe picked up the *Herald Trib* in the Galleria. On the front page, above the fold, there was a report that the body of an unidentified, middle-aged man in an American-made suit had been found floating in the Bay of Naples. Lee wondered sadly if it had been wearing a yellow tie.

Celeste, resplendent in pea-green palazzo pants and a cotton-candy-pink jacket, giggled with delight as she hugged Lee and Joe at the Newark arrivals gate. "Guess who's meditating? Stefan!"

Joe stepped back from the lunge of her embrace, frowning. "Where's Das? He was supposed to pick us up. In our car."

"Oh, I called the house to be sure you were coming home today and he said he was cutting a class to pick you up on time. So I told him to go to the class and I'd meet you. He'll be here in an hour, so let's have a drink. Lee, you look fabulous."

"I *love* your news. Stefan meditating. *That's* fabulous."

She would wait for their real conversation, for their inevitable phone connection, to hear the story with all the details of how Celeste had managed to get Stefan to a TM meeting, to find out if he'd changed yet, as Joe had.

She would tell Celeste about the Good Joe who stayed present through-out the trip, if you didn't count one bout of silent rage, and a few narrowly averted crises. Not once had he broken something, or threatened to fire her from her job as Signora Montagna.

Later, on the phone, she would tell Celeste what the Maharishi had said about seeing God and how it would now be easier for Stefan to be good.

Pundits in the
Carriage House

Lee eased quietly across thick Persian carpets in the massive, dark bedroom with the stunning view of blue water and gently gliding sails. Bunny's grand old house on Marblehead Neck had emptied out, the Maharishi being off somewhere in Boston, Bunny and all the other house guests drawn along in his wake, every Chosen One determined to stay as close as possible to the Master. Still, Lee moved carefully, listening for sounds that would propel her instantly out of this room, the guru's private space.

She wasn't sure what she was looking for, some clue perhaps to who the renowned yogi was and what he was really up to, if that was not, as he said, the bringing of the dharma to the west, a gift, no strings, no hidden agendas.

She knew that he was bringing *her* calm times, the daily sessions when she stepped away from any fear or anger, the times when Kate stopped tumbling and, with Lee, became peaceful. Lee was sure those moments of the days made it possible for her to do her best in all the others.

Joe was still distant, even when they were in the same room, the same bed. It wouldn't matter to him that she was miles away now. She was ballooning larger by the day, and moving deeper into preparations for the book on meditators. Joe was removed from these things, had even hired a freelance writer to take on Lee's MAA work, leaving him and Lee with no shop talk to share, leaving her free to go to Massachusetts. The pregnancy had been between her and her obstetrician since Dr. Carver had let slip that Kate would arrive by caesarean. Lee had been assuming the same no-drugs, wide-awake delivery that had brought Toby into the world; Carver had assumed she knew that a 39-year-old woman who had undergone a myomectomy must have a surgical delivery.

She had instantly regretted the surgery that may have made being pregnant now possible, but just as quickly saw the absurdity and withdrew her regrets; she would accept whatever the terms now were for birthing Kate. She just had to hold onto her until September, when the uterine strain of a full-term baby combined with the force of labor contractions could cause the myomectomy incision to burst. Carver warned her sternly that her infant could drown, that Lee herself could die, that there wasn't an OB in the country who would let her go into full labor and give birth naturally.

Lee was holding Kate, and yearning to be held herself; Joe's response was yet more distance. She understood. He had been through a disastrous birth before. Van's crumpled body and damaged brain were enough sorrow for one parental lifetime. But this baby would not be flawed; she would be perfect, Lee would see to it. She just wished Joe would embrace the challenge—and his worried wife.

She would never understand his absence from whatever was at hand. Thinking of the book, *Be Here Now,* she realized that Joe could write one called *Let's Not Be Anywhere Near Here Any Time Soon.*

She laughed to herself, but it was sad, really. Happiness was always over the next hill, coming only with a great goal accomplished. The small, immediate beauties that gave life flashes of joy were overlooked, unfelt. If Joe kept meditating, maybe, just maybe, he would come to taste an aged reggiano or a perfect peach, hear a Diamond symphony filling a room, take in the astonishing beauty of sun hitting gold, of a lavender rose petal dropping from a vase, of a wife growing steadily toward being two beings, a mother and a daughter.

As it was, Lee had only her lifeline to Celeste, the frequent calls that linked Lee's concerns to Celeste's "I know, I know. You must be so scared. I sure would be." Lee could tell her that she felt Joe had slammed a hatch on her, setting her up to go down with the ship, while he rowed away in his own private lifeboat. She could say she wasn't as sure as she pretended to be that she could handle all this.

The previous evening, grateful for a breeze moving across Bunny's park-sized lawn and onto the broad, roofed porch that encircled the house, Lee had been escorted to a wicker chair next to one in which the great little man sat, smiling. He had surprisingly expansive answers to all her questions about meditation and its effects, seemingly enjoying himself. When she came to the end of her questions, she closed her notebook and eased forward in her chair, thanking him for his time. He stopped her with his voice.

"You must prepare yourself for great changes that will not be easy for you. As they unfold, know that you are strong."

Of course. She was clearly adding an infant to her busy life. Still, she thought it kind of him to be so personal. He held his palms together, *jaigurudeving* her as she made way for the next seeker.

She looked around his room now for signs of his occupancy. There seemed to be none. No robe across a chair, no books or magazines on the tables, no papers or trinkets or personal effects of any kind. She opened the closet and found only a row of handsome wooden hangers that bore no clothing. The drawers of an early colonial highboy held nothing but pomanders and lining paper.

The room was dominated by a canopied bed, a bed so high that three steps stood at each side to allow any occupants to reach the mattress. The linens were so startlingly white in this room of muted rugs and mellow wallpaper that Lee guessed they were all newly bought, for the Maharishi's visit.

She stepped into the bathroom and found there stacks of new thick towels and washcloths, all equally white.

The man *wore* only white. Maybe there was some rule that colors could not touch his skin. Maybe cloth that had touched other bodies could not touch his, so all linens had to be new. Maybe he didn't require any of this and it was just Bunny and the other devotees knocking themselves out, hoping to please him.

At the bottom of the steps on one side of the bed, a pair of worn leather sandals was neatly aligned. Lee put a foot beside them and saw that they would be too small for her, wondered if the owner had gone off this morning shoeless, or perhaps owned two pairs, a shocking excess.

Her eyes moved to the bedside table where a fat, tattered, hand-sized notebook sat next to a phone. It was undeniably personal and much-used. She took a deep breath and opened it.

Page after page held names and numbers, country and city codes for people all over the world, each one entered in a small careful hand, the tidy effect spoiled by indecipherable notes that ran up the sides and at angles across each sheet. Bits of paper were tucked everywhere, making the book bulge, its cut edge a full inch thicker than its spine. Lee turned the pages gently, making sure nothing fell out.

What would she say about this in her book about meditators? Nothing. She was not supposed to have such a thing in her hands. And the only question most readers would want answered was, What are the Beatles' phone numbers? Not something she would print, though she smiled, seeing several numbers by the name George Harrison, along with more of the Hindi notations. The guru's notes to himself about this most spiritual of the Fab Four?

The phone rang, shrill in the silence, the sound of the outside world catching Lee in the act. She stared at it, wondering if the caller would know what extension was being picked up. Of course he/she wouldn't. She lifted the receiver.

"Hello?"

"Oh thank goodness. I was afraid you'd be napping. Lee, darling, you've got to rally the pundits."

There was a phalanx of monks traveling with Maharishi, to what purpose Lee was not sure.

"OK, Bunny. And what am I rallying them for?"

"We're at MIT in a computer lab. They're letting Maharishi play with some contraption that does a visual printout of sounds. And he wants the pundits to come and chant into it."

"All right. What time do they need to be there?"

"Soon. It's a half-hour drive, so get them organized and come along as soon as you can. There are keys in the minibus."

Lee wrote down Bunny's directions for driving from Marblehead Neck to MIT, studied a map in the glove compartment of the minibus in the carriage house, revved the engine and pulled it out onto the gravel. At least six Indian monks were ensconced in the rooms above the cars. Being female, she could not enter their quarters to discuss her mission with them, which left her standing under the windows, wondering how to get their attention. *Ahoy, pundits!* did not seem respectful.

"Uhh, halloo? Gentlemen?"

She considered looking in the house for a dinner bell, but settled on calling up to the windows again.

"Maharishi says 'Come now!'"

Discerning no movement or sound in the rooms, she considered barging in, rules or no rules. How good were these holy men at being celibate if they couldn't handle being in the same room with a woman? Especially a big unsexy pregnant one? Maybe none of them spoke English and she was just making unintelligible noises. Maybe she'd have to use the Harpo approach and honk the horn.

The door at the bottom of the stairway opened and a round brown man with a walking staff stepped into the courtyard, smiling broadly. Lee opened the door of the little bus and, with a gesture, invited him to board. Six more Indians in white togas followed him at a sprightly pace, settling quickly into the seats of the bus, looking forward expectantly.

One way or another, she would deliver them to the boss. She just had to drive this thing into and across Boston although she'd never driven a minibus before and didn't know Boston from Buenos Aires. But she'd studied a map, and she thought she had the gears figured out. She nodded to the pundit beside her and turned the ignition key.

Lee hadn't calculated on the mental insularity of Marblehead Neck, the inability of highway engineers to communicate, nor on the madness of Boston drivers. The tiny island was hosting an enormous number of sailboats for a week of racing, but none of the boats must be manned by strangers—or they had all arrived by sea rather than land; signage was cryptic or nonexistent and Lee circled the island twice before finding the way off it to Marblehead proper. It was, she decided, like the price of a yacht—if you had to ask, you'd disqualified yourself. People on Marblehead Neck didn't need signage to know where they were going.

She had memorized the major turns she needed to make, knew she had to bear west and southwest. Which made things dicey when signs with the right road names on them also carried the words North or East. She considered handing the map to the round brown fellow in the passenger seat but was deterred by the fact that he had said not a word to her and had looked neither left nor right but only directly ahead, since taking his seat.

Somehow the van arrived in center-city Boston, which Lee verified when they passed, as promised, City Hall Square. Every narrow, lumpy street in the city was filled with manic drivers, two of whom almost sideswiped the van as they darted through traffic at astonishing speeds. Once a Plymouth blowing off a red light would have rammed the bus broadside if Lee hadn't slammed on the brakes, sending the pundits into tumbles of togas on the floor. Frozen in a sound wash of blasting horns demanding that she move on, Lee was startled to find her arm in front of the passenger-seat pundit, protecting him from the dashboard. She checked her passengers, found them all back in their seats, smiling, totally unperturbed.

They were unshaken by the several near collisions, by the repetitions of passing landmarks as she struggled her way through the maze of narrow streets, by the godawful heat that had Lee drenched and sticking to the seat.

As they pulled up in front of the right hall at MIT, the front-seat pundit turned to Lee. "Thank you, Mrs." He was grinning broadly. "Smashing fine day. Quite like Calcutta." There wasn't a bead of moisture on him.

Lee gave him the hall name and room number and watched the group file toward what was probably the right building before setting off to find a parking place that would accommodate the minibus.

The half-hour journey had taken more than three times that. But the Maharishi was unperturbed, delightedly cueing the pundits into song at microphones on lab tables. When the printed patterns their voices generated were handed to them, they laughed like little boys, enchanted with this wondrous new toy.

Lee stayed on the edges of the spectators, not wanting to catch the Maharishi's attention. She didn't want to be identified now as the person who couldn't handle such a simple task as delivering the pundits on time. This was no time for fouling up. In the weeks ahead she had a book to start and a baby to finish and Joe was going to be no help with any of it—she was on her own.

Deliverance

Lee opened the door so the massive draft fan in the attic could pull night air into the window and across the bed. The light chill felt lovely on her damp skin, but now the tune and the words came in the open door, joining the bass notes that had been pounding on the floor, up through the bed frame, for hours. *I'm going to Kansas City, Kansas City here I come.* She considered hauling herself back to the door to shut Trini Lopez out, but it was too hard to move anything but her thoughts. And if she closed the door, the attic fan wouldn't be able to pull in this cooling air and she would go back to suffocating.

She made a stack of pillows, piling Joe's on top of her own, and maneuvered herself up onto them. He would be pissed—if he ever came to bed. But she needed her head to be higher than her enormous belly, so the burning in her throat would stop. There was no way to make this blimp of a body truly comfortable, but at least she might stop the burning. The smell of Celeste's Virginia Slims was coming in the door and traces of Joe's aftershave were on his pillows. She managed to twist around and shove them to the bottom of the pile. *The summer wind came blowing in, from across the sea.*

At least she couldn't hear their voices, only Sinatra's and Trini's. Her belly turned to stone again, and she checked the time—2:11. The last one had been at 1:13. So it was still Braxton-Hicks fake-labor contractions. The real ones would be close together, and might not start for another week.

Lee had told them she couldn't stay awake any longer and they had both said not to worry—they'd be celebrating the imminent arrival of Kate Montagna, within call, right downstairs. As if that helped. Her thoughts lashing out at them, Lee was sure they were not celebrating but drowning their own sorrows—Celeste's fairly serious—a broken wrist—Joe's ridiculously small—a bruised shin. Poor, poor thing.

Anything but a calm meditator, Stefan had decided in a rage to take back Celeste's mega-emerald and had broken her wrist in the process.

"At least I can hide it in a sleeve. That's better than a messed up face."

"Wait. He's hurt you before?"

"Well, yes."

"No, no. That's not an 'Of course' kind of thing. You never said he hit you. I can't believe this. Joe has never, ever hit me."

"You're lucky. I've never known a man who didn't hit. I think it's the price I have to pay to not be alone."

It could not stand. Lee insisted that Celeste leave New York immediately.

"The doctor must have reported Stefan to the police when he set your wrist, so they're going to be looking for him any minute now."

"I told the doctor I fell. And Stefan's in Wyoming now. Or maybe it's Idaho. Somewhere there's a mining company he took public."

"You have to get some protection before he gets back. Call the police right now."

"They never help. I used to think they would. In tenth grade, when my boyfriend broke my jaw, I went right to the police. They wanted to know what I did to make him so mad. They probably beat up their own wives. Really, I have never known a man who didn't hit."

"But I've never known one who *did*. How can this keep happening to you? I don't understand."

"I know, I know. I'm putting something out that pulls this in. I shouldn't get within a hundred feet of any man. Something about me makes even the sweet ones start hitting."

"Doesn't matter. Doesn't matter. The important thing is to get you out of there. Get in the car and come down here."

"That wouldn't be fair to your family, Lee. Or to you. You've got enough to worry about right now.

"Toby's visiting my parents for a couple weeks, until the baby's born, and Das is visiting a cousin in Cleveland until classes start again. Maddy's actually visiting her mom and Van in Georgia. So it's just Joe and me here. And it's not like Joe and Stefan are big pals, I mean Joe wouldn't stick up for a guy who hits his wife, even if he *liked* him. Hitting girls is against the rules, you know? And Joe's big on the rules. I think Stefan is too, in his own way. There's no way a nice Greek boy would hurt a big old pregnant lady like me, so I wouldn't be in any danger either. You see? Stefan might come after you, but he can do that now, at home. And he might take Joe on, but I think Joe'd enjoy that. He could be the Knight Protector of a damsel in distress. This will work. Get in the damned car."

Celeste had not come then. She'd come two days later, an hour after Joe called to tell her that he'd smashed his leg on a tennis net post. He couldn't possibly drive if Lee had to go to the hospital, if real labor started before it should. So her friend Celeste had come, not to protect herself from a raging Stefan, but on call, to drive Lee to the hospital if real labor started early, to help her friend. She had arrived with her cast, an overnight bag, a cane, a bottle of codeine, an ice bag, an astrological reading Joe had asked her to do, and her new puppy.

Joe loathed dogs, only tolerating Ivan when Toby was around to take care of him and to play the happy boy living in the country with the beautiful dog his loving dad gave him. With Toby in Carolina, good old Ivan was exiled to the kennel, hanging out with his friend and savior, Doc Murray. But here was Joe, in host mode, petting Mr. Shadrack, a cute dog with a cute name and a cute baby blue ribbon Celeste had tied around his neck, deep in his cute fur. Lee knew that if Ivan were home, he'd take care of this absurd creature in one bite. Lee was not in a good mood.

But she told herself to get over it; she smiled at the fluff ball and at her friend's pleasure. Celeste was loving and lovable; it was good for her to spend the afternoon mothering the adorable Mr. Shadrack, filling her ice bag for Joe's leg, listening to his account of his mishap on the tennis court and to his concerned advice on how to deal with Stefan, the meditator who still hit his wife, because seeing God had not been enough.

Early in the evening, Lee refilled the ice bag she'd had on Joe's leg before Celeste arrived, and handed it to her friend. "It's only been a few days—your wrist must still hurt." Celeste thanked her with tears that Lee thought were not about the pain in her wrist.

Joe insisted that Celeste remain in their guest room until she could find an even safer place, one where Stefan, when he returned from his time in Idaho or Wyoming, would never think to look for her. Joe had come up with quite a good idea of where that might be.

"Tate's family has a house in the Hamptons, Celeste, and they're closing it up this weekend. That's it. It's still nice out there, I'm sure Tate would be glad to help, and Stefan doesn't know the Altridges."

Lee had urged Joe to call Tate and arrange it. She wanted Celeste to be safe. She could also see that Celeste's wrist was seriously hurt and the bruise on Joe's leg was huge and ugly, but she found it hard to focus on these things. The possibility of Kate's death and her own was taking up the foreground of her mental landscape. But her part of their day had been pure sitcom—a pregnant Lucy who would have to be rushed, amusingly, to the delivery room by Desi/Ricky and best friend Ethel.

Lee thought the reading Joe had requested might be about her and Kate, might help him understand, and pull him back to her. But she was not privy to the reading, which Joe delayed until Lee had gone upstairs, completely done in by an after-dinner glass of the champagne Joe had opened saying it beat all hell out of codeine as a painkiller for the walking wounded, for him and Celeste, Celeste who would be safe now. He would see to it.

Stuck now to the damp pillows, hearing the ever faithful mourning doves still audible under the music, she considered her support team: both full of Korbel *brut,* one limping along with a cane, the other with a cast, thankfully on her left wrist; she could drive with the other hand. And there was Mr.

Shadrack—he'd be quite a help. But it didn't matter. Lee knew that. None of it mattered. She just had to get through this hideously hot night, just had to keep Kate alive. Settling back on her pillow pile, she knew she was the responsible party, and that she was strong. Wimping out was not an option.

She ran down Witherspoon Street wearing a green track suit that covered her hands and feet but wouldn't close in the back. No matter how fast she ran, Dr. Carver's office was still blocks away, though his voice was close. "We'll do the caesarean at 8 AM on the fifth, well before your due date and several hours before my regular Friday tee time. But if you start into labor before that, you must get to the hospital immediately or you and Kate will die."

As she ran, her great green belly was turning boulder-hard, off and on like a strobe light. She tried to run faster, but her webbed feet stuck to the sidewalk, holding her in place. She looked for passing cars, but the street was empty and no lights went on when she called out to the dark houses. From one of them Trini Lopez shouted that he was going to Kansas City to get a pretty woman. Her arms and legs were stuck with pins to a lab table so a teaching assistant could give the class a demonstration on dissection technique. "You can kill it quickly and maybe painlessly if you cut decisively into this spot right here in the belly." Dr. Carver watched the TA uncertainly, a pair of sewing shears poised over her greenness, lashed to a narrow, hard table.

A door slammed, the bed lurched, and Joe was sprawled face down across the mattress. His outflung arms, his new cane, and the smells of wine and cigarettes left her no room to be and nothing to breathe.

"Joe. Joe, please lie straight. You're pushing me off the side."

Turning onto his back, he dropped a fist heavily onto her leg. She eased away, thinking that Celeste had taken the guest bed and the beds in Toby's room were covered with clothes and books. Maddy's room was unthinkably filthy. Only the big down-filled sofa in the living room was available. On the sofa, she wouldn't have to listen to Joe snore, wouldn't smell him, or have to dodge his arms and legs. She held the turned doorknob so it would close silently; she didn't want to deal with this Joe awake.

Going barefoot down the stairs, she came into a blaze of lights and the mingled smells of cigarette butts, wine, and dog. There were tiny puppy turds on the needlepoint rug and a pee stain on one corner. A half-empty bottle stood sweating on a mahogany end table; she stumbled on an empty Korbel that rolled noisily across the bare floor.

Moving around the room slowly, she emptied ashtrays, gathered up bottles and the tumblers they'd been drinking from, scooped the turds onto a newspaper. She had to get all the smells out of the room. Someone had said soda water was good for cleaning animal pee. She poured some on the pee but when a fierce faux contraction hit, she thought better of kneeling down to scrub at the spreading stain.

It was important now to stay above the dark slow run to the waiting dissecting table. With Celeste and Joe dead to the world, she must keep watch. She would just rest. Kate wouldn't know the difference. Lee could call a taxi if the big contractions came faster. Joe would wake up in the afternoon and find her gone. He and Celeste wouldn't know what awful thing may have come of their negligence, but she would be alive, she and Kate, far from smoke and smells and irresponsible people.

Another strong one hit, and she decided to leave Desi/Ricky and Ethel a message. She opened the *New York Times* on the kitchen table, then got the Lopez and Sinatra records off the turntable and cut across their grooves with a paring knife, in a nice star pattern. One ruined record made a good base for three champagne bottles. The second record fit nicely on top of the bottles. Around the base, over pictures of Nixon and Idi Amin, she sprinkled butts and ashes and an artful border of tiny turds. It was eloquent, and rather handsome. This is what they would find instead of her. They would know that they had been stupid and frightening and that she was angry.

She began to laugh. Now would she go out in the garden and eat worms? She could picture Joe coming into the kitchen, knew that the message she was sending would not be the one he'd receive. She'd just be the bitch who made scenes, the disloyal friend who had turned on kind, injured, loyal, imperiled Celeste. She would be the crazywoman who wasn't good enough to be his wife. She gathered up her creation and dumped it into the trash, tying the plastic liner tightly shut.

"What the hell were you doing down here? Bottles clanking. Doors opening and shutting. Don't you care that your friend was trying to sleep? Jesus, she drives down from the city to help you and you can't let her sleep? I know you don't care about my leg, which is killing me, but you might show some consideration for Celeste."

She opened her eyes and looked at him, wondering who he was. She needed to go back to sleep, to get under the sea, where she was safe. She closed her eyes and tried to turn, surprised that it was hard to do.

Oh. That. Kate, how're you doing? Here we still are, eh?

She said nothing to Joe. It was going to be a very long day. She struggled up out of the hollow she'd made in the soft sofa cushions and pulled herself up the stairs to the now empty bed. Joe slammed into the bathroom, blasted a radio, sang in the shower. At least it wasn't "The Summer Wind."

She needed to talk to Celeste, but preposterous though it was, Celeste had crossed over. There was no one to throw a lifeline to. Celeste was Joe's ward and nursemaid now, under his protection, tending to his much bemoaned pain, as Lee withdrew, unwilling to point out that her need was greater. Nor would Lee remind Celeste that Joe had a pattern of making promises of help that he didn't keep, and of co-opting Lee's female rhythms. Celeste knew that when Lee was at lowest ebb each month, Joe would get the flu, sprain a wrist, have a business crisis, go ballistic. Celeste knew that.

Now he seemed to be upping the ante to match the stakes that Lee was dealing with. Lee wondered if running into a net post could be a prelude to stepping in front of a car. A foot-long bruise didn't mean his life was in danger. But hers was. Kate's was. She wanted to tell Celeste that Joe's problems didn't matter right now. Celeste had understood, yesterday.

"Joe, I need to talk to you. I am really really scared and I need your help."

He pushed her hand off his damp arm and took her shoulders in a furious grip.

"Stop it. Stop it right now. You're making up crap to get attention." He turned for the door.

"Joe, you were there. With me. You heard him. What am I making up?"

"I won't put up with this. If you can act civilized, come downstairs. If not, stay up here. I'm firing Carver. Call him up and tell him I want a final bill. If Celeste will be kind enough to drive us, we'll go to New York, to a doctor who doesn't have his head up his ass. Now I'm going down to make breakfast, since you don't seem to be heading in that direction."

"I'm sorry to have to agree with your previous doctor, but I can't allow you to deliver naturally." Sam Steinmetz, deliverer of Ashley and Glenn's Robert Martin, frowned at Lee, sternly disapproving. Joe had wanted to call Carter Burnside, the ultra-chic OB who delivered Priscilla Altridge, but Lee had pleaded for Steinmetz, citing Judith Bridge's endorsement, and Joe had relented.

"And you are in no condition to undergo the caesarean. You're not sleeping well?"

"I'm afraid to sleep."

Joe shifted in his chair, his arms crossed tightly across his chest.

"She's been a little upset, doctor," he said soothingly. "The weather you know, and she doesn't want this caesarean." He gave her an indulgent smile.

"You're going in for observation, young lady." Steinmetz picked up his phone. "And to get the rest you'll need."

Celeste brought the Buick to a stop in front of the Admissions sign and Joe laboriously pulled Lee out of the back seat, grimacing from the strain on his leg, withdrawing his hand as soon as she was on her feet. He stayed by the car and gestured Lee toward the door.

"You'll be fine here. I'll call you."

But she wouldn't be fine. They were going to put her in a room with no air. And she still wouldn't sleep.

An orderly insisted that she sit in a wheelchair to be taken to Admitting. She tried to see around him, but the Buick was gone. A taxi had taken its place at the canopy and a pregnant woman was being helped out by her husband. He pushed her wheelchair toward the desk, bending over her, talking into her ear, giving her cheek little kisses.

The phone rang through her undersea song. A wrong note. Jarring. She swam up from great depths and reached an arm out of the cocoon she'd built against the icy blast of the air conditioner.

"Lee? Lee, goddam it, talk. What's happening there? Have you had the baby yet?"

"I was sleeping, Joe. It was wonderful. Safe. There were no frogs."

"What the hell is this? Frogs? Do you know what it's costing me for you to sleep?"

"You didn't call yesterday, Joe, or the day before. Anything could have happened and you wouldn't have known."

"I was busy. Someone's got to work you know. Someone's got to pay for all this. And if you don't cut the crap you're going to damage the baby. Another crippled kid. Just what I need."

"Joe, are you drunk?'

"I am not an alcoholic, Lee. Alcoholics are drunk all the time. We had some wine at dinner and now...."

"We?"

"Now we're having a cognac."

"Joe, for somebody who's so concerned about what people think, that's extraordinary. Why isn't Celeste in the Hamptons?"

"If you weren't such a self-centered bitch, you wouldn't ask. My leg, remember? How am I supposed to get around?"

"You have Dasya. Classes started two days ago so I know he's back. You have a driver named Dasya, right upstairs."

"I'm not going to talk to you. You're a goddam crazywoman." The phone clicked off in her ear.

She looked at the clock in the church tower across the street. Dawn was five hours away. Kate turned once, ever so slowly.

She managed one journey into the world each day. Down the elevator, out the lobby door, turn right onto Seventh Avenue or left along Central Park South, round the block slowly, stopping to look in windows when she felt she couldn't go on. No crossing streets; she might not make it all the way before the light changed.

"Exercise and fresh air" seemed absurd when she was barely moving and the air was so heavy with heat, fumes, and dirt, but she was obeying orders. It would help her sleep, Steinmetz said, this daily excursion that she made walking as she always had, refusing to do the caricature pregnant-woman, backward-leaning, toes-out waddle. She held herself tall and pointed her feet straight ahead, no matter how hard it was to sustain.

It was September but not yet Autumn in New York, no excitement, no crisp resurgence from summer's oppression. It was just the grim end of summer and she was in the Dead Zone, just her and a phone in a borrowed corporate apartment. Vi the Voice called her twice a day with her messages; she'd stopped offering Joe's after Lee said to hold them for his call. Now Vi had ceased to be professionally detached. "But Lee, where is he? You're stuck in New York, the baby's coming any minute and where *is* he?"

Lee parroted his story. "There's this big negotiation, round-the-clock. They're not even breaking to go to restaurants, just having food sent in. It's a tough business."

"Well, there's a stack of messages here." Vi sounded unconvinced. "And some of them look important. Are you sure you don't want me to read them to you?"

"Wouldn't do any good. My brain's gone. Just hang onto them. He'll call."

"Well, all right, but you call me now, if you need anything. I'll figure out how to help."

Ah, a lifeline thrown. By a woman she'd never met, who was fifty miles away. But it was something. She could call Judith, who had come through with the apartment, or Ashley, Naomi, Pam, *someone,* but then that someone would ask questions Lee didn't want to answer, didn't know how to answer. It had been awkward enough calling Judith from her room at the hospital.

"Who do we know who hasn't come back from the country? I need an apartment for a few days." Judith had met her within the hour at a Central Park South apartment her ex-husband's company kept for visiting buyers.

"Maid service included, so don't even think of making the bed or tidying up. Here are menus for at least a dozen restaurants that deliver. So just rest."

"You're an angel and this place is a godsend. Are you sure nobody needs it?"

"Not till next week. And if you're still here, he can go to a hotel."

"Don't say that. This *has* to be over by then."

"My Michael was three weeks late. You have books? Magazines?"

Lee was rested, and Kate had moved into position. Now it was more waiting; Steinmetz believed that babies should knock first before a caesarean. "Babies should be born as close to their time as possible, not when the doctor wants them born, or when their parents want them born." He didn't mention working around doctors' preferred tee times but Lee thought the knocking thing was a reasonable idea, though a little unnerving, given the situation. "Don't worry," Steinmetz had insisted. "Yes, the uterus is precarious. Yes, it could split in heavy labor, but I live three minutes from the delivery room. You just get there when the contractions are coming at half-hour intervals and we'll have this baby out in the world before the uterus could break. You're really looking *much* better."

She charged the Princeton number for a call to Carolina, hoping to talk with Toby.

"Yes, I'm fine, feeling much much better. Is Toby OK? It's like he's been gone a month." Her mother was sorry she'd missed him; Toby was fishing with Uncle Punk. On the extension phone, her father asked where they were to park when they joined her to wait for their new grandchild.

"There's a garage under the building, Dad. You'd just tell them apartment 11N. But I don't think you can make the drive that fast. I'll be at the hospital, I'm sure, with the baby. And Toby's classes start Monday so he's got to get home. Just go straight to Princeton, OK?"

She did another slow foray around the block and returned gratefully to the cool lobby and the sleek elevator. As the mirror-lined box rocketed upwards, two portly men who smelled of cigars tried unsuccessfully to avoid staring at her, but the mirrors betrayed them. At the 11th floor, as the doors closed behind her, she could hear them start in.

"My God, she shouldn't be walking around like that. She could have had it in the elevator!"

"I wouldn't have let *my* wife...."

The steel doors closed on the ascending sound as the walking, talking refrigerator made it to the door of her temporary warehouse.

Someone was blasting holes under the park, the explosions thumping at the building's glass walls. At her feet, the television showed her masked assassins machine-gunning Olympic athletes in Munich and the new Miss America weeping in Atlantic City. Somewhere out there in the darkness, Toby and her parents were rolling toward Princeton. Somewhere Celeste was hiding from Stefan, and somewhere there was Joe, working that bitch of a negotiation. Somewhere where there was no phone, no way for him to reach into this isolation chamber where nothing would ever happen.

She rubbed a fingerprint off the polished steel arm of the chair, counted the shrill colors in the huge abstract painting over the sofa. Not her style, but she'd have to get used to it; she was never going to leave this apartment. She could almost see a No Exit sign over the door to the hall. Kate stretched her arms and legs, making lumps move across Lee's belly. "Right. You and me, kid. Right here. Just like this. Forever."

She aimed the channel changer at the set, cutting off a quiz show host's fatuous chatter. The loony face of a British music hall comedian beamed in.

She liked this channel-changer thing, part of the apartment's high tech gear. Aiming it at the phone, she clicked for Joe to go to a phone and call her. A click at the apartment door, so he'd come through it and get her out of here. Another click for the phone to bring in the Celeste she'd known so long, so she'd have someone to talk to when Joe didn't call or come through the door. The Brit put his foot in a bucket.

Her eye settled on her mountainous midsection. Maybe the clicker signals couldn't make it across the Hudson or out to the Hamptons. She snapped the changer at her belly, trying every number. Kate should come out, come out. Didn't she want to come out and play?

Without this weight she wouldn't be pinned down. She could get up and get out of there. She could go find Joe. Kate ran a leisurely foot along Lee's ribs and settled back into stillness.

"Goddammit I don't have a friggin' sore throat I'm in labor!" The cabbie had lurched to a halt at the entrance to the Eye Ear Nose and Throat Clinic, blocks from the address she'd given him for Lying In. A contraction of Mack-truck force bent her in half.

"It's all right, dear. It's all right." Commander Palmer patted her hand pacifyingly. "Driver, my daughter asked you to go 17th Street and Third Avenue. We are now between 21st and 22nd Streets, on Second Avenue."

He was taking charge, this father of hers who had driven directly to New York, not stopping in Princeton despite her assurances. Just hours after her parents and Toby arrived, the Commander was responding to the red alert that her water had broken by manning his battle station with steely competence. He buzzed the doorman to flag down a taxi, told her mother that he'd be back for her and Toby soon, assured Toby that his mother was fine, picked up the suitcase Mrs. Palmer had packed and placed just inside the door, and escorted his daughter down to a waiting Yellow Cab. His dignity was not dented by being with a frantic woman in labor who was moving as fast as she could waddle with a bath towel gripped between her thighs, an unladylike woman who cursed at taxi drivers.

When they arrived at the right hospital, he helped her settle into a wheelchair, and got her through the admissions process. He'd be alerting the people on the neatly folded list in his wallet: Gert and Big Joe, the friends and clients whose numbers he'd gotten from her, and Violet Mercurio at the answering service, the only known way of informing his son-in-law. He would then be waiting outside her room, with her mother and Toby, when she completed the task at hand. Ernest Palmer ran a tight ship.

"Let's get that boy out of there." Steinmetz was tying on a face mask, much too slowly. Kate was definitely making known her intentions to emerge; Lee knew her body was about to go into final stage and start pushing, whether or not the contractions would burst the uterus and kill them both.

"Girl. You're going to get that girl out of there."

"But I have a fifty percent chance of being right, don't I?"

His eyes smiled at her over the gauze, appreciating his own jolly-obstetrician banter, the same attempt at humor she'd heard from Carver and from the guy who had delivered Toby. Maybe it was part of their residency training. Make em laugh, boys, make em see what a fine fellow you are so they don't kick you out of the room and go back to midwives.

She looked up into a battery of screaming lights and the eyes of another green-masked man, this one with huge brown caterpillar eyebrows.

"I'm Dr. Noddings, your anesthesiologist." He was holding a gas inhaler.

"I don't want that."

"Fine." He brushed off her insult to his art. "Well, it's here if you change your mind."

She was annoyed with Carver, Steinmetz, Noddings, the lot of them—all these officious, you're-on-our-turf-we-know-what's-best-for-you professionals. The room was freezing, it was lit like a movie set, the crew was mob-sized, the table narrow and hard, and there was an enormous window at her feet opening onto a roof where workmen walked back and forth with buckets of tar. "Eyebrows" turned her on her side and told her to be absolutely still. He was about to put an enormous needle into the base of her spine. No one was holding her steady. What if a contraction hit as the needle went in? She gripped the table hard, sure that if she moved she'd spend the rest of her life paralyzed. Joe wouldn't like that. He'd had enough of cripples. She'd be in a wheelchair forever, raising Kate alone.

A screen was put across her body at rib level, cutting off her view of everything but the lights and Noddings' eyebrows.

They were doing absolutely everything wrong. She wanted to stop the action, get up off the table, and get things in order. This crowd needed a blue storm of edit tags. They had to lower the air conditioning or at least blanket the patient's legs and chest. Couldn't they see she was shaking, turning blue? They must lower the lights and the blinds; no show today for the roofing crew outside the huge window at her feet. They should certainly bring in a larger table that she wouldn't fall off if she moved. And for Christ's sake hold her steady for this spinal!

Eyebrows moved out of sight range and asked, "You feel that?"

"Feel what?"

"How about that?"

"No. Nothing." Not even a contraction. Eyebrows was back at her head. He nodded to Steinmetz and whoever else was in the mobs on the other side of the screen and out on the rooftop, way too many witnesses to her sudden scream.

"Oh for heaven's sake. You can't feel that." Steinmetz sounded annoyed but slightly uncertain.

"I can! You're cutting just to the left of center, below the navel." He didn't stop. She felt the downward pressure of the knife, fought back the noise rising in her. He was wrong. She could feel exactly what was happening. But she realized there was no pain. She clenched her eyes shut against the klieg lights and talked sternly to herself. There was no pain. No pain. There was no pain. Just pressing and tugging. Breathe breathe breathe. Keep quiet. There was no pain.

She was glad Joe hadn't come. There were only strangers in scrubs and tar-stained overalls to witness her cowardice, her craziness.

The center of her body was turned inside out, everything in her wrenched away and an orderly walked away from the table with his arms outstretched, carrying a baby in mid-air, huge hands wrapped around its middle. Two arms, two legs. And something else. Too many parts to be Kate.

Lee reached out to stop the orderly, to take that baby and hold it as it should be held—firmly, eyes shaded from the light, cuddled, safe, warm, like the place he'd just come from. But the orderly and the baby were gone. The silent baby. The crowd beyond the screen was jabbering about clips and sponges. Lee looked upside down at Eyebrows, who was fiddling with machines behind her head.

"That wasn't Kate."

He said nothing. She slipped into confusion. People were talking about the World Series and the row house someone had just bought in Park Slope. Steinmetz clipped and pulled and stitched and she felt it all as it went on and on. It was never going to be over. She wanted them all to get away from her, to go talk about sports and real estate somewhere else, maybe the nearest bar. She'd refused the tranquilizers and gas that were supposed to float her through this. Drugs could have hurt Kate. Now she just wanted to be put to sleep, to miss the endless tugging, and the talking. She looked at Eyebrows.

"Dr. Noddings, I've changed my mind. I'd like the gas."

"What for? We're just closing up."

She cursed them all and wondered if the baby that went by in the air was alive, wherever they had taken him.

The flowers in her room lined the windowsill and covered every table. There were cards with them, dear messages from Marina and Phoebe, from Judith, from Big Joe, eager to come back north from their retirement community in Daytona and meet his new grandson, from Tate and Pru, from the Clays, from her parents and Toby, MAA clients, from Vi the Voice, and even Abe the Vet. But nothing from Celeste, who probably didn't know. Nothing from Joe. He'd be bringing flowers in person when he came, and her pink coral ring from Florence.

And then he was there, suit rumpled, eyes bloodshot, his hands jammed in his pockets, his hair longer than she knew he liked it, curling over his collar.

"Have you seen him yet?"

"No."

"Did you tell Celeste?"

"The phone out there is shut off, and I don't even know if that's where she is. Where's my mail?"

She took the stack out of her night table drawer. "Dad brought these in this morning."

He shuffled through the envelopes, opened some, pocketed checks and threw the rest on the foot of the bed.

"You look OK. So there wasn't any problem in the delivery."

Exactly. He'd been right all along. She'd just made up the alarm to get attention. She had to divert him from this track he was heading onto.

"He's right in the front row of the nursery. Why don't you go down there and meet him?" He shrugged an If-you-insist and, staring at the floor, set out to see his son.

With breathing space back in the room, Lee picked up the note Toby had sent her. "Dear Mom, Thank you for the little brother. I promise to teach him only the good things I know and never to beat him up. Love, Toby" She was smiling when Joe again took over the room.

"He looks Irish. And he's a Virgo, so of course he's going to be a pain in the ass. What's his name?"

Lee had no idea. She'd been watching him as he nursed, talking to him as he slept in her lap, hoping she'd get an idea of who he was and what his name should be. He was quiet, stocky, broad-jawed. There were curving, crowblack lines on his head and no lobes on his ears. On her first woozy walk down the hall, she had looked at him among his neighbors in the nursery, mostly Puerto Rican, Asian, and black babies, and realized how pale his skin was. He was, after all, seven-eighths English, so the last name Montagna seemed more than enough to cover that part of his identity. His middle name should be Palmer and she figured his first name should be English too. But there she stopped.

"You have any thoughts on boys' names, Joe?"

"No. Name him anything you want."

He pulled out a checkbook and scrawled across it. "Give this to Steinmetz, OK? I'll be by the house to get the mail and some clothes next week. This has all been really hard to take, my leg, the negotiations—which are going OK now, not that you've asked—that crap with Papandreou, and now this. I need to be alone for awhile, to think about things. I can't do that around you and your parents and Toby and that baby. I have to be alone."

"And now this"? Did he mean now this male baby who was not damaged like Van but perfect, a perfect Montagna son? How could this beautiful infant be an addition to Joe's list of woes?

Before she could say anything at all he was out the door, leaving no forwarding address.

"Mr. and Mrs. Johnson" and their newborn son stepped through the door of the house-for-sale in New Hope as the agent presented the benefits of the place.

"There's a lovely creek running through the property and as you can see, the view is exquisite."

But "the Johnsons" weren't looking at the view. Stefan picked up a section of a Sunday *New York Times* that was in a pile in the living room and held it up to Lee. It was dated the day of Gabriel's birth.

The agent was apologetic. "I'm sorry the place is so untidy. You know how it is with renters."

Stefan had made the appointment as a prospective buyer; the agent arranging a viewing time when the renters promised to be absent. And Stefan had insisted that Lee come with him on this excursion.

"I know it's a hard time for you, Lee, with a new baby and everything. But you have to get real. Face how bad it really is. Stop making up fairy tales about these terrible people."

Joe's clothes were on the chairs and hanging from the tops of doors. Celeste's filled the closets. Stefan moved through the house, slamming doors and cursing. The agent was staring at him in alarm.

"My antiques aren't here. Where the hell did the bitch stash my antiques?"

He had come home from his journey west to find his apartment empty not only of wife, but of furnishings and paintings as well. They'd been part of his investment strategy, each piece chosen for him by a savvy dealer who assured him its value would soar. Lee thought he was angrier about losing his Aubusson rugs and his de Kooning paintings than about losing Celeste, so angry that he'd hired a detective who had traced her, and Joe, here, to this Pennsylvania house with an exquisite view.

Lee stood quite still, in the bedroom, where mail to Montagna Altridge & Associates spilled from the table on the left of the unmade bed, topped by the Tiffany watch and cufflinks she'd given Joe. Two paperbacks on astrology and a *People* magazine were stacked on Celeste's side, and the pillows still held the hollows made by their heads. On the dresser, next to lipsticks and mascaras and a hair dryer, there was a long white christening gown with a tiny matching hat. This was not the way Lee had imagined Gabriel's first visit to his godmother's house.

She felt his sleeping breath coming in small puffs and sniffs against her neck. She had to get him out of this place, before he inhaled the mendacity and treachery that filled those rooms. He must not take it in that these two people who were supposed to love him had instead betrayed and abandoned him. She held him closer and carried him back to the car while Stefan gave the angry realtor a hundred bucks for her wasted time.

A week later, Lee was holding Gabriel as she answered the ring of a uniformed constable standing on the porch at 99.

"Mrs. Montagna, ma'am? I've been told to serve you with these. Sorry ma'am."

There was a lien on the house from Gino Rovinato, citing unpaid painting bills, and an action for divorce from plaintiff Joseph V. H. Montagna, charging defendant Lee P. Montagna with desertion. She stared at the word, uncomprehending, until she heard Joe pontificating on the art of negotiation. His main point had always been that the best defense was a roaring offense.

It seemed enough for one day, but the afternoon mail brought a pay-or-remove-the-student notice from Toby's day school and a small box that held Joe's watch and cufflinks. The note with them said, in Joe's confident handwriting, "These were beautiful gifts when I received them, but considering what you've become, I don't want them anywhere near me. JVHM."

She stared at the note but it remained incomprehensible, no matter how long she held it. She wondered what it was that she was supposed to have become.

She wanted to become a person who knew that no matter how out-gunned she was, up remained up, and down was still down.

The earth still revolved around the sun, and the fixed point in this particular universe was Lee Montagna, standing in the foyer of a house on Underwood Road, holding Gabriel Palmer Montagna. The deserter was Out There. And he had to be out of his mind.

Silence and Slow Time

It became important to avoid the phone. Lee's automatic quick reach for the nearest receiver became a recoil. It might be the bank. Or the mason. It might be a friend eager to hear about the new baby at the Montagna's happy home. It might even be Joe, demanding to know what mail had come in. She couldn't cope with the invasions, well intentioned or ill, couldn't imagine any words to say, or having the strength to say them. When she absolutely had to engage the world, she must be her recognizable self, jaunty and wry—the effort was exhausting.

The answering service took all incoming calls between eight AM and ten PM on week days, noon to six on weekends. Lee had asked Vi to pick up on the second ring rather than the fifth, to take messages, to call through with a three-ring signal only if Toby needed her.

"And Joe, yes?"

"No, Vi. Not Joe. Just give him his own messages. I'll try to check in with you every evening for mine."

Vi was silent, then spoke very quietly. "Lee? Are you OK?"

"No. I guess I'm not. You're good to ask."

"Anything you need, anything at all, you just tell me."

>*Answering service as bodyguard. No. Sanity guard. Vi the*
>*Voice, my protector, my spokeswoman.*

"Thank you, Vi. Just... thank you."

Lee stared at the list Vi had read off to her. She went to her back-bed-room office, closing the door against the questioning her mother would start if she overheard Lee talking to Tate. For weeks, Tate had believed Joe's calls from the road, supposedly from clients' offices, from hallways outside of mythical meetings. Lee hadn't returned the calls Tate made to the house until he'd left far too many messages with Vi to ignore. There was, "I bought a new tie. I'm ready for the christening." And, "Joe missed the staff meeting today. Is he sick?" There was even one that said, "We have to come down to introduce Pris to Gabe. If he likes older women, we'll settle on the bride price." When Vi read that one to her, Lee had managed a smile, imagining Pru's reaction to the idea of promising her Priscilla Altridge to a Montagna.

Lee hadn't known how to begin a reality conversation with Tate. But it had to be done. He was the co-owner of MAA. Pulling together the necessary documents and thoughts, she had called and briefed him quite formally on the bills coming in, the lies being told about work done, the possibility that his investment in the company was being lost.

To her surprise—and to his credit—Tate had stopped her. "Lee, what about you? The baby? Tobe? What are you going to do?" He was more than Joe's partner, she reminded herself. He was a friend, and Gabriel's godfather.

He had agreed, reluctantly, to make a try at reasoning with Joe. He would get him to meet for a one-on-one lunch and he would see what he could do about this mess.

Today the Tate-message Vi read to her was, "Had that lunch today. Call me."

"Ah, Lee, thanks for calling." Tate's voice was full of suppressed laughter. Lee wondered what was amusing about "Hi, Tate."

"He did get my message to meet me at the Yale Club for lunch this afternoon." This too seemed highly entertaining.

"Did he show?"

Tate laughed. "Oh yeah, he showed."

"And?"

"Well, everything was fine, perfectly normal, talking about work like we always have. You know. A contract I'm finishing up. Some prospective clients he's meeting with. But then I said, 'Look you've got a new baby at home and you haven't been there for weeks. I never know where you are. The company's getting all these strange bills. What's going on?'"

"You said that straight out? What did he say?"

Tate let out a guffaw. "Nothing. Not a word. He just stood up and turned the table over. Then he walked out. Just left. And I'm sitting there with my lunch on the floor and my thumb in my ear."

Lee could see the room, see Tate shrugging and grinning at the assembled Yalies, all staring over their white table cloths at this unseemly occurrence.

> *How ungentlemanly. How Lower-East-Side barroom. How*
> *neatly that fit into your program of being the renegade, the*
> *Altridge with the strange interests and alliances.*

She said nothing.

"I didn't find out anything at all." This was the height of hilarity. "Sorry, Lee."

Lee was sure he was sorry that he'd now lost his work-and-play partner, perhaps even sorry that there had been no ground the two of them could stand on to have a conversation about real things in their lives. Hearing that simple, "What's going on?" must have seemed an impossible breaking of the rules to Joe, just as saying it was for Tate. There was no going back to their ritual, playful distance. Life had intruded and the game was over.

She must not now penalize Tate for his ridiculous unease, this incessant, nervous laughter, must not flail the water hoping he would be there in any personal way, for her, for her sons. Pru would be all over him with I-told-you-sos. Tate's inappropriate friendship with the Montagnas had crashed with that upended table. But she was Secretary of a corporation; Tate was Co-chair. They must collaborate to protect the business. She talked with her fellow corporate officer about invoking whatever rules might stop Joe from further destruction. Tate would handle it all. She was not to worry about MAA.

She thanked him for trying to talk to Joe about his family, and said goodbye. As she moved the receiver toward its cradle, Tate Altridge's laughter sounded joyless and immensely distant.

Commander Palmer sat in the wicker rocker in the nursery, his grandson across his knees.

"This baby's hungry."

Gabriel's cries, still the distinctive, thin sounds of the newborn, had brought Lee hurrying up the stairs to see what was alarming him. She stopped in the doorway, watching her father and her frantic son, whose doll-sized feet and hands were thrashing the air wildly.

"I think he's just scared he's going to fall on the floor, Dad. You're not holding onto him."

Her father didn't acknowledge her words, but put a large, damp hand over the baby's middle.

The heat of September had stretched into late-October, as had the Palmers' annual visit to Princeton. The air was unendingly heavy and sullen and everything, everyone, was bedraggled, moist to the touch, exhausted.

"He's hungry. He's hungry all the time. Look how he kicks."

Lee stared at her father. He thought her kid was hungry? Well, she could handle that. She had, damn it, done this before.

She'd been rattled about breast feeding all those years ago when Toby was on the way. Though set on natural childbirth, an oddity in that time, and on nursing, equally odd, she was quite prepared to fail, lacking as she was the basic equipment. Nursing was for the earth mothers, for real women.

When she was pregnant with Toby, in the pre-Lamaze era of Grantly Dick-Read, Lee had found an obstetrician who promised not to knock her out and a veteran Kentucky midwife who was running natural-birth training classes. When she had asked the midwife about a flat-chested woman's chances of successfully nursing a baby, the answer had been a smile and a hug.

"Honey, the hills where I delivered all them babies was full of skinny women. When that hungry baby is in your arms, you're gonna be amaaazed at what little breasts can do. And don't you listen to the nurses at the hospital. They'll tell you the first days don't matter, that you don't have milk then, so they're going to give bottles to your baby. But what you got those days is bettern milk— it's everythin a baby needs for a good start. So you get ahold of that baby and you two snuggle up, right away. And when they come at him with bottles, you shoo em off. You got to get the process going, the stronger he sucks the more milk you'll make, so don't you let them cut his hunger down any."

Lee had actually blossomed up to fill an A cup during the pregnancy, but she'd still had her doubts, until she'd indeed snuggled up with her hungry, newborn Tobias and then seen him hiccup a stream of liquid butter down his miniature shirt. It was a revelation. She could do this, she could provide what this tiny being needed to stay alive, and thrive. She was invincible.

Now she watched as her father shifted this new son's tiny body into the crook of one arm and put the plastic nipple of a bottle into the wide, noisy mouth.

"C'mon little feller. Grab on. That's good stuff there. You'll feel better now."

The infant jerked his head away and howled. Lee was proud that her boy wasn't going to be tricked into drinking junk. But the holes in the stiff plastic leaked some warm liquid into his mouth and he quieted down, began trying to suck the thing. The fake sustenance would mean he would not be hungry again for hours, and Lee would engorge painfully with unneeded milk. She would have to see to it that her father got no more opportunities to feed his grandson. One intervention would not do permanent damage, but there must be no more. She closed the door and went downstairs.

She reached for the phone in the kitchen, dialed 212-BU and stopped. The number she could find in her sleep was supposed to bring in the quiet voice that would understand the undermining disrespect of her father's foray out for bottles and Similac, would understand Lee's fear of the mounting stack of bills she didn't know how to pay, would be appalled that the check Tim Pitt sent every month didn't even cover the cost of Toby's braces, would understand why Lee wasn't returning the calls Vi was intercepting from good people who would have too many questions. Celeste would understand about there being no palm branch held overhead to protect Lee and her sons from the elements, about the escalating need for her to do something herself to protect them, and her inability to imagine what that was. Celeste would understand that Lee had to act but that there was nothing she could do. She would understand that Lee's life had become her monthly doldrums magnified and unrelenting, making every day the one on which the world would end. Lee needed to say that she was not a good judge of men, or of friends, that it was safest to lie low and not talk to anyone at all. People, any people, might add to the dangers, or take away something she and her boys needed to survive.

She stared at the number pad, knowing that if her hand moved in the familiar pattern she would hear not Celeste's gentle "Yes?" but Stefan's harsh "Papandreou" and its implied "What the hell do you want?" When she would say, "This is Lee," he would commence ranting about the latest reports from the detectives he'd hired, which he hated to pass on to Lee the Madonna, Lee the Wronged, Lee the Perfect. He would tell her that Montagna Altridge & Associates had been charged for jewelry, for a sports car, and for astonishing bills at department stores, but as an officer of the closely held corporation that owned MAA, Lee knew that, and knew that Tate had revoked Joe's company credit card, shifting all the renegades' expenditures to the personal American Express card she was being dunned to pay, including the costs of two weeks at a stunningly expensive resort in the Caribbean.

Stefan had warned her to expect bills for cosmetic surgery. "She's addicted to it. I paid for a new chin and a new shape for her eyes. Cost a fortune. She'll do something else on Joe's ticket. Like the jerk in LA who paid for the boobs."

"Wait. You're saying they aren't real?"

"Hell no. How could anybody that skinny have boobs that big? God doesn't make real women shaped like that."

But Lee couldn't imagine anyone deliberately shaping herself so oddly, remembering all the times she'd been concerned that Celeste might tip over from the weight of those massive appendages. It seemed there might be many things she had not known about this friend she had so treasured.

If she told Stefan anything positive about something Joe had done, he would dismiss it, as when she'd reported that Toby's school had just received a year's tuition check from Joe, and Stefan exploded.

"Big friggin deal! He registered him at that school himself, right? Before all this? Why the hell shouldn't he pay the damn bill? And on time so the kid isn't worried he'll get kicked out."

Stefan, who didn't know her well at all, would think her a saint for not sharing his fury. He didn't understand that Joe and Celeste, the two people closest to her in the world, had only done what anyone who got to know her that well was supposed to do. They had walked away.

The heat in the kitchen was appalling, the fan Lee had set up on the counter making little difference.

"Toby thinks he's coming back, you know."

"I know that, Mom." Lee would explain everything to Toby as soon as she could think of what to say, something that would make it clear to him that it wasn't his fault, something that would not break his heart. She closed the dishwasher door and told herself not to forget to come back after everyone else had gone to bed. She would run it when it wouldn't increase their discomfort in the steaming kitchen.

This never-ending summer was particularly hard on her mother, a woman who had never liked heat, and could tolerate no sun whatsoever. Mrs. Palmer's once auburn hair had been white for some years and her always pale skin had lost every bit of its peach tint to pigment-killing vitiligo. Now described by Lee as the whitest woman alive, Emily Palmer was softened, the sharp edges of her younger self smoothed away. She had become, in her sixties, almost as striking as the husband who had for so long drawn all eyes.

"Do you want your father to talk to him?"

Lee imagined the stiff-upper-lip, you're-the-man-of-the-house-now talk the Commander would give his 13-year-old grandson. If there was anything she was sure of it was that Toby was a child and must remain one until it was truly time for him to take on adult burdens.

"No, Mom, really. It's my responsibility and I'll do it. Soon."

"I wish we could help more, dear. You should have had rich parents."

The Palmers had been buying groceries and gas, slowing the drain on the funds Lee had managed to protect from Joe. "But I'd like to treat you to a shampoo and set at a beauty parlor. Wouldn't you like that?"

Lee hadn't been to a hairdresser, even for a cut, in months and wondered where but in the South one could even find a "shampoo and set." She'd been tying her hair back with a rubber band and wearing no makeup. It was, she realized, distressing for her parents, whose only compliments to her, ever, had been on her appearance. She had inherited her father's fine features and her mother's youthful auburn coloring; it was unseemly, ungrateful to let herself be unattractive. She must be, at all times, their beautiful daughter.

Sitting in the breakfast nook, the muu-muued Mrs. Palmer held Gabe and made clucking sounds at him. He watched her, listened carefully, and smiled.

"How can Gert miss this? Holding this darling. Her new grandson." Mrs. Palmer frowned. "He must look exactly like Joe did. Look at the chest on this baby."

And the black curls. The eyes that are getting lighter every day.

The ears with no lobes. Oh yes. Joe is still here.

"Gert doesn't care, Mom."

Mrs. Palmer gave her daughter a Now-now look, but Lee was sure it was true. Gert would be out spending money on useless things, yelling at Big Joe—no one was missing from her life, not Gabe, not Lee, not any of her scattered grandchildren. And much as Lee loved him, she knew Big Joe would just follow Gert's lead, intimidated by her tongue lashings. Gabriel was going to be very short on relatives.

But, to Lee's surprise, he was going to have *two* siblings, a big brother and an even bigger sister—Rory. Rory who had come to the hospital every day, and had come down to Princeton with Pranko, her mad Croatian sculptor. Rory who told Lee that she didn't want to see her slimy father ever again, that she was sticking with Lee, Toby, and her new little brother.

"He left us, he left you and Toby and Gabe, and he'll leave that bitch Celeste too. It's what he does. The creep."

There had been no evidence of Maddy in the house when Lee brought Gabe home. Her room was emptied out; the grad school dining hall reported that she hadn't been at work in weeks. Rory dismissed Lee's concern.

"She told me she liked Atlanta after all and she was heading back there for good. Girl's an idiot," her sister decreed. "She'll OD or kill herself with a coat hanger and there is nothing anybody can do about that, OK? We have to just move on, just move on."

Lee was astonished by Rory's declaration of allegiance, but expected no one else from the life she had shared with Joe to choose her over him. Like Tate, they were tied to Joe and would be gone from her world, as soon as they knew.

They sat in the soft light that filled the kitchen, the four of them tucked into the breakfast alcove, serving dishes arrayed in front of the Commander, who had carved the roast chicken deftly.

"Toby, you want the drumsticks, right?"

"Yes, Granpa. But no salad."

"Yes, Granpa, *please*."

"Drumsticks, please, Granpa."

"That's better."

He put rice, slices of beefsteak tomatoes from the garden, and chicken slices or parts on each plate. Lee was grinding pepper onto her tomato when Mrs. Palmer said quietly, "Ern?"

"Yes, dear?"

Lee saw that there was a plate under her father's and that her mother had not been served.

"What is it, Emily?" he asked pleasantly as he raised a forkful of rice.

Mrs. Palmer's hands were folded in her lap. She started to cry.

"I don't understand, Emily. What seems to be the matter?"

Lee took her mother's plate from under his and held it out to him.

"Oh. Oh I see. Sorry, dear." He handed his wife the empty plate and continued eating.

Mrs. Palmer held it in two trembling hands for a moment, looking at the serving bowls and platters of food she'd prepared.

"Oh God, Ern. Oh God." She stood quickly to leave the table but he was in her way and didn't move. She held her napkin to her mouth to muffle the sound.

"This way, Granma, over here." Toby pushed his chair back and helped her by.

As Mrs. Palmer climbed the stairs sobbing, Lee stared at her father. One gray eyebrow was twitching, and there was a tiny curve of a smile on his lips as he reached defiantly for more salad.

She tried to see in him the romantic young lieutenant with the new gold braid, buying a gardenia for the love of his life, treasuring every second of the days that might be all they would ever have. There was no sign of that enthralled lover in the man he had become, in the decades they had been given.

When the Palmers packed and headed home, the weather at last cracked open into fall, the trees snapping overnight into reds and golds, the air crisping into something breathable and conducive to the wearing of soft, dry sweatshirts after far too much time in damp chambray. It was a welcome change that changed nothing else. The days remained solidly the same, each one coming, staying for long leaden hours, then ending, nothing having happened.

By daylight Lee was treading water, her nose just above a flattened sea. But on rare and fortunate nights, she dove down to the safe, radiant undersea world, where soft voices told her she was with her kind, welcome there.

More often her nights were spent not in the glittering sea but roaming dark, rain-whipped streets, the passing cars illuminating the faces of not one but two shivering sons looking at her with unspoken, unanswerable entreaties. Each morning began another day whose only form was shaped around them.

The call to begin again was the sound of Gabe stirring in the canopied bassinette. She would reach for him from the single bed in the nursery where she had slept since bringing him home, avoiding the master bed, which Joe often occupied, taking too much of the space, when she slipped away from knowing he had left her. She must remember this. There was no reason to cut articles from the paper that would interest him, or to buy foods that he liked. On some days, she was holding in that reality.

Before Gabe could cry, she would nurse him, the urgency of his need pulling her into the world of walls and floors and air and sorrow. When he was full and smiling, she would carry him down to Toby's room, sit on the edge of the older boy's bed and talk to him until he woke.

Gabe would kick and wave in the Infanseat propped on the kitchen table as she put a breakfast together for Toby. Was his homework in his backpack? Did he have his gym socks? Lee would watch him, there in the clean, dry house, reminding herself that this was the actual Toby, not the wet, dirty boy who stood in the rain staring up at her on those terrible nights.

Then he was gone and she would sit at the table staring at the *Times* while she drank the orange juice he hadn't finished and Gabe dozed off in a pool of warm morning light. The reports of horrors the world over reminded her that she and her sons were alive, together, healthy. There had been no 7.5 earthquakes in Princeton. No outbreak of malaria. No one was napalming their village. Her country was not in a civil war. She wondered if her Saigon neighbors and co-workers were even alive as Vietnam continued to bleed—her students, so young, so desperate for safe lives—what was happening to them? The young man who invited her, his teacher, to his home for dinner and to ask for her help in getting a scholarship in her country. His house was built of printed tin that had been made to become orange juice cans; there were images of oranges everywhere. His mother made hundred-year-old eggs and one-minute chicken, and served them to her son's teacher with all her hopes for her precious boy, hopes that Lee had no way of fulfilling.

Lee knew her life, in the larger scheme of things, was charmed. Gratitude was in order. She recognized the idea, but did not experience it. Even giving thanks could endanger the precarious balance that held her in place, minimally afloat, making only the simplest, required moves. Nothing must be tampered with, changed, altered. She'd even stopped subtracting the color from what she saw, making a scene switch to black-and-white. Now, that was not amusing. Now everything must be stable, simple, the same every time. Putting a clean diaper on Gabriel, reminding Das to pick Toby up after football practice, taking a shower. When clothes-changing seemed beyond her days-end strength, she stepped out of her jeans and slept in her sweatshirt and underpants. She was vaguely aware of the election campaigns, and of a burglary at the Watergate.

When she remembered that nursing mothers had to eat, she would put things she knew were healthy in the blender, absenting herself from the taste as she drank the mess down. There were careful drives to the A&P, slow walks around the block pushing the carriage. There was sitting with Toby to watch *The Waltons*, trying to stay with the story, and with her too-quiet son.

More often, she lived in another story, one that was not unfolding where she was but where they were, Joe and Celeste. It was a story in which Good Joe moved tautly across a room Lee did not recognize, passed broad fingers through his black curls, looked with blue-sky crescents at the beautiful woman who made him happy, the woman who did not see or point out his lapses of taste or grammar or manners, who never challenged him, who instead gave him roadmaps to his future, which she read for him in the moon and the stars. It was a happy story.

When Lee's own world asserted itself, there were moments in which she saw dust balls and fingerprints as possibly removable and she would find the broom and sponges—never the roaring vacuum cleaner. Once, she rubbed all the smudges off the upper half of the kitchen door and stared at the amazing difference between the top and the bottom. The change made no sense to her. Nothing she did could make anything change. Lee the Fixer could fix nothing, could assemble no books, edit no pages, unblock no writers.

She had not been surprised when she opened Publisher's Weekly and saw that two books had been sold to major houses on the effects of Transcendental Meditation. Of course. Such things were not to be done by the likes of Lee Montagna. She did not clean the bottom of the door, but sat on the floor witnessing the mystery of the difference between the two halves.

For the first time in her memory, music not only did not help, it was intolerable. Music took her places she must not go. Too many of her favorite classical works were filled with cellos that mated with her sorrow, with brasses that mocked her with their brightness. Only silence was safe and she could only find it in snippets of time. When cars approached she tensed until they passed, wondering if they carried someone bringing another threat. She jumped each time the refrigerator or the furnace went from dormant to active, and the doves, mourning whatever new tragedy had befallen them, were worse than cellos, with no button she could press to turn them off.

Deep into her pregnancy, Lee had actually researched dove lore and learned that they mated for life, that the male bird did more parenting than the female, nesting on the eggs and feeding the hatchlings longer than the mother. She had then thought more kindly of them and their near constant soundings. Now, she just wished they'd shut up.

Sleep was dangerous, opening her to the nightmare she fought to escape or to the sea dream she wanted never to leave; Lee put off sleep as long as possible, reading into the night, dropping off with the bed lamp still on, a book sliding to the floor.

Meditating was dangerous too. Alarmed by her unwillingness to return from that good place, when her sons so needed her, she stopped meditating.

As more and more things fell away, things Lee no longer had the money or the strength for, and things that were not safe, Dasya skirted a wide circle around her, hoping, she realized, to go unnoticed as Joe's no-longer-needed driver, hoping not to become one of the quiet amputations that were clearly being performed. He drove Toby to school, diffidently offered to run errands for Lee, bicycled to his classes and quickly home in time to get Lee's Volvo, pick Toby up, and advise him on his homework.

As he made his almost silent way toward the attic on a late afternoon, Lee called up to him.

"Das, wait just a moment, please."

He stopped and came back down a few steps, still treading lightly.

"I'm worried about Toby, Das. Has he talked to you about what's going on?"

Seeing the bicycle pants clip he'd forgotten to remove from the leg of his neatly pressed chinos, he reached down with a narrow brown hand and popped the clip quickly into the pocket of his orange and black windbreaker.

"Oh yes, Mrs. M. But just a little."

"I've told him Joe's not coming back and that we're going to be all right. How do you think he's doing with that?"

The young man hesitated, frowned, and decided to proceed.

"He is sad. And he would like to be happy. He says it is much better at Connor's house than here. I am sorry to tell you that. I would like to help in these difficulties. Please tell me what I might do."

She was puzzled by the his assumption that she would know what could help, but a thought did occur to her.

"I know you're all snug up there in your bed-sitter but would you consider eating with us down here? If we could switch from room and cash to room and board, it would help me a lot. I don't know much about cooking Indian food but we could figure it out."

"I can cook! Hamburgers. Spaghetti. Grilled cheese. Not to worry, Mrs. M. I would be most pleased to assist and to join the family table. It is very lonely in the attic."

Dasya was beaming at her, square white teeth bright in his cinnamon face. Of course. Dasya had told her he'd grown up in a house with five siblings and three grandparents, plus assorted aunts and uncles. He couldn't afford to go home for any holidays and here he'd been for months, alone in the attic. She must pay attention; she wasn't the only person in her world who was hurting.

Every evening Lee called Vi to collect her messages, putting most in a Later pile, returning only those she must. After too many unanswered calls from Aiken, she dialed her parents' number.

"What have you heard from him?" Her mother remained incredulous, coming as she did from a world in which men spent their lives with the women they had married, stayed, and provided for the children they had fathered. Mourning-dove fathers, never abandoning their mates, even if they might peck at them painfully and tinker annoyingly with their offsprings' lives.

"Well, has he sent any money? What are you going to *do*?"

Mrs. Palmer's questions roiled the waters and Lee would sink deeper. Joe sometimes paid the bills she forwarded to the post office box number he had deigned to give her, and sometimes he didn't pay them, always leaving her off balance. All her Third-World frugalities now seemed vital to survival rather than just the stinginess Joe had mocked.

Every morsel of food unserved at a meal became ingredients for a later dish; there could be no freshly shelled peas dumped in a garbage can. She found a consignment shop where she bought clothes for the boys, good ones, at a fraction of the cost of new. She mended clothes that tore, socks that sprang bare toes. Paper used on one side was turned over for more use; she sharpened pencils down to their erasers. The savings were minuscule, not capable of keeping her household afloat, but her dislike of waste had mutated into an offering to the gods; every penny quietly, carefully pinched was proof to Them that she was doing the best she could.

The most destabilizing time was when the service was off duty and Lee had to pick up, in case it was an emergency at Rory's, the Palmers' or at Connor's, where Toby spent so much of his time. It had happened just last weekend. Joe's voice was soothing, cajoling, ordinary.

"What's wrong, Leedle? That was such a sad 'hello.'"

His questions were confusing. He ignored the messages from Lee that Vi had relayed to him—lists of bills due, questions about his plans for paying them. Instead he chatted about how hard he was working, about his parents, who were visiting, about what Celeste was cooking for dinner.

"We don't eat much meat. Mostly fish and vegetables. It's healthier, you know."

She thought of all the times he had demanded well marbled steaks or bacon sandwiches with mayonnaise. She couldn't understand why he was telling her such a thing. She heard a crash.

"Are you OK?"

"Fine, fine. Celeste was just heading for the door to give my suits to the dry cleaner and she knocked over a lamp."

Why should Celeste Papandreou be giving Joe Montagna's suits to a cleaner, broiling bluefish for him, taking his mother shopping? That word "we" was the worst thing. It made no sense. His voice dropped to a whisper.

"It was an awful lamp. You would have hated it." He chuckled confidentially. "Nobody has taste like we do, Leedle."

Another "we" that made no sense. Joe had a bullfighter painted on velvet over his mantle when she met him. He was probably back in polyester shirts. How could he be mocking Celeste? If he was so concerned about good taste, why was he living in tacky Atlantic City with a woman in a sequined gauze jumpsuit? Most of all she could not understand why he was showing her, his wife, this world he was making, detailing this new domesticity.

"We went up to Queens yesterday to see the Clays. *Your* friends, Leedle, Ashley and Glenn, and their little Robert Martin who's a really cute kid. So I guess I'm not as bad as you think, eh?"

Lee put her hand very quietly in the cradle of the phone, breaking the connection. There must never be another call like this. She would explain again the ring-through code to her parents, to Rory, and to Marina, Connor's mother, so she could reach Lee if Toby needed his own mother for anything.

She might be all right if she stayed still enough to be a closed anemone, pulled in tight, no fragile tendrils floating pink in the currents caused by passing creatures, opening her to incoming predators. She burrowed into one corner of the down sofa that faced the fireplace. A blanket she'd gotten from the linen closet, the same cream as the sofa, made her invisible. She wriggled farther down into its folds, pulling it up to her eyes. It scratched her face, being the wooly llama one from Peru that had been on her bed when she was a child; the one her father had brought home from a shake-down cruise around South America. It had never been on the king-sized bed upstairs. She tried to remember if Joe had ever touched it, but she didn't think so. It felt safe. Almost.

The fire was seeping through her blanket barricade, warming the front of her as her back warmed the sofa. No longer feeling zero at the bone, she sensed her arms easing, her neck, her toes uncurling. She would watch the fire for answers, for what she was to do. Or for a door out of having to know. Of even wanting to know.

She watched carefully, breathing slowly into the wool across her face. That log there, the lowest one, the oak round, that would be her, lying still, waiting, doing nothing, docile, and omnipotent. Two splits of lighter wood were above her oak, leaning into each other for support, the flames dancing around them. They would both fall when either burned way. They were standing together but only for now, only for a while. While her oak lay still, steady, burning only just enough to outlast them.

On a Sunday deep into winter, when Vi was not standing between Lee and the dialing world, Lee sorted bills on the kitchen table, her operating speed revved toward normal by three cups of Medaglio d'Oro.

She could figure this out. She had the energy, even if it was caffeine-driven. There had to be a way to raise some money, something she could sell. What if she made an apartment out of the 1920s wing of the house? They could manage without the guest room and the den. The rent might be enough to cover the property taxes. There was the thread-and-shell sterling; that could be worth a bundle if she got it into the right auction.

Without thinking, she reached for the insistently ringing phone and heard coins dropping, city traffic passing.

"Lee please don't hang up! I don't have much time before... before I have to meet Joe. I'm on a street corner, at a pay phone."

"I wouldn't hang up on you, Celeste. I've been worried about you. Are you OK?"

"Me? Well, yes, I mean I guess so. I don't understand. You're worried about *me?*"

"Of course I am. You're in terrible trouble."

"What do you mean?"

"I mean that Joe is crazier than Stefan, and he's smarter. That's a very bad combination. And I know what scares you most, worse than being hit. It's being poor, right? And there you are with Joe who's got kids to support and a business that's down the toilet. Did he tell you that Tate's split off on his own? Do you understand that Joe's blowing what he has left of the company's most important contracts?"

Lee made herself stop rapping her coffee spoon on the table.

"Stefan's losing his seat on the Exchange."

"Actually, he's not. He sold it. For twice what he paid for it. And he's taken ownership of that mining company's assets. He is very, very rich and he's got private detectives trailing you. That's how he tracked you to New Hope. And he's got photos of you coming out of the Atlantic City house together. Wherever you are now, he's right behind you with a warrant for grand larceny."

"My God. Grand larceny?"

"He says you stole half a million dollars worth of antiques and paintings."

"You won't tell him where we are?"

"Not even if I knew. How would I support this baby if Joe's dead?"

forr"He'll always take care of you guys. He promised me."

"He's promised a lot of things to a lot of people. I don't think you should believe him."

"I have to."

"It's better not to. Like if he's promised to marry you? Italian men don't marry women they can't trust. You're cheating on Stefan so in Joe's eyes—no matter how unfair that is—you are not wife material. But he'll tell you, so sincerely, that up is down and night is day, that the sun revolves around the earth so you don't know who you are or what's right. Believe me, Celeste, you need to get on a plane. Go home to LA, go anywhere you're safe."

"I can't do that. He needs me."

"Of course he does. If he owns you, he thinks he owns the future. You can tell him what's coming, so he can use you to get a drop on the competition, to be top dog. But what about *you?*"

"This is not making sense to me. I... I have never in my life done anything so bad to anyone. You were counting on me and I sold you out. Why don't you understand that?"

"I understand how scared you were about Stefan hurting you and about being poor if he went bankrupt or if you just left him, with no one to go to. I understand that you were desperate. And I know Joe can convince anybody of anything. He's never the one doing anything wrong. I'm sure it's all worked out in his mind that this is totally my fault. I understand he could make you think so too."

"No. I'm afraid not. No, he hasn't been able to do that."

"Get away from him, Celeste. He'll ruin your life."

"I think I've already done that myself. You be well, you hear. *None* of this is your fault—you are the best friend I ever had. He *will* take care of you and Toby and Gabriel, I *promise*. I'm... I'm going now."

Lee carried the Chemex to the sink and, with shaking hands, poured out what was left of the Medaglio.

"What do you *mean* she called you? And you *talked* to her?" Marina Seton towered over Lee, fists on hips, her face fierce with disapproval. Lee kicked herself for even mentioning the call. It wasn't like anyone was going to understand how this had all happened. Marina didn't really know Lee, much less Celeste and Joe. And Lee did not want to explain it all.

And here was Marina, this woman to whom Lee was just a neighbor, a fellow hockey mom, here was Marina furious on Lee's behalf, assuming her anger, puzzled at not evoking it, in chorus with her own. Lee would not tell her the long, complex story of why there was no heat in her feelings. That would require strength, and trust. Lee wanted only to go to sleep and wake up to find five years, maybe more, had passed.

She cried under everything she did, but it was from grief and fear, not anger. She was scared that nothing she could do would bring in enough money to support her kids. She cried because the bill collectors were circling closer. She cried because she was such a bad judge of people that she'd have to be alone forever to be safe.

There was a rightness, an inevitability in what had happened to her. Her prayer had been answered for the secret Joe to leave her life, but he had taken with him the other Joe, the one everyone knew, the one she wanted to keep. She was not the innocent victim others saw, deceived, harassed, bearing up, carrying on bravely. She had driven both Joes away with her endless editing of his every move.

She knew she must never again let anyone come close enough to find cause to leave her. She would show herself to people only as an amusing, friendly person, moving agreeably through life, not being critical, giving no advice, never straightening their pictures or correcting their sentences, and needing nothing from them. But now she had let slip mention of Celeste's call, and now talk of anger was expected of her, here in a neighbor's warm yellow kitchen, over a steaming cup of Earl Grey on a day that was supposed to open spring but had brought instead, snow.

She put an end-of-topic firmness in her voice. "Good people can do some godawful things."

"Present company excluded, of course." Marina accepted the stand-back message gracefully. "I don't think I'll ever understand my fellow human beings. But I keep trying."

Lee thought the photo portraits that lined the halls of the Setons' house made it clear that Marina was doing rather well at understanding people. Within each frame there was a glimpse of a human soul, captured in light and shadow. Marina was as talented as her mother, the phenomenal Phoebe, whose abstract canvases covered the dining room walls, whose venturesome nature had now taken her into the Hindu Kush for an exploration of indeterminate length and breadth. Marina had found a way to be as good as her mother, without imitating the inimitable, without competing. Marina knew a lot about her fellow human beings.

The artful portrayer of character picked up a large pottery bowl from the counter. "Meanwhile, we can wonder why the goddess has screwed up the schedule and sent us all this white stuff on the first day of her new year. It's March, damn it. My daffodils are confused. I am confused. But in my continuing efforts to become unconfused about *humanity*, I found this really interesting psychology article the other day about stories people take in and then use as patterns for their lives."

Her arm moving in one long arc, she put the bowl on top of the nearest cupboard. Lee laughed. "You know you'll never be able to sell this house."

"I'm not planning to, but what are you saying?"

Lee stood in front of the sink. "Come on. This kitchen is a dream, but it's only for giants like you and Oscar. Look. Regular people can barely reach the faucets." Marina squinted down from her full 71 inches.

"It's not *that* bad. You can always use that stepstool we got for Connor."

Lee poured herself a glass of water, feeling odd at being in a room with only another adult, someone who did not need sustenance from her but offered tea, and that suspect commodity, friendship.

She wondered if she could really trust Toby and Connor to call from 99 the minute Gabe woke up. Toby, so long the youngest, had not been at all sure which end was up on such a small person but Dasya, the veteran eldest child, had been a good teacher. Just months into big-brotherhood, Toby could hold Gabe confidently, proud of making him laugh, balking only at diaper-changing. He could certainly handle things for the minutes it would take Lee to get her boots on and walk a few doors down Underwood Road.

"So what was the wonderful psychology article about?"

"Oh, it said that you could find out a lot about people by asking them suddenly, you know, with no chance to think, to name a fairy tale. I popped up with one immediately but my dear Oscar said he couldn't think of one at all. Isn't that strange? Maybe his parents never read to him. I don't know." Marina turned back from her cupboard-organizing. "Lee, what's the matter? Are you sick?"

"I'm trying not to be. But this *is* sickening."

"What is? Did I say something?"

"Oh yes. You said something. Fairy tales. I can't believe this. I got one. Instantly. I mean the minute you said that."

"What?"

"The Little Mermaid. The Little Freaking Mermaid."

"And?"

"You don't know that one? You're lucky. It's a *terrible* story."

"OK, OK. This is good." Marina pulled the cozy off the teapot and the To Do pad from its magnet on the refrigerator. "Sit, sit. What we do now is you tell me everything you remember. Everything that stuck from that story. Then you're going to get the whole book and compare it, you know, so you can see what you left out. That's what the article said."

Lee's hand shook as she picked up her Earl Grey. "I don't want to. I can't do this."

"You have to. This is obviously important. You don't have any blood in your face."

"I feel like I don't have any anywhere. Somebody pulled the plug."

"So we attack. We wrestle this to the ground. Start talking."

Lee looked at the note pad. "That won't do it. I've got a real gusher here."

"Fine." Marina pulled open a drawer and grabbed a tape recorder.

She lowered it in front of Lee and pushed Record with a long, elegant finger. "Talk," she ordered.

"My God, my God...." Lee gulped down some tea, focusing on the warmth and the scent of bergamot, and tried again. "This isn't a fairy tale. It's a script. I've been playing it out since I was what? Nine? Ten years old? This is horrible."

"No it's not. If you figure out what you've been doing, you can decide to stop."

"It's that simple, is it? As we say in the city, 'From your mouth to God's ear.' What do I remember? All right. The mermaid found a handsome prince who was drowning. His ship sank and he was drifting down into the sea. I see him falling in big slow spirals, down to where she lived under the sea. And I see my father sitting next to me with the book in his hand. His ship had been hit in the Pacific and he was waiting out the repairs. We were in San Francisco. He read the story to me."

"Was your father a handsome man?"

"You know he was. Is. You've met him. He looks like some movie star. Please, Marina, don't smile."

"All right. I am without expression. I make no comment. I will not mention the name 'Elektra' or...."

Marina stopped abruptly, seeing tears move down Lee's face.

"Oh no, I'm sorry, Lee. This is really serious." She reached across the table and pulled Lee's hand away from her mouth. "It's OK. It really is. You need to remember everything he read to you."

Lee shook her head slowly. "Some bedtime story. I think it put me to sleep for the rest of my life."

"That's OK too, my friend. Just talk."

Lee closed her eyes. "The mermaid swims to shore holding the prince up so he can breathe. He's unconscious the whole time. She pushes him onto the sand and watches from the water to be sure he's OK. Just as he's waking up, a beautiful woman with long dark hair—oh shit—walks down the beach and the prince looks up and sees her. The mermaid figures he's going to be fine because someone has found him, and she goes home. But she keeps thinking about him and she wants to be with him. But land people have legs. So she goes to a sea witch and asks for legs. The witch—there was a picture of the mermaid talking to a horrible old crone—the witch wants to be paid and the only thing the girl—the mermaid—has that the witch wants is her voice. Oh right, that part—the mermaid was famous for her beautiful singing."

Lee stopped, moving an upright hand back and forth in front of her face, fending something off.

"No, Lee, don't stop now. You can do this. What happens next?"

Barely audible, Lee went on.

"She buys it. The idiot buys it. She wants to follow the prince so badly that she gives the witch her voice. She gets the damn legs, swims to the beach, and walks off to find him. And of course he has no idea who she is or what she's done for him. And she can't *tell* him. She dances her story but he doesn't get it. Oh. She's not just dancing for *him*. The brunette from the beach is with him. He thinks that she saved his life and he's about to marry her. The wrong woman. And the brunette's going along with it, the bitch. Everybody thinks the mermaid is this kind of nice house pet. 'Poor little mute, isn't she sweet. Let's get her to dance some more.' But the dancing *hurts*. The damned witch has set it up so the mermaid feels daggers in her feet every time she takes a step.

"There's something else. A real hook. The deal with the witch was that the mermaid had to be *married* to the prince to survive. If he marries someone else, she dies at the following dawn. She's gambled her life on his loving her. I can't stand it. In her world she's a singer, has a beautiful voice that her people love to hear, has her tail and fins and moves up, down, in every direction. It's perfect. She's understood, she's not alone, but for this stupid prince she gives it all up, comes out of the water, into the air-and-land world, where she stands to lose everything. Stupid. So stupid."

Lee stared through the glass doors into the whitened garden. A small brown bird made tiny fork marks across the curving surface of the snow.

"And he did it. He never understood who the mermaid was and he married the imposter. Then. *Then* he took the mermaid along as a guest on the honeymoon voyage. Like you'd bring a lap dog. The sun is setting and she's standing on deck knowing she's lost him and that she'll be dead in a few hours. But her sisters, yeah, her sisters appear in the water with their arms stretched up to her, pleading. They're calling to her that they want her to come home, back to the safety of the sea. *They've* made a deal with the witch. All of them traded their long hair for a magic knife. She can have her lovely fishtail and her beautiful voice and her whole world back—if she'll just kill the prince. They throw the knife on deck. The mermaid picks it up and walks into his cabin. He's asleep with this woman in his arms. The mermaid looks at him and all she can see is how much she loves him and she really can't blame this woman for loving him too. She drops the knife and she just walks out."

Marina watched Lee expectantly, but was met with silence.

"Lee? Lee, did she die?

"Yes. Maybe. I think she did. I don't know." She concentrated on the cream and sugar, moving them a quarter inch to the right.

"Lee?"

She looked up to see Marina's long arms stretched high above her, tears spilling from her navy blue eyes.

"I know, Marina. I know. I have to pick up the knife."

"Yes, dear woman, you really must."

Marina went to the wall phone.

"Oscar, you've got to find Toby's mom a really good divorce lawyer. A knife-fighter, you know? That bastard's got to be blown out of the water."

As she listened, Marina wiped her eyes dry, circled a wet hand into an OK sign to Lee and beckoned her to the phone. The chair tried to hold Lee in place. She pushed hard against it and walked heavily across the room.

"Oscar, hi. This is Lee. I want a divorce." She stopped and said again, louder, "Yes. I want a divorce." She listened a moment.

"Desertion? Yes, I guess that's accurate. I'll have to countersue because he filed already. He says I deserted *him.*" She took a deep breath. "He's missing mortgage payments and I don't want to lose the house. I may need a corporate lawyer too. He's been blowing our company's money on a woman."

Marina jutted her jaw forward and gave her a rigorous thumbs-up.

"Well, it's more than just marital community property. The company owes me a couple years' back salary. I can sue for that too, right? We were building the company together. For our future. Now the wrong woman's in the story."

Lee listened, staring at the floor. "Yes, I can document it all. I've got bills and itineraries, receipts forged "Mrs. Joseph Montagna"— they all come to the house." She hesitated. "And her husband's got photographs."

Marina scrawled quickly on the To Do pad and held it up to Lee with an enormous grin. It said, "Happy New Year!"

On a dogwood and tulip morning, the untimely snow gone, Lee carried Gabe into the children's stacks at the library and put him belly down on the carpeted floor next to her, where he immediately began what looked like swimming, chortling as his arms and legs flapped.

She searched the G's, but the mermaid was not in *Grimm's Fairy Tales*. She moved to the A's and found a single-volume picture book of *The Little Mermaid*, but it had the wrong pictures. She closed it, not wanting to lose the drawings in her mind. She sat on the floor, leaning back against the shelves, her knees bent to support an old copy of *The Complete Hans Christian Andersen*, tightly printed texts punctuated with the line drawings Lee recognized. And there she was. A small figure in the sea looking to shore, where the prince was waking to see the dark lady standing over him.

She reached out to pat Gabe but he was not where she had put him; he was in the aisle at the end of the stacks, a librarian in perfect Talbot's attire looking down at him, smiling. "Who do you belong to, little one?" The voice was friendly but foreign, not Lee's. Gabe howled in alarm and Lee dropped the book and dived after him.

"Wow, look at you. You didn't know you could do that, did you. Your first solo trip into the world."

She was laughing, delighted with his accomplishment, and surprised that such an unfamiliar sound had come from her own mouth. The librarian in her tweedy wrap skirt and Shetland cardigan moved off, but Gabriel howled louder until Lee cuddled him, first humming, then quietly singing the words of the song that always calmed him, brought him to shuddering little gasps of air, and then to forgetfulness of whatever had gone wrong. "... When evening falls so hard, I will comfort you, I will take your part, When darkness comes and pain is all around...." With the second chorus, the tired bluesky eyes closed and his breathing went deep and steady.

Lee moved the book to the floor next to her and turned the pages with one hand, her other hand circling slowly on Gabe's back as he slept face down across her lap. She began the story, telling herself she would read every word, slowly and carefully. According to Marina, the parts she had not remembered were supposed to be important, and the parts she had remembered wrongly might be even more revealing.

Coming to the last words of the tale, she closed the book and put it back into its wide space on the shelf. She stood up, Gabe heavy in her arms, her clothes weighted with sea water. She would go home now. She would think about all this later. When things were calmer. When she didn't have so much to do, to figure out. There were papers to find for her knife-fighter lawyer and the car was about to be repossessed, Toby was having trouble with the news that he couldn't go back to his day school in the fall, and she must get Das to help him prep for an algebra exam.

In the parking lot, putting Gabe into his car seat, she stopped, overwhelmed by fury. Hans Christian Andersen was a manipulating, life-destroying sonofabitch. She turned sharply and carried Gabe back into the building, going straight to the Children's Section and taking the fat volume to the checkout desk.

The librarian who had discovered Gabe smiled at them both, above her Peter Pan collar and gold circle pin. "Bedtime stories?"

Lee looked at her in surprise. "Heavens no. I'd never read these to *children*. This is research."

"Ah. Education thesis."

"Sort of. Yes. It is. My thesis on Hans Christian Andersen as a despoiler of innocent lives."

The librarian handed her the date-stamped book with a frown. "Whatever you say."

That night, under the sea, mermaids, all with long, undulating hair, surrounded Lee, all of them singing a jubilant song that Lee had been almost hearing, all of her life.

Walking the Mermaid

Lee froze at the top of the stairs. There was someone moving in Joe's office, someone opening drawers and taking things out. It was a school day; Toby and Das were in class. And they wouldn't ever be in Joe's office. The door opened and he moved into the foyer, looked up at her.

"Is this all the mail? I'm expecting some checks that aren't here."

Lee stared at him, unable to speak.

"It's really important, Leedle. I have to get checks quickly or I can't take care of all the bills."

He smiled up at her, ran one wide hand through black curls. He was wearing a bolo tie.

Lee moved cautiously down the stairs, aware that Gabriel was sleeping in the nursery behind her. She stood on the last step, blocking this intruder who must not move toward her young. She willed Gabe to not wake up now. He must not make a sound that would tell the intruder where he was.

Joe held up a flyer from the McCarter theatre. "They're doing some good stuff, kind of things you like. You want to go? Oh and what about the hockey clinic at Tobe's school? I think we should send him."

We. We should send him. He had questions, ideas, plans. Lee stared, listened, saying nothing. This was Good Joe, Loving Joe, the man she adored, and he was here. Wearing a bolo tie.

"I got season tickets for the Mets. Just for me and Tobe. Good seats. I didn't think you'd want to go. Looks like they'll be pretty good this year."

He would be back by the end of the month, he said. Back. As if he'd been on sabbatical and would now return, as planned, to campus.

"Why?" The only word she could manage.

"Because this is home, Leedle." He smiled a big, loving Of-Course and reached a hand toward her face. She stepped back so quickly, she lost her balance, her spine hitting the stair edges behind her. When he tried to help her up, she wrenched herself away from his grasp.

"You can't be here."

Tate knew. Toby. Dasya. Rory. Her family. Vi. Connor's family. There were witnesses. Others who could confirm what she sometimes knew to be fact. This man smiling at her—good Joe—was not real, and the real Joe had done something unforgivable.

"Don't be silly, Leedle. This is our home. We have a business to run. We're a family." His voice was caressing, reassuring, demented.

"Celeste is your family now. Go home."

The black brows became one angry bar over slits of blue ice.

"You're all she has, Joe. Go take care of her."

She stood on the bottom step, looking down at him, her arms making a barrier from wall to banister, as his furious hiss ordered her to cancel the Food Mart account, to forget about good clothes and restaurants, to stop work on the unfinished house, all things that she had done months before. She was not to send him bills for the *Times,* for the answering service, for Dasya's salary, her car payments, the mortgage, for Toby's tuition. And she'd better start looking for a cheap place to rent. The cords in his neck were stretched taut, his face was flushed, and he was sweating. He had crushed the letters and bills in his broad hand.

The rage broke through to a shout as he reached the door. "That's *it*, bitch!" The slamming door woke Gabriel with a cry, and she moved quickly up the stairs to his room. Gabriel was real, and he was hungry.

Joe's colle ction of bulldogs stared back at Lee from the top of the mahogany highboy that was still full of his clothes. A small wooden pup, its head cutely cocked, stood with a Churchillian one of painted china, several ceramic monstrosities, one glass piece that was almost nice. She opened the top right drawer and took out a stack of monogrammed handkerchiefs. JVHM. There were JVHM's on everything. There was a JVHM on the door of his car, on his shirt pockets; it would have been on the antique sterling, had she not burst into tears over the idea. The monogram, the name. Never Joseph Montagna. Always Joseph van Heugel Montagna. You had to know he was not your ordinary street-corner wop.

Lee opened the large drawer at her waist, took a breath, plunged her hands into his undershirts and shorts, and dropped them quickly into the Remy Martin box at her feet.

In the shallow top-left drawer there were safety pins and collar stays, and the cufflinks and Tiffany watch that he had sent back to her in the mail. Rich gifts wax false when givers prove unkind. He was too injured by her cruelty to wear these things that she had given him. The watch floated on her hand, so thin she had been amazed that it functioned. The face was white, the numbers Arabic and graceful, the black lizard band beautifully grained, and on the underside of the watch, words engraved into the pale gold:

> *To J*
> My *favorite*
> *40-year-old*
> All *my love*
> L

She put it back into the now empty drawer, which she closed with two careful hands. He'd mailed the watch to her with that venomous note; she would not now include it in the boxes she would stack in the garage where he must pick them up by the end of the coming weekend, or she would call a charity to come for it all. But not the watch. And not the pillow of 40 squares that she had needlepointed. She had presented him the watch, in its Tiffany robin's egg box, resting on this pillow that had taken her months to make, the pillow he had dropped on the floor, as if it were wrapping paper. The pillow would stay in the living room, its history erased from her mind, its beauty and the care with which it had been made remaining.

Her forehead pressed into the top of the chest, she pulled in air. Looking up she came eye-to-eye with a genuine-hand-painted, hideous ceramic bulldog pup. Celeste had given it to Joe. On his 40th birthday.

What was it doing in this house? And why were there Yale symbols all over the place? Anybody could be a Yalie. What did a straight-A CCNY grad want with this crap?

But they were his. They were part of the way he wanted things to be. For whatever mysterious reason. And he was making a whole new world that was entirely the way he wanted it, with no damned editor, no critical female eye squinting at what he did, blue-tagging his clothes and his manners and his speech. Instead Celeste's constant I know, I know, her unrelenting approval and encouragement, and her steady telling of what was to come.

Lee put bulldogs in shorts, bulldogs in socks, bulldogs in handkerchiefs. But not Celeste's ceramic, not the terminally adorable one that he could take out of the box and hold up and coo over. Oh Celekins. Here it is. The first gift you ever gave me.

Lee hefted it in her palm. About the weight and size of Toby's softball. She tossed it from hand to hand a few times then pitched it overhand and hard out the bedroom door. It hit the wall in the stairwell and shattered onto the steps.

The underwear carton wasn't very large or heavy, despite its concealed cargo of dogs. She lifted it to the stair railing and let it fall into the front hall, saving a trip down the stairs and back, saving time and strength for all the rest of the work it would take to rid the house of him.

She noted that there was no point to such behavior. Except that it was exhilarating. Except that it was time for sweeping up the heart, for putting love away, time to make war not love. *Oggi mi sento un toro*—Today I feel like a bull. Or a no-longer-to-be-messed-with mermaid.

Libraries had always been homes to Lee, from the first grammar-school days when she discovered the open stacks of the public library on Coronado Island. Now her reading narrowed to one subject: the mermaid. Reading Andersen's entire tale on the public library floor in Princeton had been so unsettling, she had needed to bring the book home, to circle it cautiously, until she could open it again and confirm what she had not included in recounting the tale to Marina.

She had not remembered that the mermaid didn't die, but tried to. On her painful legs, in her human form, no longer a water creature and unable to kill the prince, she had thrown herself from the deck of his honeymoon ship, expecting to become foam upon the water, disappearing, as decreed by the witch.

But lo! She was taken up by a group called the "daughters of the air," who were so impressed by her self-sacrifice, *they* offered her the deal they operated under—she could do good deeds for 300 years, not in her own water element but with them in the air, and earn a soul after all. Lee hadn't remembered that the mermaid needed the prince's love not only to live, but to have a soul.

Then followed the perfect guilt-hook for the child reading the story—every time a child is bad, the poor, pitiful mermaid loses time-served and is set back years from getting that soul. The hideous hook Andersen had set for his young readers, the hook that added to the destructiveness of the tale itself. You, kid, the one reading this story—you'll not only expect females to give up their own voices and walk in pain to win The Prince, you'll know that if they fail at that they are nothing, don't even have souls, unless they find another way to give up everything they have and are. You'll also, on top of all that, know that if you, kid, do anything deemed off-track, sinful, or self-serving, you're damning the mermaid to more soulless years of servitude. It's all your fault, you little wretch.

Seeing the complete story, realizing its full power and the grip it had so long had on her, had Lee chanting Sonofabitch, sonofabitch, sonofafrigginbitch. Which was beginning to feel a lot better than her lifelong *Mea culpa, mea culpa, mea maxima culpa.*

Finding this programming for self-abnegation, determining to fight against it, was not enough. She had to know what had prompted the writing—and her acceptance—of such a story. She had taken in and taken to heart a template for female helplessness, sacrifice, silence, and soullessness, without resistance or rage. Why had she done that? Why had this dreadful tale been written, told, and accepted as beautiful by generations of children and the adults reading to them? There had to be a history here, and she would find it.

Stacks of mythology and folklore books covered the nightstand by the narrow bed where she slept, in Gabriel's room, and by her chair next to the living room fire. She read through every reference to mermaids in the town library and dispatched Dasya into the University's more abundant stacks to ferret out still more, compiling notes on every manifestation of the mermaid that she found.

It was astonishing. The mermaid appeared again and again, in every culture and every age it seemed, and she was consistently not Andersen's wimp and not the cute Dolly Delius that Disney had drawn for her father's ship. She was instead an incomprehensible, malevolent force that endangered men, threatening their lives and, more chillingly, their souls. Lee found Atargatis, a Babylonian sea goddess of 5,000 BC, who became the Greek Derketo who became Aphrodite, born-from-the-sea. She found Nammu in Sumeria, Amberella in the Baltic, Tanit in North Africa, Bheara in Ireland and Scotland, Ilmatar in Finland, Mami-Wata in Ghana, the Sybil of Warsaw, and KoKwalAlwoot of the Samish, here in the "new world." Around the Orkneys, Papua, Iona and Hokkaido, in the Rhine and in the fjords, mermaids had tempted good men into sex, death and eternal hellfire.

Everywhere, again and again, innocent men were lured to their undeserved doom and damnation by soulless, sexy Loreleis, havfraus, asparas, nixies, vateas, sirenas, nereids, ris, ilkais, harpies, ningyos, nixies, tritonids, melusines, oceanids, mami watas, vateas, roans and selkies, ondines and undines, mergens and morgans—all mysterious waterwomen with beautiful voices that floated over the sea, calling men to come into their bodies, die—and go straight to hell.

How scared of life did men have to be to come up with such crap? And the rationalizations of the doubters—they were even sillier. All those sailors had really seen manatees and dugongs, not mermaids. How drunk would they have to be? No. Such explanations wouldn't do.

The mirror that was so often in the mermaid's hand echoed the shape of the astrological glyph for Venus, the sign of all things female. A mirror—the simple and universal symbol of vanity. The mermaid's hair was always long, beautiful, enticing, entangling, and therefore deadly. The comb was put into her hand by the Greeks, further evidence of her self-involvement, but also because their words for comb and vulva were the same. The Greeks always had a word for it. And one Greek word meant vain cunt. So succinct.

These ancient mermaids were unrelated to Andersen's gentle, timid twit. Hans Christian to the rescue of frightened men! Since his rewrite, the mermaid was not a force to be feared but a self-sacrificing house pet, no equal to male power. She was sub-human, spiritually inferior to males. Well, it was one way of dealing with the problem: men could stop demonizing the female and telling fear-filled tales about her—they could just make her cute. And stupid.

Male fear accounted for there being no merboys or merlads with the mermaids, no merwomen for the mermen. The female had to be named with a diminutive, denying her power. Merwomen. The full-grown women of the sea, keepers of the mysteries of love, sex, birth—mer*women* were not allowed to enter the world, respected, embraced as equals, by men brave enough to meet them eye-to-eye, strength for strength.

Lee inserted a title page in the binder of notes she'd been making:

Findings on the True Meaning of the Mermaid

or

A Case of Mistaken Identity

OR

How Guys Got the Story All Wrong

She sat on a long bench at the dingy office in Trenton, one of many women with clipboards on their knees, working their way through layers of forms.

All of the others were black or Hispanic, orbited by or draped with children. Lee was reminded yet again of her good fortune; none of these women lived in big old houses with an attic studio they could offer to a live-in student in exchange for child care.

But there was no money in the big old house. She had engaged The System, filing for a divorce settlement that would keep her household afloat until she could relaunch her life. Still, the hearing was months away, there was no job she could imagine doing, and there was no money in the house.

She'd been pulled out of panic by the memory of MAA reports she'd written on public assistance—there was a safety net that caught people plummeting toward hunger, toward homelessness, toward living the nightmare.

Approaching that net, she sat on a bench in an office with filthy windows painted shut against the late-Spring day that was trying to happen outside. As per written instructions on the forms in her lap, she'd added up her outstanding debts, averaged her monthly expenses, listed her sources of income, written numbers on appropriate lines. A small, deep-brown hand touched her wrist.

"Leroy, don't you be bothering the lady." Lee grinned at Leroy the explorer, whose black eyes were studying her seriously. She smiled at his anxious mother, a young, heavy-set woman with the south in her voice and an infant on her lap. "He's OK really. I like kids." She looked back at the boy. "What are you, four?" He held up three small fingers. "Wow, you're very tall for three." He laughed and stood on the toes of his ragged sneakers.

"Lee?"

A ruddy, balding man with a pulled-down necktie and rolled-up shirt sleeves was looking expectantly across the roomful of women waiting on the benches. He looked again at a paper in his hand.

"Lee Montagna?"

She started, then stood, gathering up her clipboard, coat, shoulder bag, and the file of documents she'd assembled. "Bye, Leroy. Gotta go." As she moved past his mother she whispered, "Good luck." The woman looked surprised but quickly said, "You too."

In his tiny cubicle, the balding man, a social worker assigned to her "case," introduced himself.

"I'm Mr. Fairfield. How can I help you?"

Lee looked at the name plate on his desk.

Charles, Charlie, Chuck. But we've never met, have we,
Chuckie. And there's not a reason in the world for us to call
each other by our first names. Unless one of us has a habit of
being extremely disrespectful.

"I am in temporarily dire straits and would like you to see if my children and I qualify for some assistance."

Fairfield looked at her warily before picking up her forms and documents. He frowned his way through them, looking puzzled. "This address...."

"I know. But I don't have title so I can't sell it, and we can't eat the shingles."

He spread papers across his desk and re-checked them, shaking his head. "I think you not only qualify for food stamps, you could get welfare and Medicaid. At that address. In Princeton."

Lee cocked her head, raised her shoulders and spread her hands, palms up, a What-can-I-tell-you? look on her face. Charlie Fairfield smiled, and Lee knew he'd taken the first step to being an advocate for her family's survival.

A key scratched in the front door. Lee reached for her coat. On the count of three, there was a long angry blast on the doorbell. On a count of seven, she opened the door, stepped out into the spring chill, closed the door, and moved past him, before he could speak.

"We'll talk at P.J.'s. See you there." After an unmoving, uncomprehending moment, he followed her across the bright green grass, still damp from Toby's watering the night before.

"Lee, why doesn't my key work? What do you think you're doing?"

She didn't turn her head as she answered. "You don't live here, Joe. We do. Toby and Gabe and me. And Das. We all have keys to the new locks."

She got in the Volvo and started the engine but she hadn't locked the doors. Joe dropped into the passenger seat. Before he had completely closed the door behind him, she pulled out and headed for Nassau Street.

"What are you doing? Why can't we sit in the house and talk like reasonable adults?"

"This is reasonable, Joe. You can say whatever you need to say there. And have a pecan waffle at the same time."

"You think you can keep me out of our house? A house I pay for? That's not going to happen. Crazywoman, crazywoman!"

As he picked up verbal speed, Lee braked and put the car into a deft u-turn.

"What the hell are you doing now?"

"What I am doing now is taking you back to your car." She smiled and offered up her delighted revelation. "I no longer have to listen to this crap."

"OK. OK. We're going to P.J.'s." He spoke in the exasperated voice that said, I'm humoring you.

"I brought you some papers. You have my mail?"

"You know I pack it up every Friday and send it to your post office box."

"That's not good enough. Sometimes it's urgent stuff and I need it right away."

"You'd have it right away if you hadn't blown your life up. The mail slot is ten feet from what was your desk. Now, you'll just have to deal with getting it weekly."

As soon as their coffee was on the deeply initialed wooden table, he began again. "You have to stop telling people I'm gone when they call. We've lost three clients."

"Oh, like maybe Mayor Fisher who called to ask if I liked the baby gift because she hadn't heard from me? The baby gift, Joe? You told her that it looked great on Gabriel and all kinds of cute crap. So you think she was mad when I said that I'd never seen the romper suit, that you hadn't lived in the house since Gabe was born? I wonder why that would upset her."

"Bitch. Bitch! First you bust up the partnership. Do you know how much trouble we'd be in if Tate had wanted a buyout? We'd be bankrupt. You *realize* that, Miz Bigmouth? Even without that, I had to change everything. The letterhead. The cards. The phone. No more Montagna & Altridge Associates. Moving the office. Do you *know* how much *that* cost? And all the meetings with clients to smooth things over. You are destroying my business."

> *Good job of keeping your voice down to a hiss. Mustn't make*
> *a public spectacle. Not that any of the kids in here would give*
> *a damn what a couple of codgers like us were up to. And yeah,*

this figures. I've killed the business—your business. No more fake "we." Has nothing to do with my life, the work I was never paid for, nothing to do with anything you've done that might have made the clients suspect you're a schmuck.

Her available stores of courage almost depleted, she held her hand out, palm up. "Give me the papers you think I should sign and I'll see that my lawyer gets back to yours before the end of the month."

"No, today. It's just a draft agreement, Leedle. Not binding. I just want you to look it over and initial it. Now. And I can tell Celeste we're working all this out. She's concerned, you know."

Lee withdrew her hand, hoping he hadn't seen that her palm was shining with sweat. A little more nerve, a few more words, and this would be over. She could go home and get Gabriel back from Dasya's room. He'd be sleeping and she would take him to the rocker and hold him, humming, letting him know in his dreaming that he was safe with her, that she would not leave him and become foam upon the water, that she had picked up the knife and was protecting his world. Even if Celeste, the dark lady of this story, might be harmed. *We make our decisions and we live with the results. There are always consequences.*

Just a few more words needed. She looked at Joe over the rim of her coffee mug.

"Really? And wadllyagimme if I initial this stuff?"

"How about I tell you who that baby's father is?"

The mouthful of coffee Lee had just taken in was instantly airborne. Grabbing a wad of napkins from the metal holder, she wiped her face and began blotting the speckled table.

"You'll tell me what?"

"You heard me. I've got the charts. I *know.*"

"And *I* need *you*—and Celeste's damn charts—to tell *me.*"

She had known that he would find a way to escape all blame for turning their lives into a demolition zone, but she hadn't known quite how he would accomplish it. Business losses? Her fault for not covering for him with the clients. His desertion? The only thing he could do, poor man, given her infidelity and her outrageous idea that he should support her bastard.

This one was ingenious, a masterwork.

Lee began to laugh—at his inventing the one saving lie that could make him appear in the right, at his attempt to control past, present and future, all uncontrollable, at the foot-in-bucket slapstick of her reaction, at showing him the knife, at seeing dots of lightly creamed coffee on and around the JVHM on his shirt pocket. Try as she might, she found she couldn't stop laughing.

The front pages of the *National Enquirer* and the *Star* weren't very funny so she passed the time in the A&P line watching the checkers. There were two high school girls, one plump, the other lanky; one young man carbuncular who really shouldn't be handling anyone's food; a matron with an earth-mother bosom and, processing Lee's line, a wiry, gray-haired woman, quick in her movements like a sandpiper dodging sea surges. They all whizzed the Technicolor array of groceries along the chutes, chatting with the customers, making change, loading bags. At bat at last, Lee relayed produce, cartons, and jars out of her cart and onto the conveyor belt. The checker twitched a smile.

"What do you do with plain yogurt? I bought a fruit one and kind of liked it."

Lee told her about using the plain in any recipe that called for sour cream, though the calories in the cream might be a better choice for someone so emaciated.

"That's $47. Even."

Lee counted the amount out in the play-money food stamps. The clerk's mouth puckered, her forehead furrowed. She briskly, silently filled the bags with oatmeal, vegetables, detergent, whole wheat bread, not looking at Lee.

> *You're right, I don't look poor and I'm not. But I am dead*
> *broke, despite this suede coat. So this isn't a scam on hard-*
> *working taxpayers like you. And please note that you're not*
> *putting any frivolities into those bags. No soft drinks or chips.*
> *And no goodies from the gourmet aisle. I'm being responsible*
> *about this. I've had a change of fortune, you see. I'll get back*
> *on my feet, I assure you. But for now, thanks to good old*

Charlie at the welfare office, my kids can see a doctor when
they get sick and they can eat because of those food stamps
you're angrily stuffing into your cash drawer, along with those
of every other freeloader you've had to deal with today.

"Those new barcodes on all the packages? Do they mean that checking out will be automated? No more people doing this job?"

The checker looked at Lee, horrified. "Oh no. I mean they've told us we'll all keep our jobs. They *promised.*"

"That's good. I'm glad for you."

There was food, there was enough cash to buy jeans and shirts for Toby and a big crib for Gabe at the consignment shop on John Street when he outgrew the bassinette, enough cash to get necessities at the drug store.

She enrolled Toby at Princeton High, full of apologies for further disrupting his life, praying that his dean's list performance at his day school would go with him into this new realm, and touched by his valiant assurances that he'd be just fine. Lee was not sure he would be, if he also lost his home.

She shoved the foreclosure notice under the phone book as Marina walked into the kitchen, returning a windbreaker Toby had left in her front hall.

"No no. No hiding things. Not when I can see you've been crying. What's the bastard done now?"

Lee knew Marina was not to be deterred. Better to just get it over quickly. She yanked a Kleenex out of the pop-up box.

"It's the not-doing that's the problem. He's so behind on the mortgage, the bank's moving in. I've got to find an apartment. You want some Medaglio?"

"No I don't want any damn coffee. And I don't want you moving. Connor's never had a buddy like Toby before and here comes Samira's baby—a playmate for Gabriel. Here. In this neighborhood. You're *staying.*"

Lee folded the windbreaker, smiling at Marina's certainty, shaking her head gently.

"Lee, don't you give up. Toby's had too many of his roots pulled up already. And you. You love this place. Look at all the fabulous work you've done on it. This place is you. We can't let this happen."

"We." Charlie Fairfield had said "we" when she'd called to tell him the divorce hearing had been delayed another three months. "We'll get through this, now don't you worry. The food stamps and the welfare checks will keep coming. You just let me know when you don't need them any more."

Now here was Marina, insisting that there was indeed a "we" in Lee's life, that there were people she could allow herself to trust.

Within the hour, Marina was back, a checkbook in hand. "Tell me right now what the arrears are. And the next—what?—three months of payments? Yes, you're going to take it. Do you have any idea how much money we have? I have a trust fund. Oscar has a trust fund. His law firm is raking it in. All those stones Phoebe wears? Real. I've got a drawerful too. We own real estate in three countries. It's obscene, Lee, *obscene.* You are a smart, hard-working, honorable person and this is just a loan and you'll pay interest on it so it's not like we're losing a thing. There is absolutely no reason for you and your boys to lose your home."

It was a debt of honor that Lee knew she would pay in full, on time, without fail, and that could not be done out of the monthly welfare checks. If she was going to keep the house, she'd have to have money for more than the mortgage and the loan repayments— what if the roof leaked? The furnace failed? The losses that so filled her sights had to be pushed away so she could see around and past them, to the ways she would bring in the money all this would cost. Ready or not, she was going to have to come up with a plan.

On the morning of the court hearing, Marina appeared at the door. "Get in the car." Lee stared at her. "You didn't think you were going into that courtroom alone, did you? Come on, it's a long drive to Atlantic City. Let's go."

Lee had been filled with apprehension since learning that the judge who would hear the case was Italian. Surely he would side with Joe, two good old *raggazzi* sticking together. Lee took her place at the defendant's table as Willa Schoonmaker, the knife-fighter attorney Oscar had found for her, went through the thick sheaf of papers she had built up on Joseph V. H. Montagna complainant v. Lee P. Montagna, defendant/counter-complainant.

Lee had insisted on that "counter-complaint" though Schoonmaker had tried to convince her it was meaningless. Lee did not believe that being identified in every court utterance as the accused, the miscreant, could be meaningless. It was entirely the wrong position in a negotiation which, she knew, was exactly why Joe had made that opening move. And exactly why he had filed in Atlantic City, a place where he might still be living, where he had clients and connections and Lee knew no one.

He sat now, at the long table on the right side of the room, tipping his chair onto its back legs, looking sleek, in clothes Lee did not recognize, the picture of relaxed confidence, a silk-suited attorney beside him. On the empty bench behind him sat Maddy Montagna, her abundant curls tied back, a navy blue blazer making her look like a Young Republican. It was the look Lee had urged the girl to wear for peace-marching, the look that would make her opinion more credible to Authority. Clearly, Maddy was going to be a witness today, but Lee couldn't imagine what she could have to say.

Marina, sitting directly behind Lee, patted her shoulder. "It's going to be OK, Lee, really."

Lee thought it might well be. As they had pulled into Atlantic City, the digital clocks on the banks read 1:11, her lucky number, the time of her birth. Marina was with her, and Schoonmaker had joined the We team, muttering, "What a bastard," at every revelation as they had prepared for this day. They had a good case. It was going to be all right. If the world made any sense.

Schoonmaker was tapping a pencil impatiently. She beckoned to the hugely overweight bailiff. "We're past time here. Can you tell me what the delay is about?"

"The judge is in his chambers, ma'am, waiting for this lady's attorney to appear."

"Her attorney is here and *waiting*," Schoonmaker glowered. "Will you please inform Judge Imbarcare? *Now*, bailiff." The man's ample face rearranged itself as he registered the presence of Willa Schoonmaker, Esq.

As he waddled rapidly toward the chamber door, Schoonmaker turned to Lee and Marina. "I should have invited him into the 1970s but that would be fighting the wrong war—for today. Don't you just love the hinterlands?"

The silk suit's sad story of Lee abandoning his devoted, loving client was attested to by a small-voiced Maddy, agreeing that her stepmother had indeed deserted her poor father. Lee wondered what had happened to Joe's vaunted acuity at negotiation. In seconds, Schoonmaker's calm presentation of her client's continued residence in the marital abode, and Mr. Montagna's long unknown whereabouts, made both Joe and his daughter look not just unreliable but ridiculous.

Maddy's eyes beseeched her father's attention, but Joe did not look her way, not once. Lee was appalled. Now Maddy was not just the dumb one of her father's daughters, she was the liar, and Joe did not trust liars. He would still not love her, and he would never trust her.

Schoonmaker, talking to the judge in a tone of shared incredulity, pointed out that in his filing, Mr. Montagna had accused her client of running up an enormous debt, which was in fact the loan Mrs. Montagna had secured to cover the mortgage payments he had failed to make on the marital home, which was the couple's chief asset, aside from Mr. Montagna's considerable earning power.

"And Mr. Montagna's assertion, here in his filing, that he has given my client a house and a car? I would like to clarify, your honor, that what he gave her is a mortgage and car payments, and only intermittent support with which to pay them."

He had even claimed in this filing that Lee stole his watch. Shaking her head, Schoonmaker presented the scrawled message Joe had enclosed when he mailed the watch to Lee. She followed with a stack of American Express bills, pointing out the high-lighted post-separation expenditures for "Mr. and Mrs. Joseph Montagna"—jewelry, restaurants, a lease on a sportscar, the Caribbean vacation.

"Your honor, I call your particular attention to the rather large charges to Macauley Seaver, custom tailor."

Silk Suit was on his feet, objecting. "My client has lost a great deal of weight, your honor. Surely he has the right to dress himself appropriately as he tries to rebuild the business this woman has set out to destroy."

"There's a complication here, your honor." Schoonmaker was smiling.
"I call Mr. Seaver to the stand."

Joe pulled his attorney back into his seat and joined foreheads with
him. Silk Suit was quickly back on his feet. "Ah, Judge, we would like a
ten-minute recess."

Imbarcare's smiling face moved from side to side. "Not a chance, counselor. This I want to hear."

Seaver, a slender, impeccably dressed blond, walked to the stand. He
took the oath with right hand raised and left pressed downward on the hip
of his perfectly pressed gabardines. Lee thought that if he raised one foot, it
would be a fine yoga pose. With some pique, he answered Schoonmaker's
question: "Would you describe the kind of clothes you make, sir?"

Lee knew the answer. As the fictitious "Mrs. Johnson" once again, she
had followed the American Express trail and called Seaver, asking if he
would see her husband to fit him with a new set of dinner clothes.

"Oh, I don't make men's clothes," Seaver had told her. "No, not ever.
But if you'd like to come in yourself, we do lovely evening dresses, from
little cocktail things to fabulous ball gowns. And we have some new designs
for street wear that are just delicious...."

When Seaver left the stand, mouthing a "Sorry" to Joe, Imbarcare glared
at Joe and his attorney. "Anything else you fellas would like to try now or
can we just get on with it? You might not want to make me any angrier than
I already am, gentlemen."

Silk Suit folded.

Judge Salvatore Imbarcare, a man Schoonmaker had discovered was
putting three kids through parochial school and college on his public-ser-
vant salary, a man who lived with the wife he had married a quarter-century
earlier, was—just as Schoonmaker had predicted— outraged that a prosperous Italian-American father had dumped his wife and newborn onto the
welfare rolls and run off to blow their assets on another woman. He ordered Joe to pay all arrears plus child support until Gabriel finished college.
He ordered that the deed to 99 be put in Lee's name. He decreed five years
of maintenance for her, noting that given Joe's proven unreliability, a constable would be at his door within 10 days of a payment's being overdue.
Imbarcare then had a second thought—given Mr. Montagna's already estab-

lished unreliability, all his checks would have to be certified and presented to Probation 10 days before the first of each month.

He then looked down on Joe Montagna, aimed his gavel at him and intoned, "You, sir, have chosen to throw the world away. In consequence, the sword of Imbarcare hangs over your head. If you do not take out your checkbook, here and now, to cover these living expenses Mrs. Montagna has rightfully incurred, you will proceed from my courtroom directly to a cell until such time as you do as I have ordered."

Joe glared at him, arms folded. Imbarcare beckoned to the police officer standing at the back of the courtroom.

The checkbook appeared, the divorce was declared. When Imbarcare asked Lee if there was anything else she needed, she asked for the legal return of her maiden name because she did not want to be a Montagna. "I can certainly understand that. Granted." He stood, with one last glare at Joe. "We are finished here."

Schoonmaker shook Lee's hand, firmly and formally. "Congratulations, Ms. Palmer. He got what was coming to him. And so did you."

Marina leaned down to embrace Lee in long thin arms. "*Now* do you get it that you haven't been the one at fault?"

Lee had to admit that the judge's anger had impressed her; he did not seem to think that she was a crazywoman. Or a bitch. She would not deal right now with her fear that in five years she would have to be self-supporting and she wasn't sure how to do that. The important thing was that there was a new member of the We Team: the Honorable Salvatore Imbarcare, with his full complement of enforcers.

The Palmers had come for their annual autumn stay, their custom since Toby was small, since Lee and their first-born grandson had returned to the US from Vietnam. Every September they were with Lee, every March with her brother Ernie Jr., who ran a factory in Illinois and had two kids himself.

Now they had come to celebrate Gabriel's second birthday, the two elders moving about busily, mending, repairing, erranding, good fairies who had descended upon the household, determined to be useful, deciding what should be done and how, not asking whether or not the residents concurred.

Duct tape and aluminum foil appeared in strange, visible places, fixing things Lee had not considered broken. Soft lights were replaced by the blaze of 150-watt bulbs. Towels of odd colors manifested in the bathrooms. Cupboards were reorganized neatly according to alien systems, replacing Lee's store-at-point-of-use with schemes based on the alphabet, or on size. Toby retrieved lovingly worn jeans and shirts from trash cans and balked at wearing the stiff, uncool replacements his grandmother put in his closet. But the now-tall teen did love being off the hook for his normal chores, his grandmother even washing and ironing daily the clothes he dropped on the floor of his room.

"Enjoy it while it lasts, kid. You know in October, it's back to do-it-yourself." Lee winked at her son, who grinned back. They had understood each other on this one ever since Emily Palmer had seen Toby loading the washing machine with an armload of the rags he considered clothing. Her bouffant white head had turned to Lee in surprise. "Why is he doing that?"

"Because he doesn't have anything clean to wear?"

"No, why is *he* washing his clothes?"

"Ah, I see. I think it's because he knows how to run the machines and I don't want him growing up to marry someone he doesn't care much about just because he needs clean socks."

Toby got it. Emily Palmer did not, and every autumn, the amused boy was the receiver of perfectly washed, ironed and folded clothes for a full month. Each year, when the Palmers arrived, they made no comments on the return of what they obviously considered chaos and mistaken priorities, sighing tolerantly and setting about the task of restoring order. Lee could always, for the first week, appreciate the intended love in these alterations to her world. Lord knew, she needed help.

She had gotten on MacGregor's list of freelance editors, passed the word to writers she knew herself, and taken an ad in the *Princeton Packet* announcing her availability as a book doctor. Manuscripts were coming in, unevenly, sometimes several, sometimes none, but they were coming.

As a working-mother head-of-household, she was at her desk for long hours, and often away from the house to meet with writers. For these few weeks a year, she didn't have to steel herself to ignore the dust bunnies and the empty tea canister and the fact that she and Gabe were running out of clean clothes. Time spent on such things was not billable, and what her household needed from her was cash for the expenses that went beyond the tiny draft on the State Department credit union that Tim Pitt sent each month for Toby, and the Probation court checks that never quite covered her entire To-Pay pile. For some reason she could not fathom, editors were not paid at the rate that applied to labor consultants.

There was Toby's orthodontist, his guitar lessons, and the wisdom tooth that erupted in Lee's jaw and demanded surgery. There was the plumber who repaired the horrendous damage to the yard and the cellar when a tree root in the side yard grew through the sewer line. There was the chimney that decided to separate itself from the house and had to be lassoed back into place until Vito Frenare could be paid, in advance, to repair the old brick work.

The house was a minefield of unforeseeable expenses, but it was home, and they were safe here and she would hold it together, no matter how hard it tried to fall apart. She was keeping up, even though it was often a close call. Her once-a-week runs to the A&P were with checkbook in hand now rather than food stamps and, once in a while, she would even splurge there on vanilla soup for Toby and the Cheezits that Das loved, products she knew had no nutritional value. But they were part of a normal America household, and it was good to feel normal sometimes.

Lee was working toward "normal" for herself. With some extra money she'd made from a stint of round-the-clock jobs, she had taken herself into her lost New York, which was visitable from Princeton, for work or play. But this pursuit of normalcy was about neither work nor play; it was life-changing.

She'd almost turned back a dozen times as she walked slowly toward the clinic. She stopped for a paper. She stopped for a "regular" coffee and a bialy; in Princeton "regular" did not mean with cream and there were no such savory lumps of chewy dough. She stopped and studied the kids' clothes in a shop window. She dug in her bag for the clinic address, which she knew by heart. She did everything she could to delay, but she did not turn back.

"Have you ever been a patient here? Social Security number? Address? Mother's maiden name? You can go right in."

She was shown into a bay separated only by curtains from the other "rooms." Sitting in the single, metal-armed chair, she propped her paper against the examining table and tried not to listen to the voices around her. In a mirror at the head of the table she could see a young redhead in a hospital gown, sitting on another examining table, swinging her legs rapidly. The white uniform of a doctor came into the picture, and curtain rings screeched along the overhead rod as he pulled them shut.

"Good morning, Ms. Clancy. What can we do for you?"

Lee was grateful the woman's answer did not reach her as she dived back into the *Times*. Her stomach knotted, remembering the workmen outside the window at Lying In, when Gabriel was born. There were some things, many things, that were best not witnessed by strangers. She read a report on the acquisition of the *New York Post* by an Australian scandalmonger and a feature on the new Concorde flights between Paris and Rio.

The curtain at the foot of the exam table screeched shut.

"Ms. Palmer. What can we do for *you*?" He was young, breezy, loud.

First, you could lower your voice, boyo.

"Information, mainly. I want to know what can be done, how much time it would take, and how much money."

"Fair enough. Ask away."

"OK. I have a belly full of stretch marks on loose flesh and a big keloid from a caesarean." She stopped, took a deep breath. "And a completely flat chest."

Sitting on the examining table himself, he motioned her to stand up.

"Let's see how bad the situation is."

She stood and zipped down the fly on her jeans. "Other people have babies without being scarred like this. I know from the dressing room at the Y."

He ran a thumb along one of the inch-wide shining tracks that ran from above her waist down to her pubic bone.

"Yeah, but they don't have faces like yours. It all evens out." He motioned for her to lift her shirt.

"I've been waiting since I was 12 for Mother Nature to come through with secondary sex characteristics. I don't think she's listening."

Lee didn't say what the flat chest had cost her. The years of feeling she was worth less than abundant women.

She didn't say a word about going home from gym classes in high school instead of into the group showers to be seen and mocked by her burgeoning peers.

She didn't tell him about her Two Mosquito Bites designation in her college dorm.

She didn't talk about not trusting Danny Bailey to stay with her flat self, nor about losing Joe to a pair of waist-length breasts.

She didn't say that she considered it highly unfair that a year of nursing from round, functioning breasts had left her smaller than ever.

She didn't say that she was tired of having the unwomanly body of a child, a body that fit her old assumption that she could be patronized, used, diminutized.

She didn't say that she was ashamed that she'd never been able rise above such a vain, superficial matter, and was tired of trying to.

He pulled a pen out of his chest pocket. "OK here's how it works."

He began sketching diagrams on the exam table's paper cover.

"We can pull down the abdominal skin this way and reposition the navel. The stretch marks will be pulled below your waist, but you'll still have some on your lower belly. You end up with a smile line along here—we've got some procedures now that minimize keloiding, so the new scar probably won't go wide like this one from the caesarean. The breast enlargement is absolutely no problem. He sketched out the procedure on the exam-table paper.

"What size would I be? I mean, I don't want to be grotesque—just ordinary.'"

"What size are you now?"

"No size. There's no such thing. Even pre-teen training bras are too big."

"Look, don't worry. You'll be a B. I know what you want. Besides, if you wanted to be a freak, I wouldn't do it. We're not into that kind of thing."

Some doctors were. L.A. doctors. But Lee was pleased that someone, someone male, thought huge breasts were freaky. Normal would be just fine.

"Now tell me time and money."

"Four days. It's a hundred twenty a day, no matter what we do. No fees for physicians. You understand this is the clinic, right? We're all residents, not private surgeons."

"How far along are you?"

"Final year." He smiled. "I'll be in my Park Avenue office in a month."

"You'll do."

"Thanks. Let's get a date set up." He looked up from her file.

"You're forty-one?" He squinted at her. "The only clue you're not a kid is right here, this little bit of hooding over your eyes. You want to fix that too? While you're here. No extra charge."

She had not gone for the eye work; age was not the issue at hand. The point was to join the club, to at last feel that she was a member of the female division of humanity. And the technology was in place to acquire these proofs that Nature had failed to provide.

She had made the decision, taken the action, and a new reality had settled in. She was no longer a board-smooth girl pretending behind thick, hot padding to be a female adult; she was a woman like those in all the nude paintings and sculptures, a woman with small, beautiful breasts she could dress in light lace, feeling their movement as she walked, wearing clothes that subtly revealed the magical dual swelling and the vertical line that said, This is a woman.

Women made serious decisions about their futures and those of their families. Women were responsible for those decisions and for the fates of their children. The woman Lee was becoming was doing these things. In a woman's body.

In her responsible head-of-household role, she did welcome Emily-and-Ernest Month each year, grateful for the freedom to work so many billable hours. Toby was freed to earn cash too; he not only did no laundry, there was no after-school hedge-trimming, lawn-mowing, or trash-can emptying for him at his own house. Instead he worked his way along the block, doing yard work for pocket money.

Dasya eagerly assisted the Commander, making runs to the hardware store, returning more often than not with the wrong widget or gasket as the white-haired elder and the small brown youth competed in usefulness. Ernest Palmer would thank the smiling young Indian graciously and later slip into his car to make the necessary exchanges.

Cars were a September sore point. The Commander's huge silver Olds-mobile was ever diligently maintained, cleaned, and waxed, its every intake of fluids recorded in a small notebook in the glove compartment. Lee's car was lucky to have its windows washed— until each September, when it would be washed, dried, waxed, and serviced to a fare-thee-well.

But Lee finally had to break her silence about the changes that were being made after she hurried to her shiny clean car, determined to not be late for a meeting with a German economist at the grad school who wanted to talk about a draft he'd just finished, something about Keynes and Fried-man. From her phone conversation with him, Lee suspected his imperfect English meant months of work would be needed on the manuscript, and there was a long empty stretch opening up in her schedule—she needed the job.

Rounding the walk to the garage, looking through her bag for the German's address, she came close to colliding with unfamiliar wood. The 60-year-old garage doors had not been closed in recent memory—they were mounted on large iron wheels that had been locked by rust for decades. Putting all her weight into each side, she managed to muscle them back to open. Silk shirt damp, two fingernails broken, Lee grabbed for the driver's door, and found it locked. She would have to dig for the backup keys she kept in her handbag, just in case the set that was always under the driver's floor mat should disappear. But she might not have transferred the keys when she switched from the canvas tote she used for errands to the old Bottega bag she polished up for meetings. By the time her hand felt the familiar metal shapes, it was trembling. She threw the bag on the passenger seat, started the ignition and put the gears in reverse.

The car did not move. Mystified, and late, she examined all dials and levers for the answer and found the emergency brake on. On the flat floor of the closed garage, in a locked car, the emergency brake was on.

Returning that afternoon, Lee had found her father in the living room, teaching Toby to play cribbage.

"Watch him, Toby. He's a master of that game."

"But Toby's getting better each time. He'll win soon." The Commander moved his peg and laughed. "That's fifteen for two." Toby gave a mock groan.

Lee knew that her father would always play to win, with no quarter given in consideration of a child's tender feelings. But her Toby had mastered chess well enough to beat the equally competitive Joe Montagna. Lee would put money on his besting his grandfather at this far simpler game.

"Dad, I need a favor."

"Certainly, dear. Anything at all."

She explained how old the garage-door wheels were and how hard it had been for her to open the heavy doors, but she knew the matter of the locked car doors and the set handbrake were best not mentioned. She would never convince him that there was nothing worth stealing in the car and that it was unlikely to roll around on the flat garage floor. It would be enough if she could convince him to leave the garage doors open.

The Commander cuffed his grandson on the shoulder. "Well, Toby, I guess you and I better find some new wheels for those doors. And I think we should get a good strong padlock."

The effort it would take to stop him didn't seem worth it. She would simply have another set of innovations to undo in October, when the garage doors could again be kept open and unpadlocked. And her car ready to roll.

Emily Palmer's contributions were making steamed eggs, scalloped potatoes, and Swiss steaks, and crocheting squares for a bedspread to go on the small bed where Lee now slept, in a repainted, refurnished master bedroom that contained nothing from her Montagna years, all of it gone in a tag sale, replaced by pieces she'd found at lawn sales all over town.

She'd finally gotten to the shabby maid's room off the kitchen, too long filled with things she'd stored from her childhood, from Vietnam, from the Congo, from Maryland, from New York, things for which there had been no room in the world of Joe Montagna. The cartons were all unsealed now, the books and music and mementos within them settled into place all around this dear old house, where there was nothing of Joe's and no thought that things that were hers could simply be thrown away. The BVM was on the wall of her bedroom, next to Dolly Delius. The living room bookshelves were filled with her books and recordings. This was Lee Palmer's house.

Now she was setting up the small room off the kitchen to host the television set. It would be the place of *détente* and Soyuz, the Khmer Rouge and Karen Quinlan, the disappearance of Hoffa and the capture of Hearst, the fall of Saigon, and Mr. Rogers, her Gabriel's daily stand-in for a loving, attentive dad. The living room would be freed of all that. She could work in that living room in the evenings, a manuscript in her lap, instead of being driven back to her second-floor workroom by the voice of Captain Kirk entreating Scotty for more power to the warp engines. When there was not urgent work to do, the quiet living room would be the place to enjoy her own music and books, and crackling winter fires.

There would be evenings when her day had been strong enough that she could risk Gershwin's "Second Piano Prelude" or Miles Davis playing *Sketches of Spain*, days when the sorrow in such music would not pull her down and drown her. In the times when she didn't feel she could withstand that draw, it would have to be Chuck Berry and Bill Haley to the rescue, pumping up the energy in the house, and in Lee. Toby, a devoted fan of the Rolling Stones, would tease her about this "ancient" music. Lee did not tell him that his fave Brits rocked but didn't roll. It would all be perfect, but first she had to create this place where television could be sequestered.

"Dad, please. I am not stupid."

Commander Palmer did not look at his daughter but slowly, with great dignity, put his corner of the carpeting down and stepped silently out of the room. Toby looked from the doorway to Lee.

"It's OK. You and I can do this. Edge that end a little more toward you."

She squatted on the rough-board floor of the almost finished room, her hands on the fat roll of crimson cotton as Toby straightened the lead edge along the wall.

"OK!" She sounded far too enthusiastic as she tried to remind the puzzled boy that this was supposed to have been fun. She grabbed his hand and got him kicking with her at the long roll. It unwound perfectly, filling the soft yellow room to the corners with its rowdy scarlet.

"Wow. *Look* at this, Toby."

Lee whirled around, taking in the new colors, reveling in their exuberance. "Let's not put the furniture back. We could just sit on the gorgeous floor."

"Maah-um. The sofa's upside down on my bed."

"Oh, right. I guess you want a place to sleep tonight, don't you? OK. Hard part."

She made a show of rolling up her sleeves and popping her knuckles before the two of them maneuvered the sofa back through the door of Toby's bedroom, adjoining this new television room, which would also double Toby's space in the house, a good thing now that so many large teen-aged boys seemed to be piling into his room, doing homework, playing rock, raiding the kitchen for sustenance.

Lee threw the cushions into the frame and collapsed onto them; Toby stood in the center of the scarlet carpet, watching her.

"Is Granpa going to leave?"

Lee started to answer with a flip remark but stopped herself. Another man might be leaving Toby's world. That wasn't on Lee's list of wishes, but neither was letting her father condescend to her, letting him sigh in despair over her inability to understand the right way to do things. His way.

But this was her home. She was head of this household. She had found the carpeting at a discount store, earned the money to buy it, knew how to cut and move it so that it would settle into place perfectly. And it had worked. Without Ernest Palmer's orders; without even his help. He was not in command here.

And she was not a deckhand, not her timid mother, not a cute Dolly Delius. Most of all, Lee was not a self-annihilating Little Mermaid. Not anymore. She had outed the mermaid from the hiding place from which she had determined Lee's actions; Lee was walking that twit up and down the avenues of her mind. The spell was broken, the brainwashing revealed, and overcome.

"Grandpa's used to running things, that's all. And I didn't think his idea of how to do this was as good as mine. So he's mad."

He was being mad silently, like a good Englisher should. No yelling, no smashing doors, breaking glass. Just the averted eyes, the silence, the look that said, You unworthy, despicable pond scum.

"What's he going to do?"

Lee hugged Toby quickly. "Nothing. Really. Don't worry."

The next day Commander Palmer left the house the minute Lee came home from a morning meeting with Claudia Havstrom. The writer was blocked again, this time on a contracted memoir about her career, intimidated by the advance and falling into a deepening conviction that she would never write another word.

Lee had talked her through an opening chapter, getting the older woman to tell stories, saying again and again, "There, that, write that down. It's wonderful, just as you said it." She knew Claudia would agonize for days over every paragraph she had now gotten on paper, but it was a beginning; there were a few draft pages next to Claudia's typewriter.

When Lee returned home, the Commander left on foot and walked for hours, circling the quiet block, then walking farther afield, back and forth on other blocks in the quiet neighborhood. They could see him pass by the house, first from the left, then the right, an old man in exile, cast out into the elements, his head held high despite the perfidy of his daughter. He came and went through the back door and ate only when Lee was gone. Mrs. Palmer wove between them, trying to thread them back together, nibbling at two versions of every meal, her eyes ever more pleading as the muffins and chops and baked potatoes came and went.

Arriving home on the fourth day of her father's demonstration, Lee passed by the garage and nosed her car around the block. Rolling up and down the shady blocks, she finally saw him, sitting on a bench by a creek, on the grounds of the grad school. She stopped the car and opened the passenger door for him, but he continued staring into a clump of red rhododendrons. Leaving the engine running, she stood directly in front of him.

"Mom can't take any more of this."

He glared at her as if to say, And whose fault is that?

"OK. I'm sorry I hurt your feelings. I really am. But you mustn't treat me like an idiot in my own house. In front of my son. It's important to me." He watched her mouth moving then looked back to the flowers.

"Come on, Dad. Let's go home." She held her hand out to help him up. He shook his head, standing up slowly, his eyes blinking rapidly.

"I'll walk."

As she pulled away she saw him in the rearview mirror, blotting his eyes with one of the soft linen handkerchiefs she'd given him for his 65th birthday.

He was quiet at dinner. Polite. Soft spoken. A red rhododendron stood at the center of the table, in a mayonnaise jar.

Riding Seaward, Making Pearls

She saw the rust velvet chair in the furniture store window as she hurried past on icy Nassau Street. Half a block onward, she stopped. It looked comfortable, the perfect by-the-fire, snuggle-into chair, an old paisley shawl over your legs. She walked back to the store window. She liked the chair. The on-sale price was quite a bit less than the extra check she'd just gotten for fast-tracking a travel book. Even without that windfall it was, she realized, within the budget of a household in the fourth year of court-enforced child support, temporary maintenance, rental income from an ancient professor in the "south wing," and one hard-working parent. And there was no one to persuade, argue with, ask permission of, before buying this fine chair she was looking at.

The next evening it was by the fireplace, adding to the construct Lee had made for an evening without tears. Sorrow lurked in the brief times when she was not working on a manuscript, not doing something for the boys, not fixing a broken part of the house. She must make these unbusy, vulnerable times so pleasant that tears would be impossible.

She would not think about being alone, probably forever, since she was incapable of knowing a good man from a demented one. Other women raised their kids alone; she must not feel sorry for herself that she must do this too.

She would not think about the couples everywhere in her life, men and women together, committed to each other, even happy.

She was equally determined not to drift over into the alternative universe where Lee Bailey was having no problems at all; Lee Palmer had no rational reason to believe that Danny Bailey's view of her, and his devotion, would have lasted all these years. Lee, the ultimate bad judge of people's character, had probably been wrong about Danny too.

She would stay right here, right now, with the right music, the right book, a fire, and now, a perfect chair; she would not ruin this evening with any more damned weeping.

She put a Jobim LP on the stereo, knowing that *Corcovado*—"Quiet Nights"—her favorite bossa, was the fourth cut. She'd picked up *The Recognitions* and *Tinker Tailor Soldier Spy* at the library—if Gaddis became too gnarly, she would fall back to the intriguing Le Carré. The wind outside warned of coming snow, ice, sleet. She put an oak log on the fire she'd kindled and settled into the new chair, her chair, un-sat-upon by anyone else. Gabe, in his flannel sleepers, appeared in the doorway.

"What happened, sugah? Bad dream?"

"There was a bird in my window. He was awfully loud."

The "awfully" made her smile. She put her books down and held out her arms. Gabe climbed onto her lap and snuggled in, compact, congruent, each curve and angle fitting to a compatible part of his mother's body. The top of his head nestled into her neck, one small square hand patted her shoulder. She inhaled the sweetness of his skin as she stroked the silky sphere of curls. His soft breath made a warm-cool pulse against her heart. She was lucky. This wasn't one of those greased-lightning kids you couldn't get your hands on. Gabriel gave as good as he got.

The warmth of the reading lamp sent the acidic sharpness of chrysanthemums to mingle with the scents of burning oak and sleeping child. Having bought herself an easy chair, it had been a small thing to buy herself flowers. As "Quiet Nights" played, the beauty of the evening, the sense of her journey to this moment and her enduring fear and grief, commingled in silent, perplexing tears. No matter how beautiful this evening was, she could not stay present to it, falling out of current time into the bruising past, then leaping from the pleasure of now into the perilous future. It was unreasonable, intolerable.

She catalogued all that was going astonishingly well, and could see that her life was a good one. She had enough work to get by most months, making up for the slow times with spurts of all-nighters. Closing off the den and guest room, renting them out, covered the property taxes. She was making it through. Now. Her five years of maintenance would end soon. But now, right now, she was making it.

Her household was peaceful, filled with laughter, good food, music. No one was raging through the rooms, breaking treasures, spreading fear. It was a joy to step through the door, into warmth, beauty, and safety. She kept Joe's office off the foyer locked, trapping in that one space the malevolence that had once filled every part of the house.

The writers she worked with were usually pleasant enough; some even became friends, despite the persistent wariness that told her to keep people at arm's length. Marina had long before broken through Lee's guard, a mer-sister in good standing. There were people in her life who chose to be with her, Lee Palmer, on her own and as herself, not as Joe Montagna's wife. This was a fine thing to know. No matter what might someday develop in any of those friendships.

Most of all there were Tobias and Gabriel, two growing males who moved through the world lovingly, who would always do so, perhaps making up for the wind-up hit man Gert Montagna had loosed upon the unsuspecting populace. Lee was sure her sons would not be drawn to women who were, as Lee had been, self-deprecators with Little-Mermaid programming. Her sons would have the strength and confidence to choose strong partners.

Tobias Andrew Pitt was man-sized, a running back on the high school's junior varsity football team, able to pick her up and carry her across a room, which he'd done on a recent afternoon, laughing. "I'm really angry with you."

"What? What did I do?"

"Nothing. That's the problem. All my friends are so mad at their parents they don't talk to them. Those guys can't wait to leave home. I can't find anything to be mad at you about, so I'm mad."

Lee had worried about his loneliness when he had stopped sharing day-school classes with Connor, when his wonder dog Ivan had moved to a farm in the countryside, after being caught fuzz-mouthed from eating a neighbor's Easter chicks. Ivan needed wilder spaces than gentle Princeton afforded.

Toby assured her that sports and studies and work left him little room for spending time with friends or pets. Nor did their straightened circumstances seem to distress him. He did not ask her for money or lavish gifts, was reluctant even to accept his allowance. He had moved on from doing chores for neighbors to bussing weekends at the Alchemist & Barrister pub. Lee worried that his grades would suffer, but seeing his grin when he bought himself, with his own earnings, a fine new guitar, she decided that the self-confidence he was learning might be more important than an A in botany.

His nose was taking on an emphatic form as his face grew to fit the huge green eyes. Braces had left him with a fine smile and Lee thought him even handsomer than Timothy Pitt. It was partly the addition of her roan hair, but it was mainly his own bright-spirited engagement with the world that made the telling difference.

She discovered that others might share her assessment of him when Marina told her, in a conspiratorial whisper, that she'd seen Toby with a pretty Asian woman who was significantly older than he was.

Lee and Toby were removing leaves from the front lawn, she raking, he bagging, when she asked him to tell her about the girl he seemed to be dating.

"Well, yeah, Mom. I met her at the Alchemist."

"A customer. And therefore of drinking age."

"She's a grad student. At the Woodrow Wilson school."

Lee leaned on the rake and watched her son push the crackling leaves into a debris bag.

"And does she know you're 17?"

He stood, tying a knot in the neck of the bag.

"I told her. She doesn't care."

Mother and son looked each other in the eyes and Lee began to smile, remembering the recent day she'd seen a figure approaching on Witherspoon Street, a tall young man in a three-cornered hat, a cutaway morning coat, no shirt, torn jeans, and construction boots, a new guitar over his shoulder. It was her Tobias, who was clearly not turning out to be a dull, run-of-the-mill fellow.

"Mom, you're not pissed at me?"

"Hmmm. I'm trying really hard but I'm not finding anything to be mad at you about."

Lee silently hoped that he was being well instructed by the pretty grad student—and that there was no 16-year-old girl with a lifelong crush on him, pining vainly for his attention, like the girl who had loved Daniel Quinn Bailey and dreamed of him for decades.

Gabriel was a walking, talking measure of the passage of time since his father had gone missing from their lives. She had made herself see his birth-date each year as the anniversary of an exchange, a red-letter, to-be-celebrated day of one enchanting male's arrival and a toxic one's departure. Gabriel was a person now, full of opinions and adverbs. He had pulled himself up the rungs of a kitchen chair to walk at eight months, said "Wow" at nine, grown broad and sturdy, a miniature, revised-and-improved edition of the father he had never met.

Lee delighted in seeing him become a force at the Institute for Advanced Studies pre-school, holding together the multi-lingual children assembled there. When she called one October morning to tell his teacher that he had a cold and wouldn't be coming in, the teacher insisted that she bring him, germs and all. "He's the only one who can deal with the Turks—I can't handle them without him."

Gabe, Lee learned, rocked the homesick Turkish boys when they cried, led them from place to place in the playrooms, holding up objects and giving the boys the English name for each of them. Every morning, when Lee took Gabe into the school, the dark-eyed brothers ran to embrace him. "Hello, friend Gabriel." "I am happy now."

He'd not been as successful with a tiny white-haired girl with transparent Scandinavian skin. When Lee arrived one afternoon to take Gabriel home, he'd eagerly pulled her to the howling little Swede, put his mother's hand on the child's rigid back, and directed Lee to "Fix this right now." She was startled by the vote of confidence, then realized it was merited. When Gabriel cried she, his mother, could indeed make his pain and fear go away.

Dasya took a magna and was accepted into a Masters program that would prolong his exile from India, and his time with her family, for at least another year. His cooking was expanding to include curries and stir fries made of the vegetables from the kitchen garden that he and Toby had planted, a major source of sustenance for them all. Lee could see that though she earned like a peon, her family's fare was royal.

On many a weekend Rory and Pranko came to visit, for the last year, as an actual married couple. Lee had hosted their wedding reception in the garden at 99, watching in astonishment as the buffet table was assaulted by a mob of young New York painters and sculptors so hungry they had emptied all the platters before any family members approached. The Commander was outraged by the impropriety but saw Lee laughing and actually joined in. As soon as the bride and groom departed for their honeymoon at an inn on the Delaware, the Commander announced that since the remaining family members were all dressed up and quite hungry, he was treating all hands to dinner at Lahiere's.

Lee smiled at the memory of taking her sons into the city to meet Rory and Pranko for the San Gennaro street fair. The dark-eyed, olive-skinned Croatian had hoisted pale, blue-eyed Gabriel onto his shoulders so the toddler would not be submerged in the crush of bodies. When they'd stopped for the zeppoles Lee loved, the vendor handed Pranko the bag with a quizzical smile. "Man, your kid sure doesn't look like you." Pranko's arm stayed outstretched for a moment, as he sorted out what he had just heard. "Oh. Him." He looked up toward the child whose hands were locked under his bearer's bristly chin. "That's not my kid. That's my brother-in-law."

Good times. Satisfying times. Even times of heartfelt laughter. And there was, beneath it all, still, grieving. The damned grieving. And the fear. When she was alone, in the car or somewhere in the house, off her guard, she would hear the doves and replay some past horror, imagine some future one, losing her current place in time. Sometimes it came upon her in public places, triggered by the sight of a man and woman simply walking together. She told herself that a woman needed a man like a fish needed a bicycle, but she was not convinced. Some women, women perhaps with too many planets in the house of partnership, those women might need a man in their lives.

The most unacceptable times were when there was no trigger at all, yet tears welled up from some deep cistern of grief she carried with her, spilling down her face, choking off her voice. It was embarrassing. Shameful. Self-indulgent. There was no excuse for such unreasonable, unrelenting sorrow, but her efforts to erase it were not working.

Brigid, one of Lee's writers, had reason to mourn. To weep anywhere, any time. Brigid had halted a session with Lee over her lagging manuscript on the suffragist movement, overcome by some trigger unknown to Lee, unable to go on. They put aside the struggles of 1910, made coffee, sat over steaming cups while Brigid both told a story and pushed it away, the telling was so painful. Her beautiful son, a scholar and an athlete, a charmer named most popular in his class at Princeton High, a boy filled with plans and promise, had disappeared years before. One day he was gone. Just gone. Bus stations and airports were monitored, posters circulated, rivers dragged. There was never a trace.

Lee could still hear Brigid telling her that the worst thing was never knowing. If she and her dear Lech could be sure their son was dead, no matter how horribly he might have died, it would be over and they would somehow absorb it. But there was no end to it. A decade after the morning she had waved him off to school for the last time, she was still getting into her car, rolling up the windows to shout out her fury, to wail in agony.

Lee shivered. That was pain. *That* was loss. Beyond bearing. Lee, who was just another single mother, had no right to the days when she could not read the words in front of her on the page as she worked, all of them blurred by inexplicable, inexcusable tears. This was not the way of the brave, strong woman she wanted to be.

There had to be something people did when they had too much sadness, just as they could apply for help in Trenton when they had too little money. She pinned her hopes on the daily meditations that she had returned to when the house was empty—when Gabe, Toby, and Dasya had gone off to playschool, high school, college. But the sorrow awaited her when she returned from these 20-minute time-outs from her life. There had to be something more intense and effective than the gradual grace of these small interludes. She needed a total reaming out of the old, useless, maddening emotions.

She knew only one person who looked as if she could move always in serenity, even if a chimney might be falling off her house and a check was late for work she'd done and her kids were looking to her for everything and she had no partner to share the decisions with and no one to hold her and say everything was going to be alright. Only one person in Lee's world seemed ever steady, centered, tranquil, and fully present. The yoga teacher at the Y. Lee knew her only from those classes but could not imagine the woman being pulled back into sadness or forward into fear. Lee asked her how she maintained such serenity and the smiling woman began to tell Lee about someone named Jahnu Kedar, the Indian guru who was her teacher. Lee cut her short.

"It doesn't matter. Whoever he is, whatever you're learning, clearly it works. Just take me with you next time you go?"

Lee wondered if Brigid, who could well be the best writer in Princeton, would survive if she lost her husband, Lech. The two of them were bonded in sorrow, sharing the open wound of their missing son. For Brigid to lose Lech too would be beyond bearing. This evening was the first break Brigid had taken from her long vigil at the hospital where he was recovering from a massive heart attack, emergency surgery, and the implanting of a pacemaker. She looked exhausted, her wide face showing newly drawn lines from forgetting to eat and to rest, her graying hair caught in a rubber band—for these weeks nothing had distracted her from her focus on Lech.

Lee was pleased to see her here with fellow writers, assembled for a warming winter evening of pasta, wine, and talk at Lee's big round dining room table. The light was from candles, not hospital fluorescents; the talk not about arteries and valves but contracts, agents, deadlines, and the possibility that the Feds would succeed in declaring royalties to be "unearned" income.

"Like we don't work our butts off for the money." Porter Quarmyne was for drawing up a letter to the President on the spot.

"Like it's so much money," Brigid interjected wryly. "We're all Peter Benchley, making out like robber barons." It was a sore subject, that. Of all the writers living in Princeton, "the shark guy" was seen as the least serious and was the one making far and away the most money.

Quarmyne himself came a close second in the not-serious category, with his annual bound-for-the-back-list novel on a topic *du jour*. Lee knew that no one here would say that out loud. Porter was the best of company, a solid friend, ace poker player, a buoyant presence, the only adult Lee had to ask not to bring grass into her house. She smiled, thinking of the times she'd watched people in restaurants or theatres look around trying to figure out who was smoking weed, never suspecting the smiling old guy with the beard and the pipe. If he'd found a way to make a comfortable living churning out forgettable titles with two-dimensional characters, no one here was going to begrudge him. Not when they all looked forward to his annual Happy Conception Day greetings, insanely funny doggerel poems that arrived each year exactly nine months before their birthdays. Not when they knew that with a little nudging they could get him to recite the entire lineage of US presidents, to a boogie beat. Everybody loved the ebullient Porter Quarmyne.

Looking at the people around her table, Lee saw book titles, magazine articles, screenplays, and poems. Kathy and Irv taught English at Lawrenceville and at the Hun School, for now. Kathy had written two movies that had made it into a few art houses, unnoticed and unprofitable; Irv expected his five volumes of poetry to go wide someday and free them both from doing lesson plans. Friends counseled them to hang onto their day jobs. The new economics book Lee had edited for Klaus was doing well; it had just been chosen as a text at MIT and Cal Berkeley. Brigid had turned from decades of writing feature pieces for magazines to doing her full-length book on the suffragists. She'd gotten a decent advance from a good house, but Lee worried that years on the same subject would be impossible for her—Brigid was a fine sprinter trying to marathon.

"I don't see I have much choice," she explained to her dinner companions. "When I started, magazine writing was the way to go, not books. I sold my first piece to the *Saturday Evening Post* for $3,000 in 1940. My last one went to *LOOK* for $1,800 and they folded before it was published. Think about that. Do any other professionals work for less now than they did over 35 years ago?"

Now Lech's illness was erasing her book advance, her writing schedule, and her time to be in this comforting, friend-filled room. Brigid had checked her watch three times since the salad.

Claudia Havstrom Quarmyne was listening, saying little, ever the reporter, though she hadn't worked since *World Watch* too had folded. Lee thought of the articles she'd read when Claudia covered Latin America, articles that foretold the rise of the Colombian cartels, and revealed the Church's complicity in the oppression of the *campesinos*. Lee was still so in awe of Claudia Havstrom, she was repeatedly surprised that the woman was a little less than life-sized—she barely came up to Lee's ear. As they worked together on Claudia's memoir, on organizing a fundraiser for NOW, and doing ad copy for a Congressional campaign, Lee's unasked question— What happened to the reporter?—had been answered as she witnessed the older woman's gut-level confusion.

"This being-a-wife thing. How do people learn to do it? I mean I started late but it's been years now and I still don't understand running his laundry, giving dinners for his friends. He just assumes I'll do all kinds of things. And I do them. But I keep thinking, why shouldn't *he* be doing *my* laundry?"

Claudia was Faye Dunaway trying to be Debbie Reynolds, and failing. The more Porter laughed and cavorted through life, the darker Claudia's Nordic angst became; twice since becoming Mrs. Quarmyne, a first-time bride at 45, she'd sunk into depressions so deep she'd been given electroshock therapy. It was all a mystery to Porter who came to Lee, as Claudia's friend and sometime editor, for her advice. "Why why why? We've got it knocked. Wonderful house, great friends, money to do whatever we want, and I adore her. What the hell is the problem?"

Lee had no answer for him that she thought would be understandable, not then, not now. The rise of feminism was changing so many rules, confusing so many people, Lee wondered about the ultimate effects. Some of them would not be good, like the faculty wife she'd heard about who decided she was meant to be an attorney and took to her bed in a deep funk rather than enrolling in law school. Neighbors were lending a hand at seeing to the bewildered children of the would-be attorney.

Clearly, not everyone was weathering the upheavals easily; the jostled souls were everywhere Lee looked, even perhaps back to the Danny Q who had not been able to understand her pre-feminism drive to have a degree, and to do her own work. She had certainly jostled Joe Montagna's sense of the world when she moved away from his interests and into her own; her plan to put together a book of meditators' writings had, she was sure, been one of the things that sent him looking for someone who would devote herself entirely to him.

She went to the kitchen to see if the Jamaica Blue Mountain had dripped through the Silex. Klaus had brought her a pound of the precious stuff, along with his last check for her rewrite of his book. One delicious cup each morning was all it took to make her feel she lived in luxury. She put the beaker, a sugar bowl, and the room-temperature cream on a tray, inhaling the gorgeous fragrance as she backed through the door into the dining room.

"Why would a publisher pay a serious money to an old writer of experience, should he be able to get a young one to do the job for nuts?" Klaus, the master of global economics, had the table's annoyed attention.

Porter cocked an eyebrow at the German. "It's peanuts, Klaus, not nuts."

"Peanuts, yes. But the important question is for Brigid—was your check cashed at the bank before *Look* was kaput?"

Brigid smiled wryly. "Yes. At least that part worked out."

Lee thought but didn't say to Klaus, that perhaps editors should pay veteran writers more because they brought so much more to the page, because what they'd seen and felt and known could be valuable.

And why was their conversation this evening about money? They were *alive*. If they were in Cambodia, all these educated, literate people, they'd be dragged out of the house and killed—for having degrees, for wearing glasses, for being able to write their names, for heaven's sake.

She imagined her guests trying to convince a squad of thought police that they were illiterate. Only wily Porter, she decided, might succeed in bullshitting them into thinking he was a happy peasant, Porter, in government-issue pajamas, tilling rice fields in the sun, singing some revolutionary anthem. But the rest of them....

Porter passed Brigid the cream. "How are your suffragettes doing? Any new and exciting break-throughs?"

Brigid looked at him as if she didn't understand the question. "Suffragists. 'Suffragettes' is demeaning. And you *know* that Lech's in the hospital."

It was Porter's turn to not understand what was being said. "Yes, of course. And?"

"And I haven't been writing. I haven't even *thought* about writing."

Porter stirred his coffee, considering this information. "Nothing stops me from writing."

Lee looked quickly across the table and was relieved that Claudia was arguing intently with Irv, who thought *Carrie* was a more important film than *Chinatown.* Lee wanted to say Shame on you to Porter, but settled for silently thanking the gods she was not a writer, which she quickly amended to not a male writer. Her female writers were good souls. And she was Lee the Fixer of words, for all of them, having none of her own to offer the world. She had some support value to those who did have something to say, enough to keep her employed, taking in manuscripts, which all too often reminded her of the grandmother who had taken in soiled laundry and returned it, washed, ironed, sweet-smelling, for a fee. Lee pondered putting a bottle of rosewater on her desk, in memory of that hardworking ancestor.

Brigid hurried away to the hospital; the others settled in, enjoying each other's company and the enormous box of *marron glaces* Klaus had brought along. When Lee finally climbed the stairs to her bed, she found herself trapped in sleepless fatigue by too much Blue Mountain. She tried to dive into any kind of dream, but found herself weeping for Brigid and Lech, for his heart and for their son, weeping for Claudia and her depressions, weeping for Cambodia, and for herself and her sons, who had only her to see them through the shoals and riptides that beset the lives of every living soul.

Jahnu Kedar was a *swar yogi,* working with sound and breath. A tall, bony man with splayed teeth, he was seated cross-legged in his tract house across town, giving Lee a rundown of how *swar* worked, even though she had not asked. A decade in this country had accustomed him to inquisitive Americans unwilling to proceed without detailed information. The work was, he explained, about sound waves affecting the human nervous system for good or ill. *Swar yogis* matched therapeutic Indian music to the state of an individual human's chakras, readable in the spine. He showed her a chart that looked like a stack of I Ching figures, seven of them, each made up of closed and broken horizontal lines. The spine of an enlightened being had no closed lines, but the rest of us had dozens of closures, in patterns that affected our behavior. At a *swar* session the yogi felt the closures in a person's chakras, chose one to be opened, and the *raga* that would accomplish that. The closures and openings were physical. The effects of their being open or closed were psychological and spiritual.

Lee knew the human body was full of electrical exchanges, synapses firing, enzymes and muscle twitches triggered by incoming information. How arrogant was it to insist that because the effects on the body of chanting shamans had not been blind-tested and replicated in Western lab conditions that there were therefore no effects? It seemed more scientific to make no judgment, more politically intelligent to avoid condescending to an ancient and sophisticated system. And there was the anecdotal evidence of her radiantly serene yoga teacher. Lee would give this a go.

Kedar motioned her onto a padded-top wooden bench. He put careful fingers along her spine as she lay face down on the padding, then chose a cassette from the wall of tapes and snapped it into a player. As Kedar slipped out of the room, speakers within the box began to resonate Lee's entire body with the unfamiliar sounds of India.

When the tape ended, Kedar returned with instructions he assumed Lee would follow. Every morning she was to play a tape he handed her and, "This one in the evenings. Do not mix them up." She would rise before dawn and perform the set of yoga exercises he had listed on a sheet of paper. She would dress in the color of the day: pale blue for Monday, red on Tuesday, green Wednesday, yellow Thursday, white Friday, black or navy on Saturday, and the sun's gold on Sunday. She would of course eat no meat. She would sleep on her left side, which would naturally open the right nostril, which meant energizing the left-lobe, the rational side of the brain, which would balance her sleep and her dreams. Upon awakening she would turn her head to open whichever airway should begin that day, determined by the lunar calendar he added to the collection of things she was to take away. On dark nights of the moon, she would join others at Kedar's home for a sleepless night of music and meditation. She would, if she could afford to, leave a contribution in the tray just inside the front door.

She did it all, moving into as formal a practice of Hindu *saddhana* as an American householder could do. She did not research the traditions involved nor seek translations of the sounds that filled her mornings and evenings. If they worked it would not be because she understood them intellectually, it would be because they were physically valid.

The music drifted out of Lee's room in the early morning and late at night, causing a frown to form on young Dasya's small face. No, he did not want to meet this Jahnu Kedar, his fellow countryman. The rational mathematician was embarrassed by his country's export of shamans and mystics. All of this "mumbo-jumbo" was, for Dasya, the Old Ways that progressive, educated people such as himself had turned away from. Lee surmised that "the dharma coming to the West" may have been for lack of interest in the East.

She did not see the occult or superstitious in this, nor in much of what was dismissed as nonsense by scientists. Thousands of years of experience and observation stood behind the practices of yoga, behind acupuncture, herbal remedies, a whole range of "nonsenses" that might include astrology and were, Lee speculated, as-yet-unexplained physical realities.

There were Aishas and Priyas and Ganeshes around Kedar, all Americans who had been renamed by Kedar and had taken up the wearing of saris and kurtas and forehead markings. Lee found that unthinkable for herself. There was a reason she had been born in this country, not Kerala or Kashmir. Lee she was, in American jeans and American sweatshirts, though those shirts were now in the designated colors of the days.

Jeans and all, she became a Lee who did not react to incoming threats and dangers with adrenalin spurts, a Lee who reacted instead with calm efficiency, seeing immediately what her move should be and making it, in a state of calm assurance. She became a Lee who did not weep in the aisles of grocery stores or absent herself from present joy to live in remembered pain. She was present to her world, fully present. And that world was full, in every moment. Nothing was missing, nothing not present was needed.

Lee had no understanding of the mechanics of what was happening; she had only the evidence. Even living without physical love had been transformed. Celibacy, real celibacy, became simple. It was not about resigning yourself to living without sex. It was being so full of what you did have that there was no room for wishing you had anything else, no room for visiting alternative universes, nor for drifting away from a now that was bursting with reality to dwell in memories of what was lost, or in dread of what was ahead.

She pitied priests and nuns sworn to sexless lives and given no practices that would remove the feelings of sacrifice and deprivation. Come to think of it, there were all those seminaries and divinity schools graduating "men of God" who had only proved they knew scripture; they were not required to connect to Spirit in order to be called Reverend or Father or Pastor.

She knew now that people who aren't centered, grounded in spiritual practice, get pulled into the magnetic fields of those who know with certainty what they want, whether for good or evil. She did not think that this would happen to her, ever again.

Toby, wearing a T shirt and cutoffs, flushed from the heat, his chestnut hair soaked brown along his neck and forehead, had almost finished polishing the silver mug when Lee came into the kitchen.

She caught herself before she called him Toby. This morning he had asked that she call him by his full name; "Toby" was childish.

"Hey you, too hot out there to finish the grass? When you've got that cup done you could start on the knives and forks. They all look like pewter."

He grinned and kept rubbing. "I don't think so, Mom. I cut all the front, and this afternoon I've got football practice. But I have to get this outside. There's this guy and I think he's really thirsty."

He filled the now-gleaming cup with water from the refrigerator. The silver frosted over as he put the cup on a small wooden tray.

"Guy? What guy?"

"Out there under the tree by our walk. See?"

There was indeed a man sitting on the curb in front of the house, in the shade of the sycamores. Enchanted with her Tobias—and concerned about who "this guy" might be—Lee joined in the water delivery.

"This is my mom, sir."

The man rose and nodded to Lee.

"Jake Waterman, ma'am."

"Lee Palmer." She extended her hand. "How do you do?"

He wiped his palm on his jeans before shaking her hand.

"Not too well, actually."

This Jake Waterman was a stocky man, maybe in his forties. He was clean-shaven, his graying blond hair close-cropped, his white shirt pressed, his jeans worn but freshly laundered. The work boots he wore seemed too warm for the day, and they looked as if he'd actually polished them.

Lee and Toby joined him on the curb, in the shade of the trees that arched over Underwood Road, as he explained why he was "not too well." It seemed that he was a logger and for almost a month he'd been walking and hitching, trying to get to Princeton from Oregon, a man on a mission.

"I was reading this book and it hit me. So I had to find someone who would understand and I figured the only place where I'd find people who could do that was the Institute for Advanced Study, you know, because Einstein worked there, so there must still be people at his Institute who would understand."

He opened the briefcase that seemed to be his only baggage. In it Lee saw a carefully folded twin for the white shirt he was wearing, and a copy of Korzybski's *Science and Sanity*. Korzybski. She was sitting on a curb talking to a logger who read Korzybski, and had hitch-hiked across the country to seek out Einstein's colleagues.

Lee had tried at least five times to read *Science and Sanity* and had abandoned ship fairly quickly every time, remembering only "the map is not the territory." Jake Waterman didn't fit any pictures Lee had of loggers.

"So you're going down there to ask for a meeting?"

"I already did. No one would talk to me." Waterman's voice was faint.

"That's awful!" Toby hit the ground with a fist. "How could they do that when you came so far? When you *walked* so far?"

Lee looked at the logger and said quietly, "What was it you wanted to talk to them about? Something unclear in the book?"

"No—something the book *made* clear, for me. See, I'm an epileptic. I have seizures a lot...."

Toby was wide-eyed. He knew what seizures were like; he'd seen Van go into a *grand mal* the last night that he'd been part of their lives.

"But you're a logger," he interrupted. "You climb huge trees and cut them down. If you had a seizure, you'd fall."

"I have never had a seizure on the job." Waterman spoke deliberately. "Never. "That's what I wanted to talk to these professors about. Reading this book I realized *why* I don't have seizures when I'm working. See, I know exactly what to do then and I know I'm good at all of it. I can get up a tree and top it faster than any guy out there. I can make a tree fall exactly where I want it to fall. It's supposed to be high-pressure and I should be flipping out, but it's all a piece of cake. The guys I work with don't even know I'm an epileptic."

Waterman stopped, looked at them, and said slowly and deliberately, "I Have Seizures When Action Is Both Impossible and Imperative."

Lee blinked and stared at him, wishing she'd gotten through Korzybski so she could understand the connection, if there really was one, but hearing the logic in what Waterman had just said, realizing that the only seizure she had ever witnessed was of a being in just such a dilemma.

"No doctor ever told me that—I don't think they've figured it out, but when I read this," he patted the book, "I got it."

Lee's mind was racing. "That could help a lot of people, Mr. Waterman."

"Yes, I thought so. That's why I decided to come here." He turned away and ran the back of a rough hand over his eyes.

The three of them were quiet. Toby punched the grass again. Waterman closed the book and replaced it carefully in his case. The driver of a passing car stared at them. No one sat on the curbs along Underwood Road. One had one's garden for sitting outdoors.

"Mr. Waterman, would you consider having lunch with us?" Lee asked, immediately adding, "We're just having tuna sandwiches and canned minestrone, but you'd be welcome."

Toby smiled at her gratefully.

"Please say yes, sir. She makes really good tuna sandwiches. With little pickles chopped up."

There was a flicker of warmth in the sad, blue eyes.

"That would be very nice. Thank you. If you don't mind, I'll sit here a little longer before I come in."

As Lee made two more sandwiches and Toby set another place at the table on the back porch, his indignation was still bubbling over. "I can't believe nobody would talk to him. What about Professor Newman across the street? He's nice. Maybe he'd talk to him. Or any of the dads from Gabe's playschool. They're all brains."

Lee put a booster in a chair on the backporch and called to Gabriel and Das to come in from the yard.

"I know it's harsh but he probably didn't get past the receptionist or the security guard. They just figured he was some nut and brushed him off."

The same possibility was bothering Lee now. What if a clever maniac was about to sit down to lunch with her children? Nonsense. He was clearly a good-hearted fellow trying to do something that would help a lot of people and he wasn't getting anywhere. He deserved a hearing and all she had to offer was lunch. On the porch.

"Toby—Tobias, go tell him it's ready, OK? And don't say that Dr. Newman will talk to him—he's an astrophysicist. I don't think he knows about epilepsy and metaphors."

Toby was back quickly, alone and looking stricken.

"He's gone! I looked in all directions and I couldn't see him." He brightened a bit. "Maybe he went back to the Institute, to try again."

Lee sighed and wished her elder son didn't take everything quite so to heart. "I don't think so, sweetie. I think he's gone back to his big trees."

"That is not *not* fair." He described their encounter with the logger to Das, who was intrigued by the equation the man had described. He took out a pen and notepad to show Toby how it could be expressed mathematically.

They ate quietly, aware of the empty place at the table. Gabriel looked puzzled when his usual bids for attention evoked no responses. A breeze started to move the dogwoods shading the porch.

"You know what I think, Toby?"

"Tobias. What?"

"I think you should try Atlanta information and see if you can get a number for Van's house."

He stared at her, quickly swallowing tuna and rye.

"You mean it? You wouldn't mind?"

Despite all, Toby had cared about Van. And there were enough missing persons in her son's life without keeping this almost-brother on that list.

"Yes, I mean it and no, I won't mind. And, what if—his dad's hard hat, from the textile plant? It's still on a peg in the garage. Maybe Van would like it if you sent it to him."

Imperative and impossible.

Like when you're a kid who wants his dad all to himself and that's not working out and he wants to walk and he's scared of the operation that will make that happen and his mom is tugging at him to always be her Tiny Tim.

Like when you know that your mate's destructive actions outweigh all the good he could possibly do but you want to hold onto the good version of him and you don't leave him even though you know you must.

Like when you know that you're all your kids have got and they're in danger and you freeze instead of fighting because you've got some invisible mermaid-programming that a guilt-dealing Scandinavian Christian story-teller implanted in your operating circuits.

Like every time you feel that a thing cannot be borne and know that it must be borne.

Lee knew something about those unbearable, pivotal moments when something must be done and nothing can be done.

Right now, she *could* do this thing of reaching out to Van, letting him back into Toby's world, despite Van's imperative/impossible choice of life with his mother, life in a wheelchair.

But for months she had been stymied by something new that had been growing larger, more impossible, more imperative for her—the go-don't-go of loving this home while yearning for New York.

She wanted to be at the still point her sons needed, the still point without which there was no dance. She wanted them to dance through strong, confident lives. She had secured this reliable, unmoving place, this good old house. She had filled it with colors, images, sounds, tastes, and touches that made it Home. She had made herself strong enough to hold it.

But the city was calling to her, there, to the north, the place where strong people went to exercise their gifts, to build careers, to see if they had what it takes. It was imperative that she go. It was impossible that she go.

When the midsummer night downpour broke through at last, she moved through the house, closing windows, checking to see if Gabe might be calling to her under the thunder and the rush of the water. Standing in his doorway, she watched him sleeping on his back, his arms and legs splayed in total relaxation, oblivious to the crashes and roars. She moved back down the stairs to get herself ice water from the jug in the refrigerator.

Crossing the foyer, the worn Bokhara cushioning her steps, she smiled, realizing that this rug would come close to filling the living/dining room of the New York apartment she had found. She checked the dampness of the soil in the ficus pot. The towering plant would never fit in the low-ceilinged apartment. In the living room, she righted the fallen Japanese fan that filled the gaping fireplace in summer and remembered all the healing evenings she had spent by that fire. Fires were good. There was no fireplace in the apartment.

The big round table in the dining room filled in her mind with the good people who had sat around it, talking, laughing, sharing their work and their lives. There was no place for it in the apartment. So small. Not even an eat-in kitchen. No special room for television-watching. And no long stairs up to five bedrooms and three baths. It was CPW VU, Lv/Dr, 2 Br, 2 Bath, Pre-war, Drmn. And the tiny space cost more every month than this dear old endless-roomed house. Rent money, wasted money, unlike the mortgage payments that made the house more hers every month.

She stepped out onto the front steps, moved along the curving brick path. The impatiens she had planted at the beginning of this day had survived their first out-of-the-hothouse, real-world dousing—they were standing themselves up after the pounding rain, leaves and petals diamonded with light from the streetlamps. Gabe's small training-wheeled bike leaned against the trunk of an old evergreen, inside the ground-sweeping branches that walled his pretend house, the place where she, Toby and Das had joined him for cookouts of mud and sticks. She sat on the low seat of the bike and looked at 99 through openings in the branches. The mass of the place, being such a dark brown, came close to disappearing in the night, but the lamp in the newly green office glowed from the window closest to the door, and there was a pale shine from the night light that chased any wild things out of Gabe's upstairs bedroom. Far to the left on the ground floor, Tobias's room was all darkness, night lights being unneeded by an 18-year-old about to be a college freshman.

She circled round to walk between the garage and the house, to the dog-wood clump she had edited into a spring-flowering outdoor room, her own arborial pretend house. From the second floor, her night-table lamp cast a warm plank across the grass, almost reaching the circle of dogwoods. She sat in a wrought iron chair that faced the house. The professor in the east wing had left the lights on in his downstairs sitting room. The next week, all his windows would be dark; he had taken a chair at Northwestern, and Lee would have to find a new tenant. If she stayed.

She must go up to bed at some point, but not until she had either signed the apartment lease or torn it up. It was perfect now. She had edited away the one-sidedness and she had scratched through the lines that asked for her co-signer's signature. They could just try putting that one back in. She'd sue their socks off. They couldn't tell an income-earning adult with banked cash from a house sale that she needed a co-signer.

She wouldn't sue of course; it would be entirely too expensive. But such suggestions seemed to be quite effective. When American Express refused her application for a card in her own name, she'd asked the company rep on the phone who he thought had been seeing that their bills to Mr. and Mrs. Montagna were paid on time and in full all those years. Had the company looked at her bank statements, her recent record of solo bill-paying? She assured him that a judge would find this information telling. There was now a gold AmEx card in her wallet, warranted she was sure, not by her only so-so finances but by her mentioning the word "lawsuit."

By some shift in currents that Lee could not fathom, doors had begun closing in Princeton, starting when Claudia Havstrom killed herself.

The call had come in one morning—Porter, sobbing. "She's killed her-self. I was away. I got back and she was dead. She left a letter. Long. One thing is she wanted you to have her clothes. Come please and take them. Come now, Lee, please. I want everything out of here."

Lee found him in the kitchen of their ultra-modern house, devastated, boiling mad, making bets with his poker chums on the Penn/Yale game, their presence a sharing of his grief. They were all with him in the spacious kitchen: Irv the poet, Abe the vet who had saved Ivan, and Milt Stein, the internist who had decided Claudia's ill health was not physical and had referred her to a psychiatrist.

Porter slammed a cupboard shut, after taking out a mug for Lee and aiming her to the coffee. "You guys keep Delafield away from me, OK? WASP bastard just called and told me to keep my chin up. You Jews, you understand pain."

"*Us* Jews, Porter. We made you an honorary member years ago, remember?" Abe's voice was as gentle as it had been when he bundled away Ivan, the wounded puppy.

Porter wept as he answered yet another phone call.

"No no. She really meant to do it. She didn't give anybody a chance to stop her." She'd given no hints, not even to the neighbor who phoned after she'd taken the pills, a week before Porter was due back from a book tour. Her body had lain there, a Penelope awaiting her husband's return, but swollen, blackening, rigid, in their bed. Now he wouldn't come into this room where they had loved and fought, wept and laughed. He was sleeping on a bedroll in the storeroom downstairs, the farthest he could get from this now tainted room and still be in the house.

Lee stood alone in the eerily empty bedroom Porter and Claudia had both fled, blinking at the bright morning light pouring in. The door was closed quietly behind her by Milt Stein. She looked at the vast white bed, reflecting all this sunlight. It had been a cold, rainy night when Claudia lay her down to sleep, and stepped into the morningless void.

All around the bed, the room rocked with the colors of laughter and curiosity. The stinging pinks, oranges, and limes in the rugs, the pictures, the curtains, all sang raucously of Claudia's beloved Mexico. Lee thought it all looked like the bright brass music Porter was pumping through the stereo system, "to remind us we're alive."

The white bedcover had been his wife's door out of the giddy spirit of this place. Claudia had lifted that door and pulled it closed behind her, blanking out all the pigments and sounds that might have convinced her to stay, choosing instead to fall into colorless silence. Lee pictured Claudia, days dead, there in the white bed, and shuddered. She turned away quickly from this invasion of her friend's privacy and walked to the closet doors.

She wasn't sure she could do this. She wanted Claudia in her life, not her clothes. Claudia as daring reporter, Claudia as byline adventurer, Claudia as proof of what was possible for a woman on her own.

Lee was wary of the clothes. They could envelop her, drain her growing strength, replace it with Claudia's despair. They could leak darkness that would revive her own semi-conquered fears and sorrow. She couldn't risk it.

But she mustn't seem ungrateful. She would take something away with her. Maybe she would find the Moroccan leather satchel Claudia had been hauling, stuffed with papers, the last time Lee had seen her. The papers were, Lee hoped, good pages for the memoir, but Claudia shook her head No. They were useless, would all have to be thrown away. Lee's opinion that they might in fact be good did not break through her friend's desolation.

For all the rest of the clothing, Lee would organize and pack and move it all out of the house, to Claudia's friends, to the thrift shop. She would start by sorting the closet's contents into categories.

Plan in mind, she opened the double doors and gasped. It was a walk-in dressing room, exploding with a chaos of dresses, suits, pants, gowns, and robes. Sandals, boots, pumps, and slippers climbed the backs of the doors. The shelves were stuffed with sweaters, handbags, towers of boxes for hats, and still more shoes. Colors shrieked, giggled, and purred. Satins and cashmeres invited the hand. There was every length and purpose of garment, enough cloth and leather to dress a battalion of women, to wardrobe a dozen plays set in the last 40 years of events in the western world. A pale blue Chanel-style suit with a Cassini label recalled Jackie. A long length of silver light, sequins shoulder-to-ankle, was the perfect look for accepting an Oscar.

Lee pulled down a Mr. John hatbox, the kind models had carried as they ran between assignments in Manhattan a quarter century before. The witty, feather-banded fedora inside would be perfect for a production of *The Front Page*. Lee decided to add the McCarter Theater to the distribution list. And the hatbox would hold Lee's inheritance from Claudia. She looked along the jumbled shelves for the tooled Moroccan bag. What had Claudia been trying to do, buy up the world? How did she ever find what she was looking for in all this?

The fine merino texture of a white sweater pleased her hands, and Lee started to drop it into the hatbox but stopped short, realizing she was wearing its near-twin; a copy was not needed. She and Claudia had joked for years about loving the same stuff, often ending with their hands reaching for the same hangar after scanning a store together. A cloud of *Cabochard* floated up from the sweater as Lee smoothed and folded it for the boxes she would fill.

She tugged on a black sleeve hanging down from a higher shelf. It fell into her arms, a cashmere with a cowl neck, thick and soft, a Persian cat of a sweater. Lee held it up and smiled, recognizing it as the one Claudia had been wearing at the Howe's party, on Lee's first evening in Princeton. It was a perfect *memento Claudia*. Elegant, sensuous, dead-on New York. Dead on.

But this was not a store. These were Claudia's things, gloriously beautiful, and terrifying in what they said about her life, and her death. There had been no lasting solace for her in the subtlety of this moiré skirt's interplay of lavender and rose silk, in the perfect line of this black wool tunic, the lovely curve in the arch and heel of this pair of suede pumps. Though they may have kept the void away for a few moments, none of it made Claudia's pain go away long enough. But the pills did.

Lee couldn't imagine the burden of tending so many garments, the sewing on of buttons, the dispatching to the dry cleaners and the shoe repair, the mothballing for the winter. She sorted, folded, and stacked, covering Claudia's death bed with tall piles, wondering who had made the bed up so neatly after Claudia's rigored body was removed from it.

In the dresser drawers there were tumbles of beautiful underthings and, in among the lacy bras, slips, and underpants, Claudia's prosthetic. In one of their work sessions just weeks before, Claudia had described to Lee an after-mastectomy hospital visit by her surgeon.

"Well, old girl, I guess your other boob is in the trash."

"Dear God. Did you slug him?"

"I was too groggy. But that's a good idea, in retrospect."

At Lee's insistence, she had included the incident in her draft for the memoir, as well as the assignment Porter got from *World Watch* to write about having a wife lose a breast.

"But, Claudia, it was *your* body. Your story. Your *magazine*."

"Don't I know it. But my old buddy editor thought Porter would have an interesting 'angle.'"

And here was the silicone-filled faux breast that slipped into the beautiful lace bras and made all the lovely clothes continue to fit, as if nothing had happened. Lee wiped tears from its surface and wrapped it in tissue paper. There would be a single-breasted woman somewhere who could not afford such a saving disguise; Lee would see that she got a posthumous gift from Claudia Havstrom.

When the dressing room and the chest of drawers were emptied, there were 19 white sweaters neatly stacked in the window seat. Nineteen. Lee had begun by making piles of sweaters of all colors but quickly saw that there could be a full box of just white ones. They were cotton, lambs wool, cashmere, silk; long-sleeved, short-sleeved, sleeveless; turtle-necked, crew-necked, V-necked. And all of them were white.

Every surface in the room was covered with categories of clothing. Lee tallied up the boxes and wardrobe cartons she'd need to remove it all from the house. She could report to Porter that the job was almost complete. Opening what she thought was a door out of the room, she found herself looking into another walk-in closet filled with women's clothes. As were the spaces behind sliding doors in the hallway. The coat closet on the first floor held more boots and hats and dozens of jackets and coats.

"Yes, the attic too," Porter confirmed. "And she filled up the guest room closets and dressers. So many beautiful things. Anything she wanted. I just don't understand."

Lee reached, stooped, sorted and folded for three full days. By the time she found everything, she had filled dozens of large cartons. One of them held 37 white sweaters. In the Mr. John hatbox she took away with her, there was the black cowl-necked cashmere, the Moroccan satchel, and a Mexican ring, two dark jade spheres in severely modern silver. It was enough for Lee, as all the things in all the boxes had not been for Claudia..

The memorial service at the Unitarian church was filled with journalists Claudia had worked with, with friends and neighbors from New York and Princeton, with celebrities she had interviewed and retained as friends. The famous Mexican novelist told the gathering, "You have no idea how important Claudia was to us. She was 'our beloved gringa.'"

At Porter's request, Lee stood and spoke of how much it had meant to her as a girl to know there was such a woman as Claudia Havstrom, of what it meant to her in recent years to work with Claudia and be her friend.

"I thought the work we were doing together might help keep her going. But nothing I could reach could do that for her. Nothing any of us could reach." It seemed wrong to speak as though it had been the cancer that killed her, or some accident. "The darkness that overpowered her was too strong for *anyone* to stop. *L'chaim*, dear Claudia. *L'chaim.*"

Porter had doubled over in his chair, his arms crossed over his belly, his whole body spasming with sobs. Within weeks, he had closed the house and moved to Oahu.

It was the first loosening of Lee's ties to Princeton. As the winter ended and spring burst through, the life Lee had built there had continued to come undone, each breakthrough of blooms and light seeming to bring another undoing.

Jahnu Kedar married a pretty American heiress he renamed Naimah, and went off to start an ashram in the Berkshires. Marina's navy-blue-eyed grandson, who was to have been the perfect pal for Gabriel, took to kicking and scratching, and Gabriel refused to play with him. As graduation approached for Toby, his college applications had produced acceptances at several places that were affordable, most of them far from Princeton, except for Hunter, which was now accepting male students and would be pleased to have him, just up the road, in New York. Connor was going to Yale, and Toby's public high school class of '76 was dispersing to Rutgers, Carlton, Howard, Stanford, Swarthmore, and all points in between.

Marina and Oscar bought a three-master they would sail around the world as soon as Connor left in the fall; the indomitable Phoebe was going along, delighted with the prospect of painting on deck, from the south seas to the Mediterranean. Dasya, so long the third son in Lee's household, was accepting a job offer to teach math in India; after so many years, he would be at last with his own beloved family. The professor in the guest wing had given notice, after three years of providing the money Lee needed for property taxes.

And as the trees had come out of skeletal rest, generating buds and tightly curled leaves, Joe's proud little New Yorker of a tree had stayed just as it had been all winter. The ailanthus, the "tree of heaven," that could grow even in a sidewalk crack, the unkillable, unstoppable trash tree, had decided not to live in Princeton.

Lee told herself that these changes need not be omens. There were other playmates to be found who didn't kick and scratch, other professors who needed housing, other neighbors who might become friends, other scholarship students who would swap chore time for room and board. There were even other yogis.

The sudden changes in time and money were more concerning. She'd finished two faculty books and had found no replacements for her work queue. The locus of her earnings had gone north; reaching for it was costing her serious time out of her sons' lives.

Brigid's suffragists were at her publisher's and the author's enthusiasm for Lee's involvement had brought in a query from the book's editor. Would Lee take on another of his writers who seemed to need a coach? It would mean frequent sessions with her in Brooklyn Heights. No, Lee wouldn't make a trek that long, but she did agree to meet the writer at a coffee shop near Penn Station every Thursday.

On Tuesdays and Wednesdays she was doing half days at MacGregor's, going through proposals and advising Asa Chandler, now a senior editor, on which ones she thought could become good books, perhaps might even sell. Lee was sure the work was Asa's apology for introducing Celeste Papandreou into her life. Whatever the cause, she was taking the jobs, racking up the hours, praying that they would be enough to match the bills that had to be paid each month.

Commuting would be better, she realized, if she had a transporter and could beam herself to the coffee shop or to MacGregor's. And a replicator to supply her guys with meals on verbal command. With the inferior technology of her own times she had to put her body into the Volvo and drive to the "dinky," the rickety two-car train that linked this town to the mainline, change at Princeton Junction for the long stretch into the city, repeat it all in reverse in the evening. And then manage the household, rallying the boys to assist.

If they lived in the city, at the source of this trickle of new work she was getting, if she were no longer commuting, there would be no time lost in trains, no furnace to repair, no garden to weed, no snow-shoveling or flat-tire changing. She and the boys could use the time she gained to go bike-riding in the park or over to see the knights in armor at the Met. She could picture Toby explaining that collection, his favorite when he was small, to his awed little brother.

Aside from the matter of time, there was the issue of normalcy. In the city, instead of being surrounded by households in which women stayed home and Lee was "odd," she would be a New York woman, who was of course in the work force.

The outrageous alternative to anchoring forever here in this dear old glowing house was to come about and race through the crack in time that was appearing, so briefly, into the maelstrom of action that was being played out just minutes from this silent, peaceful street. With Gabe ready to start kindergarten, she had an opening that would feel closed for 13 years, if he locked into this place. She'd been to countless schools herself, but she'd had two parents, and Gabriel had to make do with one. She wasn't going to set his life up to be any harder for him than it had to be—settling on a school and sticking with it was high on her agenda. The idea of not living where he had always lived, was confusing to him. When he'd seen the building in Manhattan where she had taken away a lease, he'd told her that people must get lost in such a big house; he had no concept of "apartment."

Taking that apartment meant possibly living more fully than she ever had; it also threatened her with being sliced and fried by the city, rejected, sent packing to spend the rest of her years not with a respectably wistful, un-fulfilled dream, but with the sure and certain knowledge that she couldn't make it in the center ring.

She'd set the bar as high as possible against that dreaded discovery. She might go back to New York if there were a place for Gabriel in the kinder-garten at the Rudolf Steiner School, and everyone knew the city's private schools had waiting lists pages long.

She might go back if Toby chose Hunter College and was willing to live at home, sharing a room with his little brother, and what new freshman wanted to do such a thing?

She might go back if there were an apartment with dawn windows across the park from Steiner and Hunter, in her old neighborhood, an apartment she could afford—a complete impossibility.

It all had to be in place or she could pull back from the brink and rest easy, here in her downy, cooing, minimally challenging life.

To her astonishment, Toby had quickly said he'd be glad to choose Hunter and live with his family instead of with other freshmen. He had missed New York and was eager to be back in its excitement. He loved Gabe and wanted to be around to do big-brother things with him. His mother couldn't believe her ears.

Gabriel had so charmed the Steiner interviewers that they'd offered him, on the spot, a place in their next kindergarten. More than a little unnerved,

Lee had taken his hand and walked from the school on East 79th Street, across the park on the 81st Street transverse, toward the West Side. Emerging from the park, she saw a large sign just north on Central Park West—

OVER 400 APARTMENTS

AVAILABLE SEPTEMBER 1

The Standish Hotel, a grande dame of the 1920's, was being renovated, mustiness removed, kitchens installed in what had been closets, and long-term tenants recruited. Given a tour of the building, Lee stood in the little two-bedroom suite on the southeast corner of the eighth floor. The eighth floor, low enough to reach by stairs if there were a power failure, high enough that slaughterers could not come in through the windows.

It was those windows that had captured her, more than the eerie fulfillment of her unreasonable requirements. The old many-paned wood frames were cracked and peeling and were to be replaced with steel-rimmed expanses of thermal glass, but even through the old panes, the content of the windows astonished her. In the living room and in what would be her bedroom, it was all sky and clouds at the tops, all green trees at the bottoms, with the Manhattan skyline dividing the two, a magnificent array, from the 80s on Fifth to the Essex House on Central Park South. The Plaza, the Chrysler building, Citicorp, the Sherry-Netherland—it was Oz on parade.

A person living in that apartment would not be burrowed down in some airshaft, looking out at brick walls, able to hide from the city. A person living there would know she was "on." There was no way Lee could awaken in apartment 811 of the Standish and not know where she was, and the level of performance expected of her in the day ahead. Exposure. She would be exposed, the city looking back at her, calling her forth to try her hand.

She was sure that she couldn't afford both the apartment and tuition bills until she remembered the number the real estate agent had suggested as an asking price should Lee want to sell the house. She had renovated it so beautifully it now fit perfectly into this grand Princeton neighborhood, where houses rarely came on the market and thus commanded top dollar. Lee would have money for rent, tuition, and all their other expenses—for a while. For the time she'd need to get a serious, properly paid career going.

Looking at the view from 811, she'd been forced to acknowledge that all her terms had been met in her bargaining with the gods. She frowned at the building's rental agent. "All right, all right. Let me see a lease."

Lee wiped her rain-damp sandals on the mat outside the kitchen door and eased inside. Bilbo the Second was atwitter in his cage in the breakfast nook; Lee put on the cage cover that silenced him. "Shush now, little guy. You were supposed to be asleep hours ago."

Bilbo was eligible for transfer to the city, though he'd have to be in the living room; the apartment's kitchen was far too small to include a birdcage. Lee made a mental note that she'd have to talk to the boys about moving Admiral Perry to the field near the Institute for Advanced Study where wild land turtles seemed to thrive, hoping Toby wouldn't ask if the Admiral was of the same breed. It was a detail Lee preferred to leave in the realm of hoping for the best.

Life was clearly offering her a do-over, in New York. It was possible she could be this brave. She was after all, someone who had turned and faced down her terror of water. Could being a head-of-household in Manhattan be more frightening than being under water? And she had done that. She had gone past a lifetime of fear and she had come to love being in water.

Back in her new office, the smell of paint lingered. She took a book from one of the cartons on the floor and put one finger to a shelf. It stuck. Still not ready for holding books. She looked at the one in her hand and saw it was her mermaid-research journal. Thumbing through it, she read an entry near the end of the pages, dated the previous June.

I see that in so many of these stories, water is the female element—the deep liquid darkness where creation begins and anything is possible. It's where we are at home, strong, fearless. It's where we are completely ourselves and therefore terrifying to any man who's insecure, whether openly or under his bluster and bravado—foot on chair, forearm across thigh, looking so certain. For that insecure man, there is a fairly paranoid nightmare that would scare the shit out of anybody—a merwoman's eyes see everything a man wants to hide. They see. They know. They know. Your deeds. Your intentions. All you've done. All you plan to do. She seeks nothing from you, needs nothing you have to offer her. None of your bargaining chips draw her into your game. The sea gives her all she needs. But if she chooses, if something about you does please her, she will draw you in, extract your seed, and raise the child with her sisters. And you? What was your name? She never knew and would not remember if she had.

Poor Yeats setting his Wandering Aengus to spend his life searching for the little fish who became a glimmering girl, called his name, and disappeared. Poor Donne asking to be taught to heare the mermaid's singing. Poor, poor Eliot whose J. Alfred Prufrock knew that they did not sing for him.

Female independence, women's indifference, are horrors worth preventing if you have the power to make them submit—which men, over millennia, have made sure they have had.

I don't aspire to indifference, but I do want to function at full, independent power. And I, a woman, am afraid of water. This must not stand.

Lee had never been more to-the-marrow frightened than when she'd signed up for swimming lessons for aquaphobes, at the YWCA. With every step between the locker room and the pool's edge she told herself that she should run for her life. She made it into the shallow end only on the promise to herself that she could simply climb out at any moment.

The broad-shouldered instructor introduced herself. "My name's Serena Seeger and I've taught a lot of people to swim who are scared to death of water. I hope we can start with you believing you can be one of them." Lee smiled thinly, shivering as she stood waste deep in the chilly water. "Apologies that the water isn't warmer—it would be a lot easier for you if it was. But the competition swimmers insist on keeping the pool at this temperature. So OK, in addition to being so damned cold, there are lots of things that are odd about being in water instead of air. One thing is it *sounds* funny. Would you be willing to put one ear in the water and listen?"

One ear. Still standing. In the kiddie end of the pool. Just bending down. Lee held her breath, clenched her eyes and twisted her body so that her mouth and nose were as dry as possible, and listened to the water. She had not drowned when she did that. She decided not to leave the pool.

Session by session, small bravery by small bravery, she had pushed herself further and further. She agreed to let Serena's outstretched arms hold her on the surface of the water. "Inhale, Lee, *breathe*. I've got you. Relax, relax. Stone doesn't float. Soft floats. Easy floats." On the first day she had let the water hold her up, without her teacher's intervening arms, Lee wept in wonder.

In time, she discovered that water in the mouth and in the nose were not fatal but expellable. There were, she also learned, other ways to move in the water besides the aggressive, competitive crawl. As Serena gentled her along, Lee learned to move under the surface sleekly, gliding along with the barest of movements, relaxed, easy, watching the lights, the speed swimmers whipping by in the lanes beside her as she gradually approached the far wall. And she could, as of her most recent lesson, somersault in the water when she touched that wall, heading herself back for another slow traverse of the pool.

Nowhere did she find the clutching hands of demanding, dead mariners she had not saved, not in the water, and no longer in her dreams. There was only now the good sea dream, where she moved freely in water, soaring, spiraling, at ease, in her element. Every day now, she thought longingly of water, often going to the pool when she had no lesson, lying down on the water, trusting it to hold her.

Lee sat at the old desk, took up a pen and wrote a new entry in the journal—

I am a swimmer, at home in water, peaceful there, thrilled with the beauty of it. The dream is real now, and no longer mysterious.

I see you, mersisters. I hear your good song. I understand you. And you're not maids, you are women, fully, confidently. I'm getting there. I am, after all, named for a grandmother who was named for a sea goddess.

Grandmother Morgana didn't live as the artist she was. None of the women before me lived their dreams. Not even the great Claudia Havstrom. Their agendas were all superceded by their men's requirements.

But what if I can have my own agenda? What if I get to try my hand, using whatever strengths I may have? I could stay here, tending my garden like a world-weary Candide. That's the responsible-parent thing to do. I know that.

But I haven't taken my shot yet. I don't know if I can do New York on my own but I didn't think I could ever swim—now anything is possible. It's a dare, Palmer. A double dare, the biggest one ever. I'll never know if I don't take it.

It will be difficult, even perilous, and I'm going to need all the strength I can summon.

Morgana, let's see if we can live up to our name.

Merwomen, walk with me.

Lee looked at the clock. It was 1:11 AM. The midsummer night was ending and jocund day would soon arrive, bringing back the light. She turned to the last page of the lease, where there was a space for the tenant's signature, and another for a representative of Waverly, Depthford & Pescecane, Landlords. She laughed and signed.

Morgana Lee Palmer June 22, 1977

...the rude sea grew civil at her song
And certain stars shot madly from their spheres,
To hear the sea-maid's music.
—Shakespeare ~ A Midsummer Night's Dream

"If you wrote from experience, you'd get maybe one book,
maybe three poems. Writers write from empathy."
                                                    —Nikki Giovanni

Afterword

As I warned you before you started all this, writers are thieves and liars. Giovanni adds, more kindly, that we are empaths. We have our own experiences and we take in the experiences of others, then mess with them all. What's truth got to do with it? Only that we create new truths out of all that experiencing, absorbing, and tinkering. *Outing the Mermaid* is as true as I can write.

The thanks have to start with the writing group that met every Tuesday evening in my New York living room. Not being able to cut a meeting in my own apartment, I had to write something short and readable every week. Those pieces came to be known in the group as the "Lee and Joe stories." The assembled writers kept asking for more, so I figured the scenes were of some interest. I kept writing them. Then I threw them in a drawer. But thanks for the encouragement, John Graham, Elizabeth Harlan, Richard Marshall, Nina Rothschild, Eric Utne, David White, and April White Wolf.

Years later, living on an island far from Manhattan, I opened a box and found the Lee and Joe stories. With the distance of time, I read them and thought, Oh. That's why the group liked them—they're pretty interesting. They were, however, disjointed. The process of putting them into a coherent (possibly) narrative, took some doing.

The brilliant editor, Barbara Sullivan, gave me perfect notes on how to structure the story so that it worked optimally for the reader. The early material on Lee and Joe's courtship was written at her instigation; she was sure that readers had to be entranced by Joe at the same time Lee is. Otherwise they'd be wondering how such a smart woman could do such a dumb thing. I'm interested to know if that worked for you. If you were Lee, would you have succumbed to the Knight's Gambit? Any glitches you found in the story are my doing, not Sullivan's.

As I stitched the Lee & Joe stories together, many a Dear Reader gave me feedback on *The Mermaid's Song*, *Boobs*, *Finding the Merwoman* or *The Mermaid's Tale* (the title mutated a few times before it settled into *Outing the Mermaid*). My thanks go to Goody Cable, Gary Croft, Chris Fisher, Lianna Gilman, John Graham, Malory Graham, Susan Gray, Mary Ella Keblusek, Diane Kendy, Hank Murrow, Peter Newbould, Ruth Pittard, Anne Marie Santoro, Mary Schoonmaker, Susan Scott, Neal Starkman, Cynthia & Ted Repplier, and Peter Tavernise. Special thanks to the males—we all know the stats that say women buy/read novels, not men, so having men read, enjoy and comment on this novel was truly encouraging.

Going even earlier in time, Charles Martin, wherever you are, living or dead, thank you for flunking me on work I did in your writing class at the University of Maryland. The anguished cries of this previously straight-A English major led you to educate me out of being "facile, glib and mindless." You insisted I learn to think.

Every writer should have a teacher like Charles Martin and a partner like John Graham, who's been with the stories since the writers' group days and has given feedback that's been precious, since he finds most novels not worth reading. That feedback—and his standing at the bottom of the stairs yelling, "Food!" made it possible for this writer to get to the finish line.

I am something of a Phi/Fibonacci junky, fascinated by the beauty of the spiral, which appears everywhere, from galaxies to our human DNA, with holdable manifestations like shells, in between. I must have hundreds of images of nautilus shells, but I was looking for still more of them as the question of a cover image for this book came up. And there, online, thanks to Google Images, was the stunning photograph you see on this book's cover. I had never seen a more beautiful take on this most perfect of forms.

When I started tracking down the photographer to buy the reproduction rights, I made it onto the site of someone named Drew Bedo, in Rosenberg, Texas. Bedo had never sold reproduction rights before; he markets prints. So he had to figure out a price, and terms. All that settled, we just talked. And he told me he's blind. A blind photographer. Working with antique cameras....

You must go to his Quiet-Light Photography website (www.quietlight-photo.com) to read about how he works, and to see his other photographs. His tagline: "Come inside and see what I see."

Google made me whoop with delight again when I found Galileo's finger not in Florence but in a Google search to see if *Eppur si muove* was on his tombstone. Seeing that reliquary on my screen has to have been one of the best moments in a lifetime of research, and certainly the funniest.

Overwhelming thanks to the Hedgebrook retreat for women writers. The days I spent in Fir Cottage there were the most nurturing and productive of my life as a writer. See why at www.hedgebrook.org.

And now thank you, Dear Reader, for taking up *Outing the Mermaid*. But you're not quite finished. We are living in the era of interactivity—talk to me.

—Ann Medlock
amedlock@whidbeyisland.com

www.ingramcontent.com/pod-product-compliance
Lightning Source LLC
Chambersburg PA
CBHW061511020726
47502CB00006B/2018